YOSEMITE RISING

Julie Dawn

Zombie Publishing

This is a work of fiction. The events described are imaginary. Real places are used fictitiously. Any resemblance of characters and events to real life is coincidental.

Yosemite Rising
Copyright © 2015 by Julie Dawn

All rights reserved.
No part of this book may be reproduced, distributed, or transmitted in any form or by any means, or stored in a database or retrieval system, without the written permission of the author except in the case of brief quotations embodied in critical articles and reviews.

Zombie Publishing I Eugene, Oregon

ISBN: 978-0-9962795-0-5
Library of Congress Control Number: 2015941175

Edited by Cheryl K. Smith
Photographs: *corbis_micro, stokkete, Andrey Kiselev* and *Zacarias da Mata* - Fotolia.com

Printed in the United States of America
First Edition Paperback: July 2015

For my brother, JIMMY,

I've locked our memories away, so they will never be lost.
I miss everything about you.

Happy Reading

Julio Dann

Acknowledgements

To my husband, Dan, for supporting me through this rollercoaster. I couldn't have done it without you.

To my son and daughter, for letting me steal your time and love. Because of you, I'd fight like hell to survive a zombie apocalypse.

To all of my family for all your support.

To my first readers, Lisa, Mandy, and Diana, thank you in so many ways for walking through the trenches.

To my editor, Cheryl, for making my words sparkle.

To my writer friends, Bill, Carla, Charlie, James, and Roni, for being brutally honest and making me feel normal.

To those who protect the legends, true history, and spirit of all who came before us.

To the Ahwahnee Indians, who once lived, may your legends and memory be carried on.

CONTENTS

The Great Grey Owl	1
Meadowlark	18
The Lost Legend	49
Yosemite Rising	82
Nowhere to Run	112
The Moon's Glow	149
The Empty Waterfall	178
Awanata	213
The Ahwahnee	237
The Return of Coyote	266
Moonlit Trail	297

THE GREAT GREY OWL

1

"WE SHOULD'VE TOLD HER A LONG TIME AGO."

"Margaret!" Jack grabbed hold of the travel bags. If they didn't hurry, they'd miss the plane. There wasn't time for wallowing. He stopped halfway down the hallway, let go of the bags, and returned to the bedroom.

Margaret sat on the bed, hanging her head low.

He joined her, wrapped his arm around her waist, and pulled her in tight. "She wasn't ready until now. Let's go. We don't want this to turn into more regret."

She took his hand and swept Elizabeth's present from the bed. It wasn't until that awkward moment just before the car starts—that quiet moment, where everything that should be said finds its chance—that he spoke.

"You were a good mother." He rested his hand on her knee. "You *are* a good mother."

He knew to let go; holding on any longer would make her crumble. It was an hour's drive to Oregon State University, then two hours more to the airport. He pulled out of the driveway as she stared at the modest ranch, the place they had hidden their daughters for a decade. He glanced at the house through the rearview mirror, watching all their memories fade behind them, and noticed a black Hummer pulling away from the curb a few feet back.

2

MARGARET TOOK A BREATH AND TRIED TO AVOID HER reflection in the side view mirror. Jack was being so sweet, so patient. She looked at him. His eyes were glued to the rearview mirror more often than the road. She turned to look out the back.

"No. Don't," he said.

She sat back and sank a little in the seat.

"They've been following us for a long time."

She laughed. "You're not thinking...."

"They pulled out when we left the house."

"They're probably going to town, just like us."

He glanced down at the gift in her hand. "Do you believe that?"

She didn't know what to believe anymore.

The edge of Corvallis emerged in the distance. Jack sped up. They needed more time; she needed more time. At the first intersection, he cut the car left like a maniac. She slid up against the door. As the car straightened, she turned around. The road was clear behind them. Jack slowed a little. He smiled at her and she smiled back. It was only paranoia. Since Elizabeth was born, it had felt like someone was watching them—following them. There never was anyone—not that they knew of—just a feeling she had. But Jack felt it, too. The past few days the feeling had grown stronger.

Jack's driving returned to normal and he stopped at the next light. He let out a sigh and smiled at her. "You know I love you."

She grabbed his hand and leaned to kiss him. The light turned green. He took his foot off the brake and sat back up in the seat. Something moved in the corner of her right eye. A vehicle was speeding down the side street toward them—the Hummer. It crashed into the passenger door. The car's momentum shifted all at once and the world spun into darkness.

3

"HE'S DEAD," SAID A MALE VOICE. *IT WASN'T JACK'S.*

Margaret opened her eyes to a grey sky. Rain dripped down, stinging her eyes. *Where's the car?* She turned her head to the direction of the voice. Asphalt scraped her cheek like sandpaper. Two men stood beside her car looking at their feet, blocking whatever drew their attention. Their uniforms were identical—solid black like those of a SWAT team.

"You go deal with the public, use the terrorist bit. That should smooth over any questions. I'll take care of her." The man turned around and his partner went to control the crowd now gathering.

"Margaret, something tells me you've been expecting us."

She didn't recognize him. He looked ex-military, clean cut. His eyes were dark blue, reminding her of the sky that was hidden nine months out of the year.

He stepped closer, exposing the accident behind him. *Jack.* Her husband's body hung limp in the driver's seat. His warm eyes had gone hollow. She tried to move—to run to him—but couldn't. Pain flooded her right side. She reached for its location but only her left hand moved. When she touched her right side, her fingers slid into blood.

"Who are you?"

He leaned down beside her, placing his hands against her ears.

"What do you want?" Raindrops pelted the cement around her.

"Your daughter."

She looked up at the sky. High in the clouds, something flew—something moved. She squinted.

4

I HAD PLANNED ON MEETING MOM AND DAD AT LA Café. It was right across the street from campus, so I wouldn't have to miss my next class. The café's bright yellow bricks stuck out bold against the grey sky. Amber light radiated through the large front window, its etched glass sparkling around an Eiffel tower design. A car gusted by. The wind pulled at my umbrella and rain drenched me before I could gain control of it. Maple leaves tore from a sidewalk tree and followed me across the road, smacking the side of the building.

I could see a man sitting in the back of the café through the glass. *How the hell did Dominic beat me?* His class didn't end for another 15 minutes. I spun the new ring on my finger with my thumb. My Dad forbids me or my sister from marrying before graduation. Dominic knew this. The ring wasn't much—a gold band with a cubic zirconium—but he had promised that in two years we'd be married. Mom would be so excited. I nudged the door open and shook the umbrella off to the side. A small bell hanging above the door jingled. Then I realized it wasn't Dominic.

An old man sat at the back of the café. His skin looked like crinkled autumn leaves. He wore jeans and a blue plaid shirt, but he looked uncomfortable in them. His grey hair was pulled into a ponytail, except for a piece below his right ear, which was twisted into three turquoise beads securing an eagle's feather.

Normally I wouldn't care that out of the whole empty café he chose *my* seat. Since I had started college, my sister met me every Thursday for lunch and we always sat in that seat. It was lucky.

The mosaic dragonfly, hung where there should've been a window, glistened in the light. I had only missed sitting in that seat one time since freshman year and I flunked that day's test. Out of all the tables, he had picked that one.

The scent of fresh-baked cookies carried from the back kitchen and filled the room. Every other booth was empty. If he left soon, I would still have time to take his seat before my next class. A teacup sat in front of him. If he was ordering breakfast there wouldn't be enough time to switch seats. *Shit.*

He stared at me.

The busy sidewalk outside would be a distraction for ignoring that guy. I swung my backpack into the booth framing the front window. It hit the side of the wall, hard. *Shit, my phone!* I couldn't afford to fix another screen on that damn thing. It had taken two weeks to pay for the last one.

The door opened behind me. The little bell jingled with a cold rush of wind. Thank God for another customer. Before I could turn to see who it was, warm lips pressed against the side of my cheek. I closed my eyes. I'd known that feeling since freshman year.

"Hey. Sorry I'm late, babe." Dominic was across the room ordering before I could turn my head. A pencil-thin girl stood behind the counter smiling at him and of course he was eating it up. He looked back at me. "Do you want whipped cream on yours?"

"If you can fit it in." I bit my lip. *I'd like to try whipped cream sometime while he's fucking me.* I glanced over at the old man. His eyes widened. *Did he hear that?* His eyes rested for the first time since I had gotten there, directed at his cup. Clearly I had gotten up too early for entomology—eight-fucking-o'clock in the morning.

I looked away, through the etched window. Maple leaves flapped as they clung to their branches. As soon as they let go, they'd be dead. Wind pushed the incoming rain against the windowpane. The metal napkin holder reflected the light above the table. Its placement was no less than perfect to capture the old man already two steps from the back of my head.

He stopped behind me and I had no choice but to face him. His voice was strong, not at all withered like his skin, "A-wah—"

My heart choked and sweat built in my palms. My ears felt like they were on fire, burning as I tucked a few curls behind them.

"Do not become the moth." He rested a hand on my shoulder. A moment of peace—pure contentment— washed over me. I closed my eyes and let a sigh escape. The tips of his fingers ran through my hair. The warmth of the room swirled as he whispered, "Do not become the moth."

Then silence.

"One white chocolate mocha." Dominic slid in beside me.

I opened my eyes. The old man was gone.

"So you all packed for this weekend? Don't forget a sleeping bag."

I stared at Dominic.

"Are you okay?" he said.

"Where did the Indian go?" I sat up searching the room and the sidewalks outside. Pieces of half-stuck leaves waved from the cement.

"I didn't see anyone." Dominic sipped his coffee, his finger covering the black magic marker scribbled with the name *ANNA 541* —

"I bet you didn't." My eyebrows lifted. It would be fun to watch him squirm out of this one. His smile always got him into trouble. I spun the ring on my finger.

A grin swept over his face. His fingertips brushed my cheek, pulling my lips to his. The smell of his aftershave drew me deeper into his kiss. He leaned away and whispered, "You have nothing to worry about."

I glanced past him, at the counter, but the little slut was hiding in the back. Dominic sat back, switched our coffee sleeves, and rested his hand on my knee. His fingers slid up my leg, warming the wool of my stockings, pushing the lace edge of my dress up. He leaned into me, pressing the weight of his lust against my lips, pinning my head against the window.

My phone beeped, beeped, beeped.

Shit, only ten minutes. I pushed Dominic back and fumbled for the backpack behind me. As I sat up, he kissed my neck. His hand inched up my thigh. The blood in my body flowed, trying to reach his touch.

"I can't miss another class." I smiled and nudged him

off. "Besides, I might have a date with"—I spun the coffee sleeve—"Anna tonight."

"Oh, would you let it go?" He scooted out of the booth and opened the door.

The bell jingled above the doorway. I stood up. *The seat.* I almost botched the whole damn test. Rubbing my fingers across the sparkling mosaic dragonfly wouldn't be enough for an A in microbiology, but it sure as hell was worth a try.

Dominic let go of the door and joined me in the far booth. The warmth of the seat seeped between my legs. I slid my fingers over the pieces of broken mirror following the lines of putty. *Hazel loved this dragonfly. Where are Mom and Dad?*

"Oh, I almost forgot." Dominic pulled a Mason jar from his backpack. "I know its getting hard to find insects now."

"What is it?" I scooped the jar up. The ridiculous 50 insect project for entomology was due tomorrow and I had been one short. *It didn't matter. I had fifty now.* I leaned over the table, restraining the pressure of my lips and kissed him. If the table had not been in the way, my stockings would have been straddling his lap in gratitude.

My phone rang. My heartbeat skipped. It was 9:57, three minutes to make it to class. *One missed call.* My parents were probably running late. I jammed the phone back into my bag and grabbed the jar from the table. A gypsy moth fluttered in the glass. When I stood, the phone rang again. I slid the backpack from my shoulder and dug back into the front pocket. *Two missed calls.* 9:58. I was already late. *Shit.*

I slid the phone back into the pouch. *I should really buy*

a cell phone case. It rang. I looked at the screen: Hazel. *Why is she calling me in the middle of the morning?*

"Lizzy, where are you?" Her voice was loud, but she sounded distant. She hadn't called me that since we were children, the day our dog Haju died. "Where are you, Lizzy?"

I sat back down, clenched the jar in my hand, and looked at the mosaic dragonfly sparkling from the wall. "At the café."

"Is Dominic with you?"

"Yes," barely escaped my lips. Why was she asking?

She sighed. "I'm five minutes away ...."

The call ended.

I looked up at Dominic and saw that his eyes were already showing concern. The specimen jar slid from my fingers onto the table. The moth inside lost flight as it spun with the rolling glass. My stomach tightened as I exhaled all the air from my lungs. Sadness crept into every thought. The next five minutes were spent in a haze trying to make sense of the conversation, dissecting each word to the other half of me—to him.

The door opened.

Hazel's high heels beat through the threshold stomping out the bell's jingle. Her synthetic tan looked almost natural against a tight chestnut ponytail. The eyes that had given her the name dripped with mascara. We couldn't look more different. Her eyes held an emptiness— a piece lost from everything that made her whole. She didn't have to say a word.

I felt it.

My father would never walk me down the aisle. My mother would never kiss my children goodnight.

5

IT WAS A CAR ACCIDENT. THE FACT THAT THEY DIED instantly was supposed to be a comfort. *Why would it be?* There is no comfort, not in death. A piece of my heart grew dark.

My stomach hurt from crying. Every breath burned. Each step from the café blurred into the sidewalk. Rain poured from the sky. The leaves stopped waving from the ground. Puddles filled outside my dormitory. The climb to the second floor was too much; it was just too much. Dominic grabbed my hand. Warm tears dripped down my cheeks. He nodded. It was okay to cry. Hazel's heels echoed through the stairwell from behind. Her fingers locked between mine. There were no words; we both knew that.

Dominic held the stairwell door. As soon as we got to my dorm room he sprinted across the room, scooped up the "ribbed for her pleasure" condoms, and shoved them under my pillow. The top bunk was made. The bathroom, to the left of the door, was empty. Megan had already left for gymnastics.

Dominic returned to me as fast as he could and kissed my forehead. His hands cupped my wet cheeks. He kissed me, smearing the snot from my upper lip onto his.

Hazel kicked off her heels and slid into the bottom bunk. The condoms fell out from beneath the pillow onto the floor. I nuzzled in beside her. I tried not to think. I tried so hard not think about how many moments were gone, how in a matter of minutes my life had changed. Tears soaked my pillow. My sister, my co-partner in crime growing up, wrapped her arm over me.

That was enough. It is the moment I cling to—the only moment that keeps me alive.

6

WE SLEPT, WRAPPED IN EACH OTHER'S LOVE, FOR THE rest of Thursday. By nightfall, Hazel woke up, kissed me, and snuck off to bury herself in work. When Huju died, she cleaned the whole house. I was only eight at the time. That was 12 years ago—Mom and Dad were still alive. If I could just go back to that moment, change something, anything... things might have turned out different.

Dominic's warm body replaced hers. He wrapped his arms around me, securing me beside him. The red digits of the alarm clock turned past midnight. The clock's glow danced with the caged gypsy moth, its white wings swirled with red—so beautiful. She kept me company in the hollow darkness.

Dominic tossed, reminding me that I was still alive. Moonlight rippled through the trees, caressing the dorm's windowpane. The red digits fought with the moon's glow for my entertainment. What a fucking night. The corners of my lips puckered, holding back my sorrow. The world melted into darkness as I closed my eyes, but sleep would not come.

A shadow crept over me. Something moved outside. I sat up and whacked my forehead into the top bunk. *Fuck.* Could life get any worse?

"What the hell are you doing?" Dominic mumbled and rolled over. He never was much use after his head hit the pillow.

My head throbbed and pounded beneath my palm.

Minutes were lost rubbing the pain from my forehead. When it eased, I glanced out the second-story window.

A two-foot Great Grey Owl sat across from me in a tree. The darkness of the night dissipated into the shadows, leaving only the bird's feathers stained with darkness. Rain sprinkled down, tearing the orange and brown leaves to the ground. Sunlight warmed the horizon. *I had made it through the worst night of my life.*

I slid from the bed and pressed my nose to the windowpane. The warmth of my breath fogged the glass.

"Come back to bed," Dominic said.

My heart jumped. *Shit.* He scared me.

He pulled back the covers and smiled, unsure how to handle me. He still had both of his parents. He'd never understand this.

The windowpane squeaked beneath my fingers as I turned from it. He was already half naked and more than willing to fill my emptiness.

I climbed into bed and buried my face into the pillow. His hand slid up my thigh and tugged my stockings down. The tips of his fingers slid beneath the elastic of my underwear. The tightness of his boxers pressed against my leg.

Music blared into the room as the alarm clock went off.

The top bunk rustled.

I hit the snooze button, 7:45. The large owl still sat in the tree. It looked as though it were staring at me. Dominic pulled me back into bed. Sex would clear my mind, if I let it. He gently kissed me. Saltwater streamed down my cheeks. I wanted to feel something—anything. He hushed me as he inched my dress up. His body pressed against the thin cotton of my underwear. I inhaled and my chest rose against his.

Someone knocked at the door.

I pulled away from him, allowing the world to take back my warmth. I tugged the dress down below my waist and hurried to the door.

The owl screeched.

I tripped and caught myself right before falling. My fingers rested on the brass door knob.

Okay, I could do this. I took a deep breath and opened the door. One comment—one how are you doing—and my face would be pressed back into the pillow. *Don't do it, don't cry ....*

I opened the door. Zach stood outside, ready for entomology, as he had done every Friday for our eight o'clock lab. His California tan was still deep for autumn. The brown of his eyes held no sympathy, no pity. I was in the clear. He didn't know I was crumbling inside.

His sandy blonde hair had been darker when we were children. Until junior year, I hadn't seen him since we were eight—the last year at our summer home, the day he kissed me. If I stood there any longer, I would have lost it.

"Hey," I walked away from the door, "give me a second." I fumbled into a pair of jeans and pulled a hooded sweatshirt over the dress.

"Where do you think you're going?" Dominic leaned from the bottom bunk and pulled me onto him. His hand slid up under the sweatshirt, rubbing the delicate fabric covering my nipple.

"My project is due." I pushed away from him and sat on the edge of the bed. I could stay in bed wasting a whole semester, or stumble through the rest of it—two more months. I pushed a pair of flip-flops on and tied my hair into a loose ponytail. "If I don't go, I'll lose my scholarship."

"Isn't there a rule that if …." He silenced himself.

I stood up. I knew what he was going to say. My professors would excuse me. Maybe losing myself in school work would help. Hazel always did her best when shoving her emotions to the floor. Sun warmed the gypsy moth. It fluttered until I cupped the glass jar.

Dominic rolled over, cocooning himself into my bed. "I'll wait for you."

I nodded. Tears rained down my cheeks. One deep inhale stopped the rest. I held it, clenched the jar, and headed for the door.

Zach's smile faded as I joined him. "Are you okay?"

"No." I hurried past him and down the stairway, trying to keep one step ahead of him. He'd ask what's wrong—they all would. How could they not? I wore it all over my face. I flung the door open. The cold air dug down into my bones. There, perched alongside the building, was the owl. It stared at me, watching the wind destroy what warmth I had left.

Zach bumped into the back of me. I lost balance. He caught me. I looked up, but by then the owl was gone, its branch left vibrating.

"Did you see that owl?" Zach's saving grip on my arm pulled me closer.

"Yeah." I tugged the sleeve of my hoodie and wiped my wet cheeks. He let go of my arm as we walked along the usual path. It was quiet, even for a Friday morning. He was quiet. His pace slowed. I couldn't stand the silence. "So are you and Melissa going to Alex's tonight?"

He stopped and glanced back at the empty tree.

"Zach?" *Don't do this to me. Don't ask me questions. Please fill my head with idle conversation.*

"Did you know that Indian folklore suggests owls are the messengers of death?" He stepped closer and brushed a curl stuck to my cheek. "They believe that if an owl speaks to you, it is a bad omen."

I glanced down at the jar in my hand. The moth fluttered helpless within. "I'm sorry," I stepped back from him. "I can't. I just can't."

He reached for me but I ran back to the dorm. His voice faded behind me, "Elizabeth."

It became hard to breathe. My heartbeat pounded with each step. Mud splashed between my toes. I threw open the door to my room. *Dominic was right. I should've stayed in bed.*

Sunlight trickled across the floor. The empty tree past the window framed the background for the silhouettes entangled on my bed. A girl's legs were wrapped around Dominic's bare ass. His triceps flexed as he gripped the edge of the mattress, pushing his cock into her. Her hair pressed against my pillow with each thrust. He pulled her thighs farther off the bottom bunk. The purple thong that was wrapped around her ankle fell to the floor.

The doorknob slid from my fingers. The door closed behind me.

"Oh shit. Elizabeth. Wait!" Dominic pulled out of her. A ribbed condom choked the erection he had. Megan lay fully exposed, grinning at me. *Fucking slut.*

The world swirled. *How could he? I would never …* I couldn't move. My stomach tightened. I could taste the acid creeping up my esophagus. Just the other night he had promised me everything. I had given him everything—two fucking years. I had done his homework, washed his clothes, given blow jobs at his every beckoning. He had given me a cheap-ass ring. I pulled it off and threw it at his ugly, pathetic face.

I needed to get out of there, away from there. The bathroom was a step away. I went for it, but tripped and fell to the floor. My cheekbone whacked the tile. I clenched the Mason jar.

"Babe," Dominic bent over, reaching for me, his erection pointed straight at me.

"Get away from me!" I shut my eyes, but tears leaked out. He was supposed to be there for me. *Leave me alone.* I felt him back away, but it didn't ease the crushing pain in my heart. On exhale I cried. I couldn't hold back any longer. *Why? Why me? Why now? Why the fuck is everything falling apart?* My cries turned silent. Life wouldn't even grant me the release that I needed. I had nothing left. The clarity of the bathroom blurred, doused in a sheet of tears. I heaved a breath, hoping the floor would swallow me whole. Any life would be better than this. Nausea pushed through me as my cheek smeared against the tile. Numbness took hold like an old friend.

"Elizabeth," he whispered.

Blood rushed through my veins, poured into my fingertips. My fingers tightened around the jar and I hurled it at Dominic's fucking head.

It missed, hit the edge of the doorway, and broke. Shards of glass ricocheted from the wall, raining down on me.

"I didn't cheat on you. It was nothing. I didn't even finish so it doesn't count."

Blood rushed back to my heart with a pounding hurt. His subsequent words were deafened against its beat. A piece of glass fogged beneath my breath. My cheek throbbed against the floor. The lifeless moth lay at the tip of my right hand.

"This is your fault. You left me alone with your roommate after not finishing."

Why's he still talking? I pulled the white wings closer and drew the insect's limp body between my fingers. White powder smeared onto my skin. *Why won't he leave me alone?*

"I love you," he whispered. He sat in the doorway, naked, on his knees.

He'd done enough. *It doesn't matter anymore.* Warm tears drained from my eyes, whether I wanted them to or not. Light reflected off their droplets. The broken glass shined. I couldn't move. There was no place to go. I closed my eyes and released the fragile body from my fingers. A piece of glass cut into the side of my hand. I grabbed it. Its edge sliced into my thumb. I opened my eyes fully. Blood filled the seam of my skin against the glass. I shoved my sleeve up. The blue veins running down my left arm looked like the branches of a tree on white canvas. They blurred with tears. I forced the water from my eyes. I clenched the glass. Blood dripped from my thumb.

The edge of it cut deeper as I forced the jagged glass through my wrist. Blood poured from my vein and the weight of my hands fell against the floor. The tile wasn't as cold as it had been. The pounding in my head eased. The piece of glass slid from my fingers. The moth's broken body disappeared in a puddle of blood.

Then I felt the pressure of *his* hands pressed against my wrist. His fingers crushed what was left of the insect.

Do not become the moth. The old man's voice trailed into darkness.

MEADOWLARK

1

HAZEL KNEW SHE SHOULDN'T HAVE LEFT ELIZABETH, but she had to close the McAlister deal. She had spent too many damn hours on the acquisition. The commission alone would be a quarter of a million dollars. She hurried through the office. Two hours of goddamn sleep. If she lost this, she'd be with the bottom feeders again. That wasn't an option. Elizabeth would understand—she always did.

The conference room was already packed. Mr. Pierson stared through the glass wall. Flirting wouldn't help this time. She threw her large zebra-print purse beside the door and joined the group. "Good morning, gentlemen. Shall we get started?"

"Yes, let's." Mr. Pierson's wry eyes attempted to crush her.

"So on page two-forty-three you have ...."—*the same old boring speech*. She could recite the lecture in her sleep. *Sleep would be grand.* Eleven white men stared at her boobs. They weren't even paying attention. Her circus act

finished, she took a seat beside the only young guy—
Parker Philip. He was in his thirties, a bit of a tight ass, but
he loosened up after a few drinks.

"Thank you, Ms. Hutchings." Mr. Pierson heaved his
fat ass up. He loved being the center of attention. Hazel's
short spiel lasted five minutes; any longer was too much
for him to bear.

A phone rang.

Mr. Pierson stopped mid-sentence. His beady eyes
flicked over the crowd. "Whose phone is that?"

Someone was in deep shit now. It rang again. The noise
came from near the door, echoing throughout the still
room, from the zebra-print handbag on the floor. *Shit.*
Hazel forgot to silence it. Her cheeks burned. Apologizing
would only make it worse. She stumbled from the
conference chair toward the door. The phone stopped. *Oh,
thank God.*

She grabbed the purse, slid back into her seat, and
fumbled for the phone. It rang. The burn of her cheeks
spread as she pulled it out. Frustration filled her voice,
"Sorry." She looked down. DOMINIC. *No, no, no.* The
room, the deal, even Mr. Pierson's beet-red face faded to
the background.

Her hand shook as she answered the call. "Hello?"

"What do you think you're doing?" Mr. Pierson said.

Dominic was breathing heavily. "They took her to the
hospital. She tried to kill herself. I'm sorry. I'm so sorry
…."

Hazel hung up. She dropped into the chair. Nothing
seemed real. How could she be so selfish? What the hell
was she doing at work? All those old grumpy faces stared
at her. The phone slid from her fingers onto the table. She
wiped her lips, smearing red lipstick onto her cheek.

"Gentlemen, please excuse me," she said, more from habit than from forming the words on purpose. She gathered her things, walked to the door, and looked back at Mr. Pierson. His face looked like a cherry about to explode. It didn't matter now, *nothing matters now.*

She sprinted through the office toward the elevator. *What if I don't get there in time?* The door opened. *I'll never get to say goodbye.* The elevator eased down into the basement. *She's all I have.* The keys slipped from her fingers. She bent to pick them up and banged her head on the side of the car. *Lizzy, you hold on. You fight.* She fumbled with the keys and finally climbed in. *You stay with me, goddamn it.*

She peeled out of the parking garage and sped for the hospital. All the moments she regretted popped into her head. One of them was the time she chased Elizabeth through a field of buttercups. Laughter filled the warm air. The pink ribbon her sister had stolen from her bounced with her blonde curls. Hazel grabbed for Elizabeth and they both fell. Instead of crying, her little sister laughed. They lay among the yellow flowers, staring up at a blue sky.

The hospital emerged in the distance. The clouds grew darker. It felt like a whole other lifetime now. Hazel parked in front of the Emergency Room entrance. An autumn breeze swept her toward the sliding doors. They slowly crept open, taunting her patience.

"You can't park there," bellowed the receptionist.

"I'm looking for my sister, Elizabeth Hutchings."

The woman's anger faded as she cleared her throat. Her nails clicked against the keyboard. "She's still in surgery. Dr. Stein will be out as soon as they finish. You can have a seat. I'll have someone move your car, if you'd like."

Hazel slid her keys across the counter. Her hands shook. She spun to take a seat, but a dizzy spell swept over her. It was another minute before she could let go of the counter and make her way over to the semicircle of chairs. She plopped down in the closest seat, facing the exit. She never sat with her back to a door.

The emergency doors opened.

A cold draft brought two men in. Their uniforms were jet black, military or special ops. The first had dark blue eyes. His hair was a deep brown. His partner was much more plain, not as obsessed about working out. He licked his lips and stared at her.

Her phone vibrated. It was a text message from Dominic. *How is she?*

IDK, she's still in surgery.

I'm sorry. Tell me what I can do to fix this. Tell her Megan doesn't mean anything, I love her.

Hazel held in the button of her phone and waited for it to shut down. *He cheated on her? Son of a bitch! She was supposed to be safe with him. He was supposed to ....*

She shoved her purse to the floor and looked up to find both men staring at her. Mr. Blue Eyes redirected to the receptionist intently listening to the phone. His partner, however, did not. He licked the bottom of his lip again and bit it until the receptionist hung up. She nodded to them and then looked over at Hazel.

The hairs on the back of Hazel's neck stood up. She crossed her legs and arms. Blue Eyes took the seat to her left and his partner, now chewing on his lip, sat across from her. The right sleeves of their uniforms were embroidered with the word *MEADOWLARK*. An orange-reflective fabric formed a biohazard symbol around it, centered perfectly inline with the O.

The man across from her set a black briefcase on his lap. Rattling against it was a chain, handcuffed to his wrist.

From the corner of her eye, she noticed a man walking down the hallway from her right. A clear image of an old man formed. He was a fossil, dressed in pale green scrubs and a hairnet. "Dr. Stein" was embroidered into his white coat. "Miss Hutchings, I presume."

"Yes." Hazel fumbled to a standing position.

"Please, sit." He sat to her right.

She sank back into her seat to join him.

The medical words dragged on as he explained the procedure. "The surgery went well. Elizabeth is in stable condition. We have to wait for the sedative to wear off before you can see her." He glanced back at a woman behind him, "This is Miss Grady. She will be handling your sister's case."

Case?

The woman took Dr. Stein's place and set a manila file on her lap. "We need a statement from you about the events, or what you might suspect occurred."

"Um … our parents died yesterday—I had to go to work—and she was supposed to be okay with Dominic. She was supposed to be okay—she wasn't supposed to …." Hazel looked into the woman's eyes. Tears dripped down her cheek. It was so unreal.

"Has your sister ever suffered from depression?"

"No."

"Has she ever tried to hurt herself before?"

Hazel's heart sank and with the next breath, she spoke softly, "How dare you. I don't know what you're implying, but my sister wouldn't do such a thing—she wouldn't do that to me."

Ms. Grady may have said other things, asked other questions, but Hazel stopped listening. The whole room faded into the exterior of her shell. If the walls were thick enough, nothing else could hurt her. When the woman walked away, Hazel's head collapsed into her hands. The wall crashed down, bringing her sadness into the open. The lobby filled with the cry that she had so desperately tried to keep hidden. A held breath pulsated to get out. She couldn't burrow deeply enough into the musty chair. There had to be a tissue somewhere in that huge purse of hers.

"Go ahead. I'll be there in a minute," the man beside her said. The handcuffs rattled as his partner stood.

Hazel wiped her eyes, soaking the side of her hand.

The briefcase swung to his side as he followed the doctor's fading footsteps. The handcuffs looked more like a black metal than painted silver. A sword hung to his side—*a samurai sword?*

"Are you okay?" Blue Eyes said.

There wasn't enough air in the world to fill the words she needed to respond. A light nod was all she could give. Her fingertips slid to her lips, restraining any cry from escape. *I'll be okay.*

He held out an orange handkerchief.

She forced a weak smile, took the cloth, and buried her face in its fabric. The cotton soaked and smeared with mascara. *Okay, she'll be okay. I can do this. It will be okay ....* The handkerchief was a mess. "I'm so sorry. I didn't mean to—"

She opened her eyes to an empty lobby.

2

AGENT BENJAMIN SWUNG THE OPERATING ROOM doors open. A chubby nurse stood beside a young woman, unconscious, still on the operating table. It was *her*; it had to be.

His partner stood at the woman's feet and glanced up from the patient's chart.

"Is it her?" Benjamin walked over. His heart pounded.

"It appears to be." Agent Jay exchanged the chart for a key around Benjamin's neck and popped open the briefcase. He pulled a case file from the inside pocket.

Everything has to be done by the book. Benjamin tore the file from Jay's hand. The hospital chart and case file were identical.

"You better not fuck this up," Jay said.

"Find me a syringe." Benjamin threw the folder and chart into the briefcase, and then snapped on a pair of surgical gloves.

The nurse flinched. She stood like a turkey blinded by headlights, unwilling to move out of the way.

Just ignore her. Benjamin inhaled slow and deep, held his breath, and picked up a small glass vial from the briefcase. A black liquid sloshed up the sides. Jay slowly handed him a syringe. His partner's eyes relaxed at the transfer of responsibility. Benjamin embraced it.

He fully exhaled before sticking the needle's tip into the black liquid. Air bubbles gathered in the syringe. He stepped toward the women and gently flicked the needle's side. "Nurse, please roll the patient toward you."

The woman's lips quivered. She stood there unmoving.

Fucking turkey. Benjamin looked back at Jay. He closed his eyes and shook his head. Even with all the power the

United States government had given them, some still resisted. He rolled back his shoulders and moved around to the opposite side of the operating table. If he got too close, he'd end up punching her in the face. "Is the patient's name Elizabeth Hutchings?"

"Si." The woman's voice lowered.

Jay stepped around Benjamin and pinned his chest up against the nurse's back. He wrapped his fingers around her right arm, digging his nails into her fat, squeezing harder and harder.

The nurse's posture crippled slightly and she moaned out, "Si."

Jay released her and she obediently rolled Elizabeth's hip toward herself.

Perspiration oozed from Benjamin's pores as he slowly slid the needle into the patient's spine. The rhythm of the heart monitor slowed. A golden curl drifted from her left shoulder dragging the hospital gown with it, revealing the edge of a tattoo. *A tattoo?* His fingers pushed the rest of the gown from her shoulder. Black ink curved into tribal lines forming a turtle. *How could it be?* There is no mention of it in her case file. He looked up at the nurse. "Are you sure this Elizabeth Hutchings?"

Sweat beaded from the nurse's forehead. Her arms stretched to hold the patient in place, a bruise had already beginning to form beneath Jay's fingers. "Si," sounded more like a scared mouse than a woman.

He looked back down at the frail limp body. Two years tracking Elizabeth and he had never been this close. Her pale cheeks were smeared with day-old mascara. Her back was covered in goosebumps.

"Let's go," Jay whispered. He released the nurse, grabbed the briefcase, and headed for the door.

"Okay, let her down easy," Benjamin said.

The nurse rolled Elizabeth back down, toward him.

He nodded.

She returned his nod, but it was forced, full of regret.

Working for Meadowlark had its perks. Benjamin glanced down at the young woman. Her slashed skin was mended with stitches stretching up her wrist. She was far from becoming Sleeping Beauty; her fairytale was much darker.

He walked away and stopped at the door.

The heart monitor flatlined.

He exhaled with relief and allowed the door to swing shut behind him. Both corners of his mouth formed a grin.

Dr. Stein and three nurses sprinted down the hallway past him.

He stepped into view of the lobby and ignored the weight of Hazel's eyes on him as he passed. The emergency doors slid open to a black Hummer. The Meadowlark symbol stood out in orange against the passenger door. Music pounded inside and spewed from the car when he opened its door. He slid inside and rested his forehead against the window, watching the ER doors slid shut.

"Dude, what's wrong with you?" Jay yelled above the music and nudged Benjamin's shoulder. "Woo! Let's go celebrate."

The Hummer sped downtown.

Benjamin hoped Elizabeth had been awake. He wanted to see the color of her eyes. He had seen them in photographs and on Facebook, but on stakeouts he had always been too far away. The Chief of Meadowlark had described them as an ice blue, but who the hell knows if that's accurate. He was the boss's boss and no one got to see him.

Rain splashed against the window. His reflection in the side view mirror was dark, drained by the clouds. He reached for the briefcase. Maybe he had missed the tattoo.

Jay pulled up to one of those side-entrance bars— brown chipped paint, full trash bins right around the corner of the door, harmless enough to eat at in their uniforms.

Every mole and scar was listed in her file, but nothing—nothing about her tattoo. Benjamin tucked the folder back into the briefcase. Jay disappeared into the bar. Benjamin examined the empty vial and rolled it in his hand.

By the time he stowed the vial and secured the vehicle, Jay was already sitting at the bar with two beers in front of him. The sword hanging at Benjamin's side rubbed against the stool at the bar as he sat. The bartender shuffled from the back room with two clean glasses. He was in his late forties and pale, like his skin hadn't seen the sun in years.

"Would you relax?" Jay nudged a beer toward him and gulped his down.

Benjamin's fingers drummed against the counter, as he glanced up at the clock.

"We'll go get her in a few hours, and then ... case closed," Jay said.

"I suppose you're right." Benjamin chugged the beer, letting it calm his nerves.

"What a waste of a fine piece of ass." Jay swallowed a second glass the moment it hit the counter in front of him.

He pointed up his finger and another refill soon followed. "You knew taking this case that she would have to die—at all costs."

Benjamin nodded; he knew.

3

"I DON'T KNOW WHY ELIZABETH'S HEART STOPPED, but we got it pumping again and she appears to be in stable condition now." Dr. Stein's words repeated in Hazel's head.

Appears? Goddamn it. Lizzy, you fight for me. Don't give up. I need you.

Hazel's heels pounded down the corridor, easing as she approached room 205. She stopped, wiped her eyes, took a breath, and stepped into the recovery room. Her heels clinked. She paused and took off her shoes.

A nurse stood by Elizabeth's bed injecting the IV leading into her sister's good arm. Elizabeth greeted Hazel with such a warm smile. She didn't tell her how horrible she was for not being there—for skipping out on her in the middle of the night—and not holding her hand through all of it. She just smiled—that's it.

The heaviness of Elizabeth's ice blue eyes met hers. Residual tears glistened on her cheeks. Beneath the pain meds she was looking for Hazel's empathy.

It was there. *What had happened? How did we end up like this?* Hazel exhaled as she sat down on the hospital bed. She wrapped her arms around her little sister—such warmth, such pure warmth. Not even the stench of medical disinfectants could move her. Nothing could move her. Elizabeth's gown soaked with Hazel's tears.

Snot dripped from Hazel's nose. She pulled away, looking for a tissue.

Elizabeth's left wrist lay limp at her side, secured in two inches of gauze. A frown melted across Hazel's face. She had no choice but to take a deep breath and suck it up. There was no one to hold her up and keep her from falling into despair. She forced a smile and reached for her zebra purse. *To hell with a tissue.* She wiped her nose with her sleeve and heaved the purse onto her lap. "The hospital threw out your clothes."

Elizabeth hung her head.

Hazel looked into the bag and a smile took hold of her. *There it was.* What every woman needs when her life goes to shit. She held up a box of chestnut hair dye.

"You want me to dye my hair?" Elizabeth pulled at her curls and the intravenous needle wiggled in her vein. Then she smiled.

"No, I want you to do whatever *you* want. But I know for a fact that you have dyed your hair every single time you've gone through a breakup. Nothing is preventing you from starting completely over." *Just look away. Don't cry.* Hazel looked out the window and closed her eyes. *It will be okay.* She opened them. A Great Grey Owl sat on a tree outside. The night's wind picked at the leaves clinging to its branch. She looked back at Elizabeth. "Are you really going to make me go through the list and hair colors?"

Elizabeth's eyes glazed with sedative.

Hazel smiled. "Let's see, there was little Johnny and that rustic-red color …."

"Okay, okay give me that." Elizabeth grabbed the box. "Just shut up already."

Hazel helped her to the bathroom. She rested on the

toilet seat. It had been years since she had dyed her sister's hair. They used to take up a whole weekend in high school gabbing about boys and painting their nails. Monday morning, Mom would curl their hair. *Mom.*

"Are you okay?" Elizabeth rested her hand on Hazel's arm.

Tears had escaped her. She cleared her throat, slid on the plastic gloves, cracked open the first bottle, and unscrewed the second. "Yeah."

Elizabeth let go as the mixture stained her blonde hair.

The door creaked and a nurse popped her plump cheeks into the bathroom. "Are you girls dyeing your hair in a hospital?"

Hazel froze.

The woman pushed the door open and stepped into the small area. She had a bruise on her arm just below her right sleeve.

"No, Ma'am." Hazel went to cover her mouth and smeared brown dye all over her lip. *Oh my God, this better not stain.*

Elizabeth burst out with a laugh.

The nurse looked down at Elizabeth. Her eyes widened. She glanced over at her bandaged wrist. Her face turned into a forced smile and she grabbed onto the doorknob. "Keep this door shut."

It closed behind her. Any more time contemplating that moment would take away from the time Hazel was now gifted to have with her sister. She squirted the Hershey-colored chemical onto her hair and lathered it in.

She concentrated on every touch, exhale and moment spent washing her sister's hair. She wrapped Elizabeth's hair and stepped back.

"So, what do you think?" Elizabeth tugged on the

towel and it fell to the floor. Wet chestnut curls clung to her clean cheeks. The pale blue of her eyes popped.

"You look like mom," Hazel said.

Her phone rang.

"You better get that." Elizabeth looked past her, at the mirror.

Hazel's heart pounded.

"Go get it." Elizabeth smiled and looked at her. "I'm not going anywhere."

Hazel's stockings slid across the tile as she sprinted to the bed. They could sell Mom and Dad's house to pay for Elizabeth's college, but student health insurance wouldn't cover the hospital bill. Who knew how much therapy would cost. She grabbed the cell phone from her purse.

There was a knock at the door. The nurse entered.

The phone stopped ringing. Hazel viewed the missed call. *Mr. Pierson. Shit.*

The nurse walked toward her.

"I apologize if we conducted ourselves inappropri—"

"Your sister is going to need clean dressing for the first few days." The nurse glanced at the bathroom door. She withdrew a piece of paper from her pocket. "And this is a prescription for the pain. Make sure she makes a follow-up appointment with a counselor."

Hazel held out her hand. Patients are never discharged late at night.

"I can't officially discharge her, but there were these two men ..." The bathroom doorknob turned. "... The hospital has signed your sister into their custody."

"What do you mean ...?" Hazel's voice rose.

"I don't have the answers, and I don't think you should stick around to find out." The nurse glanced back at the door and rubbed the bruise on her arm.

Elizabeth stepped from the bathroom, leaning against the wall for support. The collar of her hospital gown was saturated in chestnut dye.

The nurse handed Hazel a set of pale green scrubs and hurried to Elizabeth's side. Brenda Martinez always kept a spare in her locker.

"Do you like it?" Hazel slid over on the bed, allowing Elizabeth to lie down. Her drained body looked pasty beneath the florescent lights.

"You must have had a shitty day." Elizabeth wiped a wet curl from her forehead and sank down in the sheets.

"Yep, those pain meds should be working now." Nurse Martinez glanced at her watch and wrote on the medical chart. She took Elizabeth's blood pressure and patted the gauze around her wrist. She unraveled the gauze. Her eyes met Elizabeth's. "I like it. I think it makes those eyes of yours pop. Now make sure you dry that hair and stay out of the cold. You don't need your immune system working any harder than it already is."

Hazel noticed the nurse's hands shaking as she looped the gauze around Elizabeth's wrist. The woman glanced over at the door several times.

"All done," she patted Elizabeth's knee, stood up, and handed Hazel a stack of gauze. "You might want to help her."

Nurse Martinez tapped on her watch and left the room.

"Hazel, what's going on?" Elizabeth slowly pushed herself to a sitting position.

"Apparently, we're leaving." Hazel slid the shirt over Elizabeth's head, slowly working her arms through. She should have stayed last night.

Water dripped from Elizabeth's chemical-fumed hair, saturating Hazel's blouse. Closing her eyes didn't stop the warm tears from spilling down her cheek. She pulled away and grabbed Elizabeth's hands. "We'll get through this. Okay?"

The door creaked open. Hazel's heart skipped.

Nurse Martinez pushed in a wheelchair. She froze halfway across the room. The faint sound of the elevator beeped. Five seconds, four, three, two. She glanced back at the door and then continued toward them.

"You better go now." She pulled the intravenous needle from Elizabeth's vein. Her stubby fingers fastened a cotton ball over the hole with a band-aid. She headed for the door and looked back. "I wish you the best of luck."

She left the door open as she hurried down the hallway.

"Okay, let's hurry up." Hazel's heart pounded. She grabbed the pants off the bed. Once Elizabeth slipped into the loose scrubs, Hazel held out her $300 wool coat. Elizabeth's body swayed as she stepped away from the bed's edge. Hazel eased her to the wheelchair, wrapped the coat around her, and grabbed the handlebars. Her blood pressure raced. They made it to the threshold just as a ping of the elevator sounded from the hallway.

4

THE CEMENT WALLS OF THE CITY HAD QUICKLY FADED into rich forest. The sound of the Pacific Ocean rumbled in the distance. I was unconscious for most of the car ride. A blanket of fog had drifted across the small beach town of Otter Rock by dusk. Hazel clenched the steering wheel as the SUV weaved along the Oregon Coast.

Fishing boats twinkled in a pitch black ocean. The dark highway hid my reflection in the passenger window.

Hazel led us directly where she wanted me to be. The headlights pushed through the fog as she turned down a long gravel driveway. Conifers scraped at the vehicle's metal doors until opening to a clearing and a Victorian beach house. Windows wrapped around every inch of it; even the front door was a sheet of glass.

Warm lights danced from its interior—across the porch, over the pebbled driveway—and stopped short of the car. The headlights made up for the difference. Their glow eased the water vapor's denseness. A couple sprinted toward the front door inside, it was Alex and Jan.

"We're here." It was the first thing Hazel had said since we left the hospital. She pulled the key from the ignition and rested a hand on my sleeve. She cleared her throat and opened the door, pulling away from me. "Are you coming?"

Rain began to splash against the windshield. Alex had stopped at the front door, holding it open for Hazel. Jan sprinted toward my door. Her rain boots sloshed across the river of pebbles.

She ripped open the passenger door and cold air rushed in. I slid out of the vehicle, sedative still working deep in my veins. Jan steadied me. The pebbles stung like ice against my bare feet. My knees buckled, refusing to hold me. Jan's breasts pressed against mine, stabilizing my body against hers. She reeked of alcohol. Her hug, on the other hand, was refreshingly short. "Come on, it's freezing out."

We hurried to the house as the sky poured. My heart beat heavy as we approached the porch. The rain wouldn't be able to wash away what I had done. If I stayed long enough in it, the bitterness of the dark would freeze me— forever.

Jan stepped past Alex. His tender smile washed away any dread I had conjured up. They had started dating sophomore year and he became the brother I never had.

He greeted me with a light hug. His wetsuit was dry. An ocean breeze pushed me away from him, into the house. The foyer was more like a small hallway, opening up to a large living room wrapped in windows. A kitchen sat to the right. An island with a few barstools sectioned the two rooms. Friday night's party had been canceled. I had spent so much time planning this Halloween weekend. So much wasted time with *him*. A sigh escaped me. The sedative wouldn't allow me to shed the tears that had been building.

A woodstove crackled beside a couch that faced the interior wall. A plasma television hung above a decorative bookshelf. The barstools were far enough away to leave room for the hallway leading to the bedrooms.

Hazel's voice seeped down the corridor from the bathroom.

I sat down beside Jan. She muted a commercial selling pills for depression.

Hazel's voice grew into argument.

I sat up. *He's here!*

"Relax, he's not here, Alex uninvited him." Jan looked at me with no judgment. She was the only person I knew who accepted everyone's faults—took everything she received and turned it into something positive.

Hazel walked up the bedroom hallway. Her face was red and turned to the ground. She tried to speak and at first choked on her words. "I have to go to Albuquerque." She sat down beside me and grabbed my hand. "I'll be back by the end of the weekend. Promise me you'll pick me up from the airport."

"I promise."

She squeezed my hand.

"Hazel, …." I looked down at our entwined fingers. Gauze hid the evidence of my torn heart. I had no words. There just weren't any words.

"You can tell me when I get back." She leaned over and kissed my cheek. "And I did have a shitty day."

She pulled her hand away and placed it against my cheek. "But that just means"—a tear fell, rippling down the curves of her fingers—"you owe me."

A laugh slipped out. My teeth dug into my lower lip to hold back tears.

Hazel leaned her forehead against mine. Her thumb smeared the tear running down my cheek. She gave me one last kiss before standing to leave. As she walked toward the door, her phone rang.

"Yes, I will be on that flight." Her purse fell out of her hand. She bent to retrieve it and turned back one last time. *I love you* moved through her wordless lips. Then the moment was gone. She went on to argue over the phone and walked out.

Jan elbowed me and tossed a cell phone in my lap—my phone. "I hope you don't mind that I cleared out all dickhead's stuff."

The doorbell rang.

Jan cleared her throat. "Why don't you go get cleaned up. We're leaving soon. You can sleep in the car since it's a long drive."

The last thing I wanted to do was go camping.

She patted my knee, stood, and ran to get the front door.

I schlepped myself to the bathroom. Seeing one more person would be unbearable. Let alone a 12-hour car ride.

The shower became my sanctuary, its warm water my solace. The gauze on my wrist became saturated, pulling my arm down like a broken branch. I unraveled it. The droplets of water amplified to the size of an elephant and pounded down against the line of stitches. That shit hurt, even when doped up. Hot water streamed down my back. A sharp pain cut through my spine. I stepped from the shower. Cold air rushed at me the minute I pulled the shower curtain back, tearing goosebumps from my skin. The steam gathered on the mirror and then dripped onto the sink. Humidity weighed against the sedative in my veins.

I secured a towel around me and stepped into the hallway. No one was in sight, but voices carried from the porch. There was a small, dark blue bedroom to the right. Alex's surfboard was propped in its corner. I took the bedroom to the left. It was twice the size. A king bed sat in the middle of the wall to the left of the door. A huge bay window carried the sound of the ocean's crashing waves. A long dresser held a large mirror, capturing any intruders. Pictures of a grey-haired man smiling beside his trophy wife surrounded the room. The closet door beside the dresser was cracked open just an inch. I sat on the edge of the bed, wrapped only in a towel, leaving a trail of wet footprints behind me.

"Hey you ...." a male voice came from the doorway.

Crap.

Howard Gomez was an asshole. His mouth had no filter and his brain was always leaking some new male chauvinistic bullshit. But he was Alex's surfing buddy and was only around when we partied at the beach house. He slithered into the room, stood over me, and bent down with his face directly across from mine. I didn't look up.

His hand fell between my knees.

My thighs tightened.

"I heard about you and Dominic. You're pathetic. Bitches ..."—he grabbed my jaw and pulled my whole face toward his—"like you are crazy."

I yanked my face from his grip.

He glanced back at the door and leaned closer. "Or maybe you just need a real man to fuck the crazy out of you."

"Hey, we're ordering pizza." Alex stopped as he rounded the doorway. "Is everything okay?"

Howard stood up and grinned as he squeezed past Alex. "It's all good."

Alex stepped into the room rolling a travel suitcase behind him. He heaved the luggage on the comforter and sat down. "If Howard is being a douchebag just let me know."

"When is he not a douchebag?" I smiled and nudged him. Vertigo rushed through me. "What's in the suitcase?"

Alex's face went blank. "This isn't yours?"

The smile drained from me. He had grabbed the wrong bag from my dorm room.

He stood reaching for it.

"Leave it." I rested my hand on his. *It didn't matter now.*

"I'm sorry, Elizabeth. My stepmom leaves clothes in every vacation house. Pick out anything that fits." Blush filled his cheeks. "She's about your size."

"And age," I added with a weak smile.

Alex's chuckle was more from relief that I had smiled than the poor joke. "Anyway, don't feel obligated to hang out tonight. We'll have time to nag you this whole weekend. Get some sleep. I'll let you know when the food gets here ..."—he made it to the door and stopped—"you know it wouldn't be the same without you."

I know. Warmth gathered beneath me as I sank into the mattress. A break in the clouds allowed moonlight to trickle through the window. Dust particles danced in the lunar rays. The tips of my fingers brushed the suitcase lying beside me. I rolled onto my back and a wave of pain flooded my spinal cord. Cold air started to penetrate the wet stitches. The darkest hour is being too numb to feel the coldness.

5

JAN BRAIDED HER HAIR WHILE WATCHING *Poltergeist.* Alex stepped out from the hallway browsing his phone and walked blindly over to the couch.

"This article says that the hantavirus was confirmed in eight deaths and 20,000 people were estimated to have contracted the virus." He flopped down beside her. "Are you sure you still want to go?"

"Alex, would you stop reading your phone and go pick up the pizza." Jan grabbed a bag of potato chips from the coffee table and stuffed her face.

He wasn't listening.

She kissed his cheek and shoved him off the couch. "I want to leave in an hour."

He stood without taking his eyes off the scene and walked back down the hallway.

Howard plopped down on the couch next to her and ripped the bag of chips from her hands.

"You're such a dick!" She slid off the couch, threw a pillow at him, and stormed down the hallway after Alex. She stopped just outside his bedroom. He was sitting on the bed, still glued to his phone. The master bedroom across the hallway was open. Elizabeth was lying on her side shivering beneath a towel. It had loosened and her whole back was exposed. *What the fuck is that?* Jan crept into the room. Black spider veins spread from the center of Elizabeth's spine. She slid her fingers along the cold gooseflesh of her back. In the center was a tiny biohazard symbol branded between her vertebrae.

Chills rippled through Jan. She pulled a throw blanket from the dresser. Rain poured against the window as the Pacific winds pounded to get in.

The doorbell rang.

She covered Elizabeth, tiptoed from the room, and sprinted toward the front door. Howard was still sitting on the couch with his feet propped on the coffee table. "Don't hurt yourself."

Zach stood on the porch, flooded by motion lights and pelted by rain. She unlocked the door. It opened an inch before a gust of wind ripped it open.

Zach's muscles flexed as he caught it and jumped inside, forcing the door closed behind him. Jan smirked, looking past him into the night.

"So you decided not to bring Melissa, huh?" Her smile puckered behind clenched lips. She nodded toward the back of the house and nudged him. "Go."

6

THE WARMTH BLANKETING ME SEEPED THROUGH THE cover, dissipating into the room. Pain engulfed every inch of my body as I rolled onto my back.

A gentle knock amplified from the blurred bedroom door. A masculine silhouette made its way toward me.

"Hey?" Zach's voice carried into the room.

I slowly blinked, forcing my eyes to focus, and concealed my wrist beneath the cover as he stepped closer.

"Are you ready to go?"

I turned away. Moonlight faded with the incoming fog.

"This is new." He sat down on the bed beside me and grabbed a chestnut curl. It twirled through his fingers until reaching the curve of my tattoo.

I pulled the blanket to my chin and sat up. Goosebumps rippled across my body. The tender flesh of my nipples scratched against the cotton.

Zach immediately noticed.

I looked back over my shoulder. It had been a while since I admired the turtle etched into my skin. It was no use trying to see it. I turned back to him.

His lips press against mine. The blanket slid from my fingertips as I absorbed it. His shirt pressed against my raw nipples—warmth.

"Wow!" Jan flicked on the bedroom light, her eyebrows raised to her hairline. She started to walk back down the hall. Her voice trailed, "Pizza's here."

Zach's lips left mine only for a second. They lingered an inch away. He leaned back in, but I pulled away.

"I can't." I scrunched the blanket up to my neck with a slight shrug. "I just can't right now."

"I know." His thumb brushed a tear falling from my cheek. He kissed my forehead and slid off the bed. "You look beautiful by the way."

The door eased closed behind him.

I ran my fingers through the damp curls. My head was heavy, like the weight of the fog hanging in the trees had seeped inside of me.

The dresser mirror captured the reflection of a broken woman. That damn suitcase was still beside me. *Fucking slut.* We had been roommates for two years.

I turned my focus to the closet and slid off the bed. The blanket tumbled to the floor. Tonight, I could find a million things wrong in my reflection. I closed my eyes and walked past its judgment and into the darkness. One flick of a switch and the five foot jam-packed closet lit up. Designer clothes bulged from their hangers. High heels lined the floor.

"So?" Jan walked in behind me. She tried so hard to hide the smirk plastered to her face. It was the same look she had given me after prom night.

I shrugged and thumbed through the wall of pink outfits.

"I'm sorry about the suitcase. I thought it was yours." She wrapped her arms around me—warmth. With a deep sigh she let go. "I've always wanted to rummage through Lucy's clothes."

The house creaked with the ocean winds; vertigo swayed me. There was no way I was wearing pink. A pair of jeans slid on easily. A tight grey T-shirt would hold my boobs in place enough.

Jan pulled a large shoebox off the top shelf. Something fell to the floor.

"You have to wear these." She held up an expensive looking pair of knee-high combat boots. Her grin grew.

"So did you find everything?" Alex stepped in behind Jan. His eyes went straight for my chilled nipples. "Oh, I guess she doesn't have a bra that would fit you."

Jan elbowed him in the stomach and cleared her throat.

Lucy had a boob job done the day after the first date with Alex's dad, the day after his first blow job, no doubt.

"She talked you into the boots, huh?" He wrapped his arms around Jan's waist.

My foot hit something on the floor. It was a hand-carved redwood box. I picked it up. The detail was worn, but the faint depiction of a waterfall flowed into the word AWANATA.

"Oh, that's my Dad's pride and joy." Alex ripped the box from my hands and pushed it back onto the top shelf. "He's a huge collector of Native American artifacts."

"So anyway, we went shopping with *them*, I said I loved these boots, but of course I couldn't afford them. So Lucy bought them. That was five months ago." Jan tore off the price tag. "Lace up, let's go."

I slid the boots on. They were so heavy. The whole world was heavy. I followed the couple to the car.

Jan had already braced the front door open by the time I entered the living room. "Grab my purse, behind you!"

The tie-dyed bag was tucked beneath the coffee table. I reached for it with my left hand. The swollen tendons and stitched edges of my skin burned with its weight. The bag fell to the floor.

"I'll get that." Alex stepped back inside and rushed back to help. "Are you okay?"

Any answer would be as blurred as the day had been. I stood up with no words—completely speechless.

"Oh, I had this filled for you." He dug around in the bulky purse. A prescription bottle rattled in his hand. His eyes scanned mine as he handed over the bottle. "Let's hit the road."

I could get lost for days, swimming in pills. Numbness would be divine.

He held the door open to the intermission of a Pacific storm. Cold air slapped me in the face, jolting my exhaustion.

Jan's fingers drummed against the steering wheel of a white Prius. The mileage it got would be good for where we were going. Howard sat in the rear wolfing down potato chips. Zach was still loading the trunk. I reached for the back door and his hand slid onto mine.

He whispered in my ear, "How about I sit in the middle?"

A chill crawled up my spin and shivered up my neck. His warm breath left my skin as his fingers spread between mine, softly pulling them from the door. He took the middle seat.

I tucked my hair behind my ear and sank in beside him. Remnants of sedative drowned the swaying of the narrow highway as we headed south to Yosemite National Park.

Returning here would never be the same.

7

BENJAMIN WAITED FOR THE ELEVATOR DOORS TO slide open. The stench of hospital disinfectants was overwhelming after a few beers. The evening sun had set and the corridor blared with fluorescent light. Benjamin's heart raced as he walked toward Room 205. Jay staggered behind. As soon as they gained custody of Elizabeth, their shift would be done.

A nurse stepped from a room down the hallway. Her arms were filled with a crumpled ball of bed sheets. She saw the men, froze, and then hurried in the opposite direction.

Benjamin felt an instinct to follow her, but what for? *Get the girl and get out. Forget the nurse. She's no one.* It had taken him 18 months to be in the same room with Elizabeth. Every day he had watched her—every day. *It's time for a vacation.*

He stepped into Room 205. His heart dropped. Jay bumped into his back, knocking himself backwards. She was gone. They would never find her if he didn't stay calm. "Check the other rooms."

The momentum of Jay's turn swept the smell of hair dye from the bathroom. The fresh linens on the bed and the clean wastebaskets contained vacant clues. *Shit.* He pivoted back into the hallway and shouted down the empty corridor, "That nurse!"

The stairwell door slammed.

Jay sprinted down the hall toward it.

Benjamin ran for the elevator and began pounding on the button. *Come on.* The doors inched open. He stepped inside. The walls felt like they were shrinking in on him. Everything he had worked so hard for was dissipating. The carnival box descended back downstairs. Just before he suffocated, it pinged, and the doors opened. He squeezed out and charged at the night receptionist.

"Can I help you?" The woman set a half-eaten donut down and sucked on her fingers.

Benjamin rested his elbows on the counter. He had to stay calm. They would find her. He would find her. "Where is the suicide patient?"

The receptionist stared at him, sucking the sugar off her thumb.

"Elizabeth Hutchings." He restrained the urge to

smack those sticky fingers out of her mouth. They had to find her—he had to find her. He glanced around the lobby. *Where the fuck was Jay?* He glanced back at the woman.

She stared at the emblem on his sleeve. Her lips tightened. She wiped her hands on her pants and searched the computer. "Room 205," she looked up. "Is there anything else I can help you with?"

"So she has not been discharged?" He gritted his teeth and leaned on the counter, trying to read the screen.

The receptionist's smile faded. She sat up straight, pulled in her chair, and drummed the keyboard. "No."

His hands balled into fists. His teeth clenched together. One more look at her and he would pop. "The nurse that just cleaned the room, get her down here, right now."

She stared at him, frozen like a damn turkey.

The door to the stairwell flew open.

She jumped. Jay stepped out with one hand already on the hilt of his sword. He joined his partner and drew the weapon, forcing its blade inches from the woman's face.

Her face flushed and her lips sagged into a frown.

"Miss," Benjamin eased Jay's blade down. "Where is your security room?"

She pointed at a closed door off to the side.

"Shit." Jay grabbed the phone behind the counter. He dialed 1-1-1 and was instantly connected to headquarters. "Code Black."

It was going to be a long night.

Benjamin made his way to the security room. It contained one chair jammed beneath a computer desk. Musty air filled his lungs. Black and white monitors mirrored the stagnant night. *Let's see where you went.* He stopped the record button and rewound the day.

Video of him disappearing from the hallway into

Room 205 was first. The corridor had been empty prior to their arrival.

Jay stepped in and leaned against the wall. "So where did she go?"

Time on the screen froze. *No!* Static filled the monitor. *Fuck.* Benjamin fast-forwarded back to the elevator scene. *The nurse.* The video caught the nurse hurrying away from them. The stack of sheets covered her face. She turned from the camera and descended into the stairwell.

"Hey. That's the operating room nurse," Jay said.

He was right. Another monitor captured her getting into a late-1990s Dodge Intrepid. It sped out of the rear parking lot.

Benjamin stormed from the room, toward the receptionist. "I need the names of the nurses who assisted Miss Hutchings's surgery this morning."

She stuffed the last piece of donut in her mouth and clicked through a few screens. "Betty Young and Brenda Martinez."

"Their addresses." He pulled out a notepad.

"I can't release that information." She let go of the computer mouse and rubbed her eyebrow.

"If you don't give me the information, I can't find the patient that your incompetent facility lost track of. And if I can't find her, you'll be dead within the week. So let's cut the bullshit. You know we'll just get clearance and you'll just be defending the stupid decision you made to waste our time."

Jay stepped out of the security room and pulled the samurai sword out. "Or we can just kill you."

The woman reached for the mouse so quickly it almost fell to the floor. In two clicks, the printer kicked on.

Benjamin looked at Jay. "Update headquarters, we

need to find her before the next outbreak." *Fuck.*

Jay picked up the phone.

Benjamin smiled at the woman. She had no idea what shitstorm was coming.

THE LOST LEGEND

1

IT WAS A CRISP FALL MORNING AT YOSEMITE NATIONAL Park. The faded brown, red, and yellow leaves shivered against a breeze. Dust flakes from the ancient cliffs blew by the trees lining the mountain's edge. Whispers of Indian lore curved with the wind against the land and parted at the pane of a window. Cold mountain air drifted over the smooth glass, whispering one last time before continuing on. The sleeping morning rattled with a soft beep. The rustic park ranger residence filled with hazelnut coffee brewing in the kitchen downstairs.

Ian Jones pushed a pile of park history books from his mattress as he sat on the edge of the bed. Just a few more minutes of sleep, that was all he needed. But if he was late today, Billy would surely have his ass. He rested his head in his hands and looked up at the uniform lying across the dresser. It had taken him six years to get into the park system. There was no way exhaustion would plague him now. After ironing the forest green pants, he started on the light grey shirt. The national park badge puckered as he creased the left sleeve. The badge's thick embroidery weaved into the curve of a mountain, a sequoia tree, and a buffalo. A smile filled his face. It was Halloween. He had gone trick-or-treating as a park ranger every year of his childhood.

He made his way downstairs to the kitchen. Park housing typically came with the tranquility of a campground morning, but that day fallen leaves rustled outside the cabin's front porch.

Ian set a coffee mug down and headed for the front door. It creaked as he pulled it open. The rickety screen door behind it tapped with a passing wind. He pressed his hand against the screen, stopping its beat. The rustling grew louder.

A raccoon and her two kits ran out from beneath the porch and scampered off into the woods behind his work vehicle.

He glanced down at his watch. *Crap.* It had taken too long to finish the morning's routine. He was late. There was no time for coffee. He locked the door, jumped into the white cruiser, and sped down the dirt driveway. The cabin disappeared in the rearview mirror. The same route to work never got old. Beauty ripped to the sky from the ground, forming mountains around the valley. The campground awoke as he drove by. The closest permanent residence was that of Park Manager, Billy Hanes. They had identical cabins, but his had been well-maintained over the years. The windows were dark and Billy was already at work. *Crap.*

Ian restrained himself from speeding to the Valley Visitor Center. When he got there the parking lot was crawling with people. Their clothing was torn, hair tattered, and faces sickly. He parked in the middle of the road. A woman walked by, half her fucking cheek was missing. *No ....* He pressed his face against the window. A man limped by. *He looked like a —*

The passenger side door flung open. Ian's heart jerked.

"What's wrong with you?" Billy slid in as if the outside world was only an illusion. "Oh, there's some zombie bullshit event going on tonight. It's Halloween. Let's go."

Ian stared past him at two young women. They stood on the curb taking pictures with their phones, laughing. He whispered, "Where?"

"Bridalveil Fall. There's a wounded eagle up there," Billy said.

Ian tore his eyes off the costume party filling the road and eased the car through the sea of visitors. Today would not be a typical day, even for Halloween.

Along the ride the number of zombie costumes increased. Billy grunted and mumbled under his breath the whole way. He was close to retirement and despised unofficial events the most. The majority were extreme hikers and climbers, but zombies?

The early hours of the day left plenty of empty spaces in the Bridalveil Fall parking lot. A paved trail quickly took them to the base of the waterfall. It was beautiful. Several visitors had gathered. Mist chilled Ian's face as he approached them. "If I can have everyone's attention ...."

The crowd turned their attention to him.

He froze. They looked so disgusting. The lifeless eagle at their feet looked more alive.

Billy threw a pair of latex gloves at Ian and made his way to the small crowd. "Would everyone please take five steps back from the animal? I would also like to remind each of you that it is a federal crime to take an eagle feather, so if you have one, please hand it over to Ranger Jones at this time."

The crowd chuckled. Billy let out a grunt and bent over, reaching for the bird.

Ian's stomach tightened. There was something tugging at the back of his brain, something he had read. *What was it?* He searched the faces in the crowd like they would know. *The park book. The Indian warning.* "No!"

The crowd almost snapped their necks turning their attention back to him. He stepped forward to restrain Billy, but it was too late.

Billy scooped the carcass into his arms and shook his head at Ian. Ian's cheeks burned as the crowd's eyes focused on him.

"I would like to thank each of you for visiting this beautiful park. Have a great weekend. Yosemite welcomes you." Billy held his tongue the whole way back to the car and then held out the carcass to Ian.

Ian shoved the rubber gloves into his pocket and shook his head. "I'm sorry, Sir, but Indian mythology warns against handling an eagle until four days postmortem. They believed that something living on the birds would crawl from its feathers onto the skin and—"

"And what? Turn me into a zombie?" Billy's eyebrows narrowed and squeezed lines into his forehead. "Those are mere stories. They don't apply to us. Open the trunk."

Ian unlocked the back and rested his hand on top of the trunk, looking back at the old withered face. "With all due respect, we are standing on Indian land."

"Would you like to explain that to all these people? See if modern society cares about what should be done. So, we not only tell the public that the number of confirmed hantavirus cases has increased again at the park, but we're also going to leave this dead rotting bird along the trail?" Billy looked up at the cheesy zombie costumes still crowding the hiking path. "Do you think these people would give two shits? Get your head out of your ass."

Ian started the car. The humming of the engine calmed the tension as the tires guided them back to the Visitor Center. Billy stepped out of the car the moment Ian's foot hit the brake.

"You know, I think these are probably the only people who would care." Ian looked around the parking lot.

Billy looked at him, slid from the passenger's seat, and closed the door behind him. A breeze ripped the leaves from the trees. Autumn winds had begun to sweep into the valley.

I hope they're just stories.

2

IAN WAS UNEASY WALKING INTO THE VISITOR CENTER. The stories of lost history swirled in his head until he saw a young woman standing beside the front desk. Her skin glowed like the moon shining against the dark winter night. Chestnut hair twirled between her fingers as she gawked at a group of zombies passing. The blue of her eyes was the color of a clear sky. He stepped closer and found himself standing beside her. He cleared his throat. "You know this park history program is amazing."

She looked at him. A man standing nearby nudged closer to their conversation.

"Or if you happen to be staying up at Curry Village, there's a campfire program tonight," Ian said.

"That sounds like fun," the male inched over toward

them and wrapped his arm around the woman's waist. "Will you be there?"

"Where are my manners?" Ian extended his hand out toward the pair. "I'm Ranger Ian, and you are?"

"Elizabeth." She crossed her arms and gave a light nod.

"I'm Zach." The man offered his hand.

Nobody cares about you. "Nice to meet you." Ian shook his hand, steadying his grip. He couldn't take his eyes off Elizabeth. *There's something about her.* "Hopefully, I'll see you later."

3

I WAS GLUED TO THE WINDOW AS WE DROVE FARTHER into Yosemite. Mountainous rock looked as if the gods themselves had pulled the earth up toward them. A perfectly-sliced mountain appeared through the windshield—Half Dome—its deep grey molded into the setting horizon. The famous white face stained into its side looked like a middle-aged man with a severed nose. Chills trickled down my spine.

Jan pulled into an overflowing parking lot. Conversations and laughter filled the night's air despite its chill. I would never go back to the dorm room, or my parents' house. The only path left was to follow the group. Sleep could take me from the world, if only for a few hours. In my dreams I still had a family. I'd tell my Dad that I loved him with all my heart. Every second he's not here, it tears me apart. I'd tell my Mom I miss our conversations. There will never be another person who completes my sentences more than her. Only in my dreams can I see their smiles one last time, hear their voices, feel their arms wrapped around me. If I could just sleep, life would be bearable.

"You coming?" Zach slid into Howard's empty seat and extended his hand. The open door allowed the autumn air in, drying my tear-stained cheeks. Zach took my hand—warmth.

I slid out of the car and he tucked me beside him. The first step reminded me of the pain pills I had taken an hour ago. My equilibrium leveled out and he let me lean on him. With each stumble, his grip tightened. He was everything I needed in that moment.

The entrance to the campground was framed by a wooden sign. White lights spelled out the name *Camp Curry*. Zombies of all shapes, sizes, and artistic detail filled the site. This year Halloween was supposed to be perfect. We had planned it for months. I had wasted all that time, so much time, on Dominic.

Zach's hand tightened as we stepped over a tree root, making sure I would clear it. His grip was just as real as it had been when we were eight years old. We had been playing around the lake. I leaned too far over the water's edge and he grabbed me just in time, saving me from falling. Shortly after that I started swimming lessons.

Glowing white tents with green doors lined the pathway. A stream of light drifted up along the mountain's cliff. The stars rested on a black blanket right above its tip.

Alex stopped in front of tent 667. "I think this is—"

The door flung open.

Victoria Pulaski burst out, pushing her way straight to

Howard. His hands slid into her back pockets as they slurped each others' faces. She was exactly what you would expect to be with a guy like him.

Alex and Jan took tent 668.

"What happen to you?" Victoria's voice carried from behind.

My sedated heart raced back to normal. There was no doubt she was talking to me. The crisp air failed to soothe the burning tips of my ears. I was grateful for the blanket of darkness that night had provided. My cheeks burned as a distant tent broke with laughter.

"She changed her hair." Zach pulled me closer and opened tent 668's door. I had forgotten he was there. He never let go.

"Yeah," was the only word that I could mutter without crying.

"I can see that." Victoria crossed her arms.

"Come on, let's warm up." Zach held the door open nudging me past him.

The flimsy wood slammed behind us. The tent's A-frame was identical to a monopoly game piece, just covered in canvas. A double bed was pushed up against the rear wall. Jan unraveled a neatly folded pile of linens and made the bed. Two single beds hugged each wall beside the door. I took the one on the right and flopped against its unmade mattress. Zach sat down beside me and pulled out a thinly rolled joint.

"Dude, you're going to get us in trouble." Jan playfully kicked Alex off the bed to tuck in the sheet's corner. He plopped back down almost on her hand. She joined him, pulled a makeup kit from her purse, and began smearing Alex's cheeks with a thick white foundation. The original plan was for everyone to dress like zombies; it was the whole reason we drove twelve hours.

I snatched the joint. The tent fell silent.

"You wanted to try new things." Zach held out his hand, a Zippo lighter rested in his palm. A turtle was carved by hand on its front. It was almost identical to my tattoo.

I stared at him, my mouth hanging open.

"I carved it in the car while you were asleep." He smiled. "You can have it."

I took the lighter and lit the joint with ease. A tiny flame danced until it became a thin line of burning paper. I took a drag. *Inhale and hold.* Soon enough I could rest my head and make it into the morning. *Exhale.* White smoke swirled toward the ceiling lamp. *Inhale and hold.* Minutes crept by and soon we all shared in intoxication. A little wall heater kicked on. The sides of the tent inched inward. Hazel's wool coat suffocated my pores and sweat beaded on my forehead. "You remember the time we ran from the cops in the woods?"

Jan laughed. "And you lost your shoe."

I burst out laughing. White streams of smoke dissipated. It was okay to smile. And besides, Jan and Alex looked ridiculous with their painted faces.

"This tent's freaking me out. Can we get out of here?" Alex jumped off the bed and sprinted for the door, back out into the dark, cold night.

"You up for it?" Jan stopped beside me and held out her hand.

I nodded and slid my fingers between hers. We had been friends since kindergarten. It had been years since we passed novel-length notes between classes, spent endless nights talking about boys, and lived through high school heartbreaks. But she was still there. We had planned to grow old together, sitting on a porch in our 90s shaking our canes at the young men walking by as we ogled them.

"You okay?" She stopped and blocked my path. "You're squeezing my hand."

I nodded. She knew a hug would cripple me in front of all these people. A smile was the only thing she gave before turning back toward the path. We headed for the Pavilion for food, but when we arrived a few people were gathered around a large campfire. The flicker of light was so inviting. There was still an open spot against a fallen tree. I let go of Jan's hand.

"Aren't you gonna get something to eat?" Her face filled with worry.

"No. I'll meet you guys out here." I hurried to the tree. Its hard, ridged bark gave me something to lean back on, something to rest the weight of the world against. The earth was so cold. The pitch black sky slowly turned into a sea of twinkling lights. Clusters continued to appear. Among the forest of invaders, I was the only one looking up.

Jan sat beside me and offered a water bottle. Just its sight made me thirsty, so I took a sip. The liquid burned down my throat. "Vodka?"

She hushed me and took the bottle back. More people gathered. The fire's glow danced over a sea of zombies, while drunken conversations drifted into the air.

"So what's one thing on your bucket list?" Zach climbed over the log and squeezed in behind me. He threw a handful of crispy leaves into the flames.

Nearby conversations faded to the background. The

ghosts of the past cast shadows upon nearby trees, within them my family's history. I tugged at my hair. "Dreadlocks."

"Your parents will kill y—" Jan tried to choke back the words.

"I'll be right back." Zach wiggled out from behind me and sprinted back toward the tents. Alex followed.

"Are you sure you should be making decisions tonight?" Jan took another swig of vodka, then held it out again. I declined and pulled my knees into my chest.

"You know what else I've always wanted to do?" The dancing flames were captivating, the fire's crackle so peaceful. "Stand naked in a waterfall."

Jan burst with laughter. It was good to hear her laugh.

Alex returned, stuffing his face with cheese puffs. The white makeup on his lips smeared with orange residue.

I could feel Zach's eyes on me, even through the darkness. His whole face lit up as he stepped into the fire's ring of light. In his hand was a large block of beeswax.

"Dude with surfboard wax?" Cheese balls spewed from Alex's mouth.

"Let's do it." I grabbed the plastic bottle from Jan and took a swig. Zach scooted in behind me. His fingertips clasped a curl. A sharp tingle rippled from my scalp to the tips of my fingers—warmth.

The campfire faded in and out as he twisted each strand. The colors of autumn danced within the flames while the alcohol concentrated in my veins. The pile of kindled wood looked as if it was the only thing keeping a dragon-from-hell from entering our world.

A female park ranger approached. Her young, bronze skin looked so beautiful against the campfire light. Her features and long brown hair hinted that her people belonged among the land. She looked straight at me with eyes widened.

Shit, she can probably smell the pot. She knows. A chill ran down my spine. The weight of eight tiny legs brushed the hairs on my fingers as an Orb spider climbed up my hand. I screamed and flicked it. Its body flew into the flames. The chill lingered as I leaned back into place.

My entomology professor told us of a wasp that lays its egg in an Orb spider web. It infects the spider, turning it into a zombie of sorts. The spider abandons its web design and begins weaving a web wholly to support the wasp's larva. Then the spider sits there and waits. And when the wasp hatches, it devours the spider.

4

RANGER IAN HURRIED THROUGH THE VISITOR CENTER. He stopped outside Billy's office, pacing back and forth, biting his thumbnail.

"Get in here and stop doing that. I've taken care of the eagle, and the United States Wildlife Service will be out this evening to retrieve the carcass." Billy coughed.

"I'd like to apologize for earlier today." Ian ripped a piece of his nail off and spit it out. Billy's office looked like a closet with a desk and two empty chairs sitting across from it. Ian took one. Bloody tissues filled a trashcan in the corner, spilling over the top. "Can I do the campfire program tonight?"

"Sure, I don't feel too good. I suppose the last thing I need is to be around a campfire filled with monsters." Billy forced a smile.

"Zombies," Ian glanced back at the trashcan. "Sir, maybe you should go to the hospital."

Billy shot him a stern look.

"So have you decided what we're going to do about the hantavirus situation?" Ian said.

"Tomorrow we'll redistribute the pamphlets left over from before. Mentioning the outbreak on Halloween, with all those zombie-freaks out there, could cost me my job." Billy rubbed his eyes. "Would you drop me off on your way there?"

Billy stood, bracing his weight against the wall. Ian rushed to his side, guiding him through the Visitor's Center and into his cruiser. A cloudy night sky pushed against the cliff of Half Dome in the distance. It was a short drive to Billy's cabin. The bright headlights captured his empty house. He never said a word as he climbed out of the vehicle.

"Hey, I'll drop dinner off after I'm done," Ian yelled out the window.

Billy gave a weak wave before going inside.

Ian raced the cruiser down the main road. The campfire's glow intensified as he approached Curry Village. An old, beat-up park ranger truck was parked not far from the fire. Only one ranger would drive that thing. It was the only truck with a crew cab, but it looked like a heap of junk.

"Where's Bill?" Nevaeh banged against the passenger window. Her long brown hair hung loose over her shoulders. The tan of her skin accentuated her soft Native American features.

"He's not feeling well, so I'll be helping out tonight."

"Oh, my god, this is about that girl everyone is talking

about. The one you embarrassed yourself over." Nevaeh laughed, looking over at the crowd huddled against the fires light.

"You know, I thought you'd understand more than anyone," Ian climbed out, grabbed a bundle of wood from the trunk, and stormed past her.

"Oh, Ian, don't get your panties in a bunch. Why do you think I would believe all that folklore shit?" Nevaeh said.

Ian stepped through the crowd of people into the campfire's glow. Its flame danced across the ring of faces surrounding its edge. *Where is she?*

Nevaeh cleared her throat and took a seat in front of the fire. Conversations faded.

There she is, sitting across the fire from Ian. A smile crept across his face. He threw a few pieces of wood into the flames. Burning ashes sprayed to the sky and dwindled in the cold air. Each drunken, sober, naked, and zombie-painted face stared at him. The stillness would carry his voice. "I would like to start out by welcoming all of you" —*what a unique audience*—"alive or dead."

The crowd filled with laughter and factitious moans.

"I'm Ranger Jones. And this,"—he extended his arms to the sky—"this is Yosemite." He had begun the program the same way for the past five years. That night would be different. Ian stood there speechless.

Panic washed over Nevaeh's face.

He stared at her. Her bloodline had been thinned out by two generations, but she still held the beauty of their genes. Still, modern culture had captivated her youthfulness and she had already begun to deny her family's roots.

Elizabeth's full attention was on him. The kindling

wood popped. That night the valley would hear its forgotten tale.

"All of you can clearly see the beauty of Yosemite National Park. Before the arrival of the Europeans, the Ahwahnee Indians were a pure culture immersed in the very land you stand and sit on. It became vulnerable as its protectors were pushed from its soil. These mountains still bear the scars from white men raping its ground looking for gold. But you didn't come here for a history lesson." He sat down beside Nevaeh. *They would be the only group that could possibly care about this.* "Ranger Nevaeh has an ancient story she would like to share. A story once told within these valley walls."

The fire flickered against the frozen silhouettes surrounding its flames. Their hungry eyes turned to the last of Yosemite's bloodline. The roots of the land could only be spread by her. Otherwise its history would die, completely engulfed by colonized commercialism.

5

THE AHWAHNEE PEOPLE BELIEVED THAT COYOTE-MAN created the world and led them to this valley—a long time ago—when the sky still had no moon. He lived amongst them for several generations, but immortality came with a price. Death claimed those he fell in love with and sorrow pushed him from the land.

The Ahwahnee Chief walked alone every night waiting for his friend to return. One evening he drew close to the waterfall's edge. Something was in the water. As he approached, the stars faint glow revealed a pale baby. He pulled the umbilical cord that was still attached and wrapped her in his arms.

They say that death himself tore the color from her skin and hair, and pulled the color from her eyes, leaving them dark as the waters depth. The Chief took her back to the village and warmed her by the fire. The dark sky faded into dawn. He had spent all night feeding the flames, keeping death from taking what she had left. Only when dawn broke did he pull back the bearskin wrapped around her. Turquoise eyes blinked back at him.

Twenty years he raised her, preparing her for marriage to his son. That night he could truly call her his daughter.

The ring of fire burned in celebration of her wedding. She kissed her groom throughout the day, lusting for night's end. The beat of the drum pulled the young man from her side. As he danced, she felt a presence beside her. When she turned, he was there. Coyote-man had returned.

"Give yourself to me and I will give you everything you've ever wanted," he said.

She looked back at the crackling fire, the Chief's warm smile, the trees swaying in the wind, and the sound of the waterfall. "I already have everything."

"I've waited several lifetimes for you and you've been here all along—dancing—dancing to the beat of *their* drums for twenty years."

"Excuse me ...." She went to get up.

He grabbed her arm. "I've followed mere clusters of stars against a pitch black canvas to return here—to this campfire—to you, Awanata."

She didn't know how the stranger knew her name. When he let go of her, she grabbed the arm of her groom and retired for the night. The day had been perfect until he showed up.

That night Coyote-man split the thunder from the sky and its rain saturated the land.

Awanata awoke to a pale and sick husband. The rest of the tribe grew ill and the old began to die. There had always been a cost for her life.

By the time night came, the dead rose, killing the living. Death was coming for her. She stayed beside her groom until his moans were too much to bear. She sprinted from the village, up the waterfall's path. The wet, cold earth seeped between her toes. She stepped into the freezing cold water.

"Stop!" Coyote-man stood behind her on the bank. His left hand already offered out toward her. Darkness was rising from the depths. "I will stop all this. Just give yourself to me."

"How do I know you will keep your promise?" Awanata had heard many stories of Coyote's tricks.

He covered his left hand with his right.

"What are you doing?" she said.

He removed the top hand. A ball of light sat in his left palm. He offered it to her. The flow of ice water around her feet was so familiar. Its pain felt like home, but the light was too beautiful to resist. She reached for it. Its warmth filled her fingertips spreading through her entire body.

"What am I supposed to do with this?" she said.

He looked up at the stars and smiled. "Put it anywhere you want. It's a mess up there anyway."

She cupped the light in her hand and threw it into the sky. Lunar rays spread over the valley. Laughter filled the village below.

When morning broke and the moon faded from the sky, her groom awoke to an empty bed. He rushed outside to find his bride.

Within the dark grey granite of Half Dome was a white

face—her face—stained into the mountain. Even during a new moon, the people would never forget her.

But as you can see, these valley walls have lost their people, and her legend, too, is forgotten.

6

THE FIRE CRACKLED. NOT ONE WHISPER FOLLOWED. Ian let the crowd laze in the moment. He felt so out of place in his uniform. "Feel free to hangout. We'll be putting the fire out in an hour. Thank you for coming and enjoy your stay at this beautiful park."

He had done a poor job at keeping his eyes off Elizabeth. Zach sat tightly behind her twisting sections of curls. *Why would she ruin her hair?*

All the ancient stories lying on his bedroom floor swirled through his mind. He couldn't breathe. He shot to a standing position and stormed toward the Pavilion. The Pizza Patio was closed, but the deck was jam-packed with laughing zombies. *This isn't happening.* He had crammed far too many stories in his head over the years. *They're just stories.* The Pavilion dining hall entrance was dim. A cobblestone fireplace in the lobby forced a choice of pizza parlor to the left, coffee counter to the right, or the grand dining hall behind it. Ian walked past the fireplace's stone wall. A vaulted ceiling opened up overhead.

Billy was vegan, so Ian started at the salad bar. He filled one Styrofoam container with lettuce and another with macaroni and cheese. His own was loaded with a cheeseburger and fries. He balanced the containers and nudged the door open, lingering in its threshold to admire the architecture. Ceiling lights warmed the brown paneled walls. The outside air whistled. He had never longed to stay inside so badly before.

"Hey, where are you going?" Nevaeh grabbed the door and held it open for him.

"Home, you got this." Ian smiled at her. "You did a great job." He stepped out of the doorway. "See you in a few hours."

"So you're not going to talk to her?"

He stopped. "No, she's busy. And I promised Billy I'd drop off some food."

"I noticed when she checked in ...her name—"

"I know its Elizabeth."

"Yeah, Elizabeth Hutchings." Her eyebrows rose.

Ian shoved the containers into her arms and sprinted toward the campfire. He stopped at the edge of visitors still crowding its glow. The tip of his boot slid into the ring of light, attracting a few odd glances from those around him.

Elizabeth was standing, talking to another young woman in her group. The men were nowhere in sight. Sweat covered his palms. He tugged at the bottom of his coat and walked over to her, catching his breath. "Elizabeth, can I talk to you for a moment?"

The young woman beside Elizabeth froze like a deer in headlights.

What am I doing? This is so stupid. "Is your last name really Hutchings?" he said.

"Yes. Why?" Elizabeth stepped back away from him.

"So your great-grandmother was Florence Hutchings?" She stared at him.

"She was the first white child to be born on this land." He took a step closer to her and glanced around the campfire. "Why don't you come back to my place?"

"She's not going anywhere with you." Jan stepped

between them. The alcohol on her breath filled his nostrils. She grabbed Elizabeth's hand and led her back toward the tents.

He stood there, watching them walk away.

Nevaeh was behind him. She had seen the whole thing. "Why don't you take this to Billy? Like you said, I'll wrap up here on my own," she handed him the food. "Don't lose your job over some fairytale bullshit."

She's right. He climbed into his cruiser and inched the vehicle through the crowd. The tires crunched over gravel until fading into smooth asphalt. Work never got old, but the day had become worn. Endorphins had faded by the time he reached Billy's cabin. He was exhausted.

He grabbed the food and made his way up to the dark residence. The rusted hinges creaked as he pulled open the screen door and knocked. "Billy, you in there?"

No reply.

A breeze gusted by, pushing against the containers in his hand. He searched the surrounding darkness as he balanced the Styrofoam, fumbling for his keys—the master key for the park. The cabin's layout was identical to his, opening up into the kitchen. A small living room area sat to the left and the stairs to the bedrooms were to the rear. Billy's house was still decorated the way it had been when his wife moved out. Not many people can bear the real isolation of living in the middle of a national park. A boy and girl smiled with mouthfuls of braces within the frames lining the walls. Ian brushed his finger across a picture, pushing the dust into a ball.

He turned on a dim light above the stove and placed the food in the refrigerator. Just as the rubber seal of the door touched its frame, bright streams of light fell on the counter. He cracked the door back open. A pile of bills and envelopes were spread all over the laminate surface, covered in small erratic pen marks. He thumbed through the mess for a blank piece of paper. At the very bottom was a post-it, scribbled with weak ink lines. Its back was still blank. That would have to do.

BILL, FOOD IN FRIG

He stuck it to the refrigerator. The stove's glow cast enough light to guide him back to the door.

A rustling sound came from upstairs. Ian stopped. He took a step back and paused. A dizzy spell swept through his head. He shook it. *I think I've intruded enough. I'm sure he's okay. Damn, I'm tired.*

He tiptoed to the door and pulled it shut. The porch door tapped against his back as he locked the front door. A rustling noise sounded from the side of the cabin. He eased the porch door closed. The rustle of leaves grew louder, closer. Ian held his breath and flung his body around the corner. His heartbeat tightened, but his shoulders relaxed. "It's only you."

Three pairs of raccoon eyes stared at his awkward stance. A breeze drifted down from the mountains, lifting the porch door from its hinges, slightly tapping the frame around it.

7

Jan let go of Elizabeth's hand as they plopped down on the double bed. The lantern hanging in the middle of the tent spun with the walls. Jan braced her head against her hand, leaned over Elizabeth, and kissed her. Her tears ran into the freshly twisted dreadlocks as she pulled away. She nudged her forehead against Elizabeth's. "I love you."

Alex and Zach stumbled into the tent like drunken frat boys.

Jan sat up. A spot of white makeup smeared onto Elizabeth's forehead. She wiped it off, smudging it between her fingers. Snot dripped down her upper lip. She grabbed a towel from her bag and blew her nose. "Oh my God, I have to pee!"

"Just pee behind the tent. Maybe it will keep the bears away." Alex laughed as he fell into one of the single beds.

"That's disgusting. I'll be right back." She sprinted out the door before Alex could stop her. *I'm not pissing in the woods.*

The glowing tents formed a maze through Curry Village. The distant campfire dwindled and turned into smoke. Zombie costumes filled the campground but thinned out the farther Jan walked. The trail to the bathroom grew dark. Drunken conversations weakened in the distance. She swayed between the trees lining the path.

A dim light ahead illuminated the bathroom building. Jan leaned against a tree. The bark was so thick, so uneven. She pushed off to propel forward. An orange glow flooded into the night from the women's propped-open bathroom door. A spider dangled from the frame, swinging with a breeze.

Jan dropped to her knees and crawled under the spider. *It could still drop onto my head, crawl under my dress.* Her knees banged against the tile as she rushed through.

Large wings cast a shadow on the floor. It was only a moth, flickering against the ceiling light.

She stood. The spider was still swaying in the doorway. Her heart eased. She straightened her dress. The bottom trim was soiled. Good thing it was secondhand.

She stumbled to the second stall, pulled her black

panties down, and hovered over the toilet bowl. Who knows what you could actually catch from sitting on a public toilet. Some women are just as disgusting as men, if not more.

Cold air blew under the stall, pushing her off balance, and the skin of her thighs landed against the cold porcelain. *Yuck.* Now she'd have to take a shower. What if she just got AIDS? No, that's stupid. You can't get that from a toilet seat. Probably the clap or something that would make her coochie drip.

She hoisted her underwear up, flushed, and leaned against the stall as she fidgeted with its latch. The door swung in; those kinds are the worst.

A man wearing a park uniform stood in the doorway.

"Shit, you scared me." Jan stepped out of the stall. "So you work here?"

He said nothing. The spider hung in front of him, moving with his breath.

She steadied herself to the sinks. The man tottered just outside the door, watching her. She reached for the faucet and he stepped into the bathroom. The spider clung to his cheek. It crawled up his scalp. His pale face accentuated the dark circles under his bloodshot eyes. Sweat saturated his grey shirt.

Jan froze. *What the fuck is this guy doing?* She leaned against the sink. That last shot of vodka had been too much. The man scuttled closer. She laughed. "Oh, you're good. That's funny. Great costume! You got me. Wow!"

He stepped closer. His body lurched out of focus while she laughed. Intoxication pulled her eyelids closed. She gripped the lip of the sink, restraining her fall. His body leaned in behind her. His breath pressed against the back of her neck.

"You know, I like a man in uniform." She turned and grabbed the front of his shirt, drawing him closer. He was much older than her, but drunk-fantasies always overpowered that minor detail. She pressed her lips against his. He didn't return her affection. She withdrew her kiss and squinted at his name badge. "Billy Hanes. This is an awesome costume. So Billy, do you always take advantage of young intoxicated campers?"

Before he could answer, she grabbed the front of his uniform and forced another kiss. His lips felt like sandpaper—dry and coarse, unmoving. The smooth edge of his front teeth chomped into her bottom lip. She pushed back from him.

"What the hell, man?" She wiped her lip. *I'm bleeding?* She looked at her hand; blood covered her fingers. *He bit me!* "What kind of a *freak* are you?"

She stepped for the door. He grabbed her right arm and twisted it around her back, forcing her to look at herself in the mirror. She wiggled. He nudged her wrist higher up the curve of her back. Agony shot through her body. She clenched the sink, but the pain didn't ease. She threw her head back and cracked the cartilage of his nose. Blood drained from his nostrils. He didn't flinch or let go. His nails dug into her wrist.

She screamed. It echoed off the concrete walls. He slammed her cheek into the curve of the porcelain sink and tore the back of her stockings.

She gripped onto the sink with her free hand. Her head throbbed. The drain swirled with blood. Her lip pulsated.

His weight pushed her hip against the sink's edge. His fingernails split as they dug deeper into her wrist. His knees pressed into the back of hers. She wiggled her hips. *This isn't happening.*

He forced her wrist higher up the small of her back. *Fuck!* The only way to ease the pain would be to bend over more. She tried, digging her cheek farther into the porcelain—anything to get rid of the pain. There was nowhere to go.

This is not going to happen to me. She forced all her weight to stand, but he shoved her head back down and her cheekbone slammed against the sink. Streaks of black mascara ran into the sink. Drool dripped from his mouth and pushed the black liquid into the drain. Her cheek throbbed. Adrenaline mixed with the alcohol in her veins and the pain began to disappear.

He inched her arm up, paralyzing her with pain. Any higher and her arm would break. His weight slowly lifted from her. *Now!* She stood up. *Run!* Billy's bloodshot eyes widened in the reflection behind her. His mouth opened and he lunged for the back of her neck.

She ran for the door. He grabbed her arm and yanked her backwards onto the tile floor. She crawled to the third stall, hugging the far wall, and slid the latch.

Billy pounded on the door, dropped to the floor, and crawled underneath.

Jan screamed, stepped backwards, and bumped into the toilet. She jumped up on the porcelain seat. *Shit.* There was no tank to hoist up on. He reached for her, almost all the way into the stall. There was only one way out.

She pulled herself up on the top of the partition wall, tottering on its edge. Her biceps burned and shook. His fingernails snagged her stocking and caught hold of her shoe, ripping it from her foot. She flung her leg over the top and went crashing into the next stall—to the floor.

Billy peered over the top, down at her.

She pulled the door open and sprinted for the exit.

Night's air chilled the tears falling down her cheeks. She was free. That was all that mattered. The dark outline of the trees undulated in front of her as she sprinted down the path. The trail grew darker as the bathhouse light faded behind her. Her foot caught on an exposed tree root and she tripped to the earth.

Deep moans crept up the trail from behind.

She shook her head. It was like a bad horror film. She pushed off the ground and ran. The line of trees framing the trail scraped at her with their branches. Then they ended and the sole of her shoe hit asphalt. A dimly lit cabin window penetrated the darkness. She was lost. The clouds had faded and the star's twinkle provided enough light to follow the road.

8

IAN POURED A CUP OF HAZELNUT COFFEE AS THE woodstove warmed his living room. A short nap always recharged him for midnight rounds, but tonight refreshment eluded him. His immune system was failing.

A car sped past his driveway and a dizzy spell washed over him. The hazelnut smell grew bitter in the air. He sat down and slid his boots on. The laces dangled, barely touching the floor. He grabbed a set of keys from the counter and dumped the repulsive coffee down the sink. As the brown liquid swirled into the drain, nausea flooded him. His stomach violently forced its contents up. He stood still, hovering over the sink's edge.

Leaves rustled outside the front porch. The screen door tapped with each passing breeze. The light of the living room brightened with each blink, blinding Ian's view. Pressure filled his chest cavity as his fingertips searched for the light switch. His muscles felt like potato bags hanging from his arms.

The lights clicked off and darkness covered the cabin. His pupils widened and relaxed. Only a dim light above the stove was still on. *Much better.* His system calmed.

Leaves rustled again.

Those raccoons will be the death of me. He pulled open the front door and pushed the screen door out. It stopped, hitting a dark silhouette. Ian's heart pounded. He forced his eyes to focus on the figure. "Shit, man."

Billy stood outside on the porch, staring at him through the screen.

Ian walked away from the door and headed for the couch. The screen door banged as it closed behind him. "I'm almost ready. You feeling better?"

There was no answer.

Ian sat on the couch and tied his shoes. Cold air seeped across the floor touching his hands. He looked up. Billy stood still outside. "So are you coming in? I want to ask you some questions about the park's history."

Silence carried between them.

Ian slid off the couch and returned to the door. Billy watched every move. The weight of his breath grew heavy and deep. "Billy, are you okay?"

Another dizzy spell rushed over Ian and he momentarily lost his balance. He had to refocus. The dim stove light left only the blurred edges of his friend's image. Ian grabbed onto the doorframe and steadied himself. Billy's stare was empty, unfocused, and blank. His clothing was soiled and torn, matted with leaves and twigs.

"Maybe you should go back to bed. I'll get Nevaeh to cover rounds tonight." Adrenaline coursed through Ian's veins, waking him up a little. A spider crawled down Billy's forehead and dropped to his shoulder. Ian pulled the screen door closed. Its latch clicked into place.

A breeze pulled warm air out from the house. The screen brushed the tip of Billy's nose. He slapped his hand against it. His fingers slid down the screen. His pinky slid along the trim and cut into a large splinter. He didn't yell, scream, or stop as it tore into his flesh. His fingers balled into fists and he punched through the screen.

Ian slammed the front door shut and stepped back. His heartbeat deafened any clue of Billy's movement. The window beside the door tempted his curiosity, but his eyes stopped on the doorknob. It wasn't locked.

He hit the lock and leaned to peek out the window. Billy punched through the window, glass spraying toward Ian's face. He shut his eyes. Billy's broken fingernails scraped into his cheek. The raw layer of exposed cells burned. He moved backwards and fell.

Billy's old and flabby body crashed through the window. More glass sprayed down on Ian. He sheltered his face with his forearm and closed his eyes for only a second. Billy's teeth sliced into his arm. A warm liquid drained onto Ian's chest.

He opened his eyes.

Billy's teeth sank into Ian's forearm flexor like a lion tearing at a gazelle. Billy jerked his head back and tore a chunk of skin from the wound.

A dry heave hurled Ian forward and pushed Billy off of him. He kicked Billy and stumbled to his feet, cupping the wound. Blood drained through his fingers. He staggered up the stairs.

All the doors were closed. *Shit.* He would have to let go of his arm to turn the knob. He went for the bedroom.

Blood smeared across the doorknob and the brass slipped beneath his fingers. He wiped his palm on his pants—*shit*—and tried again. It turned just enough. He slammed it shut behind him, turned the lock, and pulled the belt from his waist. His head grew heavy. His heartbeat weakened. His eyes shot around the room. *A pillowcase.* He dumped the pillow from it, dressed his wound, and tightened the belt around it. The cotton soaked with blood. He searched the room for something, anything that he could defend himself with. His eyes stopped on a book lying open on the floor.

Billy pounded against the bedroom door. The wood split.

On the page, ink curved into the image of a coyote howling beneath a moon.

The door broke. Pieces of wood sprayed into the room.

A patrol car's spotlight drifted through the tree branches lining the driveway. It was his only chance. He forced the old, tight cabin window up, but it was stuck—painted shut. He pounded around the frame chipping the paint away from its seam. It pitched open. "Help!"

He glanced back at the door. Billy slammed into him, knocking the air from his lungs. His body crashed through the window. Cold air shot up all around him.

The black sky was so beautiful, so clear, that the stars of a new moon never created so much ecstasy. His body hit the ground and went numb. Billy landed on top of him. Billy's teeth tore into his neck, but all he could feel was pressure. He stared up into the endless abyss of the universe. A passing breeze drained all the warmth from his body.

A muffled gunshot carried through the air. Droplets of Billy's blood sprayed into Ian's view, tainting the twinkling stars. The perfect image of the night sky flooded with pieces of Billy's brain. Within Ian's last gasp of air, Billy's distorted and motionless face pierced his view, etching itself into his last memory, *Coyote-man had returned.*

9

A SECOND GUNSHOT ECHOED IN THE DISTANCE. ALEX sprinted from the tent. My eyes were still on the green door when Zach pressed his warm lips to mine. His hand rested on my cheek. I inhaled until my lungs could hold no more. The weight of his kiss never left me as he unbuttoned the front of my thick wool jacket.

Cool air chilled the thin grey T-shirt that hugged my nipples. He cupped my breast and gently bit my bottom lip. I grabbed the bottom of his shirt. He leaned back and I pulled it off. His fingers brushed the gauze around my wrist and he held his breath. He leaned against me and brushed a waxy dreadlock from my cheek.

I turned away. *What the hell am I doing?*

His warm chest pressed harder against mine.

I looked back at him, braced my palms against his chest, and nudged him back from me. I let the jacket fall from my shoulders and tore the thin shirt off, pressing my breasts against him. He kissed me, pushing my body deeper into the mattress. All his weight fell on me and I cupped his ass, encouraging it.

"Are you sure? Sure you want to give yourself to me?" He kissed my neck.

Every tendon in my body tightened. I pulled away from his lips and he lifted some weight off of me. Cold air kissed at my nipples. I searched his eyes. He stared back at me, not daring to say another word. His muscles flexed in the lamplight as his hand drifted up my jeans. I pulled him closer, forcing his lips against mine.

He exhaled. I kissed his neck and grabbed the top of his pants. He pulled back for a second at the touch of my cold hands. The button popped and he forced himself closer, barely leaving room to grab his zipper. He stood up and kicked off his pants.

The door was thrown open.

All the warmth was sucked out of the tent. Jan stumbled in with one shoe. She looked like shit. Her bottom lip was puffy, her makeup smeared and her cheekbone swollen. *What the fuck?*

She bent down beside the bed, threw my shirt up to Zach, stuffed her backpack, kicked the shoe off, and grabbed a beer as she walked out the door.

I sat up and fumbled to put the shirt back on. Thank God I hadn't taken off my boots.

Zach already had the wool jacket held out to me before I slid from the bed. "I've waited this long."

I grabbed it and hurried into the dark, cold landscape. At first I couldn't see anything—it was too dark and the tent had been too bright.

"Are you ready?" Jan stood to the side of the tent. A cigarette flopped between her lips. She pressed the cold beer bottle against her cheekbone.

I stepped toward her, but she pulled away and headed for the parking lot. I cut in front of her. "Hey. What happened?"

"What? What do you think happened?" She snapped, glanced over my shoulder, and took a deep breath. "I thought I saw a bear and fell in the woods."

I followed her stare through the parking lot. Alex was leaning against the car smoking. Her bruised cheek dripped with tears. *The gauze would work.* I unraveled it from my wrist, folded the fabric, and gently wiped the mascara and foundation from her face. She refastened her tattered ponytail and grabbed my hand, leading me toward the car. I dug into my pocket and pulled the pill bottle out. She turned at the sound and I handed over the prescription.

"Hey. Did you get lost?" Alex smiled as he wrapped his arms around Jan's waist.

"Yeah, I did. Can we head home?" she said.

Alex looked to me. I shrugged his curiosity off. Jan turned to get into the car and Alex stepped closer. The darkness of the night failed to hide the contusion forming over her cheekbone. "What happened to you?"

"Oh, I tripped on a root along the path." She stumbled over the words, with the alcohol on her breath.

"Bear. She thought she saw a bear. So how 'bout she tells us the story on the way home. In the car, where there are *no* bears." I held out my hand toward him.

"What?" he said.

"Keys," I said.

He crossed his arms.

"It will just be for a little bit. I'd say I am the most sober."

Alex reached into his pocket. Jan slid into the back seat, popped a pill, and cracked open the beer. Alex stepped toward the open door, but Jan pulled it shut. She pointed at the front passenger seat. "You need to help her drive."

I concentrated on the road as she pulled a sleeping bag over her head and passed out. Drunken pedestrians weaved in and out of the road's shoulder. Nocturnal animals scampered through fallen leaves. I stopped at the main intersection. A cabin tucked between the trees across the street was lit up by a circle of park vehicles. It looked like a crime scene.

A black Hummer sped past. A reflective biohazard sign ornamented its side. It slammed on its breaks. *Shit. I should've gone by now.* I gripped the steering wheel, and pulled out.

Yosemite Rising

1

Three minutes after Victoria jumped into Howard's arms, he was fucking her brains out. The sun peeked into the valley, brightening half the tent. The night had been wasted on sex and cheap alcohol. Howard's back pressed against her shoulder. She nudged him and found that his shirt was wet. *What the fuck?* The sleeping bag he had crawled into was drenched with sweat. His body shivered like a bug in a cocoon.

Someone knocked at the door.

"Are you guys coming to breakfast?" Zach said.

Victoria wiggled out of her sleeping bag and slid into a pair of sneakers. She opened the door. Zach's intoxicating hazel irises met hers. *It's fucking freezing out.* She grabbed a ski jacket. "Howard, I'm running to the bathroom. Get up and meet us in the dining hall."

Zach wore a shitty-ass grin.

She slammed the door shut behind them. "So did you finally get a piece of ass? You know you could do so much better. Sloppy seconds, Zach, really?" *Dominic's your best friend for Christ's sake.*

"Vicky, why can't we just be friends?" Zach opened the bathroom door for her and stood beside it.

Because I want to fuck you so hard. She grabbed onto the doorknob and squeezed it as she pulled it closed.

"I promise you I'm better to look at than put up with anyway." Zach said through the door.

Howard was a freak in bed, but he didn't have a six-pack to run her fingers over. Just the image of Zach's sweaty chest brushing the tips of her nipples was enough to deepen her desire for him. She splashed her face. The mirror captured a young woman who should've gone to college, needed to work out more, and a girl who always got what she wanted—damn it. She punched the reflection staring back at her. Pieces of broken mirror formed a spider web over her face. Her knuckles throbbed. That was better. She watched the cold water run over her knuckles, easing her pain. She splashed her face and looked back at the mirror—it couldn't judge her now. She headed for the Pavilion. Inside the main lobby a cobblestone fireplace split the entrance to the dining hall. She glanced at the coffee stand. *Damn, I need a coffee.* But if she lingered, Zach would surely be done eating without her. Besides, she could easily get one on the way out.

The main dining room was much brighter than the room preceding it. The ceiling stretched up another story.

She bumped into someone. Her heart jumped. "Fuck. You scared me!"

Howard moaned.

Blood rushed to her cheeks.

His breath filled her nostrils; it smelled like shit. He was still in his T-shirt and boxers. They clung to him, drenched in sweat. A sweet-sour smell carried from behind him as a person walked by. He had on socks, but no shoes. Mud caked the bottom of his feet and seeped up between his toes.

"You should probably go back to bed, get changed, something." Victoria looked around the room at the eyes gathering on her and walked away from him. She searched the bustling dining room for Zach. He sat at a back table beside a set of exit doors. She loaded a tray with pancakes, a Danish pastry, chocolate milk, and an orange juice. There was no way she was going to drink a regular coffee. She swayed through the people and chairs, sucked down her orange juice, and sat down opposite Zach. She picked up the Danish. "Where is the slut, anyway?"

The dining room fell silent—the scraping of silverware, clinking of cups, and muffled conversation ceasing instantly. Zach's face froze. He stared over her shoulder. She dropped the Danish back onto the plate. It sounded like someone was pouring a jug of water onto the floor, right behind her. Zach clenched the fork in his hand. The smell of urine tainted the air. A chill trickled down Victoria's spine. She looked over her shoulder.

2

ZACH STARED PAST VICTORIA. HOWARD STOOD hunched like a gorilla. His skin glistened with sweat. Urine dripped from his boxers. Zach jolted up, his chair screeching against the tile floor. Howard's hands tighten into fists. He charged, knocked Victoria to the floor, and threw the table from his path.

Zach pivoted, shifting all his weight to run the opposite direction, toward the exit doors. He made it to them and grabbed hold of the doorknob. Sweat had gathered in his palms, lubricating his grip, and his fingers slipped. The room erupted with panic. He squeezed harder and forced the knob's turn. It clicked and he swung the door open. A sigh of relief was greeted with a breeze from the mountains. One deep inhale would be enough to push him forward—escaping.

He stepped onto the porch outside. Something grabbed his ankle and yanked it out from under him. Everything went black. His head throbbed against the floorboards. His eyes squinted through the pain. Then they shut. A vomit-inducing pain resonated from his heel, forcing a scream. Breakfast pushed up his esophagus.

3

VICTORIA HEAVED THE TABLE OFF HER LEGS AND scrambled to her feet. Pieces of pancake smeared into the bottom of her sneakers. She slipped on the hard floor and fell. Her nose smashed against the carpet. Blood leaked from her nostrils as she regained focus on Zach. His screams filled the campground. Howard was crouched over him, tearing at his ankle like a hungry hyena.

Victoria pushed herself up on all fours. Blood dripped into a puddle on the floor. She lunged for Howard. Her breasts smacked the floor as she fell, but her hand had reached around his right ankle. She pulled and pulled and pulled. Her fake nails cracked and ripped the real ones underneath. He stopped resisting her and turned. His cheeks were smeared with blood, drool dripped from the corner of his mouth, and snot pooled on his upper lip. He came at her. She had only enough time to close her eyes.

A flood of pain pushed against her sinuses. His weight

pinned her to the floor. Her eyes shot open, met by his. They were dry, red, and glazed over. There was nothing there, nothing behind them—no awareness, no light. They were right there staring at her. His cold nose pressed against her cheek as his teeth dug into the cartilage of her nose. The smell of shit filled her lungs with each of his snarls.

Warm blood streamed from her nose toward her eyes. Howard dug his teeth harder and deeper into her nasal cavity. She kicked her legs to budge him, but inferior strength kept her in place. She bucked her legs with everything she had. He didn't budge.

His jaws chomped at her nose and a crack-pop noise preceded excruciating pain. His sweaty forehead lifted from hers. Sweat beaded on his skin and trickled down his temples, joining the blood staining his face. He slammed his forehead back down.

Her head throbbed. Blood dripped into her eyes. A jolting stream of pressure and pulsating pain thrust down on her eyelids. She tried to open her eyes, but she couldn't. She tried again and again. She couldn't see anything but an abyss of darkness. She felt the rapid breathing of Howard's chest pinned against hers.

Her body craved the tears that she could no longer shed. Numbness penetrated her neurons as she lay still and quiet in the darkness.

4

ZACH OPENED HIS EYES TO THE GRAINS OF A WOODEN deck. The sound of an animal snarling grabbed his attention, rolling him onto his back. As he pushed up, a sharp pain shot to his head. He rubbed his jaw. Adrenaline dulled the throat-clenching pain coming from his ankle. He bore the pain between his teeth and sat up.

A puddle of blood formed around his foot. The flesh of his ankle was torn and ragged. A blurred silhouette moved in the background. Howard's sweat-stained clothes were covered in blood. He turned from the mangled thing below him. His mouth fell open and chunks of flesh and blood dripped from his teeth.

Jesus. Zach scooted backwards through the doorway.

Howard crawled after him.

A gunshot ripped through the air.

Zach's face was showered with blood as Howard's head fell facedown against the side of his shoe. His blood spilled beside Zach's foot, trickled along his skin, and seeped into his wound.

5

I DROVE HALF THE NIGHT AS JAN AND ALEX SLEPT. Orange lights draped across distant houses framing the landscape. There was nothing like the feel of Halloween through an autumn breeze. Not every house was lit with decorations, but I appreciated each one that was.

By the time we made it back to the beach house it was late morning. The orange lights had dwindled into grey skies. I practically fell out of the car and had to lug my feet up the porch stairs. My fingers ran over a strand of lights wrapped around the porch stair rail. I hadn't noticed them the other night. Exhaustion took hold of me and I only made it to the living room before crashing on the sofa.

Jan hurled her purse to the floor and headed for the bathroom. The rat-tat of the shower filled the house by the time Alex locked the front door.

"So are you going to the party with us?" He shouted from the kitchen, as the microwave radiated popcorn.

I settled farther into the couch and flicked on the television.

"In other news, Yosemite National Park rangers are still searching for the bear that fatally wounded several park visitors and staff this weekend ...."

Alex flicked on Video One and the newscaster's face disappeared into a blue screen.

Wounded visitors?

"What's wrong with you?" Alex sat down and nudged me. The microwave beeped. He jumped up and hurried around the barstools and counter.

Jan stepped into the living room wearing red fishnet stockings and a nurse's costume that barely covered the curves of her butt. The bruise on her cheek was covered with an inch of foundation. Red lipstick did a perfect job hiding her swollen lip.

The movie kicked on and instrumental music began—a trombone or something. I knew that music anywhere: *The Shining*. The film starts with a yellow Volkswagen Beetle winding through the forest, way the fuck in the middle of nowhere Colorado—even though it was really shot in Glacier National Park, Montana. The movie was released in 1980, but it's a classic. The exterior shots for the Overlook Hotel were filmed at Timberline Lodge up on Mount Hood. That movie had ruined every ski trip since.

The woodstove crackled. The beach house windows framed an approaching storm. Jan sat down and handed me the prescription bottle of Percocet. The hem of her dress drifted up her thighs, exposing the red tulle lining beneath.

"Do you want to talk about it now?" I rolled the bottle in my hand.

"Talk about what? There's nothing to talk about." She forced a smile as Alex walked over. He placed a bowl of popcorn and a six pack of beer on the coffee table. Jan cracked open two bottles and offered one to me.

Alex sat down beside her. His fingers brushed her cheek and gently turned her face toward him.

"The news just said people died at Yosemite. You guys don't find that strange?" I said.

Alex gently kissed Jan. His cotton shirt pressed against the white vinyl buttons of her nurse outfit.

Apparently not. I fumbled for my phone, slid from the couch, set the beer on the table, and headed for the bathroom. I scanned my contact list for Zach's number. I didn't have it; I never needed it. Dominic had always called him. Alex would have it. I opened the bathroom door and glanced back over my shoulder.

Alex's lips pressed against Jan so deeply that the passion almost touched my own. She pulled back from him for a breath. He kissed her neck. His fingers followed the curve of her collar to the top button and tore it open. A red lace bra tightly pressed against her breasts.

I closed the door. My heart pounded. I put the toilet seat down and rested my head in my hands. I could go to the bedroom and just sleep. That's all I wanted, sleep. The edge of the light switch slid down beneath my fingers, and darkness engulfed the room. I cracked the door open and braced its edge with my hand.

Alex's lips pressed against the red lace of Jan's nipple, barely touching her skin. He lingered in the delicate moments of her lust for him. Her breasts tightened against the lace with each long inhale. His hand followed the seam of vinyl flowing down her curves and stopped at the edge of tulle.

She placed her hand on top of his and guided his fingers up the red fishnet stockings. She chugged the beer, relaxed her knees, and leaned back. He smiled. The fishnets covering the soft skin between her legs would be warm and damp. He ripped the middle seam of threads. She tore his shirt off and allowed his body to fall between her thighs.

The flickering light of the television captured the muscular curves of his arms. He tore the top of her dress open and cupped the lace bra. His other hand scooped her buttocks from the cushion, moving the torn stockings closer to his skin. Alex's grip around her butt increased as he pulled her hips closer to his.

My grip tightened around the door's edge. My free hand pushed the shirt away from my jeans. The tips of my fingers slid down the soft skin of my stomach, beneath the cotton fabric of my underwear. The firm lines of Alex's back molded perfectly with his legs. Jan's hard nipples wrapped in red lace blurred. My heart raced as Alex threw his pants across the room. The jeans hugging my waist fell to the floor. The damp cotton of my panties slid down my leg. Alex's back curved as he pushed deeper between Jan's thighs. Her legs fell open revealing the torn edges of her stockings and the deep contact of their bodies. My hand tightened around the door.

For a moment ... I felt nothing, but the release of my lust. And then it was gone. I wiped my middle finger off on my panties as I pulled them back up. The door slipped from my grip and slammed shut. I was back in the darkness.

6

THE WIND HOWLED AGAINST THE WINDOWS. THERE was no telling what time it was within the clouded sky, but it was no longer morning. The ocean waves pounded against the coastline, overpowering the sound of a car pulling onto the pebbled driveway.

I slid from the king bed. Pictures of Alex's stepmom stared at me from the dresser. It was her jogging outfit and clean underwear I had borrowed to sleep in. My reflection judged me from across the room. I tugged at one of the dark waxy locks draped against my cheek. Jan had finished twisting the dreadlocks in the car. They looked nice, I suppose. *What happened to you?* I had lost them, my parents. I had lost a huge part of my future, of everyone's future.

Keys rattled in the front door.

I headed down the hallway passing several photographs—all staged. Not one genuine. People with money don't have to capture memories like the rest of us.

Alex stumbled into the house with a bag full of Dungeness crabs.

I turned on the television before offering any help. I looked down at the fresh gauze wrapped around my wrist. It wasn't like I could help. Jan wasn't behind him. *Where is she?* I peeked out the door and just as "where" slid from my lips, the passenger door opened. "So how was the party?"

"Dude it was awesome ...." Alex continued, but I wasn't listening.

"Is she feeling all right?"

"Not really," Jan said as she stepped into the house.

She wrapped her arms over her stomach and walked by. "I'm going to bed."

"Hangover?" Alex shrugged his shoulders. Television commercials switched back to local news. He grunted and stormed toward the television. "Turn this crap off. I swear it's playing more than commercials. I can't even get on the Internet. And when I do, it's nothing but end-of-the-world bullshit everywhere."

I wasn't really listening. Alex would eventually tell me all about it, there was no doubt about that. Jan walked down the hallway and turned into his room. If it was a hangover, she wouldn't want company or noise.

Alex flicked the television off. "You know, my Dad's getting a divorce ...."

A violent cough echoed from the bedroom.

"So feel free to keep any of the clothes." His eyes freely followed my curves, as they had since the day we met. I had never noticed it before. "Maybe now that you're single, my Dad's almost single ...."

I laughed, grabbed a throw pillow, and chucked it at his face.

It hit him and he laughed.

"I'm going for a jog." I grabbed my cell and a pair of headphones. Any jacket would only feel like a wet comforter 10 minutes into it, so I braved the cold wind.

Conifer treetops lined a deep grey sky. An old Bruno Mars song deafened any natural noise. The dirt pounded beneath my sneakers as I walked into a jog. Fog rolled through the mountains, over wind-broken branches lining the distant rolling cliffs. I stopped to watch the clouds overtake the mountain. It's so easy to lose yourself. Drops of rain sprinkled in. I headed back because there was nothing else I could do.

The orange Halloween lights were off when I returned. The smokestack gave away the kindling woodstove. The windows were dark. The pulsating beam of the lighthouse grew slightly brighter in the distance. Nine Inch Nails blared from the headphones as I tugged them from my ears. I stood at the driveway's edge. Alex's car was gone. The pebbles crunched beneath my feet leading up to the porch. I reached for the door knob. The interior was still, the door was unlocked.

The cold ocean wind shoved me through the entrance. The kitchen was as dead as the buckets of crabs sitting in the sink. The woodstove crackled next to an empty couch. The hallway had darkened with the sun's descent and Alex's bedroom was pitch black. I grabbed a pair of jeans and a T-shirt from the master bedroom. On the way to the bathroom I stopped across from Alex's room. I took a deep breath and stepped in.

"Hey, Jan, how are you feel—" I bumped into something and fell backwards into the hallway. Enough light flowed across the bedroom door to reveal a female outline standing a foot from me. I gathered the clothes that had fallen from my hands. "What the hell? You scared the crap out of me!"

She stood in the dark. Something dripped from her navy-blue nightgown. A thin layer of cold air funneled the smell of vomit out of the room. I stood and took a step back from her. "Why don't you get back in bed? I'm going to hop in the shower."

She took a step closer.

"Where's Alex?" I stepped backward into the bathroom and shut the door, pressing my back against it as I pulled the lock. Adrenaline pulsed through my veins. *Stop being stupid.* I let the shower run hot. The small room filled with steam, fogging my reflection over the sink. The smell of vomit intensified. My shirt was soaked with bile. *Gross.* I undressed and wiped the condensation from the mirror. The reflection of my mother stared back. She didn't scold me for the disobedience of hairstyle, because she wasn't really there. She'd never be there.

The light beneath the door flickered and then darkened. Warm water sprayed out of the showerhead, hissing off the ceramic walls. A faint sound came from the door, like an animal clawing at it. The mirror returned to a clouded picture. *This is crazy.* I put off any more thoughts and climbed into the shower. I didn't know it would be the perfect place to cry—to let it out—and wash my tears down the drain. I closed my eyes and rubbed the soap between my fingers. *It isn't fair.* The soap foamed and I buried my face in it.

Something crashed to the floor and broke in Alex's room.

I pulled the shower curtain back and reached for the bathroom door—an inch short. I took a step out of the shower, water sliding down my leg and pooling at my toes. I swung open the door and shouted, "Are you okay?"

Jan's face was right outside the door.

Fuck. The shower curtain tore from two rings and I tottered.

The white of her eyes was yellow, with red cracked veins. Her hollow pupils stared through me as if I were a ghost. Her cheeks were pale, darkening her bruised cheekbone. The skin of her lips was dry and peeling. Her scalp was bleeding in patchy sections. Small clumps of hair were missing.

Everything went silent, except the pounding of my heart.

Jan had a gash across the top of her foot. Chunks of hair stuck to the fresh blood oozing onto the floor.

I slammed the door and forced all my weight against it. I looked down at the lock. If I eased off the door I could lock it, but that would also leave me vulnerable. *Fuck it.* I dropped my shoulders and bolstered one against the door. It locked. I slid down to sit with my back against it. Steam began to suffocate the room, while cold air rushed beneath the door chilling my wet and naked body. I dried off quickly and fought with my damp skin as I pulled my shirt on. My dreadlocks dripped, soaking its collar. I wiggled my damp legs into a pair of jeans and forced them up. The light beneath the door brightened. *What am I doing? This is crazy. She's my best friend. I bet it's just a joke.* I chuckled.

Darkness returned; she returned.

I froze and turned the shower off. Water tapered to a drip. I sat on the closed toilet seat watching the light dance beneath the door until it stopped. The shadows disappeared and the light returned, capturing the puddle of water soaking my feet.

There is no way, no way I am going out there. What had been on the news that Alex had changed so suddenly? Damn it. What am I doing locked in a bathroom? I must be going crazy. Poor Jan is sick as hell, bleeding, and I'm cowering in here. But what if I'm not crazy and—

I lost my concentration. *Please, let me be crazy.*

I grabbed the toilet bowl brush and flung open the door. My toes slid through the drops of water on the floor. If I was fast enough, I could make it down the hallway, to the living room, and then around the corner to the front door. It felt miles away. Dry air grazed the pores of my face as I pushed all my momentum out of the bathroom.

My toes slipped across the floor tiles. I slid down the hallway and fell on my back at the edge of the living room.

Something moved in the corner of my eye.

I clenched my jaw, bearing down on the new bruises I was sure to have. Delusions faded and I reminded myself that *it's only Jan*. I laughed against the pain.

She stood up from the couch like a choked chicken, somehow walking toward me. Her skin drooped. Blood streaked behind her foot. Her diaphragm expanded like a balloon with each breath.

I scrambled to my feet.

She charged from the right and crashed into my shoulder, knocking me to the floor. I rolled onto my stomach and made it into a pushup position. If I didn't make it to the door, my life would be over.

She grabbed my ankle. Her nails dug into my skin.

My arms buckled and I fell flat to the floor, stunned by the pain. The only way out of it was to roll onto my back, twisting her grip from my ankle. With a rush of adrenaline I kicked her in the face and sprinted toward the front door. I grabbed the doorknob, but it was locked. I glanced back.

She had pulled herself off the floor.

I turned the lock and shoved my shoulder against the glass. It didn't budge.

She was coming.

I turned the deadbolt, it clicked, and I shoved the door open. A cold wind blew against my face. It tugged the warmth of the house out into the frigid air, enticing me to stay. It would be so easy to give up.

I sprang from the porch. My bare feet dug into the ice cold pebbles of the driveway. The trees blurred into a tunnel as I sprinted from the house. Every step I took mirrored the pounding of my heart. My feet touched asphalt and pushed me farther, faster, away from the house. My leg muscles burned. My heart ached, pounding out the distant roar of the ocean.

I eased into a walk. The cold of the road stabbed through my feet. I paused, rested my hands against bent knees, and took in the thick fog rolling in around me. Its blanket brought with it fear—a suffocating sense of blindness. If only I could feel that.

Two soft beeps broke the rhythm of my heart. *Another sound would give away my location.* I scrambled for the phone in my pocket. It was a message from Hazel. I searched the dense vapor looking for a sign of Jan, but the constant roar of the ocean deafened that possibility. The ocean wind pushed against the phone attempting to rip it from my fingers.

Heading to the airport now. Pick me up at 11 pm—Newport. Something was coming. Visibility had faded to a three-foot radius, but that wasn't far enough. My heart pounded and forced me into a sprint. The noise grew closer. Dim headlights appeared in the distance, growing brighter. I moved off to the shoulder. The vehicle screeched to a halt.

7

DESERT STRETCHED AS FAR AS HAZEL COULD SEE. The light brown landscape looked gorgeous behind a blue Native American bird sign bearing the name Albuquerque Airport. The sky rumbled with jets as the limousine sped toward *Departures.* The driver slammed the vehicle into park and jumped out, retrieving a single carry-on suitcase.

Hazel scooted from the back seat, catching her reflection in the rearview mirror. Her northwestern skin was sun-beaten from the foreign climate of New Mexico, despite hours of synthetic tanning. A tired and forced smile was the only tip the driver was given. Hazel dragged her suitcase behind her. The kiosk attendant received the same smile. She could have taken a later flight, but that meant another night away from home—from Elizabeth.

The only problem with security was the mascara stuffed in her purse, which was now at the bottom of a trash can. The airport was calm for a Sunday afternoon. One of the suitcase wheels broke as she rounded a bend toward the terminal checkpoint. She stopped and tucked it into the front pocket.

There was still time to stop in the small gift shop of Concourse A. She filled her arms with water, chocolate and magazines, then spilled them onto the checkout counter. She watched the people marching through the terminal as a young girl rang up the items. A line of people grew behind her. Boarding time approached. The diversity of culture and age was something she loved about traveling.

A newspaper at the back of the line grabbed her attention.

YOSEMITE OUTBREAK, ALL QUARANTINED.

Hazel practically yelled, "Can you add that paper?"

"I need to scan it," the girl said.

Hazel glanced back at a man standing beside it. His pudgy face grew red, ripening against a bright yellow sweater vest.

"Hey. You, dude, in the back." She mustered her biggest smile. His beady little eyes met hers. "Yeah, you, can you pass me one of those?"

"I don't see why people buy this crap." The man grabbed the paper and tossed it forward.

Hazel continued smiling as she said, "Thank you."

The attendant took her time scanning the paper. *Why wouldn't she? She had no place to go.*

Hazel bent over and stuffed the items in her purse. The aroma of coffee lured her farther down the terminal, away from her gate. She stood second in line when a male voice announced the boarding of her flight. She would make it—she had to—but there was no way she was going to get on that plane without a decent cup of coffee.

The same voice returned to the intercom as she grabbed the cardboard cup burning with heat. "This is the final boarding call for Hazel Hutchings, flight 1801 to Portland, Oregon ...."

Hot coffee spilled from the cup as she sprinted to Gate B8.

A young man dressed in an aviation uniform walked away from the gate's podium and headed for the passenger boarding bridge.

"Wait!" Hazel said.

The man, likely a distant cousin of her limousine driver, turned around. He looked annoyed until noticing her $100 blouse dripping with coffee. He took her boarding pass, glancing back at the computer podium and then the tunnel.

There was nothing she could say that would win him over. There wasn't enough time to play games.

"Hurry." He waved her behind him into the bridge, speed-walking. A flight attendant paced at the end of it. Her hair was a deep, Irish red. He leaned in, whispering to her, "You guys better push off—fast—before they ground you too."

"Ma'am, you're going to have to check that." The woman's green eyes glanced down at the suitcase. "The overhead compartments are full."

"But I only packed the carry-on so I wouldn't have to check anything."

"You can retrieve your luggage when we unload." The woman's hands shook as she wrapped a tag around the suitcase handle.

"Wait! I have to grab something out of it then." Hazel rummaged through the suitcase, retrieving a three-inch box wrapped in silver paper and shoving it into her purse.

"Attention!" The intercom announced over the terminal speakers and echoed down the corridor. "All flights within the United States have been canceled. Please see the closest kiosk for further ...."

The woman grabbed Hazel's arm and pushed her into the aircraft. More coffee spilled. The door slid shut behind them. Every seat in First Class was taken. *Mr. Pierson's such a dick.* The plane began to roll out onto the runway. The motion jerked Hazel back and she grabbed onto the last First Class seat before the main cabin. The man with the yellow vest smirked as she walked by.

"Please power off all electronic devices and fasten your seatbelts."

Hazel found her seat. The half-empty plane gave her the choice of any seat she wanted—a whole row to herself toward the back. The aircraft rattled down the runway and the attendants finished their safety spiel. Exhaustion blurred Hazel's focus on her phone's screen—still no reply from Elizabeth.

The cabin lights dimmed and the jet engines propelled the aircraft into an evening sky. Hazel sank into the cushions until her body was parallel to the earth again. The "fasten seatbelt" sign clicked off.

"You are now allowed to move about the cabin," the captain announced. In an instant the man in the yellow vest stepped into the main cabin and sprinted to the back bathroom, slamming the door shut behind him.

A chill seeped in from the constant rush of air outside the plane and trickled up Hazel's spine. The horizon darkened. Clear skies clouded. The cabin's light reflected against the windows and hid the beauty of the earth. The redhead's reflection filled the windowpane.

"Would you like a pair of headphones for the movie?" she asked.

"No thank you." Hazel didn't bother turning around.

"Well, how about I leave a pair here and, if you don't use them by the time the movie starts, I'll pick them up?"

Hazel waited for her to leave. She tilted her head back just enough for a sip of coffee and the damn plane hit an air pocket. Lukewarm liquid splashed up her nostrils. A hand grabbed the edge of the aisle seat. The chubby faced man stuffed in the yellow vest gazed at the floor as he climbed back to First Class.

Light pollution reached for the plane windows from a large city below. The cabin dimmed as the movie started. The flight attendant returned and grabbed the headphones from the cushion. "I would like to apologize to you."

About damn time. Hazel turned to face her.

The woman bit her bottom lip, sat down in the aisle seat, and pressed her hands between her chattering knees.

Hazel crossed her arms. There was no excuse for her mistreatment.

The attendant slid into the middle seat. Her name tag read *Shirley*.

Hazel leaned back against the cold wall of the plane.

"I live in Seattle … I have a family and kids and … there is something going on that they're not telling us." Her eyes swelled with tears.

Hazel's shoulders dropped.

"I'm sorry. I would never, ever, treat someone like that. I would never grab a person by the arm. Really, I'm a patient person. I'm so sorry. But I have to get home to my kids."

"You're freaking me out." Hazel said.

"I know. I'm sorry. I am really sorry." She snuffled and excused herself.

"Wait," Hazel grabbed her arm. The First-Class man sprinted past again. "Can you tell me what's going on?"

"I can't." Shirley kept her eyes on the man.

"What if I forget the whole pushing incident?"

She took a deep breath and wiped her nose with her sleeve before sitting back down. "I haven't heard anything official, but over the past few hours a lot of rumors have been spreading. There've been several flu outbreaks and some violent attacks in Yosemite. A few Internet videos were posted an hour before takeoff," her entire face changed and she searched the cabin for eavesdroppers. "Once they ground a flight, no one knows when they'll lift air restrictions. When I heard that announcement, I panicked."

"So what happens when we get to Portland? I have a connecting flight to Newport."

"It all depends on the FAA's decision. The captain is the only one who has direct contact with the control tower, so we won't know until we get closer to landing ... excuse me." She shot to the aisle. A shirtless man stood only a few rows ahead. She placed her hand on his shoulder. "Sir, you need to put your clothes back on."

The man rocked as he pivoted to face her. It was the

same asshole from earlier, but without his yellow vest. His complexion was drained and his eyes were swollen. The hair on his chest clung against sweat-saturated skin. His belt hung loose, unbuckled around his soaked boxers.

He leaned forward and vomited. Shirley screamed. Chunks of undigested food molded to her shoes as the bile soaked through her stockings. He slowly lifted his head, unable to concentrate on the redhead running toward the back bathroom.

Hazel cupped her mouth. A trace of the spilled coffee was the only thing that kept her from barfing.

Another flight attendant rushed from First Class with small bags and napkins. "Sir, please move to the back of the plane and find a seat."

He lumbered toward Hazel, bringing the smell of vomit closer. Every effort to hold her breath failed. The smell gagged her, but she couldn't take her eyes off him.

Shirley stepped out of the bathroom. He stood an inch from her face. She shimmied out of the way and waited to pull the door closed behind him.

Hazel slid back down in her seat. *They should lock him in there.* The miniscule city lights flowed into a sea of darkness beneath the plane. The stir of conversations faded into occasional whispers once again. She rested her cheek against her hand. The jet wind sailing over the plane's metal wings guided her to sleep.

8

THICK FOG WRAPPED AROUND MY BODY, DISSIPATING into the warm glow of headlights. I moved to the side of the road and the car coasted to a stop next to me. Alex's forehead wrinkled from behind the steering wheel. The passenger window automatically drew down.

"What are you doing jogging in the middle of the road?" he said.

I had no words.

"Well come on, get in. I can't believe you're still jogging out here ...." Laughter filled his voice until I opened the door.

I searched the blanket of fog for Jan before sliding into the passenger's seat.

"Why in the world are you barefoot?" He glanced down at my toes.

I stared at the dashboard. *What the hell was I going to say?*

"Hey, are you okay?" He placed a hand on my shoulder.

I jumped and looked at him. His eyes surveyed the car windows wrapped in clouds before meeting mine. I blurted, "There's something wrong with Jan. She's ... not acting right. She tried to bite me ...."

His eyes locked on mine, bringing nothing but silence. Then he let out a hard laugh. "Has Zach been filling your head with stories?" His laugh tapered off and he shifted into drive. "I think you need more sunshine."

I sank into the seat. The lack of sun during the winter does have an effect on people. If you can't make the change, it can kill you. Depression is a heartless bitch. Warm air glided from the heater vent across my cheek. The cold glass fogged as I leaned my head against its pane. He's probably right. *There's a good explanation. She's probably just sick. Or I'm sick.*

"So, I think I'll take Jan to the doctor when we get back. Make sure it's not that virus I read about." Alex's hands tightened around the steering wheel.

"What virus?" I sat up.

"I don't remember. Some outbreak at the park a while back ...." He slowed the car. Sheriffs' vehicles were parked on the neighbor's lawn up ahead. An ambulance siren grew louder in the distance. Alex stopped the car two driveways from his house, in front of a middle-aged cop. His uniform hugged his beer gut. His sleeves looked like they'd rip if he extended his hand any higher. His eyes focused on the house. He should've paid more attention to the road.

I slumped in the seat. I hadn't known or remembered why Hazel had rushed me from the hospital, but I did know it wasn't authorized. I pulled my feet back from the floor heater and turned away from the sheriff, looking out the window toward the house. Something lay on the lawn. The sheriff patted the vehicle's roof, coaxing us forward. *Is that a child?* Alex pulled into the driveway. The front door to the beach house was ajar. My heart sank.

"You didn't close the door?" Alex gripped the steering wheel, shifted his weight, and accelerated down the driveway. Pebbles clunked beneath the car frame.

"What do you not understand about—I was running from her?" I gestured toward my scratched and frozen feet, caked and smeared with mud.

"We need to get her to the hospital. You wait here and I'll go get her." He opened his door and walked toward the still house.

I locked the car behind him.

He turned back at the noise and shook his head with

laughter. He entered and pulled the front door closed behind him. One window after another filled with light. Smoke rose from the chimney. The moon was rising.

I pulled out my cell phone and slowly pressed 9-1-1. My thumb hovered over the *SEND* button. A faint owl's hoot jolted the plastic from my hand. It slammed against the top of my frozen foot. *Fuck.* The visible tree line was empty.

"What's your emergency?" A female dispatcher's voice muffled from the floor.

I bent to retrieve the phone and banged my head against the glove box. "Ouch!"

Alex appeared at the glass door and waved me in.

"Hello?" said the dispatcher.

I hung up the phone. The cold pebbles felt like coals burning the flesh from my feet. By the time I got to the door I jumped inside, and locked it behind me. "Did you find her?"

My phone rang.

Before I could say hello, the dispatcher beat me to it, "Hello. I received an emergency call from this number ...."

"Oh, I'm sorry. I hit the wrong number." I hung up. My heart pounded.

"No." Alex stormed back to the living room. "But why does my couch smell like piss? And there's blood on the floor."

"She cut her foot." The cushion where Jan had sat waiting for me to get out of the shower was wet. Goosebumps crawled over my skin. It felt like she was still standing there, dripping with vomit. The smell of urine pervaded the room and burned my nostrils. My toes were numb. Fatigue washed over me and sleep beckoned. "I think I need to lie down."

My fingers found the edge of the hallway and guided me to the master bedroom. The pictures of Alex's stepmom were almost comforting. A grunt escaped my lips as I threw myself onto the bed. The closet door was open a crack and its contents were completely dark. My chest beat against the mattress and blocked out any other noise. *What if she's in there?* No sleep was worth dying for. I pushed myself off the bed and stepped toward the closet, sure my veins would burst from the pounding of my heart. I shoved the door open. It banged against the wall and ricocheted back toward me. I caught it with my palm. The closet contained only clothes. Relief didn't replace the nausea pitted in my stomach.

I slipped into a pair of jeans and a long-sleeved shirt that hung off my shoulder. So much for keeping me warm. It didn't matter. I sat on the closet floor and pulled the knee-high boots on. Heat slowly returned between my toes.

The polished redwood box stuck out on the top shelf. I glanced over my shoulder. There was no noise, no hint of where Alex was hiding. I stretched on tip-toe and inched the box off the shelf. It fell. The tips of my fingers followed the curves of the waterfall running into the word Awanata. *The woman from the story.*

I opened it. Deep brown fur lay folded inside, maybe buffalo. My hand shook as I pulled back the first piece of skin. An 11-inch dagger rested at the bottom—as white as milk. The four-inch hilt was etched with a red design. Tribal bands twisted around the bottom of a 7-inch blade flowing into a full moon with a coyote howling beneath it, and wrapped into the word "Pyhij." Tribal bands ended at its bottom.

I carefully slid the dagger down the inside of my boot.

I was sure the pounding of my heart would give me away and Alex would storm into the closet. But the house stayed quiet. I locked the bedroom door and collapsed onto the bed. I grabbed my cell phone and called Jan. A faint ring let out through the speaker, echoing out from across the hallway.

9

COLD AIR BLASTED FROM A TINY VENT ABOVE HAZEL. Dreams flowed in and out with the turbulence. The aircraft seat jolted beneath her, ripping her out of sleep. The seatbelt sign flashed on with an accompanying beep. The only other sound was the faint gush of wind outside the aircraft. She sat up and repositioned the vents. The cold night's air seeped through the plane, filling the cabin.

Shirley and another flight attendant stood at the partition of First Class. Their whispers stopped and they glanced past Hazel.

"Hey, folks, this is your captain speaking. We are due to arrive at Portland International Airport in 20 minutes. The approximate local time will be 9:50 pm. The weather is rainy; temperature is 55 degrees. We ask that you stay in your seat, as we expect moderate turbulence as we make our descent." The intercom switched off and the cabin began to stir. The naked man was gone from the back, but the restroom was occupied.

Hazel clenched her knees. The coffee had filtered through her and her bladder felt seconds from exploding. She grabbed the straps of her zebra-print handbag and rushed toward the First Class bathroom.

Shirley greeted her with a smile and waved to the other attendant to stand-down. The First Class attendant kept her mouth shut, but flared her nostrils in disgust.

Hazel squeezed into the tiny bathroom and pulled her stockings down. The pressure of her bladder released. The toilet seat fell out from beneath her thighs. Turbulence bounced her between the narrow walls of the bathroom. Her stockings were soaked with urine. *Great! Just great!* She supported herself against the walls and slid the leggings off, throwing them away. She reached for the door's latch, but the plane jerked and she fell backwards.

A female screamed outside the door. Grunts of agony followed.

"Let me in." Shirley pounded against the door.

Hazel turned the light switch off to stop the deafening vent. She rubbed her temples waiting for another sound — something to indicate it was safe to unlock the door.

There was another scream. It became muffled at the foot of the door.

The aircraft began its descent. Hazel fell backwards onto the toilet and braced her hands against the walls. The plane skidded to a stop. Its landing threw her around like a rag doll. The weight of her body fell forward and her head whacked the edge of the sink. The cartilage in her nose cracked, and a bump formed on her forehead.

Pain shot through her sinuses. Gritting her teeth wouldn't ease the ache. Warm blood ran from her nostrils. The dark bathroom swayed — or she swayed. She wiped the blood from her lip, smearing it onto her cheek. The cabin was silent. She searched the floor for her purse. Her hand hit the side of it and knocked the contents out. Her fingers brushed the soft cotton handkerchief crusted with dry boogies, and she pressed it to her face. It smelled like *him*, the man from the hospital.

"What the fuck?" A male voice yelled from the cabin

not far from the bathroom. A pair of feet stampeded from the rear of the plane toward the voice. Hazel held her breath as they passed.

"Help! Ron, help me! Open the goddamn door!" The man pounded against the cockpit door before his screams overtook him.

Hazel hugged her legs into a ball. Whatever it was—clawed at the bathroom door. She had been breathing too loud. The scraping intensified. Her lungs seemed to collapse with each breath, as if the air seeping through the doorway had thickened. The rapid fire of a silencer filled the cabin. Two kicks to the door broke its lock. The bathroom flooded with artificial light. Hazel's fingers tightened around the handkerchief pressed to her nostrils. She struggled to keep her eyes open, but it was too damn bright.

A male figure stood in the doorway. The son of a bitch was wearing a black military uniform bearing the Meadowlark symbol in orange. He held a gun fixed with a silencer straight at her face. His was shielded by a tactical mask. "What should we do with this one?"

A female agent stepped beside him. Her dark brown eyes were anything but inviting. Each strand of hair was perfectly molded to her head and wrapped into a bun at the back. "No loose ends."

The room spun, and nausea rushed up in Hazel. Her forehead and sinuses throbbed. The room blurred. The handkerchief fell from her grip. Her head rested on the wall behind her.

The man lowered his weapon. "Agent Jane, you need to see this."

The woman stepped back into view. The ringing in Hazel's head echoed. The blurred figures became clear.

She could see the body of the shirtless man. Blood pooled beneath his cheek. Empty eyes captured Hazel's reflection in the abyss of his pupil. Beads of perspiration sat on his loose skin, which was stained with a red handprint that slid down his neck. His outline faded as the background lines flowed into red hair, soaked in blood. Shirley's torn and mangled body rested behind him.

The male agent reached for a second pistol holstered in his duty belt and handed it to Agent Jane. A red laser beam floated across the floor from its scope.

Hazel closed her eyes. The ringing in her ears was replaced by the pounding of her heart. *Elizabeth.* An abyss of darkness drew around her as the light spots against her closed eyelids faded into nothing.

Nowhere To Run

1

A DOG BARKED IN THE DISTANCE, STIRRING THE tranquil night. Moonlight glistened on the withering leaves outside. I rubbed my eyes and jolted to a sitting position. *Shit, what time is it?* My head pounded. I grabbed the phone lying beside me—10:13—NO MESSAGES.

I slouched back into the pillows. Maybe it had all been a dream. I looked down at the knee-high boots weighting against my feet and the shirt hanging off one shoulder—I would never wear something like this.

The dog yelped and the night became peaceful. Two eyes glowed in a conifer tree outside. The Great Grey Owl stared back at me. Its feathers blended into the dark sky, as cold air rustled their tips. It sat still. Blood pounded though my heart. I clenched the phone in my hand and slid from the mattress. The fog had lifted enough to see the tree line. I pressed my nose to the cold windowpane and whispered, "What do you want?"

The glass fogged beneath my lips. The stitches running

down my wrist throbbed with my heartbeat. I took my eyes off the creature. Moonlight trickled over the line of stitches. I pulled the sleeve of my shirt down and the collar fell farther off my shoulder.

I glanced back at the tree branch: It was empty.

The house was quiet until my stomach growled. I searched the circle of fog one last time. In the corner of the yard a silhouette stood in a cluster of trees. I stepped back and bumped into the bed. Whatever it was—didn't move for 20 minutes.

This is ridiculous.

I kept an eye on the shadows and took a step toward the window. Nothing changed. *So stupid.*

I unlocked the bedroom door; its click echoed throughout the house. Alex's room was dark. The smell of vomit was obscured by a thick citrus scent. The bathroom door was closed and no light escaped it. The hallway tunneled to a moonlit living room. The wall of windows captured what moonlight penetrated the layer of fog. The urine-soaked cushion was gone. I sat down on the remaining portion of the couch and turned the television on. The screen filled with breaking news: scenes of hospitals, car accidents lining the streets, grocery store shelves empty and looted. I sank into the cushion.

"While government officials claim there's no connection between the bear attacks this weekend at Yosemite National Park, zombie preppers insist that the recent incidents are in fact proof of an outbreak. Fears grew today after the report that an Oregon man attacked and killed his girlfriend at Curry Village this morning. Park officials state that Homeland Security has taken over the investigation.

"Skeptics believe the whole event is due to an

unofficial 'Zombiefest' that was being held at the park. Visitors have reported several 'biting' incidents. Anyone who has been bitten should seek medical attention. As I stand here, they are preparing to close down the park. Back to you—"

"Alex!" I yelled down the hallway. The remote slid from my fingers. I scooted to the edge of the couch. "You're going to think I'm crazy, but you have got to see...."

I noticed a thick fluorescent line drawn horizontally across the wall. I stood up from the couch. Something was wrong. I ran my fingers along the textured walls and followed the line around the room. The line dug into the plaster as it neared the first window frame.

A leaf fell to the ground outside.

The line continued over the glass. I squatted down, level with the mark. Moonlight trickled through the trees and over the faint yellow line as I swiped it with my finger. It was damp—fresh. *Highlighter?* My heart raced. The line continued around the room back to the edge of the hallway.

My phone beeped. *Shit, the alarm.*

It was time to pick up Hazel. The damn thing caught the edge of my pocket as I tried to turn it off. The screen blinded me. I started to slide it back into my jeans as my vision began to readjust. The night's details sharpened, but the end of the hallway remained pitch black.

The darkness shifted at its end.

I froze.

It moved closer. The flickering light of the television stretched down the hallway unable to reach it. It was Alex, inching his way toward the living room. Synthetic light curved over the muscles of his arms. His orange OSU sweatpants made his skin appear drained and loose. His chin hung down to his chest, empty eyes stared across the room at me.

I sprinted behind the couch and threw my phone at him. It ricocheted off his torso and landed on the floor. It was no use. He rushed me. The cell phone crunched beneath his foot. I hesitated at the sound and his fingers caught a dreadlock, yanking me backwards. He pinned himself onto me.

My left arm pushed at the weight of his chest, and it shook with weakness. His nails tore into my scalp as he pulled my head toward his teeth. I fumbled for the dagger with my right hand. *Damn it.* It was tucked beneath my jeans. My goddamn pant leg caught on the top of my boot. It was no use; I couldn't get it.

I inhaled and shoved him back, forced my pant leg up, yanked the dagger out and jammed the blade into his throat.

His hands wrapped around my neck. His knuckles tightened, squeezing the walls of my esophagus. I grabbed the dagger with both hands and pushed—with everything I had—against it.

He fell backwards.

I pushed it farther, through to the back of his neck. He began to choke on his blood. My thumb slid over the etched coyote as I tore the dagger out. I climbed to my feet. Blood dripped along the floor as I sprinted for the front door. I passed the kitchen counter. *His keys.* I turned back and grabbed them.

I swung the glass door open and stumbled down the porch in a blur. Wet pebbles slid beneath my boots as I skidded to a stop beside the Prius. It was locked. Alex had a key for everything on his stupid keychain. There were three possibilities. The first slid easily into the keyhole. It began to turn. Then the metal jammed. Perspiration gathered in my palms. I glanced up at the house. Alex stood behind the front door staring at me. The ocean's wind crept into my bones. "Come on!"

He disappeared.

Sweat oozed through my pores, enticing the cold air. *Come on.* I tugged on the key. The front door shattered. Alex tumbled out. I wiggled the key and tugged harder. It freed. I fell backwards. The key ring went flying. My hip slammed against the wet pebbles and the butt of my jeans soaked. *Where'd they go?* My fingers scrambled over the pebbles for them, searching the shadow beneath the car. *It's useless, I'm going to die.* All I could think about was Hazel stranded at the airport. My fingertips bumped into the metal key ring. *Yes!*

I forced the second key into the door handle. It unlocked. I exhaled, pulled it out, and slid in behind the steering wheel. The engine purred. The vehicle's false sense of security filled me. I shifted into reverse and glimpsed back up at the house. Broken glass covered the patio. *Where is he?*

I leaned out to pull the door closed. Fingernails scraped across my arm. *Shit.* I thrust all my weight against the gas pedal. The engine revved. I jammed the stickshift to reverse and cut the wheel right. Alex was pitched to the ground. I straightened the wheels and shifted to drive. The pebbled path was covered in darkness and fog until I clicked on the headlights.

Alex's lifeless body lay facedown on the driveway in front of me.

I gripped the steering wheel and rested my forehead against it. Tears rained down. *I must be in hell.* I glanced up at the stitches lining my wrist. *What have I done?* The headlights captured movement.

Alex's body twitched.

He stood. His fingers slicked back his hair and dug into his scalp. He yanked a clump of hair out. It fell to the pebbles below. Blood gushed from his throat.

I closed my eyes and stomped the gas pedal to the floor. The tires spun, flinging stones, catching enough traction that the car shot forward. The driver's door swung shut. I couldn't see—couldn't bear to unclench my eyelids. Darkness soothed me until I heard the sound of bones popping beneath the tires. The car bumped into the air, thumping over his body. I forced my eyes open. The tires hit asphalt. The rearview mirror was dark and empty. *I had killed my friend.*

2

FOG RUSHED OVER THE PRIUS AS IT WEAVED SOUTH along the dark coastal highway. A pop song blared from the radio. I cranked it louder, drowning out any thoughts. They would be too painful.

The dashboard glowed a soft blue. Its clock turned 11:00. Music faded into a reverent male voice. "Airport officials have not commented regarding Flight 1801's lockdown at PDX. The traffic surrounding this area is still bumper-to-bumper due to the immediate cancellation of flights."

This can't be happening. I found myself speeding down

the highway. Tree branches drew lines against the canvas of the night. Music returned. As I leaned just an inch to scan the radio stations, the steering wheel went with me and the car jerked into a guardrail. I swerved out of it, nearly careening over the edge into the ocean.

I returned to search the radio. Channel after channel, nothing but songs and commercials.

Streetlights began to light the desolate road. A traffic light at the edge of town turned red and I eased to a stop. A car packed with teenagers pulled up alongside me. My heart skipped. Their dark eyes grew wide. A boy in the back seat slid his hand down the window. Moans carried through the car. The streetlight faded green. He cranked the window down and reached out toward me. Laughter filled their vehicle as they pulled away.

Stoplights lined the coastal town of Newport. Each light had its own beggar. A scruffy man stood on the corner. He walked up to the passenger window, his tattered clothes sloshing against the glass. I kept my eyes forward. I never knew what to feel for them. *Was there no hope, no work? Was he too lazy, mentally ill, or a drug addict?* His palm hit the window and smeared mud down the pane. The writing on his cardboard sign dripped with rain. I cracked the window. "I don't have any money!"

Warm air seeped out of the gap and dispersed into the cold night air. Condensation formed between the homeless man's palm and the sheet of glass. His fingers pressed against the window, his nostrils lifted toward the opening like an animal's. His neck jerked and he stared at me with hungry eyes and—then—to the white pick-up behind me.

The driver drummed his hands on the steering wheel. He was in his 50s, likely the son of the old woman waving money out the passenger window. The skin hanging from her arm flapped.

The wet cardboard fell from the man's hand as he stepped closer. He reached for the money, but he didn't take it. He grabbed her arm and chomped down on it. Blood drained down the flapping skin. She screamed. Her son lost his beat on the wheel and shoved the door open. He was halfway around the truck when granny's arm snapped.

The red hue cast by the traffic light turned to green.

I turned my eyes to the road and sped off—downtown toward the bridge—anywhere the fuck away from there. Pacific rain pummeled the vehicle as it crossed the green steel bridge arched over Yaquina Bay. Outside air seeped into the cracked passenger window, creeping across my skin.

A small blue sign designated *Newport Municipal Airport* coming up on the left. It was 11:08. I took a sharp left onto a long driveway that led to a small building. Windows wrapped around the side, facing an empty parking lot. They continued around to the front, where a glass door faced the runway.

Details became clearer as I sped closer. *Shit.* I was going too fast. I hit the brake. The front tire slid up onto the curb, but the car stopped. Fog strangled the light escaping from the wall of windows. The sidewalk was still as I turned off the engine. I slammed the door and the keys rattled in the ignition.

Stale air smacked me in the face as I entered the small lobby. A door to an employee lounge was six feet ahead. A counter sat to its right, stretching to the other side of the room. At its far end sat a crystal vase stuffed with fresh yellow roses. The windows began there and ended near the lounge door.

A woman in her 40s stepped into the room and smiled. Graveyard shifts had put a few pounds on her.

A man stuffed into a security guard uniform followed. His chubby fingers adjusted his belt and tucked in his white shirt.

"I'm sorry, but we're closed," the woman said, with that same warm smile.

"My sister's plane ...," I rushed the counter, "she's supposed to be here by now .... I heard this report on the news." I took a breath. "Please tell me the eleven o'clock flight is running late." *It has to be running late.*

Her smile faded. "I'm sorry ... but all flights have been grounded and cancelled for the night."

Tears escaped me. I buried my head into my arms. The sound of a faint plane approaching from the north cut through our conversation. My head popped up, "What's that?"

"Those are private owners." She grinned, happy that her shift would be over soon. "If you can give me a name, I could run a search for you."

"Hazel Hutchings, traveling from Albuquerque. I don't know what flight. She told me to pick her up tonight, at eleven o'clock." I glanced up searching the lobby again. *This can't be happening.*

"Here it is. Her connecting flight—from Portland to Newport—has been cancelled. Her flight from ABQ departed on time and arrived in Portland at ...," the woman swallowed hard. Her eyes went frantic reading the screen, and then they fell on me. It was if someone had dumped a bucket of sadness over her. "I think you should see the news."

No. I followed her into the employee lounge. It was a small room furnished with a two-person dining set, two lounge chairs, and a small refrigerator. Everything hugged the wall, including the flat screen television at the end of the room. *No.*

"BREAKING NEWS" took up most of the television screen. There was no sound.

No. "What about my sister's flight?"

Her eyes turned away from me and she turned up the volume.

"We just received breaking news regarding Flight 1801. Airport officials have just confirmed that there are no survivors ... the CDC arrived on scene ... witnesses ... shots fired ... all are confirmed dead .... Albuquerque Airport officials are also working with Homeland Security ...."

It all faded. The whole room blurred. My heart pounded. I tried to force my eyes to stay open, but I couldn't. Tears streamed down my cheeks. *No....* I turned toward the woman and she lightly nodded. *No....* It couldn't be real. She can't be gone. *I'm alone, all alone.* I looked down at my wrist. *No, not her.*

Hands fisted and teeth clenched, I forced my goddamn eyes open. "Well, what are you doing here? Why are you still here? You need to go home, you need to pack .... You need to be somewhere safe."

"Ma'am, you're going to have to control yourself." The woman rested her hand on my bare shoulder.

Her touch felt so real.

"You have to get out of here." I grabbed her hand and pulled her toward the lobby. "We need to find a safe place for tonight."

"You need to calm down." The security guard stepped up behind me. He grabbed my arms, pulled them behind my back, and twisted a pair of handcuffs around my wrists. The metal dug into the fresh stitches and I gagged. It was all real.

The room blurred beneath a layer of tears. Cries forced themselves out with every exhale, but they deafened in my mind. Emptiness stabbed my chest, each breath caving into my breaking heart. It wasn't fair.

The security guard mumbled on about something, but there was nothing—nothing that mattered. Even the pain had numbed. I gasped for air. Inaudible cries molded me to the floor.

He scooped me up and rolled me onto a couch. I drew my knees into my chest. My chest hurt, but I didn't care. I couldn't breathe, I didn't want to breathe. *Not her. Not her! This couldn't be happening ....* I squeezed the salty water from my eyes. All the light left in the world disappeared. The abyss of grief pulled me to sleep.

Then I saw her. *She was waiting for me, in a field of wildflowers. We were only children, amazed at the beauty around us, watching butterflies and bees drift from one color to the next.*

She pressed a bright yellow buttercup beneath my chin. "Now let's see if you like butter."

The petals tickled my skin. I giggled and her face lit up.

"Wow. You really like butter." She laughed handing me the flower ....

3

MONDAY BROUGHT SUN. ITS RAYS TRICKLED THROUGH a large window on the other side of the room. It was warm, the only comfort I had. The cushion beneath my cheek was soaked and smelled like a musty basement. I turned my head, but the slightest movement dug the handcuffs deeper into my skin, into my stitches. It was still real; I was still alive. The room was different. Not that I really remembered what it had looked like. A desk sat across the couch. The open door to the right led to the lounge—no sound. Another door to the rear was closed. "Hello?"

It too was silent.

I sat up. My cheeks were sticky. The handcuffs dug into my wrists. I pressed my cracked and dry lips together, restraining the nausea pitted in my stomach. As I sat, my bladder shifted and pressure built. I yelled, "Hello?"

The woman rushed in with her finger pressed to her lips and looked back over her shoulder. "You have to be quiet."

"I really need to use the bathroom." I squeezed my knees together.

"That's not my call, but you really need to be quiet." She stepped back toward the lounge and disappeared.

"It's my call." The door at the back of the room opened. The security guard stepped out. He was a lot taller than I had remembered, and his frame blocked the entire doorway.

"Can you let me out of here?"

He didn't move.

"Did I do something wrong, officer?"

"Yes ... no ...." He took a key out of his pocket and made his way to the handcuffs. His hands shook as he unlocked them. "I detained you for your own protection."

The metal loosened, bringing a wave of nausea. I forced myself not to throw up.

Snot dripped from his nose. He wiped it with his sleeve and sat down at the desk.

I rubbed my wrist, easing the line imprinted into my skin.

His pity bore down on me through words, "I'm really sorry for your loss."

"May I use the restroom?"

He nodded toward the rear room and propped his head in his hands.

I sprinted to the bathroom and pushed the door closed, but it stopped three inches short of its frame. Across from the door were two sinks framed by a large mirror. Beside the toilet was a full-length window with its blind drawn. Muffled conversation carried through the cracked door.

The seat was up, and a thick, deep yellow saturated the toilet bowel. I added to it and restrained myself from flushing it or washing my hands—so that I could hear them.

"I have to make sure she is stable enough first," the man whispered.

"John, if you lost someone ... and like that. We can't keep her here. I don't know what's going on, but I'm going home—which both of us should've done last night after the ..." She caught me out of the corner of her eye. "So ... what's your name?"

I stepped out of the bathroom. John darted toward me.

YOSEMITE RISING

He looked like a lumberjack about to take down a tree. I froze. He squeezed past and slammed the door shut. A hoarse cough echoed beneath the door. Vomit sprayed into the toilet.

I sat back down on the couch, silent.

The woman stared at the bathroom door with wide eyes.

It opened.

John stepped out and sat down beside me. I slid over as far as I could and hugged the armrest. He coughed and wiped the sweat running down his forehead.

I looked at the woman and said, "How long has he been sick?"

"Oh, he's not sick. He just has bad allergies." Her voice shook, her hands clasped tightly in her lap, and her teeth dug into her bottom lip. She looked at me. "So, any ideas?"

"What do you mean?"

The man hacked.

My heart jumped.

The woman nodded and led me into the lounge. I paced in front of the television. She took a couple of hoagies from a small refrigerator, threw one over and headed for the lobby. "Eat. I need some chocolate."

I was starving. I devoured the whole thing while turning on the television and waiting for it to actually flick on.

"All flights have been canceled. Anyone with flu-like symptoms is encouraged to stay at home …," said the newscaster.

I glanced at the open door leading back to the office.

"All government offices and public schools will remain closed until next week. Local hospitals recommend that you stay in bed and not seek emergency medical treatment unless clear life-threatening symptoms appear. Again, the best thing is to stay home."

Something banged behind me.

The dining chair closest to the lobby door had fallen. The woman stood beside it; her eyes were wide and she didn't move. The chocolate bars in her hands were squished in clenched fists.

"Are you okay?" I took a step back.

"There's a man walking around outside." She looked at me, but her gaze went right through me. "He just stood outside staring through the door at me."

I grabbed her arm and jerked her out of the doorway. I peeked around its threshold—the lobby was empty. The wall of windows captured a two person airplane parked on the runway. There was no man. I grabbed the door and eased it closed. "There's no lock?"

She shook her head.

I pressed my back against the door and looked around the room. "Did you see where the guy went?"

"No. He was just there," she paced in front of the office door, "at the front entrance—just staring at me."

The security guard coughed.

We froze and turned our attention to the office. He sat hunched over on the couch cushions, drooling in his sleep.

"How long has he had that cough?" I said.

"I don't know. It started after our lunch break yesterday ... well actually during lunch break ... we ... he started coughing while he was . . ." She blushed.

John's body began to convulse and he fell to the floor. His eyes rolled to the back of his head. The woman rushed to his side, but I tackled and restrained her until he lay limp. His chest filled with a deep moan. I let go of her. She dove to his side, shoved her arm under his, and attempted to pull him up. "Can you help me?"

Fuck no. I shook my head. There was no way I was getting near him.

"Please?" she said.

Fuck. I supported the damp pit of his arm and helped heave his body back onto the couch. His perspiration smeared around my neck as I sat up. He let out a deep moan. I sprang off the couch.

"Elizabeth Hutchings is still wanted by police in connection with the murder of Alex Muir. Anyone who knows her whereabouts is urged to contact Homeland Security." The soft newscaster's voice carried from the lounge.

My heart jumped. I froze.

"What are you not telling me? Is that your name?"

"I should go." I headed for the lounge.

She cut me off. "Please."

"You'll just think I'm crazy."

"You might be surprised." She glanced over at the man she had been screwing around with for months. She nodded to the lounge and we moved into it together. She offered out her hand and I shook it. "I'm Tina."

She sat at the table. "I've been up all night watching the news. You've missed a lot. Aviation has shut down, government offices and schools have been closed. They say it's an attempt to stop some superbug. But before Facebook and Twitter went down, people were saying that—this is the zombie apocalypse."

"Facebook?"

"Yeah, well I think so. Everything is down for routine maintenance." She paused, her eyes widened. "Excuse me."

4

TINA FLUNG THE BATHROOM DOOR CLOSED BEHIND her. It slammed shut. She shoved her stockings down. Her nail nicked the fabric and a small run began to spread. The toilet seat was cold beneath her thighs.

The window blind tapped against the glass. Cold air seeped from its bottom. Passing gusts sucked it toward the window and blew it back out again.

She grabbed a clump of toilet paper.

Something banged against the windowpane from outside.

She sat still. Another breeze sucked the blind back against the glass—thump—then another pushed it away.

She tugged at the toilet paper roll slowly, listening. The smell of rotting flesh blew through the seams of the blind. She leaned back against the toilet tank. Another breeze pushed itself into the room chilling the dampness of her wet bottom. She leaned forward and peeked around the side of the blind. A solid glass panel filled the top two-thirds of the window. The remaining third was open—a hopper-style window that popped up and out.

A man—the man from earlier—stood hunched on all fours beside the window. His hair dripped with rainwater, his hands pressed into the mud outside, and his cheek pressed against the bottom of the screen. His nostrils flared.

Tina pulled her feet back toward the base of the toilet.

He sat up. Yellow-crusted and swollen eyes watched the blind.

She kept still. If she let go of it now, he'd notice the movement.

His nose pressed against the windowpane, condensation formed beneath his dry and cracked lips.

She waited for the next breeze to suck the blind, let go, and then stood.

If she could make it to the door before he crouched down again, she would have a chance. She went full force toward the door, but the drawstring of the blind snagged on the hem of her skirt and drew up. She had only taken three steps before realizing it was caught. She froze with her back to the window.

Menses ran down her leg. She glanced over her shoulder.

His grotesque eyes followed the blood dripping down her inner thigh. It soaked into her stockings.

A small space heater kicked on behind her, pushing the room's warmth through the open window. The man became an animal—snarling and tearing at the window screen. His fist broke through the mesh, but the opening's size trapped him from her. He stood and released a fierce groan.

Her hands shook as she reached for the string caught on her skirt. The plastic thing at its end unhooked and the string swung free. The blind rushed down the window. It stopped five inches short of the bottom and tapped against the glass. She sighed and turned back toward the door.

The window shattered behind her. Pieces of glass showered against her back. The man pummeled into her like a freight train. Her body went flying. Her head smacked the floor.

5

"ARE YOU OKAY?" I TAPPED AGAINST THE BATHROOM door. She had been in there forever. "Tina?"

No answer.

I flung the door open. It slammed against the bathroom wall. Her limp body was laid out on the floor. Her eyes were open facing the door—facing me—but there was no life left in them. A man was bent over her legs and his face was pressed between her thighs. He looked up. Pieces of torn flesh and blood slid down his chin.

I stood still, only stretching my fingers for the doorknob—I got it, slammed the door shut, and spun around. My nose brushed against cotton—the security guard's shirt. His body walled me off from the rest of the room.

Without thinking, I ducked under his love handles and ran for the lounge. The door leading into the lobby was still closed. I tried to stop, but momentum hurled me into the door. *Shit.* I bounced off just enough to regain balance and rip it open. The exit was only a few steps away. I went for it, clasped my fingers around the doorknob, and pulled. It didn't budge. I turned around. The worn exterior of the security guard stood in the doorway behind me, nothing more than a hollow shell. He stepped closer and groaned. I faced him and pinned my back against the door's glass.

The flowers. I sprinted for the yellow roses at the end of the counter. He followed. His groan morphed into a growl. I could smell his breath behind me as the tips of my fingers slid into the water of the crystal vase. I swung it around. It slammed into the side of his skull, slipped from my hand, and shattered against the wall.

He fell to the floor.

I jumped over the counter and knocked a mug of curdled coffee over.

He stood up, crushing the flowers into petals. Blood oozed from his temple, dripping down his cheek.

I landed behind the counter and reached for the coffee mug. I grabbed hold of its handle. He clawed at me from across the counter and his fingernails tore into my bicep. Before he hurtled the countertop, I rounded its side and threw the cup at the front door. Glass rained onto the floor. The mug skidded across the sidewalk and broke.

Shards of glass created a barrier to the outside—a sick version of a door in a funhouse. It was pain or death. I charged the opening with my shoulder. At the last second, I stopped, my shoulder continued through the door enough for my sleeve to catch on a piece of glass. I pulled back and my shirt ripped, leaving both shoulders bare.

The security guard rushed from behind me.

I faced him, bent my knees, and braced for his impact.

He lunged.

I shifted all my weight to the left.

He crashed through the jagged glass and fell on top of the shattered mug.

I jumped through the door, landing on his leg, then lost my balance and fell to the ground beside him. He stood up, never taking his eyes off me. Pieces of porcelain protruded from different sections of his cheek. The mug's handle dangled from the torn flesh beneath his eye. My pulse accelerated. The walls of my vision focused in on the Prius. I went for it. The soles of my boots slipped on the rain-beaten pavement.

I slid across the hood of the car. Beads of water soaked into my jeans. I tore the door open. My breasts squished up against the steering wheel as I forced the ignition. I stepped on the gas and tried to shift. The car revved. *Goddamit.* I stomped on the brake. He moved to my side of the vehicle and ripped the mug handle from his face.

My window shattered. Pieces of glass sprayed against my left cheek. His fingernails tore into my shoulder. I slid into the passenger seat and fumbled for the door handle—got it—and the door swung open. I fell to the ground. There was no doubt he was already halfway across the seat. I scooted back from the car like a crab. My lower back scraped into the asphalt. *Shit, that fucking hurts.* A stabbing pain pushed the partially digested hoagie halfway up my throat.

Every second counted, but they were wasted, crippled by nausea. The security guard fell out onto the ground and grabbed for me. His fingers touched the sole of my boot. One more attempt and he'd have full control. I forced myself up.

Rain started to drip from the sky and pelt the wax of my dreadlocks. I froze. *Not yet. I can't move, not yet.* It was all about timing.

He closed in. Infection had seeped through every cell of his body—the hollow capsule.

Just two more steps.

He took them.

I ran around the front of the car.

He moved more quickly than I had calculated—too close for me to get behind the wheel. I pushed myself until my lungs hurt, rounded the back of the car for the passenger side door, and then slid across the seat. Pieces of glass rolled beneath my jeans.

I gripped the steering wheel so tightly that my fingernails dug into the skin of my palms. I threw the car

YOSEMITE RISING

into reverse and spun it around, speeding off down the driveway toward Highway 101. I turned right—not thinking—heading north—never looking back.

Newport's seaweed-colored bridge climbed higher over the bay as I drove back into town. Every building looked beaten by the sea. Vacant shops lined the main stretch off the bridge. The first light turned red. *Where do I go?* There was nowhere to go. *Where do I go?* The light changed. I forced the gas pedal down and accelerated to 30 miles per hour, blowing through the next two street lights. A small sign on the right pointed to Corvallis. I headed east—home.

The small beach town quickly faded into rural mountains. I passed by the smaller town of Toledo. Light rain clouds darkened in the distance. It was a long drive through no man's land.

The red "check engine" light lit up. The fuel gauge sagged to the bottom line—empty. The car slowed and then stopped. I pressed all my weight on the gas pedal. It was no use. There was nothing left to give.

A cloud burst. Rain poured into the broken window and I slid over. Mist accompanied the autumn air rushing across the seat for me. Goosebumps covered my skin.

Sunlight poked through the clouds, calming the weather. I searched the car. Nothing. It was empty, except for a pack of condoms in the glove box. I slammed it shut. Walking for miles was better than sitting there vulnerable and freezing to death.

I threw open the door and continued east. Desolate houses stretched between the miles, until there was a clearing—a rest stop. I sprinted across the street and down the pull-off road. A wooden sign labeled the land as Ellmaker State Wayside—halfway home.

A building sat on the other side of an asphalt loop. Cement panels covered the exterior, giving it a creamy, refined wood-like look. A storage door segregated the women's restroom to the left and the men's to the right. A privacy fence shielded both doors from the road.

I was in the middle of nowhere and the sun was setting. Anything could be hiding in the woods. *Anything.* The dark clouds that had been following me blew faster across the sky. I ran into the women's restroom.

I wasn't safe, not yet. The brown door led into a two-stall room with a single sink. Fluorescent lights flickered, lighting each corner. Rain poured against the roof. The door closed behind me. I pinned my back to the door frame and slid down until my butt hit the floor. My heart jumped. I forgot to check the stalls. I leaned over, laying my cheek against the floor—no feet.

I stood. All I wanted to do was sleep, but it wasn't safe, not yet. I shoved the first stall door open. My heart pounded so loudly I heard no other noise. A plunger rested beside the toilet. I grabbed its sticky handle and moved to the next stall. I pushed against its door. It didn't budge. *Shit.* I glanced back at the front door and bent down, sticking my head beneath the stall—nothing. Exhaustion overtook me as I staggered to the sink. I grabbed its edge, letting it bear my weight. I looked at the woman staring back at me in the mirror. She had lost everything; there was nothing left. Tears fell down her cheeks and I felt them fall.

I turned on the faucet, drowning out the growl of hunger. Ice cold water trickled through my fingers and flowed over my cupped hands. I splashed the saltwater from my cheeks. The mirror's reflection could have killed me, but I hit the light switch. Three small privacy windows on the side of the building captured every dimming ray of daylight outside. It danced, as it always has.

I huddled in the corner closest to the door, beside the sink. The floor sucked out all my remaining body heat. I loosened each lace of my boots before kicking them off. Steam from my toes wafted into the rising moonlight. The dagger stashed in my boot fell to the floor, cast in shadow. My stomach's growl echoed against the walls. I closed my eyes. For tonight, even death would be too exhausting.

6

A CAR DOOR SLAMMED, AND THEN A SECOND. MY head throbbed against the wall. The damp bathroom air had filled my lungs all night and coated my throat. I shoved my boots on and picked up the dagger, sliding it back into my boot. I pressed my ear against the door listening for anything. The men's bathroom door creaked. I held my breath and strained for the slightest evidence of conversation—nothing. If it was two men, I was screwed.

I cracked the door open; there was no one. A black Hummer with tinted windows was parked out front. A biohazard symbol framed the word Meadowlark on the passenger door. Unease enfolded me. *But it's a vehicle.* I didn't wait to contemplate choosing between being a good girl and escaping from two men in a world with no laws. I sprinted for the Hummer.

The men's bathroom door creaked open. I had reached the back passenger door before looking back. Two men dressed in some sort of black military uniforms stepped out. When they saw me, their conversation stopped.

Something banged against the window behind me.

I squinted through the tinted glass. Someone was in

there. A woman smacked her forehead against the window. A piece of duct tape covered her mouth and stretched halfway over her cheeks. *What the fuck?*

"Get her!" One of the men yelled.

Adrenaline shot through my veins. I sprinted toward the road. The clearing faded back into a wall of forest along the highway. The air was heavy in my lungs. Bile sloshed in my cramping stomach. My muscles burned. I had to get away, but I couldn't—I couldn't go on any longer. That was it. I stopped and rested my hands on my knees. My muscles tightened as I braced for impact.

One of the men plowed into the back of me like a bulldozer. My cheek slammed against the ground. Every particle of stale air freed from my lungs. I tried to replace the lost breath, but couldn't. His weight pinned my back.

"You shouldn't have run," he whispered behind my ear and got up.

I gasped for air and dirt filled my mouth. He tore my left wrist back and slapped a handcuff on me like I was a criminal.

His grip tightened around the cuff and the metal dug into my wrist. "That's for running."

I clenched my teeth, restraining tears. I wouldn't be weak.

He nudged my wrist up the small of my back. It fucking hurt. I dug my cheek into the mud trying to alleviate the pain. I screamed out. The man ripped my other hand back, cuffed it, and let go. He helped me stand and spun me to face him. He was much more attractive then I thought he would be. His eyes were a deep blue. They studied me as if searching for something.

A car horn blasted.

The man pushed me toward the Hummer. His

partner's eyes were locked on me the whole way. The woman in the back seat had her cheek pressed against the tinted windowpane. She didn't turn her head or move her eyes as we walked around the vehicle. The man's grip tightened around my arm as he opened the door behind the driver.

I hesitated. The woman's hands were handcuffed behind her back. I stepped back and bumped into the man standing behind me. I turned and faced him. His uniform was embroidered with a matching biohazard symbol and the word Meadowlark. A samurai sword hung at his side. He rolled back his shoulders. I met his eyes but he looked past me, saying nothing. I slid into the back seat.

The driver was stocky compared to the other man, a bit older and less concerned with appearances. He tilted the rearview mirror down and I could see the reflection of my nipples. *What a pig.* I collapsed down in the seat.

The Hummer pulled out into the road and did a U-turn. I leaned my head against the window. A grey, rainy day was perfect. It mirrored the life I deserved. We headed west. They were backtracking all my steps—all the distance from yesterday, all of it wasted away as a moving picture. I turned to look at the woman beside me. Mr. Blue Eyes was staring back at me. At least my mouth wasn't duct-taped.

Alex's abandoned Prius appeared up ahead. The driver elbowed his partner and stopped the Hummer in the middle of the road. Both men jumped out.

I faced the woman. There was something familiar about her pale green scrubs. "Hey, are you okay?"

No answer.

"Hey." I nudged her leg with my own.

The nurse's forehead skidded against the windowpane

as she turned toward me. She looked so familiar. No fear filled her eyes despite the duct tape sealing her lips. Her eyes widened and she lunged across the back seat. I screamed and tried to scoot against the door.

Her face landed on my thigh, her teeth gnarled beneath the duct tape trying to rip into my skin.

Mr. Blue Eyes tore open her door, grabbed hold of her handcuffs, and threw her to the ground. She rolled, struggling to stand up. He pulled a gun from his holster and slammed the car door shut. I couldn't see her. A shot blasted out.

His partner returned to the driver's seat and his eyes went right back to the mirror. A shitty-ass grin filled his face.

Mr. Blue Eyes slid back into the car—calm. He showed no remorse for the life he had taken. They drove away, just leaving her lying in the road.

I had left Alex—his crushed and broken body—lying in the middle of that pebble driveway. I forced my eyes to the moving pavement outside. Rural houses dotted the edges of Newport. They took Highway 101 north. My stomach knotted. The vehicle slowed as it approached the beach house. *Why are we here?*

He pulled into the pebble driveway.

I didn't want to see Alex's body—see what I had done to my friend. I turned my face to the window and closed my eyes. I waited to hear their reaction. The pebbles crunched beneath the tires. *What the fuck are we doing here?*

"We're here, get out." The driver pushed his door open and the Pacific winds pushed back. Once he managed to get out, he pulled me out of the back.

The ocean wind teased the goosebumps of my skin. I

took a step. He blocked my path and pushed me up against the car. His chest pressed against mine. He grabbed my breast. The tips of his fingers rubbed my cold, hard nipple. It hurt. He bit his bottom lip and pushed his other hand up under my shirt. The warmth of his skin was almost inviting against the nauseating cold.

"Hey!" Mr. Blue Eyes shouted from the porch.

The tips of the driver's fingers reached the bottom curve of my breast. He pulled away and pushed me toward the house.

I looked back, down the driveway. I had to know, had to see. But it was empty: Alex was gone. Rain had washed away all the evidence of my crime. The surrounding woods creaked with the wind. The house was dark. Overhead the autumn clouds swelled with rain. Fallen branches cracked on the forest floor. I climbed the steps and stood outside the front door. I had made it out of that house once, but there was no guarantee that I would be allowed a second.

I stepped through the shattered door, glass crunching beneath my boots. Cold ocean winds had filled the house. The smell of crab grew strong as I walked toward the kitchen. The crab legs were still sticking up out of the bucket in the sink.

Across the counter was a tattered female body, slouched in a barstool. Her hands were cuffed to the chair behind her back. She lurched her head up, her pupils mirrored pools of darkness. *Jan!* She stared at me. There was no kindness, no warmth. The rose color of her skin had drained and the remaining patches of her hair were drenched in sweat or rain. My friend was gone. The grotesque creature slouched against the counter barely resembled the woman I loved. The navy blue nightgown clung to her frame. Chunks of food coated in bile dripped down her breasts.

"You see this?" The driver grabbed my arm, yanking me closer. He drew a handgun and aimed it at her. "This is Code Black. This means," he waved the gun between himself and Mr. Blue Eyes, "we're the only law left in your world now."

He pressed his dry, cracked lips against mine. His saliva smeared into the creases of my skin. The smell of shit seeped from his mouth to mine, filling my lungs. He pulled away, admiring the gun's beauty and power.

I stepped back from him.

"Do you think I won't take what I want?" He shoved me to the wall, pressed the tip of the barrel to my jaw, pushing my bruised cheek against the textured paint. His other hand grabbed the inside of my thigh. He forced the gun harder, while his fingers dug into my jeans and slid up my leg. *Son of a bitch.* I turned my face toward him— letting the gun's barrel dig deeper into my cheek—and spit in his face.

He pulled the gun away and wiped his cheek. Rage filled his face. He clenched the weapon, swung it back, and with full force punched me in the face.

The room flashed into a tunnel of darkness. I felt nothing.

7

WHERE AM I? THE CEILING MOVED AS MY BODY bounced, draped in someone's arms. I tilted my neck an inch and my ears began to ring, my head pounded, and my left cheek pulsated. He carried me down the hallway and turned right, throwing me onto the king bed. My slutty roommate's suitcase bounced as my jaw skidded across the soft blanket, tearing into my throbbing cheekbone. The mattress sank behind me with his weight. I rolled onto the floor, trapped between the wall and the bed, hidden from his view.

The door slammed shut.

Stillness rose. Then there were footsteps—inside the room—coming for me around the bed.

Deep blue eyes looked down on me as he rounded the end of the bed. I dug my heels into the carpet and kicked myself backwards into the corner. I was too weak—tired and heartbroken—to fight anymore. He kneeled. I shut my eyes and pulled my legs in. The soft skin of his cheek brushed mine as his arms wrapped around me.

"Please don't," I whispered.

The warmth of his fingers brushed my hand and grabbed the handcuff.

I winced. *Don't.*

"Relax. I'm not going to hurt you." His words kissed my cheek as the cuffs fell. He backed away, giving me the same look as before. "What's your name? I'm Benjamin."

"Carol."

"You should get changed, quick. We're leaving and you'll be coming with us."

"Why?" I stood.

"Because you look like shit." He chucked a prescription bottle toward me. *My prescription.* My heart dropped and my cheeks burned, pounding with blood beneath the bruises. "Perhaps that will help with the pain."

"No. Why do I have to go with you?" I clenched the

bottle as he stepped closer. I glanced past him at the closed door—to the animal waiting outside. "Can't you just let me go?"

"No offense, but you don't look like the type of girl who could survive a zombie apocalypse without a lot of help." He stepped past me and rummaged through the dresser.

I searched the room for a piece of reality, something to ground me. *A zombie apocalypse? No. Shit.*

"Catch." Benjamin threw a whisky bottle from the drawer.

I smiled. Alex's dad liked to drink on rainy days, trapped inside with his young wife who never shut the hell up.

Benjamin looked at me, narrowing his eyes.

I took a swig, forced a pill down, and headed for the closet. The light was dim with incandescent light, but I closed the door—for privacy. Darkness seeped from the corners as I peeled the shirt from my torn shoulder—it scraped against my cheek. I threw it to the floor. A faded Beatles T-shirt caught my eye. Cold air rushed under the door taunting my bare feet. I traded the torn jeans for a new pair that could be worn over the knee-high boots, and transferred the dagger. The jeans flared enough to pull the pant leg down over the laces. There was no way they would suspect anything.

I grabbed a brown corduroy jacket off the back of the door and rejoined Benjamin.

He had emptied the suitcase out onto the bed—*her* suitcase. My stomach knotted. Purple lace underwear lay beside a blue vibrator. A red silk nightgown lay on top of a Tool band T-shirt—Dominic's fucking shirt. Blood rushed to my cheeks. I focused on the pain throbbing within my left cheek—it hurt less. I slid my fingers beneath the corduroy jacket to rub my shoulder.

Surprise flashed over Benjamin's face. He froze and nodded. "Did you come in contact with any body fluids?"

The past 24 hours were a blur. I had lost everyone—everything. I was not going to relive any part of it. It would cripple me.

"Saliva, blood, sexual excretions?" He rested his hand against his holster. "Were ... you ... bitten?"

I shook my head. "No, it's just a scratch."

He crossed his arms and went back to studying the items dumped on the bed.

The pain medication kicked in, invitingly numbing my mind as I sat down on the mattress. A wave of vertigo rushed over me. I grabbed onto the comforter, stabilizing my place. It passed and I focused—on his uniform's logo. Then it blurred again. "What's Meadowlark?"

"In 1864 President Lincoln established the Yosemite Valley Grant Act. Within it, Meadowlark was established." He lifted a velvet jewelry box from the suitcase.

My eyes filled with tears. It was identical to the box my ring had come in.

"You see, the Indians who lived there believed Coyote created the world—this world."

The weight of my body shifted, a chill crawled up my back.

"The story begins after Coyote had created the world and its creatures. Coyote and his friend, Meadowlark, were taking a walk in the forest and came across the first creature to die. Coyote's empathy pushed him to resurrect the animal, but Meadowlark told him not to. Its body and energy should return to the earth from which he had made it. Coyote agreed."

He popped open the box. "It was Meadowlark who ensured that the dead would remain dead, and Coyote was to keep his promise that the dead would never rise."

"So you're zombie hunters? That's why you're here?"

"I suppose that's an accurate statement." He pulled a bracelet of freshwater pearls out. My heart skipped a beat, but I exhaled in relief that it wasn't another fucking ring. He slipped it into his pocket. "And a Keeper."

"A keeper of what?"

"Elizabeth Hutchings," he said.

I jumped up from the bed and walked toward the closet. My face burned. *Me?* My voice cracked even with restraint, "Who is she?"

"A woman we've been searching for, for two days." He took a step closer. "Look around for anything out of the ordinary."

I looked back at him through the dresser mirror.

8

JAY HAD BEEN BENJAMIN'S PARTNER FOR 18 MONTHS. They had an agreement that when shit hit the fan, Jay got first dibs. But Benjamin had grabbed that girl and headed for the bedroom so fast—*son of a bitch*. Jay kicked the kitchen cabinet and popped a beer. He chugged half of it and sat at the second barstool.

The disgusting, infected woman sat slouched and unmoving beside him. He pulled a pack of cigarettes from his front pocket and slid a condom out from between the cardboard and plastic.

He tapped the box on the counter to compact the tobacco. The woman's hard nipples rose and fell with each breath. Jay took out the one cigarette that was upside down—the lucky one of the pack—and lit it. It burned and smoke swirled in the room. *Fucking Benjamin.* Jay glanced down the hallway at the closed door. He clenched the cigarette between his lips and stood up. He bent down and grabbed the woman's swollen ankles, forcing them together behind the chair's front legs, and cuffed them. Her skin had a blue tint, a corpse tone. He tore the condom wrapper open. The cold, wet rubber slid down the soft, warm skin in his hand.

The curves of her breasts perfectly centered her nipples. The soaked nightgown hid nothing. His fingers slid through the pieces of vomit and grabbed her collar, ripping open the gown. Her pale breasts were as cold as the beer bottle. Her knees were spread. His damp fingertips slid the bottom of her gown up, exposing navy blue silk underwear. He tore them from her, the elastic cutting into her skin.

He grabbed the beer and poured it between her legs. She squirmed. He stepped closer. The condom slid between her thighs. The dryness of her skin ripped the rubber. His raw skin brushed against the sides of her vagina. *Shit.* Panic washed over his excitement. He looked into her yellow eyes. They were already tearing at him over duct-taped lips.

His skin throbbed as he pulled out and pulled the prophylactic off, throwing it to the floor. *Fuck it.* Standing naked and erect, he pushed himself back into her. He stared at the pale breasts bouncing beneath his momentum. He let the spit run from his mouth onto the seam of their connecting skin. His body grew warm against the dry creases. He pushed against her upper thighs, spreading them wider, harder—deeper into her. The friction of their skin moistened as he released himself, filling the lining of her walls. He pulled out, zipped up his pants, and kicked the barstool backwards.

Her head whacked the floor.

He took the cigarette from his mouth and puffed, then noticed the condom. *Fucking bitch.* He spit on her and kicked the rubber underneath her back. Her used body convulsed and then stopped moving. He bent down to uncuff the bottom restraint and noticed a cellular phone under the sofa.

The bedroom door opened.

His fingers slid across the cracked screen as he pulled the phone out.

9

Benjamin stepped out of the bedroom door ahead of me.

I wanted to clench the dagger between my fingers, but it wasn't possible. I couldn't take them both.

Jay stood at the end of the hallway and tossed something at him. "Call headquarters for the serial number."

Benjamin caught the cell phone—my cell phone, turned around, and stepped back into the bedroom. His one-sided conversation carried from the room as Jay walked toward me. My shoulders rose to my ears. Benjamin stepped beside me and they eased back down. "It's hers. A Code ZA20 has been officially issued. We are to report back to the office and head out with the whole team."

Jay continued toward us and stopped two inches from me.

"Dude, let's go." Benjamin scooted around us and nudged Jay's shoulder.

Jay grabbed my wrist and slapped the handcuffs on me, binding my arms in front of me. His lips leaned toward mine. "Let's go."

The handcuffs hung loose enough around my wrists, but the swollen skin of my stitches rubbed against the metal.

Jay pulled out his gun and nodded in the direction of the front door. "Go."

I stepped from the hallway. There was a puddle of blood at the top of a fallen barstool. I gasped. Jan's corpse lay lifeless.

He pointed the gun at her.

"She's dead, for Christ's sake." I stood like a brick and closed my eyes trying to wipe the image of her cracked skull out of my head. If I moved, I would regret my actions later.

The barstool scratched against the floor. I opened my eyes. Jan wiggled back and forth. I cupped my mouth, trying to restrain another gasp. The noise stopped, then she stopped and looked at me. She rolled the chair onto its side and kicked, pushing toward me. Her long hair mopped through the blood oozing from her cracked scalp. I ran for the door. *She was my friend. She was my friend ....* I stepped out the door into the splintering cold wind. It sucked all the warmth that clung to me. I didn't want to go on. I wanted to give up, fall to my knees, and allow the hard pebbles to dig into my skin—let the rain pour over me. But there was no rain.

Benjamin leaned against the car's hood, waiting—so fucking calm and peaceful.

"Aren't you going to do something?" I charged him.

He opened the back door. A gunshot ripped through the fog. I nearly fell jumping into the back seat. He slammed the door and climbed up front.

"Do you know what we're supposed to do with people like you?" His hand braced against the driver's headrest as he turned to look back at me. "Code ZA20 is what someone like you would call ... the beginning of the zombie apocalypse. See, the virus is spreading at such a rate that it is now considered irreversible and uncontained."

Footsteps crunched across the pebbles, headed for the vehicle—Jay was coming. I kept my eyes on Benjamin.

He faced front. "It's actually lucky for you."

Jay hopped behind the wheel and peeled out, down the driveway.

My body rocked, unconfined by a seatbelt.

The house exploded.

"In any other situation we'd have left you in that house." Benjamin glanced back, past me, through the rear window.

Pieces of wood shattered against a smoke-blackening sky. Jay readjusted the rearview mirror. His dark eyes narrowed at my reflection.

The Moon's Glow

1

THE HUMMER FOLLOWED THE WINDING COASTLINE north. I swayed as the vehicle hugged the mountain's cliff. Moonlight shone over a clear ocean, painting the darkened landscape with stars. The tires weaved over the center line and back toward the shoulder. Jay's head bobbed with each gust of wind. We made the descent to the flat beach of Lincoln City. Portland's summer getaway was a ghost town.

Oregon 18 East took us past paved sidewalks and shopping centers and then flowed into forest. No streetlights, no shoulder, and no other cars. The headlights captured a mere five feet ahead in an abyss of darkness.

ZA20. "So why the twenty? I get the ZA, but why the number?" I asked.

Something stepped into the headlights on the right side of the road—a man. Jay's head hung to the right and bobbed back and forth with the vehicle's motion. The Hummer swerved, clipped the man, and flew over the edge of the road. I would have slouched down in my seat, but there was no time. We careened into a tree. The impact threw me into the back of the passenger seat. I fell, prostrated on the floor. I couldn't move. A ringing in my ears engulfed every sound of the night as adrenaline pounded through my veins. Gradually, I pushed myself back onto the seat.

Benjamin's body hung over an inflated airbag. A crack in the windshield branched into a large hole over the steering wheel. Jay was gone. The headlights glared off the side of the tree trunk and captured a bed of leaves on the forest floor.

I leaned over the front seat and dug my fingers into Benjamin's front pocket. The tips of my fingers hit something metal. *The key!*

The leaves moved. A shadow emerged in the headlight. Jay stood in front of the vehicle. His nose was broken and dripping with blood. A large piece of glass stuck out of his head.

I leaned back and the key slipped from my fingers. It fell down the center console. By the time my butt sank into the back seat, Jay had stumbled toward the back window opposite me. He pressed his face against the glass, his eyes eating through it.

I hugged my knees in. *This is it.* Then my hand touched the hilt of the dagger beneath my jeans.

His breath fogged up the windowpane.

My bound hands fumbled to pull the jeans up over the goddamn boot.

The window shattered, glass spraying across the seat. He climbed through the broken pane. Shards of glass tore at the flesh of his shoulders. His fingers dug into the seat cushion and he hurled himself toward me. The edge of his belt caught on the window frame.

My fingers slid around the dagger's hilt. I hesitated. His hips broke free and he lunged at me. I stomped his face and fumbled for the door handle. I found it, pulled, flung the door open, and fell to the ground. The fall knocked the wind out of my lungs.

Jay pummeled me, his sweaty skin smearing against mine. I clenched the hilt again and jammed the dagger between his collarbones. Blood poured out, soaking my corduroy jacket. I pushed him off, ripped the dagger out, rolled away, and sprinted up the hill for the road.

Fuck. What have I done? I wanted to drop the dagger, but if I did I would have no protection. I focused on the deep tire streaks carved into the soil leading back up the hill. The crevasses created by my boots filled with mud as I slid against soaked leaves.

The forest was dark. A hidden moon escaped the clouds that had imprisoned it. The pit of my stomach knotted. I looked up. Death formed into a dark figure stumbling down the tire track toward me.

I stopped, rested my hands on my knees, and caught my breath. The dark silhouette walked closer. "Oh thank goodness. These men took me captive and I need someone to take me to the hospital. There was a car accident and ..."

The figure quickened down the hill. Moonlight rippled through the trees. His arm hung to the side, swinging out of the socket. A gust carried the scent of decay down from the road. The angle of the path was in his favor. His body plowed down like a bag of bricks straight into me. My head hit the ground, mud smearing into my deadlocks. The dagger slipped from my fingers. I fisted my hands and shoved the chain of the handcuffs across his neck to shield myself. He lunged harder, choking. Drool dripped from his mouth. My biceps burned. His weight bore against the metal chain and inched closer.

2

BENJAMIN'S HEAD THROBBED AGAINST THE AIRBAG—A splitting fucking headache. He pressed his palm against it, but the pain wouldn't ease. *What the hell?* He sat back. Cold air brushed his left cheek. Jay was gone and the hole in the windshield gave him a good idea of what had happened.

"Are you okay?" He glanced into the back seat.

The woman was gone. Adrenaline pounded through his veins. The driver's rear window was smashed and the door behind him was wide open. There was no telling how long he had been unconscious.

Each Meadowlark vehicle had a keypad in the glovebox. Benjamin pressed 2-7-6 and the bright-red stereo glowed ARMED. He jumped out of the vehicle. The pressure in his head shifted, flooding his nose. He took a step and his boot kicked something.

He pushed the back door closed. Jay's corpse rested at his feet. There was no time to figure out the crime scene. He sprinted away from the Hummer. She would never make it without him; she was probably already dead.

He looked up the steep tracks. The silhouette of a man was crouched in the distance, attacking the ground. Benjamin had done the job long enough to spot one of the infected. Meadowlark had used homeless people for years to train agents.

He charged the figure. The woman's petite frame was pinned beneath the animal. Her handcuffs, holding the man back from her face, shook with the strain of her muscles. Benjamin drew his gun and shot.

3

I COULD TASTE THE SALT IN HIS BLOOD AS IT DRIPPED onto my tongue. My saliva thickened, diluting the cells. The creature's body went limp, and my muscles gave way. His dead weight fell and pinned me to the ground. The stitches in my wrist burned with each beat of my heart.

"Let's go. We have to move." Benjamin kicked the corpse off, grabbed my hand, and pulled me up. He looked down at his hand. Moonlight glistened over the blood dripping from his skin. He drew his gun and pointed it at my face. "Take it off."

Cold blood dripped down my hand from the jacket cuff. My fingers trembled as I unbuttoned the heavy corduroy. It slid down my shoulders, caught on the handcuffs, and stopped at my elbows.

He reached into his front pocket. "You took it?"

"I dropped it." Thick saliva balled in my throat. "Just go back and get it."

He looked down the path. "That's not an option."

"Just go get it!"

"That's not an option." His voice rose and he took a step, getting ready to walk away.

"The knife." I turned my cheek guiding his eyes to the bone dagger. It had slid into the moonlight. The red lines of the etched moon and coyote glowed a light blue.

Benjamin grabbed it and walked back toward me. His

shadow blocked the lunar rays from the dagger. The bone's glow faded back into red. He kept walking, right past me.

"Where are you going?" I yelled.

He turned back. His eyes held a million questions. They looked past me—down the hill. He sliced through each jacket sleeve, freeing its weight and warmth from my arms.

I turned to see what he was still looking at, but there was nothing but tire tracks. The thick forest hid the car accident. Even if the world hadn't gone to shit, no rescue team would have saved us. I looked back at him, but he was gone.

I sprinted up the hill, slipping on his footprints. Each time I fell, soil caked between the chains binding my wrists. The last time my hands hit the ground, it was against asphalt. I had made it to the top.

Night's natural glow was so much brighter without headlights.

The highway curved west around the mountain, leading back the way we came. So I continued east. *It has to be east: he had to have gone east.*

An explosion erupted behind me.

I ducked in pure reflex. That's when I saw Benjamin in the distance. The dagger glowed in his right hand. He kept walking and never once looked back. Adrenaline or anger built in my veins and I ran after him, finding myself screaming again. "What the fuck? You're just going to leave me?"

"You're here, aren't you?" His eyebrows raised and he continued walking.

I shut up. He was right. I had nowhere else to go and no idea where I could find a key for the handcuffs.

Silence accompanied us for miles. Every time a twig snapped, a leaf rustled, or a gust of wind howled, unease roiled in my stomach. Clouds swept over the earth's celestial body as we approached a quaint little shack. Its woodstove filled the crisp night air with aroma as smoke trickled to the road. A rusted, two-door 1957 Chrysler sat in the south side of the yard—nearly buried in tall grass—its weathered windshield wipers faced the street.

Benjamin crossed the yard—trespassing.

I stood at the grass's edge. Crossing onto private property was not something that I did.

He crouched in the tall grass beside the driver's door. It didn't creak as he inched it open. He left it ajar and slid over into the passenger seat.

My heart raced. The dim light from the house danced on the front lawn. There was no telling how many people were inside, how many creatures could surround me—ripping the skin and muscle from my bone.

I focused on the open car door and stepped onto the property. There was probably a bear trap just waiting to chomp off my ankle. *Just get it over with.* I sprinted. I grabbed onto the door handle as I slid across the Chrysler's cracked, white leather seat. It snagged at my pants. Benjamin took such care to open the door; I felt it should be eased closed.

My nipples were hard from the cold, raw from rubbing against my shirt.

He swirled the dagger between his fingers and stowed it under his duty belt.

My heartbeat slowed. The car sheltered us from the wind. I was so tired.

He unbuttoned his shirt. Hours spent at the gym had chiseled his chest muscles. The Vee of his waist led my eyes to the beltline he untucked. He pulled open his shirt and held it them open. "Come here and warm up."

My heart raced to a pound again. The cold air pushed me against his skin. His warmth was the only thing keeping death from me. Nausea pulled against the lining of my stomach. He wrapped his arm around my shoulder, allowing sleep to engulf me.

A bloodcurdling scream ripped me from slumber. The sky was still black. Benjamin's hand was cupped over my lips. His warm cheek pressed against my ear and he shushed me.

A porch light had flicked on. A woman sprinted from the house, heading for the car we were in. Benjamin pushed my head down onto the driver's seat pinning his temple against mine. The car swayed as the woman tugged on the passenger door's handle. It clicked, but didn't budge. I heard her palm whack the glass and then, another scream. It was right outside the window. I was breathing too heavily, sure they would hear.

Whack—the second noise sounded like bone snapping. I twitched with each crack. I tried to look up, but Benjamin forced my head down. The woman's screams shrilled.

"Shut up! Some of us are trying to sleep in here." A male voice spoke from behind us.

Benjamin sat up and allowed me to follow. A wrinkled old man sat in the back seat. The flannel blanket that had concealed him was bunched at his waist. The odor of vodka spewed with each breath.

The lawn turned silent.

I couldn't breathe, couldn't move. A husband stood over his wife. Blood dripped from his mouth and her body convulsed against their lawn.

YOSEMITE RISING

"Go," was all I needed to hear from Benjamin.

I cast the driver's side door open and jumped into the cold.

"Dude, what the hell?" The drunken man's raspy voice faded behind me.

There were no bear traps leading back to the road — and if there were, it didn't matter. I ran until my boots hit the pavement. The house's glow faded behind me, but I refused to glance back, not even to see if Benjamin had followed. All that mattered was getting as far away from there as possible. The old man's screams echoed thorough the forest after me. Headlights rounded the bend far into the distance. I stopped. It could be anybody.

Benjamin plowed into my back and knocked me to the ground.

What the hell? My palms slid across the pavement and my knee scraped along the road's edge, tearing my jeans. He threw the drunk man's blanket over me, rolled, and crouched beside me on the asphalt's edge.

He drew his gun. The vehicle was halfway to us. "Go into the road and get them to stop."

This is a bad idea. I pulled the blanket over my shoulders and stood up.

"Go," he yelled.

The headlights were closing in fast. It was now or never. I stepped into the middle of the road. The vehicle showed no sign of slowing. The headlights became brighter and I sheltered my eyes with my arms. There were worse things to die from. The tires screeched and the horn blared. I clenched my eyes, my jaw, and every muscle in my body. My thighs felt warm all of a sudden. I opened my eyes.

Steam dissipated off the headlights four feet from me. A tall, skinny man stepped from a 1987 Bronco II. It was light blue with the bottom half dipped in white paint.

I held the blanket up, shielding the bright light from my face. The man was in his late 30s. His beard and crewcut divulged his Oregonian authenticity.

Benjamin stepped up behind him. The smile on the man's face faded. He held up his hands.

"Don't hurt me. My name is Wyatt Brown. I have a wife and three small children. You can take the car, money, whatever you want."

Benjamin holstered his weapon. A branch snapped a few yards away. The Bronco's headlights had drowned out the moon and the forest had seeped into a pitch black background. He looked at me. "Get in."

Another branch cracked.

I pushed Wyatt out of my way and sprinted toward the open driver's door. A third branch snapped at the forest's edge. Benjamin nudged me into the passenger seat.

4

THE MOUNTAIN CLIFFS ISOLATING THE COAST flattened into a rural valley. Wyatt hugged the right side of the car in the back seat. We were 26 miles out of Portland, at the edge of Dundee. It was a small town placed in the middle of nowhere. Its only purpose was to cater to the farmers spread in every direction around it. Modernization had started to seep from the city, building up its eastern side.

The Meadowlark agent driving Wyatt's Bronco sped toward a new gas station on the right. Its owners spared no expense to light every inch of the property. He jerked the steering wheel and the car bounced over the curb. Rubber burned into the cement as the car skidded to a stop under the station's awning.

The handcuffed woman sat straight up, pulling the blanket tight around her shoulders. The convenience store shined with light behind a propped open door. The woman's stomach growled and Wyatt's echoed it. Maybe the remote town hadn't been affected yet.

The agent jumped out.

"You know, you can't pump your own gas in Oregon." Wyatt yelled from the back seat. "It's against the law."

The woman turned around and faced him. "So where are your kids and wife?"

"What?" He stared at the store.

"Your family."

"Oh," Wyatt laughed, "I don't have a wife … or kids. I read that type of thing helps in hostage situations." He climbed over the seat and slid out the driver's door.

"Where do you think you're going?" The agent blocked him. "You're not using the bathroom, it's too risky. If you gotta piss,"—he pointed to a small grass area beside the convenience store—"piss over there."

"Chill. I'm just going to get us some food. I'm starving." He looked back at the woman and wheezed past. "Do you want anything?"

"Hurry up. If you're not back in five minutes, we leave without you …." The agent yelled louder as Wyatt scooted into the small store.

He stacked the counter with junk food. *The driver must be military. And the girl handcuffed and beaten—probably marked as a terrorist.* It wasn't his problem, but he had just bought that damn car and spent a year worth of savings. The midnight atmosphere lingered with an eerie stillness. "Hello?"

He looked around for the clerk. The bathrooms were at the back of the store. It had only been two minutes and three was plenty of time to take a piss. He glanced out the window. The Bronco was still guzzling gas. Wyatt sprinted toward the bathroom door and pushed it open. It was dark. His sneakers slid across the tile floor and the door pulled closed behind him—pitch-black darkness. His arms flew out, stabilizing his balance.

Once he stopped, he reached out, brushing the wall, searching for the light switch. Each breath echoed. His fingers found it and the lights shot on, blinding him.

A teenage boy stood facing the back corner.

What the hell? Why's he standing in the dark? Wyatt stepped backwards, his heel hitting the door. The boy began to turn. Wyatt started to pull open the door, but the boy moved too fast. He knocked Wyatt into the air. His body skidded across the floor into the storefront. Teeth clamped down onto his left butt cheek harder and harder. Wyatt clenched his fists and spun, punching the boy's sweaty temple.

The boy fell to the floor.

The Bronco's engine started.

Wyatt sprinted for the front door and grabbed a bag of chips displayed beside it. The Bronco had already begun to pull onto the highway when he stepped out of the store. If they saw that kid following him, they wouldn't even bother to stop. He dashed like he was headed for home base. The brake lights glowed red and his chest smacked into the back bumper.

5

"NO. I REFUSE TO LEAVE HIM HERE," I SAID.

"Okay." Benjamin threw the car into park.

I opened the door and climbed into the back seat. Benjamin could have taken off, but he waited.

Wyatt chucked the bag of chips back and slouched against the window. I popped it open, grabbed a handful of greasy fried potatoes, and ate greedily. I leaned forward and offered the bag to the two of them.

"No thanks." Benjamin sat stiff behind the wheel.

Wyatt held up his hand, never looking back at me. The pavement sped by. Interstate 405 led us into the heart of Portland. The streets were empty. I had never seen so many dark windows, especially at night. Lying down across the back seat was as useful as an ostrich sticking its head in the ground. *There are so many dark windows.* I had not escaped death; it covered the empty sidewalks. Parked cars lined each side of the street. Small fires burned in buildings, in dumpsters, and beside playgrounds.

Benjamin parked the Bronco in the middle of the street. An orange *FOR SALE* sign sat in the window of a nearby building. He flung open his door. "Get out."

We were in the center of the most populous city in Oregon. I sat on the edge of my seat waiting for Wyatt to let me out of the back. Shadows wouldn't hide us for long. He slid the passenger seat forward. We weren't going to make it without being seen. He held the door open and leaned over as I climbed out. "Come with me."

Benjamin walked up behind him.

Wyatt's eyes widened with the sound of handcuffs ratcheting around his wrists.

"Let's go." Benjamin pushed Wyatt toward the building. His eyes searched the cityscape. He pulled on the door handle like it would be open, and it was. The Department of Homeland Security logo decorated the door's glass. It locked behind us. There were walls for cubicles, but they were empty, completely empty. Shadows lined the corners and a dark hallway led us to the back. Cold air moved down the walls, creeping up my spine.

Benjamin pulled out the dagger and walked toward me. "You have some explaining to do."

He continued deeper into the room and headed down the hallway.

I kept a three-step distance back from him, just enough time to pivot and run if needed. It wouldn't give me enough time if Wyatt blocked my way though, so I slowed another step behind. Wyatt stepped on the back of my heel a dozen times. His hot breath pushed against the back of my neck.

The hallway took us left, turn after turn. We came to a metal door with a glowing keypad mounted in its middle. Benjamin typed in a code. The latch clicked and the frame decompressed. The four inch metal door swung outward. He pushed me through the threshold. "Keep going."

The hallway continued on the other side, this time heading to the right. Wyatt backed off as I stepped forward. My heart pounded as the door began to close. There was no getting out. At least my hands were bound in front of me, for whatever was waiting on the other side. I brushed my fingers along the wall as I descended down the dark hallway. My goddamn heart was beating too loud. Its rhythm filled the dark corridor. A red glow appeared in the distance. A replica of the previous door stood in our way, but this one was armed with a glass pad.

I turned around. Wyatt was a few steps behind me. Darkness followed minute after minute. Benjamin could have left us in the corridor, two stories beneath the building—trapped with no way out. The air began to smother my next breath.

He stepped into the red glow and placed his hand on the glass. A bright red laser scanned his fingerprints and the door released. Bright white lights lined a cement hallway. It turned to the left, tunneling even deeper beneath the building. Benjamin stepped past us and disappeared around the corner.

I couldn't breathe. We were too deep, so deep. There was no way out. I didn't want to die beneath the ground.

Wyatt pushed past me into the next corridor.

The door began to close. My heart throbbed and my vein pounded against the tight stitches. I jumped through the threshold and sprinted down the spiraling decline. The men had just reached a third door. It had an orange biohazard symbol stamped on its front. Benjamin lined his eye up to its center and a blue laser scanned his retina. The door decompressed.

A woman stood on the other side with her hands on each hip. She was in her late 20s, solid, and fit. A badge introducing her as "Willow ..." hung clipped to her black scrubs. The Meadowlark logo was partially covered by her photograph. She looked past us, searching the hallway. "He didn't make it?"

Benjamin sighed, said nothing, and held out the dagger.

"Where did you find this?" Her eyes searched his.

He glanced back at me and walked into the bunker buried three levels beneath the building. "Run their labs."

Willow watched him walk down the hallway toward a glass door marked "Laboratory." Just before reaching it, he stepped into a room to the right. She looked back at us, down at my handcuffs, and then led us deeper into the tomb. "Follow me."

Both sides of the hallway were lined with three doors, all closed. The first one on the left had a glass window. As we passed it, I caught a glimpse of a black leather armrest.

Willow stopped at the second door on the left and unlocked Wyatt's handcuffs. "Take the next one, get cleaned up, and then I'll do blood work."

He did as he was told, taking the third door.

Willow slid the key into my handcuffs. "I'll find you something to wear."

The metal fell from my wrists. My heart sank to the floor. The indented skin burned, but I was free. The door opened to a small exam room. The table looked like it had been pulled directly out of my gynecologist's office, stirrups and all. A towel sat folded atop crunchy tissue paper. The bottom drawer was a stepstool, meaning that the next one up held the cold metal speculums. If they were in there, I had nowhere to hide to avoid being sprawled out between the stirrups and having the thing wrench open my vagina. I grabbed the towel and headed for the bathroom in the back of the room.

Its tiled wall and floor wrapped into a four-foot square. No toilet, no door, and one showerhead. Privacy would've been nothing more than a commodity. I waited for the lines of water to steam before stepping in. The warmth of the shower beaded over my frozen skin. Dried particles of blood washed away into the drain. Water rained down my back and dripped through my dreadlocks. My eyes rested, closed to the ceiling as water pounded my face. I had lost everyone, everything, and my freedom.

"Dry off." Willow stood a foot behind me holding the towel.

I wrapped my arms around my chest and grabbed it.

"There are clothes on the exam table." Her eyes loosely followed the curves of my skin. She smiled and walked out.

The water rushed to a drip. I patted it from my bruised face, torn shoulder, and scraped knees. After the towel was secured around my body, I stepped out.

Willow sat at a small counter opposite the exam table, labeling several glass vials. She waited until I was one step from the clothes. "Okay, put your arms out and spread your legs. Just like airport security."

"What?" I stopped and turned around in front of the exam table.

She stood up, walked over, and ripped the towel off my body, throwing it to the floor. I held my breath. Cold air hardened my nipples. Goosebumps rippled across my skin. I stood frozen, naked.

Willow slapped on a pair of latex gloves and clenched a small flashlight between her teeth. She went for the most obvious, the gash in my shoulder. She pressed her thumbs on each side of the wound, pulling it open. "What is this from?"

Pain shot through my arm and back. "A guy attacked me."

"You can put your arms down." She walked back to the tiny counter, filled a medical tray, returned, and set it on the exam table. She yanked my left wrist and pulled me closer. I could feel her breath against my lips. Her fingers slid over the stitches. She turned my wrist. "And amuse me, explain this."

"I don't care to." I ripped my hand away.

A dubious look filled her face and she stepped closer. The black threads of her scrubs pressed against my bare breasts, pinning me up against the exam table. The latex gloves brushed the side of my face as she pushed the dreadlocks from the gash in my shoulder. Her breath passed my cheek as she leaned for the tray. She took her time bandaging the wound, placed the last piece of tape to the gauze, and glided her fingertips down my arm.

My skin rippled with gooseflesh.

"You have such beautiful skin," she whispered. Her fingers followed the curve of my hip down.

There was a knock at the door and a trim man entered. His black hair had been shaved clear to his scalp. "Are you finished? I need to discuss some things with you."

"I still need to run labs." Willow withdrew her hand.

I exhaled.

She cleared her throat and stormed into the hallway. "What is it that can't wait?"

"Benjamin needs you to check the authenticity of the dagger. Why don't you do that other guy's labs while she gets dressed?" He glanced over at me.

Willow took a step back toward the exam room. He blocked her.

By the time he stepped into the room, I had finished fastening a pair of black scrubs around my waist and pulled the first of two black tank tops on. Despite layering them, it was obvious I had no bra. He was respectful enough to keep his eyes focused on mine. "Why don't you follow me to the lounge? Willow can find you there when its time to draw your blood," he held the door open, "and you can get something to eat."

"And then can I go?" I crossed my arms and stepped through the doorway.

He extended his hand out. "I'm Yen. What was your name?"

Shit, it started with a C. Carrie, Candice, Carol, "Carla."

"Follow me." He led me to the door with the window.

The armrest connected to a full black leather couch. A woman with dark hair sat in the middle staring at a phone in her hand. I stepped into the room and the door closed behind me.

"Hey, do you have a cell phone? I'm trying to get a hold of ...." The phone slid from her fingers and crashed to the floor. "Elizabeth?"

My stomach tightened. I held a breath, too afraid to let it go. Tears filled my eyes and blurred the figure in front of me. *It couldn't be.* I clenched my eyes, forcing the salty water from my view. *Hazel.* "Hazel?"

She rushed into my arms. Each breath tightened within my chest. I was too afraid to exhale. If I let anything out, anything go, she might disappear.

"I thought you were dead." I lost my breath. I clenched my eyes, as tears rained down my cheeks into her hair. I hugged her tighter, until it hurt. "I love you. I love you. I love you."

I was afraid to open my eyes and find only the remnants of memories.

6

MINUTES WERE WASTED AS BENJAMIN SHOWERED AND changed. There was no time to stand in the warm water, but it could very well be his last shower, so he let several minutes drip by.

A black, pressed uniform awaited him in the connecting room. Two cots lined the converted exam room. He slid into uniform. The clean fabric soothed his skin. It was time to get back to work. He walked down the hallway toward the middle exam room. It was empty. The young woman was gone.

"Ben!" Willow stepped out of the laboratory with the dagger. "It's getting worse out there. We need to leave at dawn or we'll never get out."

"Did you run labs?"

"It's the real thing." She walked over and handed him the dagger.

"And the girl?"

"She's waiting in the lounge."

"No, who is she?"

"She says her name is…"

Carol.

"Carla. I haven't had time to run either of their labs. I dropped everything to run this."

"Run the girl's first." He looked down the hallway at the lounge door and opened the door behind him. "I want to know who she is."

The room's light was off, but several surveillance monitors cast a grey glow into the dark corners. The weapons case was hidden behind the far wall and Agent Yen sat just before it. His feet were propped up on the desk below the monitors. He leaned back, balancing the chair on its back legs.

Benjamin counted the moving objects on the street. There were five, but the parking garage behind the building had too many shadows to confirm anything.

He sat down.

The young woman he had brought with him sat on the couch in the lounge with her arms wrapped around another woman, hugging her. Jay and he had followed every lead, searching all of Elizabeth's frequent hangout spots. He looked at Yen. "We never found her ..." He looked back at the monitor. "She's probably dead by now. That zone went under two days ago."

"So who's the girl you brought with you?" Yen watched the lounge monitor.

"I don't know. We found her at a rest stop not far from Zone Two."

Agent Willow stepped into the lounge and onto the monitor's scene. The young woman kissed the stranger's cheek and stepped into the hallway, changing surveillance screens.

Benjamin could feel her ice blue eyes weighing on him as she walked by the open door. He kept his eyes forward and set the dagger on the desk. "But she had this. Something feels ... off about her."

The laboratory monitor captured Willow and the woman sitting at a large conference table in the front of its room. Back in the lounge, the woman picked her phone off the floor and began to pace.

"So do you want to try interrogating the survivor of that flight?" Yen stood up making his way toward the hallway.

What?

"Oh, you haven't been briefed yet? One of the pilots from Flight 1801 survived, and a young woman. It appears that an *Event* occurred. They were coming from Albuquerque."

"And why weren't they terminated onsite?" Benjamin leaned back, slouching.

"The pilot was. But the woman had locked herself in the First Class bathroom. She was holding a handkerchief in her hand."

Benjamin looked back at the monitors. His heart fell. *A handkerchief?*

"It was one of ours."

He stood up, knocking the chair to the floor. *It couldn't be.*

"We are running tests and doing all the typical documentation before we terminate her."

Benjamin dashed for the door. Yen slid over and Benjamin hurried toward the employee lounge. *It couldn't be.*

Yen ran up behind him and cut in front his path, blocking the door. "What's going on with you?"

"I'll explain in a minute, just move out of my way." Benjamin's heart raced as he reached for the doorknob.

Yen scooted aside. Benjamin opened the door.

The woman stopped pacing, clenched the phone in her hand, and whispered across the room, "It's you."

Benjamin froze. The room melted away. *Elizabeth's sister.* Dark circles hung under her eyes and her nose looked broken, but it was her. He spun around and sprinted from the room, nearly knocking Yen down. The short distance to the laboratory felt like a treadmill track creeping beneath his feet.

Willow sat facing the door. The woman who had looked so familiar sat with her back to him.

He flung open the door. It slammed against the bullet-proof windowpane.

The young woman jumped. "Ouch."

Willow grabbed her wrist, pinned her arm in place, and shoved a needle back into her vein. The vial filled with a deep plum-red liquid.

"Are you finished in here?" Benjamin cleared his throat and gathered himself. He took Willow's seat across from the woman.

Yen closed the door and stood guard against it.

Willow moved to the back of the laboratory to run the blood sample.

Benjamin folded his hands. He stared at her irises. Photographs had never captured their perfect shade of a clear blue sky.

She shifted, no doubt uncomfortable.

"You've changed your hair."

Her eyes rushed away from his.

"Run her fingerprints."

Willow returned to the table with a thin tablet. She placed it in front of Benjamin. The woman didn't move. He scooped her hand up and held her fingers down, letting the computer scan every cell folded along their tips.

7

HAZEL COULD HEAR ELIZABETH'S VOICE THROUGH THE glass door at the end of the hallway. "What do you want with me?"

Agent Yen looked over his shoulder into the corridor.

Hazel darted into an empty and dark exam room to the

left. The laboratory door opened and she stepped farther back into the room, hiding in the shadows. Her heel bumped against something, halting her before she hit the wall. She held her breath. The surface behind her back was soft and cold. Cool air blew against the back of her neck. A cold wet liquid dripped down between her shoulder blades. A hand hit the back of her head and shoved it down against the exam table. She attempted to stand, but her head was slammed back down. Fingernails dug into the back of her neck. Her dress was pushed up and her underwear was ripped to the floor. She screamed as a naked male body pressed his erection against her leg.

Yen charged the man and tackled him. Hazel fell to the floor. The hallway light trickled over the naked and sweaty man. He shoved the agent from him, returned his eyes to Hazel, and attacked. She held out her hands to keep him away, but his weight pinned her and his hands wrapped around her neck. She pushed his teeth from her face, but the room was becoming fuzzy, gasps for air became useless and the shadows on the ceiling deepened.

Then his grip loosened.

Her lungs grabbed for oxygen. Blood poured into her throat. She choked and swallowed the liquid.

"Go get in the shower." Yen pulled her off the floor. "Now!"

She sprinted to the back bathroom and stripped. The water ran red, swirling down the shower's drain.

8

"GO SEE WHAT HE'S DOING." BENJAMIN ORDERED Willow and returned his glance back to me. He reached for my folded hands and pulled my left hand toward him.

I pulled back. His grip tightened around my wrist flooding me with pain. His fingers caught the edge of the fresh gauze.

The door flew open.

"Ben, we have an *Event*. You need to wrap this up now." Willow's voice disappeared as fast as it had arrived.

His fingers fell from my skin and he hurried after her. The door closed and the automatic lock clicked.

I picked at the tape fastening the gauze. *Shit.* I looked behind me into the hallway—nothing. *Shit.* I looked around the laboratory. The door unlocked. I tore a piece of tape loose with the edge of my nail. I turned, greeted by Benjamin and Willow. The nurse hung her head, and returned to the laboratory's far side.

"What do you want with me?"

"Stand up and turn around." He grabbed the bottom of my tank tops and pulled them up. The cold room crawled up my back as the cotton lifted to my shoulder blades. His warm fingers pressed against my spine. He pressed on my lower back. It felt like he had just cracked a wooden bat against my spine. Tears flooded my eyes. As the fingerprint machine verified my identity, he whispered, "Elizabeth Hutchings."

"I don't understand. You gave her the vaccine." Willow's face was blank as she approached reading the blood test results. "We need to head out, now. Just in case it has failed," she handed Benjamin the results. "She's infected."

"What do you mean I'm infected?"

Willow raced out of the room.

I pulled my shirt down. The fabric brushed my spine where his hand had been. *Fuck.* I faced him. "What did you do to me?"

"I've spent two years searching for you. Two days ago, you provided us with the perfect opportunity to take you into custody. We could say you died and no one would ever question it. So I administered a vaccine to you, but you escaped with the help of that stupid nurse."

What are you saying? I sat frozen, overwhelmed with nausea. The room went numb—no sound—all perception of the physical world was lost to me until cold hands wrapped around my shoulders from behind. Warm soft lips pressed against my cheek. The same eyes that I had looked into nearly every day of my life met mine—Hazel.

Willow dropped Hazel's zebra-print purse on the table and walked out.

Benjamin cleared his throat, prompting her to sit down. "I suppose you both deserve to hear this, and in a few hours it won't make a difference anyway … We believe that your attacker"—he looked at Hazel—"was infected with the Yosemite Z virus. This is what modern society would refer to as the zombie virus, if they actually knew it existed. The strain is transmitted through body fluids. It manifests as the common flu, and has a fatality rate of ninety-nine percent."

I followed his eyes. Hazel's hair was wet and out of place. Her eyes had lost something; a light was missing from them. *No.* Tears ran down my cheeks. I looked back at him. "But you said there is a vaccine!"

Hazel grabbed my hand, calming the anger, trying to calm me—to comfort me.

"Vaccines don't work like that, and they're not a guarantee." He looked down at our clasped hands.

"But you got a vaccine, too?" I looked at her. Surely if I had received one, then she had. Her eyes drew down only a second. In that moment I glanced back at him. "Right?"

"No," he said.

"How long?" Hazel coughed into her shoulder.

"A few hours to a few days, the time frame is different for each person." Benjamin stood and looked down at us. "This may be the last chance you both get together before your systems are overloaded with the virus."

9

I PULLED HAZEL INTO MY ARMS. I COULD SIT THERE forever holding her, smelling her hair, taking in that moment of pure contentment wrapped in her presence.

Benjamin closed the door behind him.

Hazel's grip loosened and she pulled back, giving a small, forced smile as if everything would be right in the world. She reached for the purse on the table, dug out a small box wrapped in silver paper, and smiled. "Open it. It's your birthday present."

I leaned back into my seat shaking my head. *I don't want it.* Salt water leaked from my eyes and burned into my cheeks. *Not without you.*

"I'm going to miss it this year." She pushed the box closer toward me.

My fingers shook as I opened it. Inside was a necklace. Twisted hemp hung from the center of a turquoise stone fox. It hung in a U-shape from the string.

"You have always been the sun in my life." She gently placed her hand on mine, flipping the stone over. An X was carved in the middle, its tips curved counter-clockwise to create a spiral effect. "Sometimes there are clouds that hide the sun, darkening the skies. But its rays eventually push through, reminding the world of its brightness."

The door opened and I shifted. Hazel sat perfectly still. The two male agents entered and stood guarding the door.

Yen took a step closer. "We have to move out at dawn or we will never get out of the city."

Hazel grabbed hold of me and whispered, "I want you to know that I love you. I have loved you since the day you were born and will love you till the second I die. I can't guide you through this darkness, but I will always be with you." She placed her hand against my chest. "Let go. And live for me."

She pulled me tight, took one last breath, and kissed my cheek. Her eyes glanced down at my mended wrist. She squeezed my hands. "We were lucky, you know. I was lucky. Perhaps this is the price to pay for allowing me another day with you. Another moment to touch you, smell you, talk to you, and love you. Cry, laugh, and hold you. I get to say goodbye this time."

She kissed my cheek and pulled her sleeve up. A two-inch tattoo was raw and puffy against her left wrist. A turtle identical to mine rested there. "Get out of here and fight. For me ...."

Her fists tightened at her side. She stood up and walked around to the opposite side of the table.

"Fight to live." She looked past me at the agents, nodded, grabbed the dagger off the table, and shoved the blade through the turtle.

No. No. "No!"

My heart fell to my feet. I propelled forward across the table toward her. Benjamin grabbed me and, in one fluid movement, he pulled me into his arms and carried me into the hallway. The lab door locked behind us. He set my feet down onto the floor. I let my body fall to the ground—shutting out as much of the world as possible. I could hear my own cries, but I couldn't feel anything. There was nothing.

The door opened behind us. A thick needle jammed into my shoulder. It was real, I felt its pain, but it was nothing compared to the emptiness filling my every being. A warm rush of sedative coursed through my veins.

THE EMPTY WATERFALL

1

I WOKE TO AN EMPTY EXAM ROOM. THE FLUORESCENT bulbs flickered as I slid off of the table. The hallway was silent. Willow stood at the back of the dim laboratory staring at a Petri dish. Yen and Benjamin were sleeping in a room to the right.

A male voice came from behind me. "Hey, do you know why I'm here?"

I know that voice. My stomach knotted. I turned and there *he* was. My hands drew into fists.

"Elizabeth?" The guy who had torn my heart out and stomped it into the ground stood mere inches from me.

Dominic's eyes widened with surprise. They followed the twisted strands of my locks. He reached for my hand. "I've been—"

"Don't touch me!" I yanked back from him.

Benjamin jumped between us. "Get him out of here."

Yen yanked Dominic's arm and forced him down the hallway.

Benjamin pulled me into the sleeping quarters.

"What is *he* doing here?" I yelled.

"We were trying to find you." He closed the door. "Listen, we leave in a few hours. If you don't want him to come with us ... then we can leave him. He's no use to us now."

I sat down on a cot.

"This is your decision." He sat down beside me. The warmth from his body brushed my arm. He turned to me and ran his fingers gently along the curve of my face. His thumb brushed a falling tear and guided my chin toward his. "Find your strength and courage."

He reached into his pocket and retrieved the turquoise fox. It twirled in the air before falling into the palm of my hand.

It was all I had left of her.

"You're going to need it." He stood and walked out the door.

I lay back and the cot sagged beneath me. Carbon dioxide heaved out of my lungs. The increased production of white blood cells within my body drained any extra energy I had. I picked at the tape sealing the gauze against my skin and tore the bandage off. The swollen wound was tightening around its stitches. I rolled onto my side and began to count them. The weight of my eyelids cleared the tears from my eyes. The necklace slid from my fingers to the floor. I leaned over to grab it and heard a faint conversation.

2

"IT'S GETTING WORSE OUT THERE." YEN STEPPED INTO the security room. Benjamin sat at the desk, motionless in front of the monitors. "What are you doing with the boyfriend?"

"I left it up to her." Benjamin spun the chair and faced him.

"You can't get attached." Yen sat on the desk blocking the monitors. "We have a job to do. You can't save her."

Benjamin stood up and faced the weapons closet. He chose a samurai sword and fastened it to his side, attempting to ignore Yen shadowing him.

"You know you'll have to tell her." He glanced over at the computer monitors. "Shit, you should tell her."

3

"TELL ME WHAT?" I STEPPED INTO THE ROOM. IT WAS half the size of the others. The wall of monitors faded into the background when I noticed the weapons closet across the room. The bone dagger sat mounted in its middle.

Yen raised his eyebrows at Benjamin and left.

I approached him and reached for a 19-inch sword. His hand rested on mine. He nodded toward the set of chairs. I turned one away from the monitors and sat down.

"Do you remember the story of Coyote and Meadowlark?" He pulled up the other chair and sat beside me. "Coyote had promised Meadowlark that the dead wouldn't return to the earth after death?"

I nodded and sank into the chair.

"Well, Coyote-man had joined his favorite people and lived among them. He had indulged in their mortal women, but never desired any as much as Awanata—a woman unlike any he had ever laid eyes on. Hair identical to the sun, eyes mirroring the sky, and skin as milky as the clouds.

Of course, the Chief had also noticed her beauty and promised her to his son, a mortal man. On her wedding day, Coyote-man approached Awanata and offered himself to her. She declined. Soon after, an illness fell over the tribe. By night her newlywed husband lay dying. When she went to fetch him water from the falls, Coyote-man once again approached her. He told her that if she willingly gave herself to him, her people would be saved. Again, she refused. But on the walk back to the village, the dead began to rise. The people grew empty and wild.

She kissed her husband's cheek, knowing that it would be the last time she would feel his skin against hers. Coyote-man was waiting beside the waterfall when she returned. Awanata demanded proof that he would keep his promise. That night he created the moon—for her."

Benjamin stood up and walked back to the weapons closet.

"The Ahwahnee Indians say that in that moment, she killed herself with this," he handed me the dagger. "Legends tell that the handle glows in the moonlight," he paused and glanced down at it. "Coyote's howl accompanied the moon that night. He freed the people from illness and allowed them to bury their dead. As for her husband, bearing the pain of the loss of Awanata was more punishment than death could've ever brought. The

Coyote-man left the moon in the sky as a constant reminder to him—and her tribe—of the decision she had made."

"But what does that have to do with me? That's only a legend." I handed the dagger back.

"This legend ceased to carry on after 1864. You see it was not because of the tribe's extinction; they still existed at that time. In that same year, a white child was born on their land. It is no coincidence that President Lincoln signed the Wilderness Act and created Meadowlark the year after your great-grandmother was born. Nor the fact that the park was protected, guaranteeing that you would one day be able to return to the land. You are her remaining bloodline. It must be your blood to save the world." He placed a hand on my shoulder. "Haven't you always known or felt that your life had more purpose?"

4

I SAT UP IN MY SEAT AND LAUGHED SO HARD I NEARLY fell out of the chair. Benjamin was completely silent. His eyes searched the room for the humor as I caught my breath.

I brushed the tears from my cheeks and slowly stood. Clearing my throat masked the heaviness of my steps toward the weapon closet. If I choose the biggest fucking weapon on the wall, I could kill them all. A small knife caught my eye. It would be easy to cut open my wrist. Then he could worry about saving this fucking world. My fingers touched the sword's hilt before I could finish my thought, but Benjamin stopped me.

"Are you trying to kill yourself?" There was no anger

in his voice, but he had realized the impact of the comment itself. "There is no way—you can't handle that."

He was just as sexist as his partner had been.

"That's not what I meant," he put his hands in the air. "That one's too big for your frame. Having the wrong tool can be worse than having nothing."

He studied my body and then rested his eyes on mine. He didn't smile, only paused a moment to look for the sorrow within them. His pity flooded me and I looked away.

He scanned each weapon quickly and chose a set of 19-inch samurai swords complete with a back holster. He slid the straps up my arms, they rested over my shoulders. "You don't have to forget her. She will always be with you. At least she got to see you as *you*. You had a chance to say goodbye, which is more than most of them will ever get."

I shoved him away. "Don't act like you know me."

He stood there.

I grabbed the set of swords from the wall, feeling my fists clench around the handles. I took a long breath and held it—letting the wall of weapons distract me from his words. The small knife's blade caught in the lamplight and I reached for it. Benjamin didn't stop me. I slid it down the inside of my boot. Its presence was weak compared to that of the dagger.

I reached for a grenade and he slammed his hand down on top of mine.

"I think I'll handle these." He released his hand and pulled my face toward his. "You need to understand a few things before we leave."

He let go and paced around the room. "We move exactly at dawn. Hopefully we will have an advantage."

He filled his pockets with weaponry. "You may start feeling the effects of the virus. Some symptoms mimic the flu at first. You're going to have to fight."

He froze, giving me his full attention. "First, initial infection occurs, like any typical flu. You feel like complete crap."

"Shit. You mean she'll feel like shit." Yen leaned in the doorway and glanced at the monitors. "Are you ready to go? It's almost light."

He pushed off with his shoulder and disappeared down the hallway. Benjamin followed and I took the only path available.

Once I stepped into the hallway, Willow squeezed by, tapping my ass. "Keep your eyes open, babe. It's going to be a long trip."

Benjamin had stopped outside the lounge, looking through the window. As I continued past him he grabbed my arm and pulled me back toward him. I held my breath. He handed me a machete and dug into his pocket. "You need to decide now"—he grabbed my other hand and placed the bracelet of freshwater pearls in it—"whether you want to bring him."

I followed his eyes to the door's window. Dominic paced in front of the couch. I grabbed the door handle and looked back at Benjamin. My fingers slid from the brass and I began to walk away. He had broken my heart, but I couldn't stop loving him. I turned back and bumped into Benjamin.

"Make it quick." He nodded and joined the other agents down the hallway.

I opened the door and stepped into the lounge. Dominic turned around. I couldn't help but charge him, pressing the machete blade to his throat. Why was he left standing in Hazel's spot and *she wasn't here.*

His eyes widened and he pleaded, "I love you."

"Shut up," barely got out of my mouth. I pulled the blade back and tossed the machete to him. "Don't make me change my mind."

He hadn't shoved the blade through my spine straight to my heart, ripping every last piece out, but each following footstep felt that way. I stepped into the corridor and my equilibrium wavered, pushing me into a dizzy spell. I fell into the wall, leaning for a moment to gain balance. Dominic grabbed my arm and I had no choice but to let him carry half my weight until we caught up to the others.

"You protect her with your life." Benjamin poked Dominic in the chest and stepped up against him. "Or it will cost you yours. This isn't a game. Its life or death out there" —his voice rose— "and you must be willing to give your life for her, or" —he pressed a pistol to Dominic's head— "I will kill you. Either way you will die if something happens to her."

Willow scanned her retina at the door. It decompressed and began to open. We followed her through two of the three doors—ascending back into reality—into a dying world. The last corridor was dark. She stopped halfway to the top. Her fingers brushed the flat wall and a panel decompressed. Light faded in from a covered parking deck. A Meadowlark Hummer sat 20 feet away. Cars littered the parking spaces. The stairwell to the right was as pitch black as the shadows. Two formed into adult silhouettes casting themselves at the far end of the parking deck.

"Get down," Benjamin hoarsely whispered.

I knelt in the middle of the parking lot, 10 feet from the Hummer. Perspiration dripped from my pores. I was so fucking cold. The dawning sunlight trickled through the deck's open windows, but my weakness—not the light— knocked me onto my butt.

"Three o'clock," whispered Benjamin.

A dark figure stepped from the stairwell. It moaned. My heart pounded, but my body wouldn't move. It stepped into the light. Remnants of a man hung in a torn business suit. His nose turned toward the air like a hungry animal. His groans grew angry and loud. A car door to our left creaked open and two secretary-type women dying of infection slid from it.

Dominic stole the gun holstered to Willow's side and pulled the trigger. Nothing happened. She ripped the gun from his fingers and smacked him in the face. The Hummer's keyless entry beeped as the headlights flashed. The figures closing in around us quickened. A grenade rolled out in front of us, stopping at Yen's feet. "Shit," rolled off his tongue.

"What the fuck did you just do?" Willow screamed at Dominic.

Benjamin grabbed my arm, drew his samurai sword, swung at the businessman, and forced me into the stairwell. The man's head fell to the floor, bounced, and rolled to a stop between my feet. Death began to look different.

Benjamin hoisted me up alongside him and then let go, forcing me farther down the stairs. I hit the bottom cement slab. His body fell on top of me, crushing my lungs. He wrapped his arms over my head and pressed his chest to my cheek. The grenade exploded. The foundation shook.

Dust filled the air. His weight released. "Keep moving. Now!"

I tried to cough in the bend of my arm, but he had already yanked it away. The lowest level of the parking garage was even darker than the previous one. Cement particles condensed in the air as dust. I attempted to grab the swords holstered to my back, but exhaustion forced my arms back down. Benjamin reached for my hand and led me through the parking deck. Darkness and dust blinded any path.

My shoulder hit something—*someone else's shoulder.* Adrenaline flooded my system so fast it hurt. My hand tightened around Benjamin's.

He pulled me into his chest and swung his sword in a circle, slicing through the particles. It hit something, sticking for only a second before he ripped it back from the darkness. The *EXIT* sign flickered with red light. Its door led into blinding sunlight. We were outside. Benjamin barricaded the garage door as it closed behind us.

An obese man stood beside a woman in the street. They gazed up into the sun, soaking it in. I leaned against the building restraining any breath, any noise. Benjamin released my hand and stepped in front of me. The woman moved more quickly than expected. She came at Benjamin. With a single swing of his sword her bowels spilled out in the center of the road. The man came next. He plowed into Benjamin. Willow burst through the *EXIT* door and stabbed the fat fucker in his chest, over and over again.

Dominic appeared from the garage holding Yen against his shoulder. Benjamin led us toward the front of the building—hugging its side—where the Bronco was parked. A couple stood beside a minivan parked at the curb along our path. Their clothes were wrinkled, saturated with more than one type of body fluid. The woman had one arm left and the man chewed on it. A young child pushed between their legs from behind. The man stopped chewing, looked down at the child, and followed its gaze toward us.

I could feel their hungry eyes tearing through my flesh as Willow pulled me toward the Bronco. How I missed the cover that night had provided us just hours before. The Bronco blurred as my eyes burned. Willow let go of my hand. I wouldn't make it. I closed my eyes, took a breath, and opened them. An old man stepped out of a store across the street. The sun warmed his wrinkled skin and his step quickened. I closed my eyes, letting the hot tears soothe them. I glanced back at the man. He was right there, right in front of me. His weight pitched me onto the asphalt.

"Help her!" Willow screamed as she elbowed the mother to the ground.

"No!" Dominic kicked the old man off me, but he scrambled back. Dominic thrust the machete down— through the man's spine—and twisted the blade. He reached down to help me up. "Are you okay?"

The old man rolled over and lunged for Dominic. Benjamin grabbed his silver hair, yanked his head up, and severed it. Blood ran into the cracks of asphalt. He stepped around Dominic and grabbed my hand. "Watch your back."

"Liz!" Dominic called out.

The child sprinted toward me. I reached for the sword over my left shoulder. My fingers touched it. *I can't do this.* My hand fell to the side as the once-innocent child rushed closer.

Strong arms wrapped around my waist from behind.

YOSEMITE RISING

Somehow I ended up in the Bronco. Dominic pushed in beside me. The tiny body was left lifeless in the street — broken.

5

BENJAMIN HAD TAKEN THE DRIVER'S SEAT AND HEADED west, out of the city. Yen sat beside him, focused on the road as the black pavement flowed beneath the car.

He angled the rearview mirror at Willow sitting behind him and tilted it down, only capturing her hands. She rubbed the sweat-soaked hair from Elizabeth's face lying in her lap. Elizabeth's body shivered with fever and easily slid closer to Dominic as the Bronco swerved through abandoned cars.

A woman stood beside the road in the distance. Benjamin sped up. She stepped into the highway. There was no time to brake. He plowed into her. The metal hood and roof clanked like a tin can as her body went flying and smacked the pavement behind them.

Cement walls transformed into squished rows of small residential houses. The plots of land increased between residences as they crept toward the coast. A long stretch of tree farms rose out of the land until the earth started to flatten again.

The pounding of the ocean played into the silence as they hit Lincoln City and headed south. The mist had begun to settle in on Highway 101. There was a break in the clouds around the tiny town of Yachats. Benjamin had to slow down to take the curves in the road.

He began to speed and shot over a small bridge, up into the winding cliff that creates Cape Perpetua.

"Don't move for them." Yen's voice ricocheted against

the windows. A pair of men decked out in athletic gear jumped into the southbound lane.

"Shit." Benjamin jerked the wheel to the left.

The right headlight clipped the closest man. He bounced off the hood, cracked the windshield, and fell over the cliff.

Benjamin repositioned his grip on the steering wheel and slowed his speed. Once the road began to straighten out, he glanced into the rearview mirror. A car swerved in the distance behind them, gaining on the Bronco. He slowed to let them pass, but the car crashed into the bumper. The Bronco shot forward into the wall of the mountain. Darkness filled the momentum of impact and his neck whiplashed. The world went dark in one blink and blinded every sense. The airbag burst against his cheek, reassuring him of life. His hand shook as he released the seatbelt, letting out a huge sigh. "Are you okay?"

Yen nodded.

"Willow?" Benjamin's shoulder popped as he looked behind him.

"Fine." She pushed Elizabeth up.

"We need to move." Yen looked at the ocean as he climbed out. Grey clouds appeared over the horizon.

Dominic jumped out and started south along the highway.

Yen stepped in front of him and nodded back toward the car. Willow pulled Elizabeth's limp body from the back seat. "Help her."

"Dude, just leave her." Dominic glanced back at the women. "She's just slowing us down."

Benjamin grabbed Dominic's collar from behind and

threw him to the ground. He drew the samurai sword from his side and pointed it at the car. "Now."

Dominic scrambled to his feet and followed its direction.

"Take the rear," Benjamin patted Yen's shoulder. A wall of rain pushed across the open ocean. It poured on them, soaking the asphalt, creating rivers down the mountain. His rubber soles barely gripped its surface.

There was a dirt driveway on the right. It led to the Heceta Head Bed and Breakfast—the lighthouse keeper's old house. A white picket fence gated its antique frame. Dim porch lights accentuated the century-old body wrapped in white paint.

The back door squeaked open as he approached. A dark silhouette filled the doorway, hidden by a thin screen door. He clenched the sword's handle.

"I'm sorry," an old woman's voice carried through the mesh.

His grip eased and he continued to the steps. The scent of a blown-out candle drifted into the night.

Moonlight revealed the woman's white hair and deep wrinkles. Her hands shook, as she tried to steady a candle in her grip. "We're closed."

"Is anyone here sick?" He stepped up the stairs to the door.

"Sir, there's no one here." She began to pull the door closed. "I don't want any trouble."

"I mean you no harm." He caught its edge, restraining its closure. "Only to get out of the rain. Then we'll be on our way."

She looked up at the sky—the rain.

Yen joined him with his Homeland Security badge

already out. Obediently she stepped aside and allowed them in. The men secured the two story house as Willow and Dominic carried Elizabeth inside. The old woman gasped when she saw her. She lit the candle and led them into the living room.

They collapsed into the couch, unloading Elizabeth.

Benjamin blew out the candles flickering on a hutch. Ocean air pushed against the rickety walls searching for a way in as he crossed the room. Its cold air howled against the thin windowpanes. Within a single puff, he blew out the old woman's candle and dropped into a chair beside the front window. It faced the fog and nothing else. Exhaustion would have to wait until second shift.

Yen left the room, taking post at the back door.

"Towels?" Willow asked, pulling Elizabeth's soaked clothing off. They sloshed to the floor. She wrung out each dreadlock, water trickling into the cushions.

Benjamin forced his eyes toward the blanket of fog outside. If she had been any other woman ... it wasn't a thought he could afford.

The old woman's steps scuffled out of the room and back in. Her arms were full with thick fluffy towels.

Willow peeled her own shirt off. A black sports bra squeezed her breasts, until it didn't. She stripped within a single minute, fastened a towel around her chest, and began to wipe the rain water from Elizabeth's naked body. "She's burning up."

The old woman returned with a damp hand towel and pressed it against Elizabeth's forehead. Roberta had worked at the Bed and Breakfast back when her skin was smooth and young. Now, her winkled hands shook as she dabbed the towel against Elizabeth's hairline. She glanced at Willow, "Go ahead, dear. Get dry."

Willow pulled a handgun from the pile of wet clothes and switched places with Benjamin. They had been trained that self-preservation came last, and she followed it by the book.

He scooped Elizabeth from the couch. "A bedroom?"

Roberta led him to the second floor. He laid Elizabeth on top of a floral quilt. The quaint room was in the décor of the Victorian era. The sound of crashing waves drew up from the fog below.

Roberta untied a knitted shawl from her shoulders and placed it over Elizabeth's pallid body.

6

I COULDN'T MOVE. MY HEAD THROBBED AND FEVER chilled me. I shivered under the warmth of the shawl. The bedroom door slowly crept open, but there was no use forcing words from my mouth. My eyes burned. If I moved the eyelids protecting them, they would shrivel. A man's hand slid up my leg, its warmth scorching my skin.

"Oh, I've missed the feel of you." Dominic's voice dug through the air.

His breath smelled like shit. My stomach knotted. I couldn't sink any farther into the mattress away from him. His fingers crept up to my knee and pushed the shawl from my thigh. The room spun as his fingers inched higher. Bile sloshed up my esophagus. I forced myself to swallow it.

"Get out." Benjamin's voice barged in with the sound of the door ricocheting off the wall. Everything was so loud. The mattress shifted as Dominic stood up. I cracked my eyelids and an old woman scooted between the two men. In her presence I rested. Minutes blended into an eternity, accompanied by the sent of her talcum powder. Pieces of *Twinkle, twinkle, little star* broke into my consciousness. Death kissed at my skin and grasped for my life.

By morning my immune system was exhausted, but when the sun rose I opened my eyes. Roberta sat in a chair nestled in the room's corner at the foot of the bed, sound asleep. I sat up. The ocean pounded at the bottom of a cliff, onto a small beach cove. Stale sweat coated my skin. Rays of sunlight brushed over the small bedroom, warming the air. I scooted under the quilt, rocking the bed. Its wooden headboard knocked against the wall, awakening the old woman who too had slept with death waiting patiently to take her from this life.

She smiled and I was filled with ease. The floorboards creaked as she stood and moved around the bed. She rested a brown T-shirt from the gift shop beside me and began to head downstairs, saying, "How about I make some breakfast?"

Willow stepped into the room. "So you made it through the night. How are you feeling?"

I tightened the quilt to my neck. She sat down next to me and brushed a dreadlock behind my ear.

"Where are we?" I pulled my knees into my chest. The quilt drew up from the bed's edge.

She looked down at the shirt beside her. "It's an amazing thing, what you're doing."

I kissed her. There were so many things I would never do—never be able to consider. The soft, delicate touch of feminine lips was difficult to pull away from. I needed to soak up a lifetime of experiences before they were all lost, before I was gone. I'd never kissed a girl before.

"Sorry." My cheeks were still feverish and burned as they blushed. "I only have a few hours?"

She shrugged and clenched her lips together.

I pulled the shirt on, grateful that its bottom reached my fingertips. I stood and vertigo rushed up the stairwell, dizzying me. It pulled me down the steps. My fingers were all I had to steady me between its walls.

"Come in here, dear." Roberta's voice lured me into a small kitchen. She set a single plate at a table meant for four. One chair was moved to guard the back door; Benjamin sat in it. His eyes went straight to the bottom of my shirt. I tugged it down enough for modesty, but my cheeks blazed with embarrassment.

Roberta smiled at us. "Oh, young love."

"Ma'am?" Benjamin pulled his eyes away and stared into the backyard.

"It's quite a long time since I've felt that." She dumped two flat eggs and a pile of bacon onto the plate.

My stomach growled despite the eggs' nauseating smell. I picked up the fork and stared down at the plate. "Thank you."

She sat down across from me. Her voice, for only a moment, reminded me of my mother's, "Eat up before it gets cold."

"No ..." I placed my hand on top of hers and waited for the worn eyes to find mine, "thank you."

She withdrew her hand and patted mine.

Yen merely walked into the room, but it sounded like a herd of elephants. He placed my clothes—neatly folded and dried—on the table.

I devoured the food, easing the hunger that tore through my stomach. I grabbed the clothes and hurried into the bathroom. The tank tops were still warm from the dryer. I slid them on and sealed in the heat with the gift shop shirt. I stepped into the scrubs and began to pull on my soaked boots.

There was a soft knock at the door.

I fell over and landed on the toilet. The first boot slid on.

Roberta held out a pair of purple flip-flops as she entered. "Those are probably drenched. Why don't you take these? You better hurry. They're all waiting for you."

I took the boot off, tied both laces together, and threw the boots over my shoulder.

She opened the back door. A mid-1990 Buick Roadmaster Station Wagon idled in the parking lot, just beyond the picket fence.

I grabbed Roberta's hand and turned back to look at her. "Come with us. It's not safe here."

Her stance firmed. She pulled me into her arms and wrapped me tightly within a single hug. "I've lived my life. Go live yours."

I was exhausted, beaten, and completely empty. The embraces of Mom, Dad, and my sister would never hold me. There was nothing left to live for.

She let go, cupped my face, and kissed my forehead.

I closed my eyes and stepped from that porch. It was what I was supposed to do.

Dominic's irritating face sat behind the empty passenger seat. I shoved the boots to the floor and climbed in. Every particle of dust lining the station wagon danced in the morning's stale air. We took a right. A tunnel carved through the mountain took us south.

7

EVEN A FULL TANK OF GAS WOULDN'T HAVE GOTTEN the station wagon to Yosemite by nightfall. Rural Northern California began to fade behind us. A single driveway was the only thing visible for miles and the fuel gauge dipped toward empty. Benjamin cut the wheel and turned down the long gravel road. It led to a run-down trailer. The closer we got, the more it looked like a piece of shit.

"Where are we going?" I hunched in the passenger seat.

Benjamin parked 20 feet from the residence and hopped out.

"Stay in the car." Yen pushed Dominic out of the back and dragged him along.

I couldn't help but laugh. Dominic looked so stupid crouched alongside the agents. They inched up to an old beat-up truck parked in front of the trailer. Benjamin disappeared around back. Dominic siphoned gasoline from the rusted vehicle. Yen stood guard beside him.

The curtains moved in the window directly behind the two. I looked back at Willow. She had already sat up on the edge of the back seat.

A shotgun blasted from the trailer.

"Get down!" She jumped behind the wheel and floored the station wagon into reverse. Halfway down the driveway the trailer disappeared from sight. She spun the vehicle around and stopped when the front tires hit the gravel's edge.

The door behind me squeaked open and slammed shut.

"Shush." She glanced back at Dominic cowering on the back seat. "Lock the doors and stay down."

I sat on the floor, slouched against the door, and tried to get comfortable. The window-crank dug into my arm, but adrenaline eased its pressure.

Willow slid out and shut the door.

I sat up. The long driveway was empty behind us. Dominic blocked the rear window with his big head and climbed into the driver seat.

"Are you really going to die for these people?" He reached his hand down around my feet searching for the key, grabbed my left foot, and pulled it into his lap. The flip-flop fell to the floor. He rubbed my skin between his hands. "Your feet are freezing."

I pulled my leg back from him, but his nails dug into my ankle, holding my foot in place. I searched the surrounding perimeter. There was no sign or hope of a distraction.

"So, what do you say?" He squeezed my ankle tighter and ran his other hand up my thigh. "How about you let me fuck you one last time?"

I scooted closer to him and grabbed the collar of his shirt. An inch from being able to feel his lips pressed against mine, I whispered, "Go fuck yourself."

I let go and stared out my window. I couldn't feel his reaction and didn't care. Anger and adrenaline restrained my tears. The thick forest framing the driveway darkened with the evening's sun. I slouched down into the seat, ignoring his befuddled stare.

He slid across the bench seat, pinned me against the door, and grabbed my knee. "Technically we're still going out."

I stared harder out the window, hoping he would disappear.

His hand slid up my thigh and his fingers dug harder into the cotton scrubs. "I'm sorry, babe."

Every muscle in my body tightened. The trees blurred as tears built within my eyes. *Fucking asshole.*

"What was I supposed to do? You left me that morning. No guy is going to turn down a girl. It wasn't my fault." He released his grip and pushed a dreadlock from my cheek, his touch almost gentle. "Let's forget this weekend ever happened."

If only this weekend never happened. I looked into the reflection caught by the side view mirror. I leaned my head against the window. The brown hair plastered to the glass. I saw Hazel's smile in it. The curls twisted into dreadlocks under Zach's fingers almost brought the smell of campfire back. The same eyes I have always looked at, that had always reflected those I loved, looked back. "It will never be the same."

The door behind Dominic flew open.

The vehicle rocked as Willow pushed Benjamin into the back seat. She chucked the keys at Dominic. "Drive!"

Her hands pressed against the side of Benjamin's left bicep. "Get his belt!"

I teetered over the front seat and fumbled with his belt buckle. He lifted his pelvis, releasing the belt from behind him. Blood gushed from his arm.

Dominic stomped on the gas pedal.

The vehicle shot forward, all my weight shifted, and I almost fell on top of the agents. The dotted yellow lines of the road bled into a solid stream.

The fuel gauge pinged. It was empty. Dominic slowed

the station wagon at first and then began to speed. The hypnotizing, blurred lines broke as the road curved.

"Hold on!" Dominic yelled and slammed on the brakes. A two-pump gas station sat outside.

A gas station!

"You hold this." Willow grabbed my arm and pulled me into the back seat. She stuck my hand over Benjamin's wound.

Blood oozed between my fingers.

"You ..." Willow kicked the back of the driver's seat, "fill up the car."

By the time she reached the store's entrance, warm blood had started to drip down my hand. Benjamin began to nod off.

"Hey, so where did you run off to?" I said.

"Kill the son of a bitch who shot Yen." He turned away.

I knew that feeling. If he didn't push back the thought—how many moments of laughter were now lost—all the things he would never be able to say—the immense regrets—his will to live would perish. I pressed harder against his arm. "Hey, stay with me."

His eyes stayed on the window.

"I won't do it without you."

He looked at me, met with raised eyebrows.

I leaned harder against his arm. "Okay, tell me something ridiculous about yourself."

The back door swung open. Willow slid in beside me, sandwiching me in. "Don't move. I'll work around you."

Dominic jumped back into the driver's seat and headed off down the road.

Willow nudged my hands away and cracked open a bottle of vodka, pouring it over them. She took a swig and did both her hands, dumped it over Benjamin's wound, and handed it to him. He chugged it as she pulled out a travel-size sewing kit.

Night fell around us as she stitched Benjamin and the car crept through the city of Santa Rosa. The streets were silent. Dominic stopped at a red light. Willow jumped out of the back seat, tore the driver's side door open, and shoved him over. She whacked him upside the back of his head. "What the hell are you doing?"

He held his anger.

She peeled off and sped toward an on-ramp. The city lights flickered. There was still life hiding in buildings, starving in closets, and dying with every second.

Moonlight brightened as we left the city behind us.

The headlights drifted off the road onto grass as we approached an overgrown road. Willow slowed the car, turned the lights off, and allowed the brake lights to guide her into the brush. She ripped the keys from the ignition and glanced back at me. "Grab your weapons and come with me."

Benjamin had passed out.

I stepped into the night air, allowed my eyes to adjust to the moonlight, and drew the swords from my back.

Willow pulled her pants down and squatted directly behind the vehicle. "Can you watch the woods?"

Blush warmed my cheeks despite the biting cold air. I don't know why I was embarrassed; she sure as hell wasn't. A stick cracked. My hands tightened around the swords. I watched each leaf rustle in the breeze.

"You should go. We're sticking it out here tonight." She walked up behind me and handed me a torn handkerchief.

I took the cotton and squatted behind the vehicle. The

air biting at my ass didn't help move things along. The passenger door opened. The interior light blinded the moon's natural glow.

"What are we doing here?" Dominic's voice pierced the peacefulness.

"Shush." Willow pulled him away from the vehicle and gently closed the door. I could see her searching the perimeter.

I let go and peed. Their bickering ceased. My face burned red, I just knew it. I stood up, grateful for the night's concealment.

Dominic slid back into the front seat. Willow opened the back door. I stepped in front of her and blocked the seat beside Benjamin. "I'll take the first watch."

She glanced at Dominic and followed him into the front. There was no protest or argument. I crawled into the back. The car had fallen silent quickly. Its passengers fell into slumber as I waited for the howl of the coyote.

8

BY MORNING COYOTE HAD NOT COME. A *YOSEMITE National Park* sign grew in the distance. I slowed the station wagon as we passed it. Three small tollbooths barricaded the entrance. Blood-splattered handprints covered their exterior. I clenched the steering wheel and looked at Willow.

"Go slow." She sat up.

The tires hummed over asphalt, and crunched over broken glass and torn body parts. My foot pressed on the gas pedal. The booths passed outside the windows but then began to shrink in the rearview mirror. Suddenly a booth door pitched open and a girl sprinted after us. I slammed on the brakes.

"What are you doing?" Willow yelled, bracing her hand against the glove box. "Go!"

I jumped out of the vehicle. The girl looked about seventeen. I hoped to hell that she wasn't infected. I yelled, "Are you hurt?"

Her deep brown eyes were wide, exhausted, and filled with fear. Breathless, she shook her head.

"Get in."

She slid into the front, taking the middle seat.

I turned to get back into the car. Something moved in the corner of my eye. I froze, grabbed onto the door and looked back down the road. Two men appeared in the distance. The dirt and blood covering them had been unnoticeable from the vehicle, but their awkward stance was obvious. One of them walked closer, dragging his foot behind him. The badge of his park uniform hung from his sleeve by a thread. The other man wore spandex that hugged the bulging muscles of his legs. In life, he had likely completed several marathons. *Fuck that.* I jumped back into the vehicle and shifted into drive, taking off.

"Stop!" Willow said.

I slammed on the brakes. We screeched to a halt and the wagon jerked forward.

Willow extended her arm and restrained the girl's body from smacking the dashboard. She flung the door open and jumped out. "We've got a jogger."

The spandex man snarled and ran at her. The tip of her blade slid through his torso and jammed between his ribs. She jerked it backwards. He stepped closer and let the blade dig deeper through him. Her fingers curled into fists as she let go of the weapon and punched him to the ground. An animalistic hunger intensified within his eyes as he reached for her feet. She stepped toward his crippled body and ripped the sword from its place, jammed it back down into his throat, and forced all her weight onto its handle.

She stood up, pushed her shoulders back, and turned her focus to the park ranger only a few feet away.

My heart pounded. I could watch or I could help. I grabbed Willow's gun from the dashboard, pushed the door open, and fell to the ground as I tried to hurry to her aid. I wrapped both hands around the gun and took a shot—three feet from the son of a bitch. Ringing deafened my ears. Willow yelled, but it was all muffled. I had missed. *Shit.* The ranger directed his assault at me. I went to turn—to run—but my feet slid within my flip-flops and I fell.

He sprang for me and I kicked him away before he could pin me to the ground.

Willow stepped beside him and thrust the sword down between the back of his ribs, clear through to the ground beneath him. Blood pooled around his body and flowed toward my feet. I sat up, scooting back from it. Willow grabbed the gun from me and spoke through clenched teeth. "Get in the car."

She took over driving and I settled into the passenger seat. We passed two open gates before a third blocked the road. Any further travel would have to be on foot. She jumped out. "Let's go."

Benjamin grunted as he slid out the back. Dominic tailed the agents, leaving no space.

I kicked off the flip-flops, pulled on the knee-high boots, and stowed the Meadowlark knife.

The girl beside me sat stiff in the middle seat. Her filthy hands were folded in her lap. Her khakis and dark green Staff shirt were wrinkled.

I patted her knee, slid out the door, and pulled both swords from my back.

"Who are you?" she said.

Tears gathered in the corners of my eyes. The question had always been easy. Her eyes searched mine for a mere introduction, but all I could do was shrug. "I don't know."

She nodded with acceptance, understanding, and restraint from crying. Jennifer had been stuck in that booth, all alone, for days. There was no telling what damage it had done.

I handed her a sword and looked at the group standing on the other side of the gate. I looked back at her. "You ready?"

"On foot? In there? Do you know how many people come to this park ... in a single day?" She crossed her arms. "I'm staying here."

I began to holster that blade, but she needed something. I couldn't just leave her with nothing. I offered the sword again. "Good luck."

Her jaw dropped as I handed over the weapon.

I jogged toward the group. Light footsteps followed.

"Wait up." She cut in front of me, swinging the sword carelessly.

"Watch what you're doing with that thing." I eased the sword down.

The road split ahead creating a one-way loop around the entire valley floor. The right side led deeper into the park, circled the valley, and exited on the left.

Willow headed right, obeying the laws of the road. I began to follow.

"Where are you going?" Jennifer stayed put and crossed her arms.

"To the falls," Willow said.

"Why?"

Willow ignored her and continued walking.

"Because if you go this way"—Jennifer pointed to the exiting road—"it's faster and ...." She waited for our attention.

The forest rustled.

Her voice trailed off, "Less campsites."

"Run!" Benjamin crossed over to the left side.

I sprinted after him. I didn't wait to see what we were running from. My heart pounded harder. Several dark-brown buildings appeared nestled between the trees. I stopped running, but the pounding continued drumming against my chest. I rested my hands on my knees and gasped to catch a breath.

Willow caught up. She pointed to the only building with a large awning attached. White letters designated the building as *Yosemite Lodge at the Falls*. Its doors were framed by glass windows. The last thing I wanted to do was walk into another dark building, but it would be safer than being out in the open.

Willow tugged on the front door. It was locked.

I searched the trees for movement. *They'd be coming soon.* My heart pounded. A branch creaked in the wind. I turned to check on Jennifer.

She was gone.

I spun around, searching for any evidence, any spot she could've got lost in. A breeze rustled fallen leaves, scattering them toward us.

YOSEMITE RISING

"Are you going to just stand there?" Jennifer's voice came from behind me—behind the glass door. The lock clicked and she opened it.

We rushed in as fast as we could. The lobby formed a rectangle. A large counter spanned most of the opposite wall, with a closed door behind it. A tiny waiting area was cluttered with lounge chairs to the left.

Benjamin swept the building, leaving the door behind the counter for last. If someone was inside, they'd be in there. Willow locked the door behind us as though it would keep *them* out. Jennifer pressed her back to the wall, trying to disappear from sight. Dominic found a lounge chair and propped his feet on a nearby coffee table. Willow marched over to him and slapped the back of his head forcing "Go" from her lips.

A smile slipped out. *Was he always such a dick?*

Willow joined Benjamin and prepared to open the door. I could hear each of them inhale as I did. Benjamin turned the knob. The door swung open and banged against the wall inside. Nothing—there was nothing but a small office.

I slid behind the counter's wall as Benjamin stepped into the room. Jennifer's tired body followed mine.

"Are you ready?" Willow stood over me.

"I'll take her at sunset," Benjamin said.

9

I STARED AT THE WORN FOREST PATH THAT ASCENDED up the mountain. Jennifer had sketched a map of the Lower Yosemite Falls trail for us. We cut onto it across the road from the Lodge. Benjamin moved quickly up the trail. I struggled to keep up. Cold air brushed my cheeks. It had silenced the insects months earlier. Peace filled the valley.

A rock slid beneath my foot. My heart jolted. A wind drifted around the canyon wall, pushing me farther up the path. Dominic shuffled his feet, one step behind me. He could thrust his machete through to my heart at any time. A chill crept up my spine. *Was there anything along the path that could distract me from the thought — the pain?*

Yosemite's history had been beaten through the land, forgotten beneath hoards of footsteps. Ours carried a replenishment of its people — its protectors. The mountain cliff lined a sky full of stars and curved into an empty waterfall. Moonlight crept over the ancient forest. Clouds drifted into the valley, trickling water over the land and our heads.

Benjamin stopped at the top. The forest was cleared around the bottom of the fall. I looked up. The distant balls of gas and dust had never looked so bright burning out in the universe. I stood in the shadow of the forest, unable to step from its edge, and took in the expanse of humanity's existence.

"So do you guys want to tell me what we're doing in Yosemite and why the fuck we're climbing a mountain in the dark, during a *zombie apocalypse*?" Dominic bumped my shoulder as he squeezed past into the clearing.

Benjamin looked back at me. I crossed my arms. He reached for my hand. "Only one person can save us — can stop all of this — and prevent the death of billions of people. Return things back to the way they're supposed to be."

I took his hand with regret. I wanted to pull back, to run away, but the warmth of his touch kept me there. He led me to the empty river bank. He turned over my hand. His thumb brushed over the stitches of my wrist and he pulled the dagger from his pant leg. He let go of me and held it out flat. "You have to be willing"—his eyes met mine—"to be with him."

I searched his eyes for any evidence that they could be wrong. "It's quiet. There is no Coyote's howl."

He grabbed my wrist, pulled me closer, and placed the dagger in my palm. "He already knows that you've returned."

"What if it's just a legend? What if I die for nothing?"

He looked down at the dagger. The etched handle filled with moonlight as he moved his hand from it. "I wish it were."

Lunar rays filled the bone's design—the coyote howling beneath a full moon. It glowed. I fell to the ground. My mouth went dry, my grip tightened around the handle. It wasn't fair. Empty winds pushed against my skin. I sat on the cold, wet ground staring at the mended wrist in front of me. *What had I put her through?* It had been so easy to give up, leave Hazel in this world alone. *Now she's gone.* I had been so stupid. I licked the tears streaming down my lips and pressed the bone blade to the edge of the first suture. I closed my eyes.

Air rushed past me. I opened my eyes and followed the movement. Dominic sprinted for the trees. He took the opposite trail, leading deeper down into the valley's floor.

Benjamin grabbed my left forearm and pulled me up. The dagger sliced through the first stitch. It stung until I noticed the large shadow emerging from the tree line before us. He stepped in front of me, pressed his back to guard me, and stood firm with his sword drawn. He whispered, "Run. Run."

The shadow formed into a large black bear. It charged. I fisted the dagger at my side.

"Run!"

Without thinking I followed Dominic's path. The trailhead spit me out into Yosemite Village, the center of the valley. The familiar cobblestone Visitor's Center sat in front of me. Its interior lights blared into the night through the glass doors. I sprinted into the building. "Turn off the lights, you dipshit."

My eyes jetted around the room for the light switch. It was to the left. I hit it and braced the wall, catching my breath. My eyes began to adjust to the darkened room.

Dominic's fingers slid between the dreadlocks on the back of my head. He yanked my head back and forced me to face him. He pressed his lips against mine and pushed me up against the wall. The dagger slipped from my fingers and slid across the floor, stopping beside a wooden bench. His weight pinned me harder.

"You should thank me." He whispered into my ear as he brought the machete to my throat. As his breath pressed against my neck, he ripped at the drawstring of my pants.

"For what?" *For cheating on me, making me feel like shit, for making me love you and crushing my fucking heart?*

"For cheating on you." He watched for a reaction.

Asshole. I pulled back my tears. I wouldn't let him hurt me again—make me feel inferior, pathetic, and undesirable. I didn't want to feel like that—like this.

"I overheard the agents talking. If it wasn't for that day, you would never have been vaccinated."

"You're a fucking asshole." I shoved my palms against his chest, throwing all the love I had for him away from me. I didn't want to love him.

I began to walk away, rounding the bench in the middle of the room. He grabbed a dreadlock and threw me against the bench. My spine shattered with pain and nausea flooded me. He laid all his weight on top of me. His cold fingertips slid under the three layers of shirts. His warm breath crept into my ear, shushing me. The chill of his hand hardened my nipple beneath it. His tight jeans pushed against the thin cotton scrubs. I searched the window for any sign of Benjamin. Dominic grabbed my face and forced my eyes to his.

"Don't take the other day personally." He slid the machete blade down the seam of my pants, cutting the fabric from my skin. He spit into his hand and rubbed his fingers between my legs. His top teeth bit into his lower lip as his finger slid into me. I turned away, closing my eyes. I wasn't there; I didn't want to be there. He pulled his finger out and wiped it along my thigh. He pressed the machete blade harder against my neck as he undid his belt. His grip around its handle tightened and he grabbed my thigh, digging his fingers into my skin. He leaned back and his pants dropped to the floor. "Besides, I saved your life, so you owe me."

I reached for the dagger.

He crushed me with his heft and pressed the blade harder against my skin. His nails dug into my hip as he pulled me to the bench's edge, forcing my thighs apart. The outside edge of my boot rubbed against the hidden knife.

The knife!

The machete's blade loosened against my skin as he forced himself into me. I loosened my thighs allowing him deeper. The tips of my fingers brushed the knife's hilt. With my free hand I pulled my shirt up, arched my back, and pressed my breasts closer to his lips. The blade of the machete lifted from my skin.

He searched my eyes before taking a nipple into his mouth. It was enough to wrap my fingers around the knife. I straightened my back, easing my nipple from his lips, and jammed the knife into his chest. His eyes grew wide. I twisted the blade and blood ran down my fingers. I knocked the machete out of his hand and forced all my weight against the knife. He couldn't hurt me anymore. Blood ran down my elbow and dripped between my breasts. His hand went limp, his breathing shortened to a gasp, and his body slid from mine onto the floor.

I stood. A bucket of his blood flowed down my stomach. He gasped on the floor. I knelt beside him and ripped the knife out of his chest. There were so many things I wanted to say. I breathed in the moment. The knife went back into my boot. I grabbed the dagger and began to walk away. I stopped, picked up the torn pants from the floor, and dug into the pocket. The smooth and imperfect freshwater pearls slid between my fingertips. Each one had a different shape, but they were all beautiful.

I chucked the bracelet at him, not waiting or caring what expression he wore on his face. I didn't care about his feelings. If this was my hell, it was going to be what I wanted.

I stepped outside. Rain clouds burst. I tore my shirts off, wiped the blood from my torso, and threw them into the mud. Cold rain washed his scent from my body. My knees began to buckle.

A silhouette emerged from the trail.

I had killed the love of my life. The dagger fell from my fingers, its glow cast upon the mud. I dropped to my knees.

AWANATA

1

WILLOW LOCKED THE FRONT DOOR OF THE LODGE and hurried back around the counter into the small office, and then locked that door too.

Jennifer sat beneath the only window ornamenting the far wall. To its left were a metal desk and a rolling chair.

Willow grabbed a stack of paper and began to tape it to the windowpane.

Jennifer sat still, biting the skin around her nails. When she accumulated enough, she'd spit the flesh onto the floor.

The pink and grey canvas of the sky disappeared behind the last sheet of paper. Willow sat down beside the girl and slapped her hand away from her face. "Stop it."

Silence recaptured the room.

Willow rested her head back against the wall. Something pounded against the front door.

Jennifer returned to biting her fingernails.

Willow shushed her from making any noise. The last light of dusk shined through the paper, casting a square on the opposite wall. As the outside world darkened, the square morphed into a synthetic yellow from the streetlights. A masculine silhouette stepped into its frame. Willow gasped and pinned her hand over Jennifer's mouth. She flattened her back against the wall, watched the shadow, and let go of the girl's mouth.

Jennifer started biting her nail again and Willow slapped her hand away.

Jennifer inhaled with pain and looked down at her nail. It had torn too low and ripped her skin. Blood filled the crease surrounding the nail.

Rain began to drum against the roof and exhaustion soon won. The man stood unmoving. The weight of Willow's eyelids grew heavy against the shadow, nodding her to sleep.

Glass shattered and Willow's eyes flew open. There was no time to restrain Jennifer. She shot to a standing position. The man outside the window tilted his head and pressed his face against the glass. Willow yanked her back down. Her foot hit the computer chair, which rolled into the metal desk with a clink.

Faint moonlight seeping beneath the office door disappeared. A stale moan pressed against its panel from the other side. Something pounded against the office door—slow knocks over and over again.

Jennifer grabbed Willow's hand.

Another piece of glass shattered from the lobby. There were at least two of the infected out there. Willow stood up. A glass paperweight shimmered on the desk. She tore the paper off the window. A man snarled at her. *Why the hell had all this bullshit not ended yet? Where was Benjamin?* The man's bloated and loose skin stuck to the window as he pressed his face against it. Condensation sprayed against the glass with each grunt.

Willow grabbed the paperweight. The man banged his head against the window. She hurled it at his face. The window shattered. She drew a samurai sword and jammed it straight through his eye socket. His dirty nails reached through the window clawing at her arm. She twisted the blade. Several figures emerged from the forest's edge. *Shit.* She ripped the sword back through the window. "We better go the other way."

A scratching noise sounded at the door.

"Are you fucking kidding me?" Jennifer said.

"It's literally now or never." Willow grabbed her arm and pulled her up.

The clawing grew louder, quicker.

Willow signaled to Jennifer. The plan was that she would open the door. Jennifer would kill the first man and continue into the lobby—

Moans deepened outside.

Willow bent her knees, her fists tightened. *Now or never*. She unlocked the door—no doubt the creature had noticed. She kicked it open and stepped back, allowing Jennifer to stab him.

The girl swung. The blade chopped into the doorframe and a man's belt fell to the floor as half of him followed. An infected woman stood behind him. Her hunched shoulders straightened and she leaped at Jennifer, who screamed, dropped the sword, and shielded her face with her arms.

Willow took a swing. The woman's head fell to the floor, while her body was left standing. Willow kicked it down. Jennifer grabbed her sword. The lobby windows filled with a horde of visitors, their decaying shells fighting to get through the broken doors.

Jennifer sprinted for the back exit.

Willow holstered her sword and drew a handgun. She aimed it toward Jennifer and took a shot. The door shattered and glass sprayed toward the girl. Willow sprinted, grabbed Jennifer's shirt, and pulled her through the back door. Night's cold air blanketed them. Willow pulled a grenade from her pocket and threw it into the building. She fell to the ground, pushing Jennifer with her. The Lodge exploded.

The tower of windows framing the adjacent Mountain Room Restaurant crumbled. Nothing moved at the forest's edge.

Willow stood, helped the girl up, and hurried for the back side of the restaurant. She rounded the corner, bumped into a large object, and fell to the ground. The dark features of a man blended with the night's shadows. His ankles were twisted inward, but his steps weren't hindered.

Jennifer stabbed the 19-inch blade into his chest. He didn't stop. She forced the blade deeper until the hilt's edge caught on his skin. Blood oozed over her fingers. She ripped out the blade and slit his throat.

Willow didn't move until his body hit the ground. She acknowledged Jennifer's triumph with a single nod.

2

BENJAMIN CARRIED ME IN HIS ARMS. I WATCHED THE stars bounce in the sky with each footstep. Then they stopped; he stopped. A figure stepped into the road in the distance. Benjamin jumped behind a nearby tree and let go of my legs, leaning my body against his. He peeked around the tree and looked back at me, wrapping his arms tight. Rain dropped from the branches and splashed against my bare skin.

Who had I become? I grabbed onto his collar and looked at my hands. I scrunched the fabric and pressed my face against his shirt. I inhaled and tears poured when I exhaled.

He hushed me.

A grenade exploded.

He pushed me to the ground, sheltering me.

A layer of fallen leaves stuck to my back. A grunt echoed from down the road. I turned my cheek to the ground. *Everything was broken. I was broken. I should've let go, should've killed myself.*

He pushed my cheek back to face him. Tears pooled in the corners of his eyes and mixed with the earth's raindrops, pelting the ground around me. He whispered, "You don't have to do this."

I turned away from him.

He sat up, unbuttoned his shirt, draped it over my naked body, and lay down beside me. He grabbed my hip and rolled me toward him. His lips barely touched mine as he whispered, "If you're going to give up ... at least save the world."

I opened my eyes to the deep blue of his irises.

"But I need you to know ..." He pressed his lips against mine.

My heart skipped and he pulled away.

"I think I'm in love with you."

I turned away from him, looked for something else, anything else but him. I sat up and peeled the shirt off, wringing it out. He didn't say anything. I worked my arms into the shirt and buttoned it. Moonlight captured the branches' shadows dancing across the road. I stood and began to walk down the dance floor.

Benjamin joined me, but stayed a step behind until we arrived at the Lodge. It had exploded from the inside out. Pieces of the building littered the clearing. The shadows beside the cabins moved. Infected campers circled the rubble. He jerked me behind another tree and pinned my back against its bark. His cheek brushed against mine as he whispered, "Wait here."

I slid to the ground, the tree bark scratching at my back the whole way down. Mud smeared between my thighs. Raindrops pelted my eyelashes. I leaned my forehead against my knees and rested. My heart jumped. I looked up and there *he* was.

The old man from the café stood at the edge of the Lower Fall's trailhead. His deep earth-toned wrinkles contrasted with a natural leather outfit. Eagle feathers filled the full headdress, hiding his long grey hair. A passing breeze caressed its feathers just before he disappeared into the tree line. I sprinted after him.

At the top of the trail I froze. He stood over a small bear carcass and tore a spear from its body. The moon peeked from behind the rain cloud, drawing his attention to the clearing sky. I joined him beside the fall's empty bank.

He stood as a perfect picture, a man admiring the beauty of the forest framing the valley walls, waiting—for the glaciers to melt—to hear the roar of pure water rushing down the mountain. He placed his hand against my cheek. "This land has been waiting along time for you, Awanata."

He looked back to the sky. The rain clouds had moved,

revealing a half moon. He studied my eyes. "Feel the earth breathe."

He turned away and headed deeper into the woods. Smoke rose into a vast sky from the mountain, surrounded by an endless forest. The old man's pace never slowed as I lost breath; he never waited or turned back to look at me. I was lost, dependent solely on this stranger. A warm cabin appeared in the distance. Wool curtains blacked out the fireplace's glow from within. The smell of burning wood swirled around a small cleared yard.

He stepped into the cabin and I followed. Rainwater dripped from my skin to the floor. Three pairs of eyes fell on me. The old man showed me to a small bedroom to the right, closed the door, and left. A single candle illuminated a towel neatly folded on the bed's bear-skin blanket. Elderberry branches hung over a hand-carved headboard. The room grew cold. I peeled Benjamin's shirt from my body.

A gentle knock preceded the man's return. Warmth engulfed me as the fireplace's heat drifted back in. I tucked the towel under my arms and sat on the bedside, kicking the boots from my soaked toes. He handed me a wooden bowl with steam rising from its liquid. He nudged it closer and nodded. Radiant heat filled my palms as I cupped it to my lips. Its contents warmed my entire body and I fell backwards onto the mattress. The bowl fell to the floor. A dreamcatcher swung from the branches above. *It drifted into a dragonfly mosaic, pieced together by broken mirrors.*

3

NEMO RESIDEO, NO ONE LEFT BEHIND. BENJAMIN HAD stood by that phrase long before joining Meadowlark. He ran up behind the Mountain Room Restaurant. They had to be in there; it was the only building he would have chosen. Infected campers shuffled through the debris. More would be on their way.

He opened the door slow and slid in, hugging the wall. Wind gusted from the dining room. The three-story wall of windows was blown out. Cold air whistled through the broken pieces of glass.

Giggles came from behind the bar counter. Playful shushing followed.

Benjamin darted to the counter and jumped over it. Willow and Jennifer sat huddled together on the floor with a bottle of wine. Willow's reaction time was off and she barely lifted the sword beside her. Jennifer laughed hysterically. He slammed his hand over her mouth, pressing her head back against the wall, hushing her.

He tightened his grip before removing his hand, making damn sure she wouldn't do it again. The snarling outside had ceased. Benjamin ripped the bottle away from Willow and pulled her off the floor. "We've got to go."

She laughed.

He slapped her and poured the wine over her head. Her eyes brightened as she gasped. He grabbed Jennifer's hand and headed back out the way he had entered. She stumbled behind him. Moans grew louder outside the exit. Jennifer squeezed his hand and stopped. Benjamin stepped back from the door and pivoted down the hall. They entered into a large kitchen and she let go of his hand.

Willow fumbled in from behind and secured the door. Benjamin caught sight of a back door and went for it. A bright light reflected off its glass window from behind him.

Jennifer stood in front of an open refrigerator.

"What are you doing?" He charged her and calmly closed its door. One more noise would allow the animals to pinpoint their exact location. He headed back to the exit and unlocked it.

Willow joined him and leaned against his shoulder. "Oh my, that was some strong stuff ...."

"Elizabeth's out there and I need to get back to her." He nudged her hand off. "Get the lightweight over here and follow me."

Jennifer popped open a bag of chips.

Benjamin waited for Willow to grab the girl. The coast was clear. He darted to the large tree just a few feet away. She was gone—Elizabeth was gone. He fell to his knees.

Willow rounded the tree. "What are you doing?"

"She's gone." He pushed his sword into the ground trying to stand back up.

Jennifer joined them.

"Wasn't that the point?" Willow stuck her hand in the chip bag.

"No, I left her here." His heart pounded. "To save you."

Willow laughed, covered her mouth, and looked around. She walked past him. "Perhaps she is with Nantai."

Jennifer bumped into his shoulder as she followed Willow up the path toward the Lower Falls.

Benjamin searched the perimeter, hoping that they were taking the right path.

Willow finally stopped once they reached the clearing and approached the bear carcass.

There Benjamin caught up with them. "Who is Nantai?"

Willow pointed up the mountain. A faint line of

chimney smoke rose deep within the forest. She grabbed another handful of chips and headed along a hidden path. "He's an old friend."

The path stretched for miles until the outline of a wooden cabin emerged. Willow ran when it came into view. Warm light from the fireplace escaped into the cold as Jennifer scooted inside after her. Benjamin held his breath as he stepped in. Willow's arms were wrapped around an old man—Nantai. The rumors that an old Chief still existed were true. His wrinkled fingers ran through her wine-soaked hair. He let go and directed her to the bedroom, then walked across the room toward Benjamin.

"Yosemite." Nantai tapped Benjamin's shoulder and walked out into the night.

4

WILLOW STEPPED INTO THE BEDROOM AS BENJAMIN left with Nantai. The old man was the last of the Ahwahnee. His children had left for the cities long ago. One grandchild returned to the land, but she didn't believe in the old ways.

Elizabeth's body was wrapped with a loose towel, limp on the mattress. Willow closed the door, barricading their eyes and the cabin's warmth from them. She stripped, took the towel off Elizabeth's back, patted her skin dry, and sat on the far edge of the bed. She wrung the wine out of her hair. It splashed onto her feet. The box spring creaked. She turned around and Elizabeth's soft lips pressed against hers. She pulled away. "I can't. You're ... well, you're *her*."

"Please. I don't want to feel him. I don't want to feel like this ...." Elizabeth rested her hand against Willow's cheek, pulling her closer. She leaned against the headboard and sank down into the mattress. Tears ran down her cheeks. "I don't want to be *her*."

Willow wrapped the towel under her arms and headed for the door. She opened it. The orange and yellow light of the fireplace danced into the room bringing warmth with it. The living room was empty. Voices carried from the porch. She tiptoed to the fireplace and wrung out her clothes, hanging them over the fire—it sizzled with each drip. She warmed her hands and looked back over her shoulder.

Elizabeth laid stoic against the mattress.

She walked back into the room, shut the door, and locked it. The towel slid off her body. She climbed into bed and warmed her hands against Elizabeth's breasts. She kissed her soft lips again and moved to the delicate skin of her nipple. It hardened beneath her tongue. She bit her lip and tested the waters, guiding her fingertips down Elizabeth's hip. The tip of her thumb brushed Elizabeth's belly button as her hand slid between her warm thighs. Her legs fell open, allowing Willow's fingertips to touch the skin between them.

Willow's lips moved from her breast, down her stomach, and toward her thighs. She grabbed Elizabeth's ass, pulled the petite frame closer, and pressed her lips against the wet skin.

5

JENNIFER SAT DOWN ON THE PORCH STEPS. A GIRL about the same age sat down beside her. Kimberly's perfectly placed black curls and manicured fingernails made it obvious that she had never worked a hard day in her life. The alcohol pumping through Jennifer's veins numbed the envy and pity she had for the girl.

Her boyfriend smoked a cigarette a few feet away, planting his butt on the ground beside an extinguished campfire pit. Moonlight crept through the small clearing above it. The treetops rustled in the wind. Dylan's worn shoes and faded jeans gave away his lower class, but he was cute enough to get Ms. Popular. He stood, stretched to tiptoe, and held his cell phone up.

"What's he doing?" Jennifer said.

"Trying to update his status." Kimberly pulled a piece of gum from her mouth and stuck it under the porch boards.

"Aren't they down?"

Dylan flopped onto the ground.

"Apparently." Ms. Popular shrugged.

The cabin door creaked opened behind them. Its noise turned the liquid in Jennifer's stomach. The forest drifted in and out of focus. She pressed her fingers against her lips. The contraction of her stomach muscles pushed its contents up through her throat. She leaned over the side of the stairs and spewed.

"She's infected!" Kimberly jumped off the steps and ran toward Dylan.

The cabin door closed. Heavy footsteps stopped behind her.

"I think I had too much to drink." She wiped the stomach acid onto her sleeve.

Sven's broad shoulders brushed hers as he sat.

She waved off the couple. "Relax."

Sven loaded a hunting rifle in his lap and stared at her. Sweat beaded on her forehead. Something dark caught her eye at the forest's edge. Both shifted their attention to the shadow forming in the distance. The trees barricaded the moonlight from identifying it. Sven steadied the rifle eye level.

"Shush"—Jennifer whispered, batting the gun down toward the ground. "Ya gotta be shush." She placed her finger to her lips, picked up the sword Elizabeth had given her, and handed it to him.

He smiled, no doubt finding her intoxication amusing, and took the weapon.

The weight change nearly knocked her over. Her stomach bubbled and a deep groan slid out, easing the pressure. Sven stood, the moonlight bright against his blonde hair. The darkness of his eyes mirrored the forest before them.

It was coming. Its head formed into the outline of claws and, as moonlight touched them, they transformed to feathers. It was the old man.

Sven lowered the sword. The wind died down. Jennifer felt at peace in the old man's presence. A second figure emerged behind him, dragging its weight. It grew closer, grunting. Sven broadened his shoulders, blocking Jennifer's view. His grip tightened around the sword handle. The moon waited for the second shadow.

"Hey, can one of you give me a hand?" Benjamin gave himself away before the moon could do it. Neither of the two moved. He stepped into the light, dragging the bear carcass from the bottom of the falls. Sven handed the sword back to Jennifer and hurried to help. Her stomach churned as the men dropped the carcass at the foot of the stairs.

"Do you know how to clean it?" Benjamin said.

Jennifer sure as hell didn't.

Silence presented itself, beckoning Benjamin's eyes toward the large man. Sven stood with his arms crossed as if not hearing a word.

"Food?" Benjamin nudged Sven, pulled out the dagger, and pointed at the bear.

"Da." Sven's one word revealed his thick Russian accent. He nodded and pulled a skinning knife from his belt.

Benjamin stepped back as the man kneeled and cut into the skin.

Jennifer covered her mouth and ran into the cabin.

6

"May I see that?" Nantai stared at the dagger with wide eyes. His hands were extended, almost touching the blade with his fingers.

"You speak English?" Benjamin said.

"I never said I didn't." Nantai smiled.

Benjamin held out the dagger and looked down at Sven. "What about you? Do you speak English, too?"

He didn't look up.

"I have only heard legends of this blade. My grandfather used to dream of it. But that was in a time when stories were still left to be told." Nantai's wrinkled fingers shook as the dagger came into his grasp. He walked toward the cleared fire pit. Benjamin followed. Moonlight captured the 7-inch blade and white bone. He sat on the ground across from the teenage couple and held the dagger into the moonlight. The red tribal bands glowed into a pale blue. His fingers circled the full moon, to the coyote howling beneath it, over the word *Pyhij,* and into the last tribal band just before its rounded end.

The girl kissed Dylan on the cheek and hurried inside. He fumbled for a lighter stuck in his pocket and pulled another cigarette out. The tobacco stick hung between his lips. "What is that?"

Nantai pulled a calumet from behind his back. The pipe reached to the ground. Feathers hung from it, displaying a semicircle. He pulled a stick from a side pouch and held it out to Dylan, who in return lit its end. A small flame burned at its tip. Nantai slid his fingers back into the pouch and took a pinch of herbs. He pressed the flame to the leaves. Smoke trailed into the dark, crisp sky. He inhaled and passed the pipe to the boy.

Dylan took a puff, inhaling the thick smoke, and handed it back to Nantai. The old man stared at the moon. He passed the calumet toward Benjamin, never taking his eyes off the sky.

It was no time for Benjamin to let his guard down, but there was no bigger honor. He sat on ancient land, beside its last storyteller. Smoke filled his lungs. Exhale drew it out into the autumn air.

Nantai took the calumet. His wrinkled lips pressed against the pipe. "It is a story not yet finished."

7

THE INDIAN HADN'T SAID MUCH MORE TO DYLAN except *you are already part of this forest*. Whatever the hell that was supposed to mean.

Inside the cabin, the drunk girl had passed out on the couch. Kimberly slept in the middle of the room close enough to the fireplace not to get burned. The perfect spot was at the base of the couch, sandwiched on both sides.

The remainder of night eased into the next day.

Dylan's underwear pressed against his pants with morning wood. A soft feminine hand slid under the covers, freeing the garments from his hardened skin. If he kept his eyes shut, he could imagine anything he wanted.

The blanket slid from his body and cold air ripped the warmth away. A smirk covered his face as her knees wrapped over him. *Bet the new girl looked hot naked.* The fabric of her panties ripped as she forced herself down against him. He clenched his eyelids, reached for her breasts, and pulled down her sweat-soaked bra. His fingers found her nipple and pinched it, demanding a moan from her, and he got one. "Damn, girl."

"What the fuck, Dylan?" Kimberly's voice yelled into his right ear.

She was lying next to him on the floor, her eyes glued to the girl bouncing on his cock. His fingers fell from Jennifer's breasts. Her fragile figure slid his body into hers. He couldn't stop the blood from rushing through him and hesitated to throw her off. He grabbed her hips to force her from him, but she resisted and he released inside of her.

"Oh, my god," rushed from Kimberly's lips as he ejaculated.

"Kim, wait, it's not what you think!" Dylan threw Jennifer onto the couch.

Kimberly sprinted for the door. He stumbled after her with his pants tangled around his ankles and fell to the floor. He rolled over and tugged them up, but it was too late. Jennifer passed him and tore her teeth into Kimberly's neck. Blood squirted from her artery. His girlfriend screamed. He turned away from the scene. Her cries died and the cabin shrank as he collapsed to the floor.

8

THE DREAMCATCHER GENTLY SWUNG FROM THE elderberry branches. Sunlight flowed through its strings. The natural light of morning beamed into the bedroom. I rolled onto my right side, the warmth confined by the covers fading from my bare skin. The comforter was tucked tightly behind my back, unmoving. Fingertips brushed the turtle tattoo on my left shoulder. Goosebumps crawled along my back. The last memory of the night was a wooden bowl touching my lips—its warm liquid taking all the thoughts from my mind—with the dreamcatcher swinging above me.

I rolled over and the fingers moved away. A teenage boy lay beside me. I had seen him before. Last night he sat beside a girl his age on the couch. He lay fully clothed, staring at me, past me. Tears swelled in his eyes.

I brushed a dreadlock beneath my cheek and my fingers shook. The white of my nails had turned yellow from the dirt jammed beneath them. The stitches created a staircase to the deep blue vein of my wrist. Sunlight danced across my arm, its warmth longing to deepen my pale skin.

He grabbed my wrist and jerked it toward him.

"You're hurting me." I tugged it back, but his fingernails dug into my skin. He pulled out the bone dagger, pinned my wrist, and jammed its tip under the second stitch.

I relaxed, looking up at the ceiling.

The blade shook as he severed the suture.

The dreamcatcher swayed. Wind gusted outside, pressing against the cabin windows in protest.

"You can't do it," said Benjamin. He stood just outside the doorway. "And it won't bring her back."

The boy's hands shook harder. The blade stopped before the third suture.

Benjamin's footsteps moved toward the bed. When I looked at him, he extended his hand for the dagger. "If you do it, we're all dead."

I looked back at the boy. His face swam with tears. His fingers loosened from my skin. I let go of my breath. Sunlight caressed the white bone as he handed over the dagger.

Benjamin guarded the foot of the bed until the boy left the room. Then he sat down beside me. "There are some clothes in the closet and food in the kitchen. We're leaving in a few minutes."

Where was there to go? Death crept from every corner of the earth. There was no place to go.

He grabbed my hand, pulled it into his chest, pinched the severed stitch, and pulled it out. His thumb pressed against the seam, dulling the sting.

As much as I wanted to stay there, I slid from the bed and wrapped a towel around me. I looked back at him before stepping into the closet. The cabin lay silent. Modern day jeans hung beside beaded, embroidery-collared shirts. A single dress rested among the male wardrobe behind a blue plaid shirt.

It was made of soft earth-tone suede. The vee neckline was framed by turquoise beads. *The necklace?* My fingers reached for my neck, but it was bare. I lost it. The necklace Hazel had given to me. It slipped from my fingers in the city … *No, no, no.* The dress fell to the floor. I could easily take its place. I picked it up and slid into the fur-lined, long-sleeved suede. It warmed me perfectly. I stepped out of the closet. Benjamin was gone, replaced by my knee-high boots. I carried them to the bed where my swords made a pair. *She didn't make it.* I pushed them aside and sat down. No matter how bright the sun shone, each dawn would carry death.

"Awanata," the old man said as he entered the room. He sat down beside me. "I've always wondered what she would look like."

She?

His hand rested against my cheek. He searched my eyes for answers. "What *you* would look like ..."—he presented the dagger—"I can see why Coyote picked you."

I turned away from him. *No.* I shook my head. *No.* I stood and paced in front of the bed. My fingers pressed to my lips. There had to be a mistake. *This isn't real.*

Benjamin leaned in the doorway.

I froze.

"Are you ready?" His eyes focused on me.

I sat down beside Nantai on the bed.

Benjamin stepped closer, looking at the old man. "What about you?"

"This is not my path." Nantai patted my knee, stood up, and walked past Benjamin. He paused and looked back. "Is it yours?"

I let myself fall back onto the mattress. He walked out and I stared at the ceiling. The dreamcatcher rocked as Benjamin lay down beside me.

"You don't have to do this." His deep blue eyes gazed down on me. His hand cupped and warmed my cheek. He bit the bottom of his lip, restraining what he really wanted to say.

I turned away. Tears dripped down my eyelashes. *I do.* I had to give up myself to save the world, to save them. But I refused to feel it. I wouldn't feel, wouldn't let it overtake me and push me down into the ground until there's nothing left. Before my thoughts suffocated me I leaned over, placing my cheek against his. The grease of his skin slid against mine as I leaned my body against his. He wrapped his hands around my waist and gently rolled my body on top of his.

He pressed his lips against mine. His hands curved down my ass and inched up the bottom of my dress. All the loss, pain, and existence of the dying world disappeared. I forced every ounce of myself against his kiss. His fingers slid up the outside of my thigh, pushing the edge of suede toward my waist. His fingertips stopped at the absent pantyline and his lips pressed harder against mine. My thighs were wet, my body demanding to feel him. His hands pulled me closer. The tips of his fingers followed the curve of my butt. He squeezed really hard and pushed me off of him. He adjusted his belt and leaned over, kissing my cheek. "I can't."

The smell of cooking meat wafted from the living room. Footsteps charged the bed. Before I had a chance to sit up, Dylan was holding a gun to my face screaming, "This is all because of you!"

He pressed the gun to my cheek. It dug into my bone with each enunciation. "Kimberly is dead because of you!"

If I focused on the dreamcatcher hard enough, it would rip this nightmare from me.

The gun fired.

9

THE DREAMCATCHER FLEW FROM THE ELDERBERRY branch as Benjamin knocked Dylan to the floor. My ears rang and deafened any sound. Willow sprinted into the room.

The boy's screams of pain pierced through the ringing as she ratcheted his wrists with handcuffs and jerked him off the floor. Benjamin scrambled to his feet.

I slid off the mattress, picked up the gun, and stepped toward the boy. I pressed the barrel to the sweet spot between his eyebrows. "I didn't ask for this."

I took a breath and exhaled my anger. My lips squeezed together as I looked around the room. *They didn't ask for this.* I lowered the weapon and looked down at the ground.

The dreamcatcher lay broken beside Dylan's foot.

I jammed the gun back to the indented circle on his forehead. "If you're going to do it—do it right."

"Elizabeth." Benjamin's voice was a whisper behind my neck. His hand slowly reached under my arm. Calmness swept through me. He rested his hand on top of mine, drawing the gun down.

I elbowed him away, pushed my shoulder into his chest, and pointed the gun at him. Then I pointed it at the floor, offered it to him, and walked away. The wet skin of my inner thighs rubbed together. "Go fuck yourself."

My heart pounded. I grabbed the swords off the mattress, holstered them behind me, and stormed out the door. The world disappeared into a blurred tunnel as I made it halfway down the mountain. Two hikers popped out of nowhere and straightened up as they noticed me.

Anger flooded my veins so quickly and carried me so fast down the path—I almost missed them. Their backpacks arched their spines back. Their eyes were filled with hunger and their heads were tilted. Then they moved for me.

I withdrew both swords and charged. The right blade sliced into the first hiker, but the other one moved from reach and I lost my balance. I tumbled down the path. Branches scraped at my face and leaves stuck to the wax in my hair. Dirt skidded under my stitches. I stopped rolling and stood.

A six-foot boulder was three inches from my nose. *That was close.* The hiker had followed me down on foot. His speed increased with the mountain slope.

I waited. My heart pounded so hard it could crack a rib.

He was a step from me.

I slid right, grabbed the back of his head and smashed it into the rock. A rotten smell leaked from his mouth with a moan.

He climbed back to his feet and stumbled closer. Blood oozed from his skull. His expression was empty.

I thrust the sword between his ribs. The blade reached for his cold heart. His fingers tore at me. I kicked him to the ground and kept kicking. Blood splattered onto the edge of my dress. My heartbeat drowned out the world.

A set of hands grabbed me from behind.

Black sleeves wrapped around my arms and the swords fell to the ground. It was Benjamin. A breeze pressed against my dress, ruffling the fur lining above my knee. He shushed me. My breasts pressed against the boulder as his body shielded me from the wind. Goosebumps rippled over me. I squirmed, attempting to nudge him away, but his arms only tightened. The warmth of his body ultimately pulled me closer.

"I want you," he whispered. The wind whistled as it passed by. His breath warmed the side of my neck, chills rippled down my spine. He loosened his arms, allowed me to face him, and pulled my waist closer. He kissed me.

I held my breath and lingered in the softness of his lips against mine.

He pulled away. "But I can't." Half-hearted he shrugged his shoulders. "You belong to *him*."

A tree branch snapped just behind the boulder.

He picked up the swords, pushed me flat against the granite, and handed one over.

A black boot stepped out from behind the rock. Green pant legs drew up to a worn park ranger uniform. It was the woman from the campfire at Camp Curry—the one with the story. She pulled a gun on us. Her jaw dropped and she stared at me. With her free hand she dug into her front pocket, digging out a folded piece of paper, unfolded it, and returned it to her pocket. "Are you Elizabeth? I've been looking everywhere for you."

Drops of rain trickled from the clouds.

"Come with me." She grabbed my wrist and pulled me away from the boulder, leading us down the mountain, and stopped at the bottom of the trail. An old beat-up truck with a vintage park logo sat silent beside the road. A storm began to blow in, carrying with it slow-moving shadows.

I jumped into the passenger seat. Benjamin nudged me into the center. Willow threw Dylan into the truck bed and slid into the back cab.

Nevaeh shoved the keys into the ignition and jammed the truck into drive. Death was close. The campgrounds awakened with movement as we drove by. Visitors began to flood the road, reaching for the windows, fighting to get at us. Nevaeh had to slow for a turn. Dylan screamed and was ripped out the truck's bed by the mob. They tore his limbs and shredded his body. His cries ceased.

A primitive camping site approached in the distance. Fabric tents were nestled between trees on the right. Nevaeh gripped the steering wheel. I could see the blood-smeared, broken tents destroyed among corpses. Their mangled bodies stirred; their crusted eyes followed us. Nevaeh cut the wheel, taking us up a driveway—somewhere too close.

THE AHWAHNEE

1

THE WINDING ROAD ASCENDED DEEPER UP THE mountain, wrapped in forest. A small cabin identical to Nantai's stood in an unfamiliar pattern of trees. There was no fire pit and no porch. Neglect had allowed the moss to grow and vines to flourish. An ax waited in a large stump before the cabin's rotting stairs.

Benjamin studied Nevaeh as she hopped out and unlocked the rustic door. She filled her hands with firewood and nodded us in. Benjamin blocked Elizabeth from getting out. "Why don't you wait with Willow?"

She sank back into the seat.

He jumped out and reached for his sword. The ax caught his eye and he yanked it from the stump. His boots clunked into the cabin. He slammed the door shut behind him. Nevaeh looked back at him from the fireplace. He stormed her and pressed the ax against her throat. "Who sent you?"

"What are you talking about?" Her chest rose with the question.

"Who sent you to find her?" He pressed the blade harder.

"A guy from the park." She squeezed her eyes shut. "There's a reward."

Benjamin lowered the ax.

She pulled a wad of $100 bills from her front pocket. "I'll even split it with you."

The folded paper fell to the floor. Benjamin picked it up. The word *Liwa* was scribbled on the backside.

"The deal is, you help me deliver her ...." Nevaeh continued to ramble.

He unfolded the paper.

"Do you know what I could do with that mon—"

"Where did you get this?" he said.

It was a printed photograph, a zoomed-in shot of Elizabeth sitting in the small café across from Dominic, smiling. Nine fifty-six in the morning. Her blonde curls bounced on her shoulders as she sat talking to him. Benjamin knew that, because he was the one who had taken the photograph.

"Where?" He ripped the money from her fingers and crumpled it.

"Are you crazy?" Nevaeh said.

"Where?" He grabbed her collar and threw the money into the fireplace.

"From a guy at the hotel." She flinched. "I don't know anything else."

"And the word?" He released her and stepped toward the stack of wood. A large matchbook sat on the floor. "What does it mean?"

She shrugged.

He lit a match and threw it onto the crumbled currency. A small line of fire ate at it.

A cell phone rang outside, from the truck.

2

DYLAN'S PHONE PIERCED THE SILENCE THAT WILLOW and I had tried so hard to keep. She looked behind her. It rang from the truck's bed. I jumped out of the truck and leaned over the side to get it. A tree branch snapped in the woods behind me.

The screen lit up with a picture of a brunette named Matilda. She looked a lot like him. Another branch snapped. The night sky was returning behind the clouds. Darkness molded into outlines of once-human figures. The small clearing circling the cabin gave little warning of the approaching crowd.

"Hello?" had already escaped my lips as two male hikers stepped into view.

"Where's my brother?"

I didn't say anything. The first hiker was so bogged down with infection that he walked with a hunch. A fanny pack hung at his waist. The hiker behind him walked with a limp, dragging a torn and twisted foot behind him.

"Where's Dylan?"

"Listen I don't have time for this shit. Where are you?" I said.

"The Chapel."

I hung up. The fanny-pack hiker lunged for me. I climbed into the truck's bed. He started to climb in. I put my right foot on the bed's edge to jump out, but slipped. I fell over the truck's side and landed on my spine. Pain flooded through me. The second hiker rounded the back of the vehicle.

Benjamin stepped from behind me, drew his sword, and sliced its mangled leg clear off above the knee.

I stood up, brushed the dirt off my ass, and faced him.

He swung the blade at my neck. A single dreadlock fell onto my shoulder and to the ground. The blade stopped just before my skin. Fanny-pack's head hit the side of my boot.

A shot fired on the other side of the truck. I ducked. A second shot fired. My heart skipped and lingered with the ringing in my ears. A loud female grunt preceded a hard punch. A third shot fired.

On the other side of the truck, Willow stood over three bodies. She holstered her gun and climbed into the passenger seat. "Let's go!"

We jumped in. Nevaeh sped down the mountain. The engine rumbled against the night's return to silence. A river of people crowded the driveway. Infection seeped from their gashes, crusted eyes, and soiled clothing. She slammed her foot against the gas. Limbs hit the windshield as the truck bounced through the crowd, leaving their shadows struggling to follow.

"Do you know where the chapel is?" I yelled over the rumble of the dirt road.

"Yeah," said Nevaeh.

"We need to get there." I felt for the phone in my pocket.

"No way. I'll take you straight to the safe house." She stopped at the end of the driveway and looked back at Benjamin.

I pushed open my door and jumped out. "Go without me."

"God damn it." She turned off the truck and followed, taking the lead through an open field. I heard Willow and Benjamin's footsteps behind us as we crossed a wooden bridge. Once we cleared it, I stopped. Nevaeh continued toward the cliff in front of us—there was no path to follow. I sprinted after her, hugging the bottom of the mountain's cliff, lost between trees, blindly trusting another stranger.

3

NEVAEH AND ELIZABETH DISAPPEARED INTO THE TREE line. Benjamin stepped off the bridge. A woman stepped onto the path knocking him to the ground. She fell beside him and quickly crawled to all fours. A piece of flesh hung from her cheek, exposing the silver fillings of her molars. Her shirt hung from her chest and her sagging breasts flopped as she scrambled for him.

A gun fired.

The woman fell lifeless. Willow holstered her firearm, wiped the splattered blood from her cheek, and helped Benjamin up.

He drew his gun, pointed it at Willow's stomach, and pulled the trigger. "I'm sorry. I can't let her die. Not now."

4

MY HEART JUMPED WITH THE SECOND SHOT. NEVAEH moved more quickly through the trees. The backside of a red building appeared ahead. She hugged its south side and we crouched toward the front—not that it would prevent us from being seen. The front faced a huge clearing. Shadows lined the trees. There was no movement, for now.

We stepped out onto the lawn, exposed, as we quietly climbed each step of the 100-year-old building. Nevaeh took the last step; it creaked. I froze. The wind ruffled a pile of leaves across the lawn. We waited for the trees to flood us to death, but they never moved.

A window sat on each side of the chapel doors like a pair of eyes watching us. Silhouettes moved inside. The right door cracked open. I had a bad feeling but, in a world saturated with zombies, it was a feeling I had to get used to.

"Who is it?" The girl from the phone peeked out the door.

"*Usted idiota,* zombies don't knock." Jasmine bumped Matilda out of the doorway. She looked a bit older. Her tight black curls tangled in large gold hoop earrings.

The chill of death rushed up my spine and pushed me through the door. The room was 50 feet deep and lined with empty pews. A man in his 60s huddled in the left corner clenching a Bible. The tips of his fingers were white, as he clung to it for dear life.

"You must be Elizabeth." Dylan's twin grabbed my hand and pulled me into a hug. "Thank you for saving us."

I stared at the door—waiting for them to open it—waiting for the other two—for him.

"I still expect to see him, walking through that door." Matilda hung her head and sat down beside the Bible-man. She pulled the last water bottle from a now-empty case and tossed it to me. "We've been stuck in here for days."

"Yeah, I've yet to grow balls..." Jasmine pointed over at the man. "And his don't work, apparently."

The door burst open.

Benjamin stormed in, slammed the door shut, and leaned against it. His chest heaved to catch a full breath. Blood dripped from his sword's blade. He stepped toward Willow and me. "Are you trying to get us killed?"

I held my breath. *What did I do now?*

"The only way we could survive was on foot." Nevaeh shielded her face with both forearms as he stomped toward her.

He grabbed her wrist and pulled her close to him.

"Oh," Jasmine bit her bottom lip, unable to take her eyes off him. "Me next."

Nevaeh's eyes clenched.

"She's more precious than money," he whispered and placed the dagger in her hand.

Jasmine's eyes shot toward me, scanning me up and down, wondering what was so special about me.

Nevaeh's eyes widened. She stepped toward the window—into the lunar rays streaking through. Tears dripped onto the blade as it glowed.

I couldn't breath. No matter how much I wanted to deny it—wanted it to untrue...to believe that I'm not....

She looked at me. "Awanata?"

The weight of the room thickened. They all stared at me, their eyes weighing against me, pulling me down.

"Meadowlark." Nevaeh glanced at Benjamin's uniform. She approached me almost with caution and shoved the dagger into my hand. She cupped my cheek.

Her eyes searched mine for something. Then she stepped around Benjamin, sprinted for the doors, flung them open, and ran into the darkness blanketing the cleared lawn.

"Dear Father—" Bible-man began.

"You," Benjamin pointed at him. "Do you know how to get to the hotel from here?"

He nodded, pulled his knees in, and rocked.

"He's not going to be any help." Jasmine crossed her arms. "My pops works here so"—her voice shook—"I'll show you the way."

"Wait! I'm not leaving. Those things are out there." Matilda jumped up, pointing at the doors.

"Zom-bees," Jasmine walked over to her. "Come on. Commercial media has been preparing you for years for this shit."

Matilda crossed her arms.

Jasmine grabbed a candleholder from a donations table to the left of the door. "Besides, you can get revenge, or you can sit in here and starve to death."

Matilda uncrossed her arms and slowly stood. "So, what's at the hotel?"

"She"—Benjamin watched Nevaeh disappear into the park—"said there's a safe house." He looked at me. "I honestly don't know what awaits us there."

"Over the bridge, through a parking lot, across a field to the trees' edge." Jasmine stepped out onto the porch. The wind rushed into the cabin. Staying still would get us killed. There was no time to waste. She grabbed Matilda's hand and ran down the steps.

I followed. Water poured from the sky. Mud encrusted the bottom of my boots as we trekked to a cobblestone bridge. I stopped. The east called to me. There in plain view was the white silhouette stained into Half Dome's cliff. My heart pressed against my lungs. The outline still looked like a middle-aged man with a severed nose, or even a witch. Nothing resembled me. There was nothing female or beautiful about the hideous face—a shrine for the pioneer assholes who had taken the land.

I fell to my knees. *They could all be wrong.* If I was alone—if they left me—it would be so easy to let one of those creatures tear the rest of me apart. Raindrops pulled the tears from my eyes and diluted the stinging of my cheeks.

Bible-man clenched the book as he sprinted by. Mud splashed across my face.

I glanced back up at the mountain. There it was— beneath the broken nose, within the witch's chin—a young woman's face. Awanata's true identity displayed for all to see, and they had never noticed. She looked like ... *me.*

I stood and leaned against the bridge. The dagger's glow rested while the moon hid behind the downpour. I looked down at the stitches. *They'd be so easy to open.* Dominic had poisoned our love; all I had wanted was to free it from my veins. I had given him myself, all my worth. *No man should have that power.* I wiped the rain from my brow and stared at the reflection. Half Dome stood reaching into the clouds and I could almost feel the mist across my cheek.

Benjamin grabbed my right arm and pulled me after the group. As we neared the north side of the parking lot, a large garage nestled between the trees came into view. Bible-man lay on the ground, pinned beneath a large maintenance worker. The man bit into his face. Jasmine tried to pull him off but he didn't budge. Bible-man kicked to scoot away and whacked his attacker with the book, but it had no effect. The worker sank his teeth into his neck.

Matilda stood frozen behind them, watching wide-eyed. I charged—jerked her behind me—and headed for the field.

Benjamin went for Jasmine.

"No! He's my Dad," her voice faded behind us as we cleared the field's edge.

Two dark shadows rushed us from the right. Everything faded into complete darkness.

5

THE NOVEMBER AIR SENT A CHILL THROUGH BENJAMIN as he crossed onto the field. Elizabeth's body lay facedown and motionless beside Matilda. Her fingernails disappeared deep in the mud, beside a puddle.

Jasmine let go of his hand and fell to the ground sobbing.

A pistol pressed into Benjamin's spine. Handcuffs slapped onto his wrist and he was kicked to his knees. A familiar female voice yelled above the pounding rain, "So, rookie, did you find her?"

"I have." Benjamin straightened his shoulders and took attention, staring forward.

Agent Jane stepped in front of him. They had only met once. She had shaken his hand and given him the badge he carried in his pocket. Jane Penelope Albright had worked for the Canadian Security Intelligence Service for eight years before becoming Meadowlark's commanding officer. She took orders directly from the Chief, someone you don't get to meet with only 18 months in.

"She is, however, lying about her identity," he said.

She nodded at an adjacent agent. Eddie Menendez had gone through basic training with Benjamin. The prick had kissed a lot of ass to get on Agent Jane's team. He stepped up beside Elizabeth and Matilda waiting for further instruction.

Benjamin had been waiting for this moment his whole career. He tried to sit straighter and taller on his knees. He had been stupid to give up his career, his dreams, for Elizabeth. He stood and walked over to her. Out of the corner of his eyes he could see they were surrounded by agents. He pointed down at Matilda.

"Take her to the Library Suite. You know what to do with the rest." Agent Jane approached him.

Menendez scooped the girl off and another agent grabbed Elizabeth.

"No!" cried Jasmine. Her protests quickly ceased with a piece of duct tape. Several agents helped assist her into the building.

The Ahwahnee Hotel looked like a Native American castle—constructed with piled stone, wood, and turquoise awnings—but its very foundation covered the remnants of the Indian village that had once lived in the valley. It stood as a shrine to America's colonization, built for the rich.

"Good work ...." Agent Jane extended her hand. She looked down at the mud puddle. The tip of her boot slid through the dirty water and hit something. She swished her fingers through the muck and pulled out the bone dagger. Her eyes lit up. She clasped it and looked up into the night sky, waiting for the moonlight. "Why don't you get cleaned up? Dinner will be soon."

The handcuffs fell from his wrists and he hurried into the hotel. It was just as elegant inside. Luxury was an understatement. It was built to separate the wealthy from the poor and middle-class and had succeeded until now— now it headquartered Meadowlark. Agents walked, oblivious, over the large tribal designs tiled into the floor. They didn't seem to notice how the desert-colored columns lining the lobby matched the tile.

The rustic red elevator doors were framed with a black tribal pattern. When the doors opened, an agent stepped in with Benjamin. He looked like he was right out of high school.

"What's your name?" Benjamin said.

"George." The kid drummed his fingers on his sword holster.

"I'm Be—"

"I know who you are." George stopped drumming. "We went through training together."

You're shitting me. The elevator jerked and settled at the second floor. "Listen, kid, I need to find one of those girls."

The doors opened.

"Please?" Benjamin said.

George smirked, nodded, and hit the third-floor button. The doors closed and took them one level higher. "Check the rooms at the end of the hall."

Benjamin stepped out and nodded at the kid before the doors shut. He walked into a sprint down the hallway. There were two doors. *Left first.* The door banged as it hit the wall. Elizabeth's naked body lay on the bed, still unconscious. Her knee-high boots rested at its foot. A female agent stood over her, folding the earth-toned dress. He stepped into the room. "Leave."

The woman flinched, took the dress, and obeyed.

He walked to the bed and picked up a towel. Elizabeth's skin was covered in gooseflesh. He dried her rain-soaked body. Blood rushed through his veins as he blotted her breasts dry. He wiped the mud from her legs and his cheeks burned. He slid the towel down to her toes, his lips brushed her belly button. The tranquilizers Meadowlark used would last for hours.

He brushed a dreadlock from her cheek and mud covered his fingers. It would be so easy to take her right then and there. He climbed into bed and slid the cover out from beneath her limp body. As he pulled the comforter over the smooth curves of her skin, he spooned in beside her. Just the warmth of her body against his was enough, maybe even too much.

6

IT WAS MORNING BEFORE THE SEDATIVE WORE OFF. I found myself once again naked in a strange bed. The bathroom door across from me was cracked and dark. I felt the warmth of a body beside me. There was no way I'd look back, not after the last time. It couldn't matter who it was anyway—not in this world.

I found the bathroom light and closed the door. I turned the shower's heat all the way up. Steam began to swirl in the room. The air grew heavy. I knew it would be the last warm shower I would ever feel. I stepped in and let the water scald my skin. I grabbed the soap and rubbed it between my hands.

There was a knock at the bathroom door and it opened. The shower curtain hid me from view, but they knew I was in here. I breathed deeply to extinguish the pounding of my heart.

"Hey," Benjamin said. He pulled back the curtain, letting in cold air. He was naked. His muscles weren't huge, but they were ripped. The stitches in his bicep tightened as his arm flexed. He stepped in and pulled the curtain behind him.

I bit my lip and restrained the smile pressing to get out. I turned and foamed the soap more, then smeared it over my face. "So from the looks of it, we made it to the hotel." I washed it off, lingering in the water. "What the hell happened?"

Benjamin stepped up behind me. I turned to kiss him, but he grabbed my hands and pinned them to the wall. His chest pressed against my back. He kissed my neck and continued to the tattoo on my shoulder. His right hand released mine, but I stayed still, holding my breath. He pulled my hips closer to him, forcing my breasts against the wet tiles. His fingers followed the curve of my back and slid between my thighs, caressing me. I moaned at his touch. My nipples hardened against the cold wall.

"Yes," slipped out of my lips.

He pulled away, grabbed both my hips, and pushed himself into me. The cold tiles against my chest dulled. His raw skin slid against my natural lubricant, deeper. *Kiss me.* He grabbed my hips tighter, the tips of his fingers digging into my skin. He thrust himself harder and deeper inside of me, harder and faster. He pulled out, resting his penis on my back. It twitched as cum dripped along the beads of water.

I stood. A deep breath filled my lungs with humidity and I grabbed the soap. His hand brushed the tattoo on my shoulder. His fingers stopped, grabbed my arm, and spun me around. He pinned me into the shower's corner and pressed his lips against mine. He kissed my neck and pushed himself back between my thighs. He pinched my nipple as he started with slow, passionate pelvic thrusts.

There was a knock at the bedroom door.

YOSEMITE RISING

"I better get that." He kissed me, pulled away, and stepped out of the shower. "I'll meet you downstairs."

The blood pumping through my body had no place to go, no release. I spread my thighs and slid my finger into the fresh lubricant.

7

THE SECOND KNOCK WAS MORE OF A POUNDING.

"Coming!" Benjamin pulled on a clean and pressed uniform. Nothing felt better—well, except for sex. He opened the bedroom door. His heart sank.

Agent Jane stood with her arms crossed, blocking the doorway. "Agent Ben, the Chief is requesting that you meet with him after breakfast."

The sound of the shower running suddenly sounded like an airport runway. She took a step into the room. "Which one is it?"

"What do you mean?"

"Which one are you fucking, Agent?"

"That's none of your goddamn business." He puffed out his chest, blocked her from further entry, and took a step, pushing her into the hallway. He pulled the lock and shut the door behind him. He stepped toward the elevator, but Jane's sword blocked him.

"You'll do well to remember your place, Agent." She brought the blade closer to his neck. "The Chief wants to see you in the Library Suite after breakfast."

She withdrew the sword and he walked away. Nearly two years with the Meadowlark division and he still had never met its Chief. He took the elevator and dropped his guard for the first time in 11 days. His shoulders dropped down; it was almost painful. The doors slid open to a busy hallway and his shoulders inched back up. Meadowlark agents filled the lobby, but none spoke. Benjamin's boots squeaked as he entered the dining room.

Thirty-four-foot pillars held up the room. An elegant green ceiling filled the space between rafters. Chandeliers hung by long chains. The left side of the room was filled with windows that stretched to the ceiling. The opposite side was lined with serving tables. Round tables filled the floor in between, dressed in white cloth. The illusion that everything was right in the world still held its place in the hotel.

Black uniforms filled every table except one. A young woman waved frantically at him. The hotel robe she wore was a blinding white. He walked over and she threw her arms around his neck, her wet hair sticking to his cheek.

"Thank you for saving us." Jasmine's hug weakened and she pulled back, staring over his shoulder.

Elizabeth walked into the room wearing an identical bright-white robe. It moved with each step and her knee peeked out as she walked toward them. The knotted belt pressed the fabric to the curves of her body. The blue of her eyes was obvious even from so far away. If anyone else knew who she was, her walk across the room would not have been completed. They would cage her, break her, until she begged for death.

Benjamin froze.

Matilda walked up behind her wearing a Meadowlark uniform. Background conversation dulled as she stormed past Elizabeth and charged the table. "Who the fuck is Elizabeth?"

Any remaining conversation ceased. All eyes were on them.

8

I STOOD BEHIND MATILDA AND PLACED MY HAND ON her shoulder. She spun around and let her anger go. She pulled me into her arms and wrapped the remaining love she had around me.

I embraced it. My fingers pressed against her hair as I kissed her cheek and whispered, "I am."

Benjamin pulled a seat out for her.

"Why didn't I get one of those outfits?" Jasmine looked at Benjamin.

He looked to the girl for an answer.

"I don't know. They gave it to me after that blood test." She shoved her sleeve up, exposing a cotton ball stuck beneath a band-aid.

The kitchen opened. The tables emptied and agents formed a line at its serving tables.

"Grab her." Benjamin grabbed my hand, leading me through the dining room, toward the elevators. We formed a chain heading through the lobby.

The elevator. I stopped and Matilda ran straight into my back. I let go of Benjamin's hand.

"What are you doing?" He hit the elevator button and reached back for me.

The red elevator doors were framed by a black and red

Native American design. The mere look of it chilled me, as if all the wrong in the world would come pouring out of its doors.

"Oh my God, it's that movie." Matilda took her hand away from mine and cupped her mouth.

The fucking Shining.

The elevator doors opened.

No river of blood poured out, but my heart knew no different. I refused to step inside. Benjamin pulled me in and Matilda followed before the doors closed.

"I'm starving. Where are we going?" Matilda waited for an answer. None was given. She turned toward me. "What do they want with you?"

The doors opened. Benjamin led us back to my bedroom. He shut the door, locked it, and pressed his back against it. "Take off your clothes."

"You're a freak. Let me the fuck out of here." Matilda attempted to shove him away from the door.

"A few days ago I was just like you," I began.

She stopped.

"Just trying to keep my head above water. Now ... now I'm expected to be some fucking savior."

She turned toward me.

I couldn't hide my face from her. My chest rose slowly with a long inhale—it was all I could do to keep from crying.

She unbuttoned her blouse. Benjamin stared.

A knock pounded against the door. "Sir, the Chief is ready for you now."

"Give me a second." Benjamin walked over toward me and swept me into his arms, untying the robe. It fell open, allowing my breasts to press against his shirt. He pressed his lips against mine, their softness lingering as he stood me up, let go, and headed for the door. "Get changed. I'll be right back."

9

MATILDA SLID INTO THE ROBE AND PLOPPED DOWN ON the bed. I was still buttoning the shirt when another knock pounded against the door. Out of reflex, I reached over my shoulder for a sword—nothing. *Shit.* There had to be something around the room I could use. *The hotel phone.* I yanked it from the wall, opened the door, and smashed it into a man's face. He fell to the floor. I stepped over him and started for the elevator.

"Elizabeth," he called.

I froze not three steps from him.

"Elizabeth."

My heart fell to the bottom of my chest. Tears dripped down my cheeks. I turned to the familiar voice as Matilda passed me.

The man stood, cupping his jaw and leaning against a cane. His warm eyes met mine with a smile.

"You're alive?" I reached out to touch him, to feel that he was real.

He stepped closer, allowing my fingers to rest against his cheek. The cane fell to the floor as he wrapped his arm around my waist, pulled me into his arms, and pressed his lips against mine.

"Is it really you?" I clenched my eyes. Saltwater dripped onto my lower lip.

"Yes," Zach said. He kissed me, allowing the tears to soak into his lips.

I forced myself back from him. "Have you been bitten?"

"Howard attacked me." He wobbled, bending for the fallen cane.

"Shouldn't you be dead?" I crossed my arms and stepped back. He pulled me back to him.

"I've been looking everywhere for you." He kissed me.

I clenched my lips, avoiding affection. He would die just like everyone else.

"Relax, babe. I'm fine. Aren't you immune anyway?" He took another step and pinned me against the wall, kissing me harder. My lips melted to his. The smell of campfire trickled through my neurons. Each dreadlock tingled in memory of his touch twisting their strands.

"Hey! Let's go!" Matilda waited at the end of the hallway. The elevator chimed. I braced Zach's shoulder, walking him down the hall. Matilda popped her head out of the elevator with a smile. "Do you think you could share one?"

We stumbled in.

"What does she mean?" Zach leaned against the elevator wall.

"It's a long story." I released his hand and picked at my nails.

The doors opened at the ground floor. Benjamin had been pacing outside of them. His eyes went straight for Zach. Meadowlark had tracked me, but was my entire past in one of their files—all the way back to when I was eight—my first kiss?

My file. Nausea pummeled me with the thought. Benjamin supported Zach and tossed a set of car keys at Jasmine. She had been sitting off to the side reading a magazine. I leaned against the wall, forced the bile of my stomach back down, and then followed the group through the lobby. The entrance doors spit us out onto a long breezeway with a red carpet rolled out beneath it. A park cruiser was parked oddly at its end.

"I'm driving!" Jasmine sprinted down the breezeway.

Matilda hurried after her and slid into the back, leaving the door open. I slid over, allowing Zach to take the window seat.

Benjamin took the front passenger seat. "Go."

Jasmine peeled out and sped down the road. The hotel faded behind us. The forest to the right was littered with boulders that had fallen from the valley's wall. The sun captured a piece of granite the size of a house ahead. It made the car-size boulder hugging the road look miniscule. Masoned stone around its edge formed a guardhouse. A black circular sign stuck out of the top. It would have gone unnoticed if not for the gold paint displaying the Ahwahnee Hotel's logo. The post on the opposite side of the street hinted at a once gated road. Something was draped across the path.

The cruiser's tires popped and deflated. The rims scratched into the asphalt. The car made it around the next bend. A Meadowlark Hummer was waiting for us, beside a pedestrian crossing sign. Jasmine allowed the car to coast to a stop as Agent Jane stepped into the road. The rims ground to a halt.

"I'll handle this." Zach flung the rear passenger door open, shoved his cane to the ground, and pushed all his weight from the cruiser. "Ma'am, if I can explain—"

"Sir, I need you to get back into the vehicle." She nodded at Agent Menendez. He stepped in front of her, blocking Zach's path.

Zach punched him to the ground, extended the cane

out in front of him and pointed its tip perfectly in line between her breasts. A gunshot blasted from its end.

Her body fell to the ground.

Zach leaned back on the cane and walked toward the Hummer. He climbed into the back seat and waited for the rest of us to follow. Jasmine raced for the driver's seat and Benjamin let her have it. Zach leaned his head back against the headrest. "Go! What are you waiting for?"

Jasmine threw the Hummer into drive and sped out of the park. We traveled an hour before reverence was broken.

Zach scooted to the edge of the back seat. "Where are we headed?"

Benjamin turned around. "Where'd you get that gun?"

Zach leaned back into the seat and crossed his arms. The town of Mariposa filled the windshield. Silhouettes showed in the frames of store windows. The Hummer slowed through the main street. Eyes crept from the darkest shadows into the midday sun. The tires rolled into a school zone. Townspeople flooded the vehicle. Children flowed from a playground to join the crowd. Their yellow, swollen eyes were caked with mud. Loose skin hung from their eye sockets, arms, and cheeks.

"Floor it!" Benjamin said.

My neck nearly snapped as I turned toward him. It was a river of children for fuck's sake. Jasmine must have given him an identical look. He held his hands up in defense and sat back as the infected mob swarmed the vehicle. The Hummer edged through the crowd, bumping their little bodies out of the way. Weak hands pounded against the vehicle doors. The sea of children grew reluctant to move. Older kids began to tug at the locked door handles.

The front doors of a nearby elementary school swung open. Two male custodians and a lunch lady charged.

"Now!" Benjamin said.

The adults pushed the fragile bodies from their path, gaining on us. Jasmine stepped on the gas and—in the moment before the Hummer shot forward—Benjamin's window shattered. An eighth-grader grabbed onto his collar. He elbowed the kid in the face and shoved him away. Small pieces of glass slid into Benjamin's cheek. The cold outdoor air pushed into the vehicle. The last small child fell away, crushed beneath the wheels.

"My lake house," Zach said.

"No, bad idea." Benjamin looked back at me. "It has to be someplace completely unrelated to any of you. Some place not in your file."

"I agree with him." Matilda sat up.

"Okay, you guys pick." Zach slouched back down in his seat, forming a grin. The wind whistled through the broken window.

10

BENJAMIN KNEW OF A GUN SHOP NOT FAR FROM where they were—situated in the middle of nowhere—down a long driveway framed with trees. The asphalt molded into a dirt road. A building emerged at its end. The windows were fastened with bars, but an ax sat beside the front door among a pile of wood. Unease filled his stomach.

"You guys should stay out here for a minute. Hank is a little quick on the trigger, even under normal circumstances." Benjamin stepped out of the vehicle, his boots sliding into the mud. The front door had a small window with its blind closed. A single line opened and someone peeked out.

"Hey, it's Ben. I'm in a situation and I could really use your help." His hand braced the door and his voice lowered. He looked down at the ground. "I lost Yen."

The door opened and he fell through the threshold, crashing to the floor. The front room of the shop still looked the same, even from the ground. The glass countertop displaying handguns and knives was still intact. Wooden panels displayed nine types of rifles up on the wall, but the Ruger 10/22 rifle was missing from its spot. Its barrel was pressed into his cheek and a 20-something man looked down its barrel. His elbows were too straight to handle its kickback if he fired. In one motion Benjamin grabbed the barrel, ripped the rifle from his fingers, and turned it on the man, aiming it at the second button of his shirt. The man had a feminine quality to him, likely brought out by his mother.

Luke threw up his hands. "How did you do that?"

"Where's Hank?" Benjamin lowered the rifle and rolled to his feet. The store was still stocked and there was no sign of a struggle. The only thing out of place was the mama's boy.

Luke's finger shook as he pointed toward the back room.

Without hesitation Benjamin climbed over the counter. He passed an occupied bathroom on his left; urine reeked from its seam. The velvet green couch he and Yen had broken as tweens still sat against the back wall—empty. The back closet creaked open. An old lady walked backwards out of it, rhythmically mopping the floor.

The bathroom door flew open.

"Ben?" Hank's overweight body looked more worn than usual. His grey beard had lightened since the last time Benjamin had seen him.

The past few years, trying to get into the Meadowlark program, had kept him away for far too long. After getting assigned to Elizabeth's case, he was considered to have no other life, at least not until she was dead.

Hank took Benjamin into his arms, just like the day when he and Yen were placed into his foster care. They had both made their way into Child Protective Services. Benjamin at the age of 12 and Yen two years prior. There weren't many foster parents willing to take on boys of that age, or at least not ones that weren't child molesters.

Benjamin smiled, patted Hank on the shoulder and let go, heading back to the front room. He pushed the door open and waved the crew in.

Jasmine sprinted in, noticed Luke, and nodded toward him. "What's up?"

Elizabeth stepped in and approached Hank with her hand ready to greet him.

"This place is a dump." Matilda stepped in with her arms crossed, guarding the entrance. The door began to close behind her. Bloody fingertips reached around its edge and yanked it open. Matilda screamed as the nails dug into her shoulder. A man in his late 40s lunged into the shop. His fluorescent-orange ball cap and camouflage outfit were streaked with mud. His purple and bloated skin was peeling. Saliva dripped from his mouth. He grabbed a chunk of Matilda's hair and yanked her backwards.

Benjamin charged them, tripped, and plowed his shoulder into the man's cheekbone. The cap flew in the air as the three fell to the floor.

Blood-curdling screams pushed into the small room as the creature's teeth tore into Matilda's stomach.

The ax. Benjamin reached out of the door for it and climbed to his feet. Adrenaline lifted its weight and he swung the blade down between the man's shoulders.

Matilda's eyes filled with tears.

Benjamin swung the ax back over his head. Infected blood soaked into her exposed and torn intestines. He closed his eyes and swung the ax back over his head. "I'm sorry."

11

I STARED INTO THE GIRL'S FRIGHTENED EYES. THE sound of rubber sliding on a wet floor turned my attention to the back room. An old woman stood a foot behind me. My heart jumped and I shoved her away.

Her body was hurled backwards. The back of her head smashed into the concrete floor. Hank's cries replaced Matilda's as blood pooled under the woman's head. The old man made an attempt to run to her, but Benjamin tackled him. Her frail body convulsed.

I stepped back, my stomach knotted. *It was an accident.* The bathroom doorknob was in reach. I pulled open the doors and locked myself into its seclusion. I lowered my head into the piss-stained toilet. The bile of my empty stomach splattered onto the rim. I pulled my face away, gasping for a clean breath of air. I tried to stand, but my knees buckled. I closed the lid of the toilet seat, sliding the tips of my fingers into tacky urine.

YOSEMITE RISING

A light knock at the door was followed by Jasmine's voice. "Yo! We're heading out. There's a storm rolling in, so you better get your shit together."

I grabbed the sink, stood up, and wiped the stomach acid from my lips. The reflection in the mirror resembled anyone but me. I tugged at a dreadlock framing my cheek. *Breathe in, breathe out.* I forced myself to open the door.

Jasmine stood guarding the doorway. Her gold hoop earrings swung beside her curls. "So is he still worth it?"

I pushed past her.

"All of this death, for a single person," she said.

"What makes my life less valuable than yours, or theirs?" I shoved my nose an inch from hers.

"You could save everyone ..." she gestured around the room, "the entire world."

"You tell me, what is worth saving?" I turned away from her. "My sister didn't die for nothing."

12

I SLID INTO THE BACK SEAT BEHIND ZACH. HE SAT WITH his feet propped up on the dashboard, resting his head back. The darkening clouds overhead had weighed his eyelids down. Cool air rushed through the broken window.

"Do you remember our first kiss?" He turned around and placed his arm over the headrest. "God, I love your eyes."

I should have smiled, but I couldn't.

"We were eight. The day was fading beneath the lake in spring. We spent all day trying to catch baby turtles. Just as dusk approached, you looked down on the water's edge and there, trapped between twigs, was a red-ear slider."

He rested his chin on his arm. "I wanted to keep it, but you insisted it should be free, given a second chance."

Tears pooled against my bottom eyelashes. I looked away. *How foolish an eight-year-old can be.*

Zach paused. The shop's front door burst open and the group headed toward us. "A chance to find his soulmate."

The stitched line of my wrist throbbed beneath my sleeve. Warm tears streamed down my cheeks. I looked back up at him. "I killed Dominic."

He faced forward.

13

BENJAMIN WATCHED ELIZABETH AS HER CHILDHOOD boyfriend turned forward. Nothing in her file had suggested Zach was anything but a good guy, but there was something he didn't like about him.

Zach had been right; they should've just gone to his lake house. According to the case file, he was rich enough to survive an apocalypse.

Benjamin climbed into the driver's seat and mama's boy, Luke, slid in beside Elizabeth. He wasn't much competition—a city boy in tight jeans. His petite frame fit perfectly in the middle of the back seat until Jasmine and Hank squeezed in.

The Hummer sped down the dirt road. It would take 30 minutes to get to the lake and 10 more to reach the house.

Something moved from the tree line. It formed into the silhouette of a man. He jumped onto the driveway, the vehicle plowed into him, and his body thumped beneath the tires. The Hummer screeched to a halt.

"No!" Hank jumped out of the back seat. "Gary!"

Shit! Benjamin threw the car into park and jumped out.

Hank leaned over the broken body. Exhaust fumes spewed into his face. His fingers brushed the man's eyelids closed. He rested his forehead against the caved-in camouflage vest.

The man's bloodshot eyes opened. He sat up straight, pushing Hank as he went. Perspiration dripped from his pores. His teeth caught Hank's arm and he bit down.

Benjamin drew the Ruger 10/22 rifle to the crusty, swollen eyes staring at Hank and pulled the trigger. A shot broke through the air. Gary's dentures, dripping with saliva, fell to the ground.

Benjamin offered a hand and pulled Hank's heavy frame from the ground. "You okay?"

The only man who had ever been a father to him nodded. "What was I thinking? You aren't hurt, are you?"

Benjamin shook his head.

Hank pressed his hand against his arm. If he had been bitten, he knew better than to admit it.

"It's just a surface wound. He didn't break any skin." Hank patted Benjamin's shoulder. "Let's go before any of my other friends try to kill me. Gary always was kind of an ass."

They took their seats. Benjamin shoved the car back into drive, looking at the old man in the rearview mirror. Hank didn't turn to watch the corpse of his friend disappear behind them.

Benjamin's eyes drifted toward Luke's reflection. Luke nuzzled closer to Elizabeth. She stared out the side window.

In 40 minutes, everything would change.

THE RETURN OF COYOTE

1

RAIN TAPERED OFF AND CLEARED THE EVENING SKY. I thought I would never return to the lake. Our house had burned down right after the kissing incident with Zach. Gossip had already taken over my new third-grade classroom the first week of school—I had kissed a boy. What a fucking year that was.

Forest hugged the water's edge. The neighborhood looked just the same as we had left it. The Bennett's brick mansion stood three stories on the right. It was old money and there was no sign that it was running out. Next was an empty lot framed by a few trees—the place our three-bedroom cottage once stood. The lake hugged the back of the property. I turned away from the window and closed my eyes. It was all gone. *They were all gone.* All I had left were memories.

The brakes squeaked and my seatbelt tightened with

the slight jerk of the car. Zach's two story cabin stood at the end of the road. Every detail of the lake house screamed bed-and-breakfast. Inside, the plants, knickknacks, and furniture sat exactly as they had 12 years ago.

Zach kicked off his shoes in the foyer. To the left, a bear carcass sprawled the length of the living room floor, head and all. The kitchen was to the right. It had the cutest breakfast nook I'd ever seen. The stairwell was directly in front of us, hiding the basement beneath it. Zach headed to the second floor and I followed. The first door led to the master bedroom. Windows filled the far wall, capturing the full width of the lake. Gusts of wind picked at the last of the deciduous leaves, dropping them to the water's edge.

"Do you know the story of Coyote?" Zach leaned on the cane to his side and lit a candle beside the bed.

I froze, my heart jumping into a race. Every muscle tightened as he hobbled back toward me.

"Coyote and the stars?" His fingers pulled my chin toward his.

I restrained his pull, staring out the window. The abyss of space framed the twinkling white dots in the sky.

"No? Well, Silver Fox had spent half the night painting the sky. She had placed each star in a specific place. Not only would her designs comfort the humans in night's darkness, but they would also remind them that there was always another stargazer out there, lying beneath it."

"All I see is chaos." I walked to the window and pressed my forehead against the cold glass.

"Just as Silver Fox turned her back—only for a second, Coyote spilled the remaining stars into the sky. And here they stand, to this very day. Most see chaos … but there are some that can decipher her painting."

The lake was a perfect mirror to the constellation's mess. "What an asshole," I said.

Zach stood silent. A grin filled his face.

"So, what happened to Silver Fox?"

"One story claims she hid on the moon, another that she hid among the Ahwahnee people. Coyote searched all over earth—in every stream and under each rock." He stepped closer and pressed his chest against my shirt.

"Did he find her?" My lips were only a breath from his.

"No." Benjamin stepped into the doorway and leaned against the threshold.

"No one knows. But they say *the answer is in Tissaack*." Zach stepped away from me and looked out the windows staring up at the clear night sky.

"What does it mean?" Benjamin straightened up.

Zach came back to me and brushed my cheek with his fingers. "Half Dome."

I held my breath as he pulled me toward him. My body screamed for his, wanting to push the rest of the world away.

Benjamin cleared his throat.

"I can wait a little longer." Zach kissed my forehead. His lips lingered and then all at once he walked away.

Benjamin unblocked the doorway.

"I can show you to your room," Zach said.

"That won't be necessary." Benjamin crossed his arms and stepped into the bedroom.

Zach took his time walking out the door.

Benjamin slammed it shut behind him.

YOSEMITE RISING

"What is wrong with you?" I said.

"I don't trust that guy." Benjamin sat down on the edge of the bed and loosened his bootstraps. "I've read your entire case file. Don't you think it's weird that your third grade boyfriend just happened to attend OSU, *after* all those years of being gone from your life?"

"I think it's weird that a whole division of the United States government was created to track me down, capture me, and force me to sacrifice myself based on an old legend." I stormed into the attached bathroom and locked the door. Marble flowed from a garden-style bathtub into every inch of the room.

A generator kicked on outside and the room flooded with light. I hurried to turn the hot water on. The water's roar echoed off the walls and drummed through the pipes. Steam rose toward the ceiling. I sank into its warmth, exhaustion and hunger seeping from me. It would be so easy to collapse into the thick liquid and drown out the world.

The lights went out.

2

ZACH PULLED THE BACK DOOR CLOSED BEHIND HIM, shutting out the cold. Mama's boy had managed to find the generator. With his help they would all be dead by morning. The noise carried across the lake, but with luck, the sound had echoed against its vastness.

Zach didn't have to wait for his eyes to adjust to the night. He went straight for the kitchen counter and grabbed a handful of long candles from the cupboard.

Luke sat across from Jasmine at the nook. Its wooden bench hugged the windows overlooking the lake. Beside the water's edge was forest as far as their eyes could see.

Jasmine had found a jar of almonds and sat stuffing her face.

Luke scrunched his nose and drew up his lip, watching her.

"Anyone else hungry?" Zach set the candles up around the room and headed out the back door to a brick patio.

"Do you need some help?" Luke followed.

"Grab some wood." Zach nodded at the boy and grabbed a stack. "So what's your story?"

Luke loaded his arms and headed back for the door.

Zach blocked the warm entrance to the house. "How did someone like you get stuck at a gun shop amid all this?"

"I was in there shopping for a gun. You know those small ones that fit in your hand?" Luke's arms wobbled, bearing the weight of their load.

Zach walked into the house. An autumn breeze swirled the stale air inside. *The old man must've loved that question.* "Like a Beretta Nano?"

"I guess," Luke said.

"Do you mind if I ask why?" Zach kindled a brick oven nestled in the kitchen wall. The only modern appliance was a stainless steel refrigerator.

"Protection." Luke cleared his throat. Silence persisted until the last piece of wood was lifted from his arms.

"Oh, what the hell ...." Zach ripped open the third kitchen drawer from the refrigerator and pulled out a Glock 45.

Hank walked into the room, releasing a loud fart.

Jasmine broke up laughing. He sat down across from her and rested his head in his hands.

"Let's go practice, shall we?" Zach smiled, handed Luke the gun, made his way to the back door, and held it open.

Luke stepped past him into the bitter night.

Zach set up facing the lake. If anyone was going to have a gun around him, they better know how the hell to use it. He stepped behind Luke, wrapped his arms around him, and brushed his fingers along Luke's hand, pushing him to hold the gun up—straight—out in front. The boy shivered. Zach whispered, "The bird house by the edge of the lake."

"Dude!" Jasmine burst out of the house.

The gun fired. It echoed through the still forest.

The silent night rang with white noise as Jasmine yelled, "I'm next!"

Zach yanked the weapon from Luke and pointed it to the ground. "You never place your finger on the trigger unless you're a hundred and ten percent ready."

Jasmine wasted no time taking Luke's place. She nuzzled her shoulder back into Zach. The cucumber scent of shampoo was still clinging to her hair. She got into position and listened carefully. Her right shoulder came back into him and she fired. Her first shot disappeared between the trees in the distance.

"I'm guessing you're a lefty?" Zach said.

"How the hell do you know that?" She yelled over the ringing in their ears.

He smiled and repositioned her hands—left on top.

She fired. The second shot blasted through the tiny wooden house in the distance. She jumped with excitement. The gun discharged again. A window in the master bedroom shattered.

"You both need to be careful. These aren't toys." Zach glanced up at the broken glass and headed back inside. Jasmine bumped into the back of him as Luke pushed them faster through the door. Zach paused and let them pass.

The darkness behind him knotted his stomach. Outside, death waited in the bareness of autumn. The cabin was their only sanctuary. Without it, the cold of winter could kill them. And it was coming. Cold air gusted across the back of his neck. He turned around. There was nothing. He took a step back and loaded his arms with wood. It would be cold tonight. He stepped inside and headed for the living room.

Luke sat at the nook, nervously rubbing his hands. Jasmine followed Zach. She slowed as they approached the bear carcass lying on the floor. It was one of Zach's favorite pieces. Its teeth had been bleached, which made the open mouth look twice as large. The walls stretched to the second-story rafters. A large fireplace spanned the opposite wall, extending to the ceiling's arch. His prize piece was a full-grown black bear, stuffed in a standing position beside the fireplace.

"So, I take it you like bears." Jasmine kicked off her shoes, slid her white socks across the fur rug, and sank into a brown leather couch.

"To the contrary." He started the fire. Its glow grew. It popped and crackled as warmth filled the room. Without death, there would be no life.

A gentle knock came from the front door.

"Are you expecting someone?" She sat up.

He drew the Glock from his pants and clenched it to his side.

The knocking grew louder.

3

WHEN THE GUNSHOT WENT OFF, BENJAMIN PUSHED me to the floor. Glass rained down on him and a bullet hole ruined the perfect view of the lake. He slid off to my side. "You okay?"

I could breathe. Cold air rushed through the broken glass, chilling the bare skin beneath my towel.

He brushed a wet dreadlock from my cheek. His lips stopped before reaching mine, and he whispered, "If you trust him, that's all I need."

I leaned up and pressed my lips against his. His body felt so warm. His fingertips followed the curve of my shoulder until finding the edge of the towel. He kissed my neck, lingering as he tore the cotton from my body. I inhaled, pushing my breasts against him. He cupped them, lowering his lips to my nipple, caressing its tip with his tongue. His pants tightened against my thigh. My knees loosened. He lightly bit my nipple and slid his fingers between my thighs.

I fumbled with his belt. My heart raced. I yanked on the buckle, freeing it from his waist. I wrapped my feet around his back, drawing him close. He wiped his wet finger down my inner thigh. All the horror in the world could disappear with a good fuck.

He reached into his front pocket and pulled out a necklace. A turquoise fox dangled from a string of hemp.

The necklace! My eyes widened and my body tightened.

He leaned over the top of me and shifted his weight to one side. He kissed me and I shut out the world. He laid the stone on my chest, fueling my adrenaline and lust. His lips pressed harder against mine as he pushed himself inside me. I pulled my lips from his and turned my head. There was no going back now. His fingers dug into my thighs, forcing them wider. He kissed my neck and rubbed my nipple.

An owl's hoot rippled through the broken window.

My muscles contracted, as my legs and thighs stiffened and relaxed around his skin.

He kissed me, leaving his lips pressed against mine. His hand pressed on my hip, stabilizing my body as he slid himself in and out, harder and faster. He pinched my nipple, bit my lip. His body tightened and pulsated inside of me. His fingers loosened and fell from my breast. He pulled out, wiped with the towel, and tossed it to me.

A second hoot filled the air.

I stood. Cum dripped from between my thighs. I ran to the bathroom. Watermarks on the mirror reflected the stains of my self-image. *Shit.* At least I just finished a period. *Shit.* I grabbed a towel from the shelf and concealed myself. Beyond the closed bathroom door was that awkward post-sex moment. I reached for the doorknob. I didn't want a relationship. I quickly opened the door and dashed for a dresser sitting opposite the bed. Top drawers are for memories or underwear, so I pulled the second. A vintage green shirt was folded in an otherwise empty drawer. I grabbed it, speechless. The towel slid from my fingers and fell to the floor. *It couldn't be.* The shirt unrolled from my fingers revealing a simple screen print, a circle that formed a tree at its center. A faint purple stain was visible on the left shoulder.

Dominic and I had been eating blackberries at a concert during the Oregon Country Fair. The sun was bright, and when he went to kiss me, I fell over. Damn berry popped beneath my shoulder and stained my new shirt. That wasn't the only thing that popped that night.

"Is something wrong?" said Benjamin. He had climbed into bed.

I turned my attention to the bedroom door. Light conversation carried from downstairs. I shook my head and climbed in beside him. The night's end was approaching. I squinted through the gallery of windows. The owl's outline hugged a tree branch. Its eyes reflected the lunar rays, watching me drift into slumber.

Benjamin pulled me close, spooning me. His warmth countered the night. Surely the owl's omen was coming, but there was nothing I could do to stop it.

4

ZACH RIPPED OPEN THE FRONT DOOR, ITS KNOB slamming into the wall. A female park ranger stood on the front porch. Nevaeh wasted no time pushing him out of the way and finding the fireplace. He slid the gun back into his pants and locked the door behind her.

She stood warming her fingers at the flame. He passed her and opened a black door, almost hidden, at the back of the room. The office space was twice the size of the living room. A grand wooden desk sat in front of a stained-glass window. A dusty typewriter sat at the far end of a bookcase. On the opposite wall was an oil painting of the lake. Zach took down the painting, exposing a safe mounted in the wall behind it.

"Where the hell did you go?" Jasmine's voice carried into the office.

Nevaeh shushed her.

Zach grabbed a wad of $100 bills, returned to the living room, and tossed it at Nevaeh. That made them both shut up.

"I went to see Nantai." Nevaeh's eyes narrowed at him. She threw the worthless paper into the fire and pulled a knife to his throat. It cut into the first layer of his skin.

A smirk replaced the fear she expected on his face. He grabbed her hand and crushed it around the handle. She fell to her knees. He tore the knife from her fingers and swung her hand away from his.

"What do you want with her?" She cupped her hand in her lap. Tears swelled in her eyes.

Luke stepped into the room. "Dinner's rea—"

"She's just an old friend who means a lot to me." Zach extended a hand down to Nevaeh. Reluctant, she slid her fingers into his. He pulled her up and handed her the knife. "Here."

Luke stepped backwards toward the foyer and Zach followed. The aroma of brick-oven pizza drifted from the kitchen to the bottom of the stairs. Zach stopped and glanced up at the closed bedroom door. He waited for Nevaeh to catch up. "Seeming how I still owe you,"—he pulled another wad of $100s from his back pocket—"here."

Her jaw dropped.

He smiled and walked into the kitchen. Money can have such a hold on people.

Hank was propped at the breakfast nook in the corner. His love handles hung out from the bottom of his shirt, touching the bench. Jasmine sat down beside him. He didn't turn or look at her; his head hung low staring at the pizza lying out before them. "Why did you ruin the pizza with all these vegetables? I can't eat this," she said.

The men didn't utter a word. She'd eat if she was hungry enough. Half a minute later she was woofing it down. On her last bite, she reached for a second piece. Luke slapped her hand. Her face turned bright red. He nodded toward the foyer. "What about the other two?"

"Eat up, we can make another." Zach stood and made his way to the back door for more wood.

"Shouldn't we spare as much food as possible?" Luke pressed.

"That's the nice thing about having a greenhouse." Zach laughed. The back door closed behind him. They wouldn't survive if things never got better.

The back door opened.

Luke came out with a candle, assuming its light would show him more than the moon ever could.

Zach blew it out and tossed a piece of firewood at him.

"You like her, don't you?" Luke said.

Zach chucked another log at him.

"It's the way you look at her. Like she could fill the last piece of your soul ... or something like that." Luke stared past Zach into the forest. He was somewhere else then, reliving a memory, perhaps.

JULIE DAWN

"Hey," Zach nudged Luke's shoulder. "You sound like you could use some rest."

Night pressed deeper toward midnight. They walked inside. Hank moaned—a long satisfied moan. All the pizza was gone.

Jasmine jumped to her feet. "So is there somewhere I can crash?"

"Anyone else?" Zach examined the old man; he didn't look so good.

Luke chimed in with a "Ditto."

Zach led the two up to the second floor. The stairs creaked as they continued down the hallway to their rooms. He stopped outside the master bedroom and rested his fingers on the doorknob. He took his time turning it. It was locked. He knocked—his heart raced—and knocked again.

5

BENJAMIN CRACKED THE DOOR OPEN. IT WAS ZACH. Benjamin stood a little straighter, smug in his tight boxers.

"Hey." Zach walked towards the adjacent room. "It's your watch."

Benjamin closed the door and glanced at the petite figure still wrapped between the bed sheets. If he refused to stand guard—

There was no time to waste contemplating it. He stumbled into his pants and kissed Elizabeth's cheek. Walking away from that bed and closing the door behind him quickly disappeared into the past. The hallway was empty. His fingers reached around to the inside of the bedroom door and locked it. She would be safe until the morning.

His boots clunked down the stairs and into the kitchen. Hank was sitting face down in an empty pizza tray filled with vomit. The smell burned Benjamin's nostrils. He ran to him. "No, no, no ...."

He slid his hands into the vomit, scooping Hank's face up. He was as limp as a sleeping child. Benjamin leaned Hank's head back against the wall. It rolled forward, bobbing on his double chin.

Benjamin slammed his elbows against the table and buried his head in his hands. The first man to show him love was gone; his father was gone. Tears drained from his eyes, diluting the fumes of bile soaked into his sleeve.

Hank moaned.

Benjamin didn't want to look up, to see him like that—an empty, savage creature—but he did. Hank's head still hung motionless sitting beside him. There was only one thing to do. He reached for the sword holstered at his side. It wasn't there. He had left it lying on the bedroom floor. His body jumped as hard as his heart. He sprinted to the kitchen cabinets and tore open the drawers. The first was filled with a phone book and old menus. The second rattled as he pulled it out—silverware and *a meat cleaver*. He grabbed it and didn't move, couldn't move. After tonight, he would have no one. He had lost Yen, and now he was going to lose Hank. He stared at the floor and braced himself against the counter.

Hank moaned. His chest raised, fell, and then stopped—nothing.

Benjamin's palms sweated as he stepped toward Hank, making it hard to hold the cleaver. He gripped it tighter, extended it over his head, and forced it down. *No!* He thrust all his weight backwards and stopped the blade three inches from Hank's neck. *I can't.* He took a breath, clenched the hilt and walked outside, pacing in the darkness. The night air filled his emptiness. It was so cold. He longed for warmth.

He noticed the pile of wood resting to the right of the back door. He bent over, stacking logs in the bend of his arm. Something pressed against the back of his pants. He attempted to stand, but a sweaty palm grabbed the back of his neck. It was Hank's cock that pressed against his pants. The wood fell out of his arm. His fingers tightened around a large log which he swung as hard as he could.

It smashed against bone.

Momentum carried him halfway around before he could stop.

Hank was on the ground. Chunks of snot filled the blood pouring from his broken nose. His chubby body rolled in attempt to stand.

"I want you to know that I loved you," Benjamin whispered. He raised the cleaver above his head and swung it down.

Hank fell to the ground moaning.

Benjamin dropped the cleaver and wiped drops of sweat from his brow. His body cried, but he stayed focused. A few more minutes and it would be over. He smeared a falling tear and reached for a shovel cornered beside the back door.

Hank mustered everything he had left and stood up from the ground. The primitive part of him knew what was coming.

"You were the closest thing to a father for me." Benjamin swung the flat end of the shovel and smacked Hank in the face, sending him back to the ground. He

YOSEMITE RISING

swung it back over his head—as far as he could—and thrust it through Hank's neck, all the way through to his spinal cord.

Hank choked against the metal.

Adrenaline blurred the moment Benjamin jumped on the shovel's head and forced its tip through to the soil. Rain dripped from the sky. Clouds covered the moon. Darkness wrapped itself around him.

Hank's blood soaked into the ground.

6

THE BEDROOM DOOR CREAKED OPEN. A MALE silhouette stepped into the room and closed the door behind him. His warmth blanketed me as he spooned into bed. His stiff penis pressed against my thigh. Soft lips gently kissed my neck as his fingers brushed the curve of my hip. I turned to kiss his lips, but his arm tightened, restraining me. His teeth lightly bit my earlobe as his fingers slid between my thighs. I inhaled, holding the moment in my lungs. My body craved his touch, begging to feel him. He pulled away from my skin just enough to roll me onto my stomach and force my hips back toward his.

He slowly pushed into me. I dug my fingers into the sheets, attempting to hold myself in place. Sweat poured from my skin as he demanded my satisfaction. Slowly and deeply he drew out my release. I let go just as he did. His hand pinned my hips to the mattress, finishing. The warmth of his body pulled away.

I hugged the pillow beneath me, catching my breath.

The stars twinkled in the night between fast-moving clouds. They had drifted me to sleep and, as if instantly, they faded into dawn. Morning had come. The warm body was still lying beside me. Sun rays danced across the sheets as I rolled to spoon him. Contentment filled my breath as I closed my eyes and guided my fingers down the front of his chest.

I opened my eyes. *Sandy-blonde hair!* My heart pounded. My knee brushed his bare ass. Benjamin's hair was dark. The sheets rolled as he turned toward me. Blush burned into my cheeks.

Zach rolled to face me. His warmth caressed the goosebumps rippling over my skin. Before I could fathom words, he kissed me, pushing my body deeper into the mattress. I melted against his soft lips, allowing them to smother me as he nudged my hips down to his.

"I can't," I exhaled. I turned my cheek toward the windows, waiting for the grey sky to numb me. But it was blue, and clouds were still pink with a waking sun.

"You already have," he whispered and kissed my neck.

I froze. Excitement rushed between my legs. His hard body pushed against my thigh. I turned toward him. To deny that moment of lust for sake of repercussions would be too painful.

He leaned in and kissed me, spreading my shaky knees. His fingers pushed my shirt up. His lips kissed my breast. I gripped onto his hair and pulled his mouth from my skin.

"I can't." I shrugged and pulled the shirt back down. *Would it really be cheating?*

Zach searched my eyes and retuned his lips to mine.

His kiss pressed harder against me and his fingertips caressed my thigh. He moved his lips to my neck and followed the curves to my breast. He paused, waiting for any disapproval. I held my breath and he continued. The sheet fell from his shoulders as he kissed my inner thigh. There was no going back. His tongue rushed the ecstasy from me. I let go. He slid his finger into me.

"Fuck." It felt so good. Cold air blanketed me as he found his way back to my lips. They were still wet, but I didn't care. He grabbed a handful of my dreadlocks, and slowly pushed himself deeper between my thighs. His grip tightened and he went even deeper. The headboard banged against the wall harder and harder. My heart pounded. For a second the whole world disappeared. My muscles contracted. His head fell beside mine on the pillow as his body pulsated within me. *I'm so stupid, what did I just do?*

The sun danced across his painted back. The image of a moon was inked between his shoulder blades. Every muscle in my body went tight. I pushed him off and sat up against the headboard.

"What's wrong?" He sat up and placed his hand on my knee.

I pulled my legs into my chest and pulled at the bottom of my shirt. I nodded toward him. "Your tattoo?"

A warm smile filled his face and he stood up. His penis hung down, but the blood had not receded from it yet. He turned so that I could see the design. The moon sat high above a howling coyote covering the center of his back.

Fuck. My toes curled and I scooted back, pinning my spine to the headboard.

He sat down and rested his hand on my foot with a sigh. "I've been looking for you for a very long time. I found you once, a few lifetimes ago, hidden with the people of Yosemite. They called you Awanata, which was quite fitting for your love of turtles."

My tattoo. In reflex, I cupped my shoulder.

"But you had forgotten who you were ... who I was. Your mortal body had come with a price. The day you sacrificed yourself, I once again lost you. So, I waited for your return. Imagine my excitement when lifetimes later a pale baby was born on the same land from whence you first hid."

Florence Hutchings.

"But she wasn't you. Decades passed and I watched each woman of your family die." He stood up and walked into the bathroom. "When you were born, I was ready."

"For what?"

Silence stretched to every corner of the room.

I ran into the bathroom after him and landed straight in his arms. The hairs on my body quivered to a stand.

"For you. So that I could join your second attempt at mortality." He twisted a dreadlock that rested against my cheek. "You see, I was afraid of losing my memory as you had, so I left myself clues. And I did forget. But your words that day beside the lake reminded me."

I will always be beside you.

"I will always be beside you," he whispered.

No, no. I shook my head. *No!* I pulled away from him, stormed for the bedroom, and scooped my pants off the floor. I couldn't get those goddamn things on fast enough. My toes managed to find every possible snag of cotton and then they caught on my butt. I buttoned them as I hurried to the door. I stepped into the boots, not bothering to tie them.

"Elizabeth!"

I stopped in the threshold and looked back.

"Awanata, you are my Silver Fox."

I couldn't breathe. The room felt like it was caving in on me. My heart was being strangled. Tears soaked my lips and dripped off their edge as I stood still.

"Stay with me."

"You're fucking crazy." I stepped out into the hallway.

"He killed your parents!"

7

DAWN BROKE AS BENJAMIN STOOD OVER THE SINK, wringing out his shirt. Despite the mandatory vaccine for all Meadowlark staff, constant exposure to infection was draining his immune system. The last bits of night grieved with him.

He walked into the living room. The fireplace—no matter how hot—could not warm him. Shadows flickered over the mantle and reached across a black wall. *A door.* He glanced back at the foyer; the coast was clear. He slowly opened it. Beyond was an elaborate office. A large oil painting framed the wall. Brush strokes captured two children sitting beside a lake. At closer glance, he noticed the girl held a turtle. A tiny metal plaque was fixated to its frame etched with the word *Liaw*.

The floor boards creaked behind him.

Nevaeh stepped into the room and sat down behind the desk. "It means lake."

He faced her. "So, did you receive your reward?"

"You were right. I now know my path. But what is yours?" Nevaeh squinted. "Where do *you* fit in?"

"I don't know." Benjamin swiped the grease of his forehead into his hairline. "So it was Zach who offered the reward?"

"Yes," Nevaeh looked around the room. Native American artifacts filled the shelves and otherwise empty spaces. "I saved him a week ago. There was an attack at the park before all of this happened."

"He was bitten?" Benjamin's shoulders broadened.

A door upstairs slammed.

He ran out of the office, through the living room, and stopped at the bottom of the stairs. Elizabeth was coming full steam at him. Her hands were fisted and her face had melted with sadness. He had been in enough fights to know when one was coming for him. She swung and he caught her wrist.

"You killed my parents!" She sank to the floor.

"How could you—*know*." He bent down beside her.

"Get away from me," she pushed the words between her teeth and stood.

He reached for her.

She tore her arm away and ran out the back door. Cold air whipped the door back open before it could latch. The cabin's temperature dropped within seconds.

He started to follow, but Nevaeh tugged him back.

"I'll go." Her eyes squinted back at him. She knew something didn't sit right.

He nodded. A girl would be able to fix things more than he ever could. The floorboards upstairs creaked. Benjamin turned his attention to the top of the stairs. His heart pounded as he climbed the steps. He shoved the door open. It slammed against the wall, ricocheting back.

Zach stood naked in front of him.

Benjamin froze in the doorway. *How could she?* He rolled his shoulders back and tightened his fists. "What did you say to her?"

Zach sat down on the used bed, too calm. The smell of sex still warmed the room. He leaned over and picked up the sword lying on the floor. "Agent Benjamin Joseph Osbourne, you've broken all the rules."

What the fuck?

Zach stood up, spinning the sword in his hand, and walked closer. "You've complicated things. And we both know what I said was true. Do you think that I wouldn't have seen this coming?"

What? Benjamin's body stiffened as the man walked closer.

"You work for me." Zach drew the sword to Benjamin's chest. "This could've all been avoided if you had made our meeting."

Benjamin stepped closer. The blade pressed against the sweet spot between his collarbones.

Zach lowered the weapon.

The Chief of Meadowlark? Some sick training exercise?

"I am Coyote." He raised his arms to the sky, brought the sword back to Benjamin's throat and stepped closer. "Now bow to me."

Benjamin stared at him and knelt to the floor slowly.

Zach leaned down and whispered, "Did you really think she would choose you over me?"

Blood boiled in Benjamin's veins and pulsated through

his fisted hands. With all his weight he punched Zach in the face.

Zach fell to the floor, clenched his jaw, and wiped some fresh blood from his mouth. He grinned and stood back up. Then he swung the sword.

Benjamin rolled. Car tires sped down the gravel driveway, instinctively turning his attention.

Zach clocked him.

Benjamin fell and darkness engulfed his consciousness.

8

I RAN INTO THE WOODS TOWARD THE LAKE. *ZACH'S fucking crazy.* Autumn leaves crunched beneath my soles. *Benjamin killed my parents.* The trees blurred around me as the sun sparkled off my tears. The tip of my boot caught a tree root and I tripped to the ground. The air was knocked from my lungs, dirt skidded across my face, and blood rushed to my head. *No.* Everything was so fucked up. He was supposed to love me—not be some crazy stalker. I felt fingertips slide over my arm. It didn't matter anymore—who it was—what it was. I threw my head down into the dead leaves. I was ready.

"You're not alone." Nevaeh's fingertips brushed my hair.

I looked up. "You left us. What are you doing here?"

"I'm sure you can understand." She slouched against the trunk of a nearby tree. "I was told many legends as a child. One was of a woman I had grown up admiring. Nantai always told me I would one day meet her. When I was little, I believed him. Over the years I lost interest in fairy tales."

She grabbed a handful of crispy leaves. "And then there you were."

She looked up. "I never pictured you my age."

She tore the leaves into tiny pieces and threw them to the ground. "But I had already promised to return you to a man. He offered me a reward—more money than I could ever want—to return you to him."

Zach. A passing breeze pushed against my body. I searched her eyes. Could I trust her? The next wind brought the sound of a car with it.

I lay my head flat to the ground and rested on my arm. Nevaeh flattened down beside me. A black Hummer pulled up beside the one already parked in the driveway. A much larger biohazard symbol covered the Meadowlark logo on its doors. A woman and three male agents stormed the cabin.

Nevaeh pressed her head to the ground and whispered, "What do you want to do? I'm not leaving your side again. But I can't tell you what to do. Your heart is your own."

"I don't know." I searched her eyes for guidance, but got none. A breeze gusted by, masking any noise leaving the cabin. It, too, showed me no path. Dirt stirred with each breath. Leaves rustled.

"Then we'll stay here until you do. But we're running out of time."

A gunshot blasted in the cabin.

I looked up. Jasmine raced out the back door and sprinted toward the vehicles. A male agent closed in on her from behind and drew a gun.

"No!" I grabbed a stick, stood up, and sprinted toward him.

He looked at me and shifted the gun's barrel straight at my heart. A shot fired.

I fell to the ground.

"Get up!" Jasmine ran to my side and tugged on my arm.

My head throbbed, but there was no other pain. My hands rushed to my chest, but there was no hole.

Nevaeh grabbed my other arm and pulled me from the ground. Each step burned with the pounding of my head. They carried me to the newer vehicle, tore open the back door, and shoved me in.

Jasmine pushed me across the leather seat as she climbed in.

The cabin's front door pitched open. A female agent stepped out, eyes growing with fury. She was supposed to be dead. I had seen Zach kill her. Jasmine had too. "Shit."

Agent Jane aimed a gun at us.

"Go, go, go!" Jasmine said.

Nevaeh had climbed into the driver's seat and at the command, slammed the vehicle in reverse.

Zach stepped beside Jane, easing her aim to the ground.

They quickly faded in the rearview mirror. We wouldn't have much time before they caught up to us.

9

"LET THEM GO." ZACH TOOK HIS HAND OFF THE weapon. After all this time, he had found her—this time it would be easy.

Agent Jane let out a grunt of frustration.

"I see the bulletproof vest worked," he said.

She smiled.

He returned to the house and she followed. He grabbed his cane and stepped down into the basement beneath the stairs. Dust powdered his fingers as they slid down the railing. A circle of candles flickered across the man handcuffed to a chair in its center. Benjamin was still unconscious, slumped.

"The way I see it is this—you have one option. Do what I say, or I kill you." Zach had no time for games. He paced in the shadows. "I get that you love her, but she is not yours to love."

Benjamin's head rolled against his chest. Moans trickled down his chin with drool—such a pathetic human being.

Zach clenched the cane and whacked Benjamin's calf.

He groaned with agony and shook his head, attempting to focus on the pair in front of him. His words were dry and broken, "You can't do this. Who the hell do you think you are, God?"

Zach grinned, stepped closer, and leaned in. "But I am."

Benjamin held his breath.

Zach squeezed Benjamin's cheeks. *He was this close to getting her, and she had slipped away. If not for this asshole, all this shit would already be over.*

Footsteps creaked down the stairs. A second agent entered, pulling Luke behind him. He threw mama's boy to the floor.

A gunshot blasted outside. Agent Jane sprinted up the stairs. She was half way when a second shot went off.

Zach pulled Benjamin's confiscated sword from his belt and stepped behind him. It clinked against the cement floor as he dropped it beside Luke. He uncuffed Benjamin and stood tall, leaning against his cane. "I need you to help me find her."

"Chief!" Jane screamed.

Zach sprinted up the stairs and the men followed. Sunlight blinded their dilated pupils as they emerged from the basement.

Jane was covered in blood. Two bodies lay on the floor in a crimson puddle. "A little help would've been nice."

White hair framed the face of Mr. Bennett. Death had swept over him many years ago and the zombie outbreak had easily taken the rest of him. His dentures slid from his gums and followed the pooling blood. Mrs. Bennett's neck was sliced just above her pearl necklace. The cabin was contaminated. They would have to move, fast.

Zach tossed the group some bags and headed for the greenhouse. "Load up, we're leaving."

Outside, beside the lake, a twelve-year-old girl slowly walked into the yard. Zach tossed his gun to Luke. The boy offered it back and shook his head. Zach stepped up behind him, shoved the gun into his hand, and wrapped his fingers around Luke's, just like the night before. He steadied the Glock in Luke's hand. The girl's head rolled to the side. Luke pulled the trigger before Zach could force it. The bullet stripped a nearby tree of its bark.

The grotesque little girl continued, unflinching, toward them.

"Again." Zach nudged his shoulder into Luke's.

Luke pulled the trigger. The petite body fell to the ground with the shot's explosion.

Benjamin erupted with applause.

Excitement drained from Luke's face.

The girl's head popped up off the ground. She pulled her body through the leaves in a wounded army-crawl.

"Finish it," Jane joined them, grabbed the gun from Luke's hand, and replaced it with a sword. "Or you're not coming with us."

Zach stepped away from him and walked toward the car with Jane.

10

"YOU'RE GOING TO HAVE TO DO THIS SOONER OR later." Benjamin placed his hand on Luke's shoulder. "Just do it fast."

Luke took a breath and, with it, Benjamin was gone, joining the others. He swallowed hard and stepped closer to the girl.

She dragged herself with one arm, while the other now hung loose at her side. Her shirt was soaked with blood that oozed from the bullet hole in her shoulder. She had probably gotten straight A's in some expensive private school. Her long, brown ponytail swayed, tattered, past her shoulders.

Leaves gathered around Luke's feet, crunching as he stepped closer.

The bronze of her skin had faded with sickness. Several scabs covered her arms. Her gums bled. Yellow crust clogged her tear ducts. Dirt was lodged beneath her fingernails. Blood gushed from the bullet hole each time she pulled forward.

He kicked her over onto her back. She sat up, growling. If he didn't kill her, he'd be left alone out there to fend for himself. He stabbed her. Her nails hooked his arm. He thrust the blade back down, again and again, until her nails loosened.

The engine revved in the driveway.

Luke clasped the sword and tore it out. She was so young. What joy was left in this world?

The car horn blared.

Luke sprinted for the vehicle. He hoped that when he jumped into the Hummer, he could leave it behind—forget he had killed a child.

Zach sped down the driveway. Dust flew into the air. Luke pictured the weight of what he had done fading with that dust, but it didn't.

The car slammed to a stop beside a mailbox marked with the name *BENNETT* that sat on a stone pillar. The brick mansion looked like a Tuscan village, sitting vulnerable with open gates.

Zach glanced back at Luke through the rearview mirror and smiled. He jerked left down the driveway and stopped in front of the grand entrance, the doors left wide open. He stepped out and the rest followed without asking questions. A three-story foyer was framed by a grand staircase. "Benjamin, food. Jane, check for ammo. Mr. Bennett was a hunting enthusiast. Luke, loot the bathrooms for medical supplies."

Luke held tight to his sword and ascended the stairs. The rest of the group disappeared throughout the house. The stairs were easy. There were no walls to block his view, no closed doors required to open. The second floor consisted of a long hallway. Bedroom doors lined each side. The bathroom was likely to be at the end of the corridor. The first set of doors was closed. He kept walking. The next door to the right was cracked open. Sun rays sneaked into the hallway from its windows. Pink walls glittered in its brightness. Teen-boy posters lined the room. Two twin beds sat adjacent to one another against the left wall. The name *Amy* was painted in big purple letters above the first headboard; *Erin* was painted in green above the other.

The closet door rattled.

The hair on Luke's neck stood up. His fingers gripped tightly around the sword. He shouldn't have stopped. Sweat built in his palm. He inched toward the closet. His fingers rested on the doorknob. He hoped for a pile of stuffed animals—even ET. The door bent a quarter of the way, then jammed. Something prevented it from opening—or someone. His heart pounded. Any noise or breathing was blocked out. With both hands, he tugged the doorknob toward him. The door popped off the track and flew open.

A girl screamed.

Luke fell to the floor.

He had left her lifeless body among the litter of leaves, yet there she cowered. Her skin lacked the synthetic tan of her sister, and her hair rested right beneath her chin, but they had been identical. He had killed her twin, but she was alive—unaffected.

She jumped over him and darted for the hallway.

"Wait!" He stumbled to stand and hurried after her. She was at the bottom of the stairs by the time he had made the first step. She was getting away. He tried to go faster but he fell, tumbled down a few steps, and twisted his ankle. He screamed in agony.

She stopped. The healthy cells of her skin wiped the image of her dying sister from his memory. She stared at the sword in his hand.

He gritted his teeth, dropped the weapon, and held up his hands.

Agent Jane stepped into the foyer with a handful of hunting rifles. She saw the girl and froze. Benjamin walked out of the kitchen hauling several trash bags of food. He saw her and dropped one. A can popped and beer sprayed all over the interior of the bag. An engine revved outside. All four turned their attention to the door.

Zach stepped from a black Dodge Challenger. "Let's go."

Little Erin relaxed and sprinted toward him. She wrapped her arms around him, nearly knocking him backwards.

He refused the hug at first, holding his arms out from her, and then embraced every inch of it. "You've gotten so big."

She smiled and didn't hesitate to climb into the back seat. Jane followed the girl.

Benjamin turned to support Luke as Zach approached. "Hey, maybe he can use your cane since you're getting around pretty good."

A gun fired. Luke felt the momentum of the bullet tear through him. He fell onto Benjamin and they slid down the steps.

Moonlit Trail

1

Without a plan or destination, we followed the road. Nevaeh stared at me the entire ride. She gave it a rest once we stopped at a bridal shop. It was guaranteed to be empty and have a bathroom. It'd be the last place they would look for us. There was no food, but the manager had hidden a bottle of whisky in her desk. It was enough to get us by for a few more hours.

Jasmine grabbed a handful of dresses and piled them in the middle of the room. She tore off her robe and stood in a circle of mirrors.

"Wouldn't you feel more comfortable using a dressing room?" Nevaeh tried to look anywhere but at her. Blush deepened in her cheeks.

"Fuck, no. I'm not risking my life so that a couple of chicas don't see my tits," Jasmine said.

I locked the front door and browsed the second row from the front. A few hundred dollars could buy a white sheet with a line of sequins around the neck or bottom. My father would've bought me the dress right off the front mannequin. Now, in this life, I could have any I wanted. I found one with no detail, no beads, no pearls, and no lace.

Jasmine twirled in a $1,000 dress. Dusk's light bathed her through the large front windows framing the store. Just enough sun escaped the sky, hitting the circle of mirrors, before it descended into night. Each imperfection of her body went unacknowledged; she looked stunning.

Nevaeh lay on a nearby bench and stared at the ceiling. We were safe and warm.

"So, where were you two during the Last Day?" Jasmine stopped spinning and flopped down on the pile of dresses.

"What's the Last Day?" Nevaeh sat up and faced her. She stepped onto the dresses and sat down behind Jasmine, fastening the pearl buttons down her back.

"You know, the day before the zombies." Jasmine said. "The last day you had with family and friends. I was skipping school to hit up this crazy party in the park."

Nevaeh's finger slid from the last button.

"Me and this guy, Julio, were getting freaky and *bam!* This guy comes out from nowhere, jumping and attacking our tent." She swallowed and stared at the mirror.

"And then what?" Nevaeh lightly nudged her.

"Now I'm here." She shrugged. "What else is there to say?"

"I spent the day with my grandfather. All morning we talked about our people, things he wanted me to know before he left with the Great Spirit." Nevaeh glanced at me. "But what I remember most is the owl sitting beside his porch. I had never seen such a large bird. It sat so still, sure of itself, determined to let us see it."

The dress slid from my fingers and brushed the stitches on my wrist. I looked down to see them, but the shadows concealed the line of stitches. *My Last Day was Thursday morning in the café.* The weight of their stares fell on me from across the room.

The entrance exploded and glass shattered.

"Find them!" Zach's voice carried from the front of the store, through the ringing in my ears.

I fell to the floor so fast that my check whacked the hard tile. I rolled under the first row of fluffy gowns, easily concealed. About an inch of view remained once my throbbing cheek was plastered to the floor.

"I can understand you're a little freaked out right now. And I'm sorry it took until now for you to know who I really am. We belong together." Zach was inside the building. I watched his shoes move toward the empty pile of dresses.

Footsteps stopped behind me. My chest pounded against the floor. Blood pushed a deafening sound to my eardrums.

"I will love you like no mortal ever could."

A hand grabbed my shirt, ripping me off the floor. Agent Jane twisted the cotton in her fist, so the shirt strangled me. I couldn't breath. She pushed me toward Zach. "Chief."

"I've loved you since before you were born." Zach nodded at her and she let go, flinging me toward him. He caught my fall and pressed his lips against mine, lightly.

I tried to resist the flood of adrenaline. My heart was sure to burst. I didn't want to feel anything.

"What about the others?" Jane cleared her throat.

He eased his lips from mine. I looked away. He grabbed my arm, tightened his grip, and led me outside. "Burn it!"

"No, you can't ... please!" I tried to free myself. His nails dug deeper.

Agent Jane stepped through the broken door. A fire ignited inside.

"Please save them for me." I tore my arm from his grip and made for the building. He caught my arm as fire engulfed the rows of dresses. I sank to my knees, to the ground.

The Challenger's engine started behind me.

With all my strength, I stood up and dashed for it. I banged against the driver's tinted window.

Zach and Jane ran toward me.

"Please let me in!" The palm of my hand slid down its glass. A 12-year-old girl sat in the driver's seat clenching the steering wheel. "Please."

The door unlocked.

"I wouldn't do that if I were you." Jane pointed a gun. Zach took a step closer. I pushed the girl into the passenger seat and stepped on the gas. I refused to be forced into anything. Flames engulfed the building as I sped down the highway. Darkness blanketed the car and the strip mall faded in the rearview.

Jane took a shot.

A triangle with an exclamation point in its center, popped up on the dash. *What the hell does that mean?*

Erin hugged her seatbelt and squished herself to the door. I pulled over and rested my forehead on the wheel. "See if you can find a manual."

"Up there, there's a four-way," she said. She knew exactly where we were.

I pulled back onto the road. A stop sign approached in the headlights.

"Left," she said.

I floored it and cut the wheel to the right. Rubber burned into the asphalt as the car fishtailed. I eased the car into a glide and coasted to a stop, avoiding any more marks. I turned the car around, followed our tracks to the intersection, and blew through it in the opposite direction.

Erin slumped lower as I pressed the gas pedal to the floor. The car shot through the darkness, the headlights capturing three feet of asphalt before us. A small building glowed in the distance. I slowed and coasted to it. Neon lights spelled out *Gene's Used Cars* above a shack. We were in the middle of nowhere. The land was paved with empty farmland as far as the moon could reach. I squeezed the car between two minivans in the very back. With some luck the night would bore us.

"What are we doing?" Erin slouched down into the seat—any deeper and she'd disappear. The glass began to fog with our beating breath.

"Waiting." I cracked my window and allowed the condensation free. We could hear the sound of tires screeching faintly in the distance. A passing breeze ripped through the crack, whistling into the car. I grabbed the keys. "See if there's a manual."

Erin popped open the glove box and took out a book.

I ripped it from her hands, thumbing through the pages. *Come on.* There it was: the triangle with an exclamation point inside—tire pressure. *Shit.* I threw the book to the back seat. My heart pounded and I couldn't hear anything else. We wouldn't make it on the road. What the hell were we going to do? The parking lot was filled with cars. We could hide under one. Erin shivered beside me.

The sound of a car racing down the road seeped into the window. My heart jumped and, with it, I pulled the key from the ignition. Headlights appeared far in the distance. Sure enough they would stop; after all, I had.

"What are we going to do?" Erin hugged her knees.

I searched the car lot for ideas.

Something pounded from the trunk.

2

A RICKETY PORCH FRAMED THE FRONT OF THE dealership. Decades of neglected paint peeled from it. I crawled onto my elbows dragging my body into the crawlspace. We wouldn't have much cover with the lattice fencing, but the piles of junk crammed beneath it should hide us. The damp soil wiggled with insects under my stomach.

The Hummer pulled into the car lot. Its headlights swept over the lattice as the tires crunched closer toward the building.

A wolf spider dropped down from the floorboard overhead.

"Ah—" Erin started to scream.

I shoved my hand over her mouth.

Zach stepped out of the Hummer.

The spider landed on my hand. I gritted my teeth and

pressed harder against the girl's lips. A November wind chilled the air and nudged the eight-eyed arachnid along my skin.

Agent Jane stepped out and scanned the scene. She sprinted toward the Challenger nestled in the back row. "Chief!"

"Check the trunk." Zach braced his cane and followed. His shoulders dropped as he approached the car. Jane slid into the driver's seat. She wouldn't find the keys. Zach reached into his pocket and pulled something out.

The spider's legs tapped across my arm. Goosebumps flooded my skin. The floorboards creaked above us. The spider crept up my arm and then my cheek, finally digging down under a dreadlock.

The car exploded. Jane and Zach made their way closer to the shack.

The spider nuzzled deeper against my scalp. My heart pounded and adrenaline was making it hard to stay still. Its little body wiggled and nudged between strands of hair.

The floor creaked again and the front door squeaked open above our heads. Zach stopped 10 feet from us. I should've looked away. The white of my eyes could giveaway our location, but it was all I had to distract me from the spider.

The steps squeaked. A pair of wet sneakers sloshed as they stepped from the porch. A dark liquid spilled over their edge, draining into the soil. A man in overalls dragged his feet as he approached Zach. His deep moan carried into the night.

Jane tossed her sword to Zach.

He threw it back, let his cane fall, and rolled up his sleeves. "Well, Gene, today is your lucky day. You get to finally meet your maker."

Jane walked away from them—toward us. My chest drummed against the ground with a racing heartbeat. She stopped at the steps and sat down.

Zach took a swing at the man. Drool sprayed from the car dealer's mouth on impact. Jane shifted her weight and pulled out a handgun. I could hear her breathing.

I took my hand off Erin's mouth and motioned for her to stay quiet. Careful not to make noise, I slid my fingers into my hair. Movement stirred the dust, tickling my nose. I dug in after the spider, grabbing its squishy body. It slipped from my fingers and burrowed deeper. All I wanted to do was scream, but I held my breath and dug down, pushing it forward from behind the dreadlock. I clenched it between two fingers, while its legs pushed against them trying to free itself. I cupped it. It ran around my palm. My jaw tightened. I leaned over a pile of rusty fenders and soggy oil filter boxes, closer to the lattice. Zach was still hammering away on the man's face. Jane's boots were firmly placed on the bottom step. I opened my hand, holding the spider out, waiting for it to grab hold of the side of her boot.

The man fell to the ground. Zach pounded all his anger and frustration against the salesman's skull.

The spider lifted from my hand.

Jane screamed, stood, and ripped down her pants.

Zach looked up.

The man bit into his forearm.

Zach screamed.

3

THE HUMMER WAS GONE. I HADN'T MEANT FOR anyone to get killed or hurt, but it had worked and there was no changing it. I climbed out from beneath the building, shaking off the creepy feeling.

Erin stood up and began to run in circles. Her hands patted every inch of skin and scraped into her scalp, ruffling her hair. "Oh my God, oh my god, oh my god. Is there one on me?"

"I really don't think I could've done that." Benjamin rolled out from under the porch. I wanted to forget he was there. If I had left him in the truck of the car, he would have gotten everything he deserved. There was no smile, no happy greeting on his face. Luke's splattered blood covered his left cheek. "Hey, I want to talk to you."

"I have nothing to say to you." I turned away from him and walked toward the road. Nevaeh and Jasmine could still be alive. There had been a back door. It wasn't too late. Nevaeh had seen the same owl, but why?

Erin stood like she was deciding which parent she would live with after divorce. I didn't care, but she hurried after me, saying nothing until we reached the end of the driveway. "Where are you going?"

"I have to know if they're dead. I have to know." I started into a run. If I hurried, I could make it back within an hour. *An hour?*

An engine revved from the parking lot and headlights hugged us from behind. Benjamin pulled up alongside Erin in a green minivan. Her lips chattered and a quick glance around at the surrounding darkness was all the motivation she needed to jump in. As the girl found a seat in the back, he waited for me.

I crossed my arms, slipped into the shadows off the highway, and began to jog.

The van inched up beside me. I ran faster and it followed. He kept pace with me and yelled out the window, "Would you like a ride?"

I stopped. Air heaved in and out of my lungs. "What the fuck do you think!"

I sprinted from him—from them. The van continued to follow. I stopped and it stopped. I leaned over, catching my breath, and scooped up a handful of gravel throwing it at the van. "Would you leave me alone? Don't you think you've done enough? You've ruined my whole life. I've lost everything."

With that, he took off down the road.

Clouds had hidden the moon, bringing bitter cold and darkness. My scalp itched where the spider had squeezed. Stillness left the perfect opportunity for my mind to stir, crippling me to the ground. My kneecaps banged against the asphalt. *Only being alive could hurt this much.* I was wasting time, so I pushed my knees farther into the road and stood up. *You're going to risk your life for some strangers—to find out more about a stupid fucking owl?* I shoved the chatter of my mind down with each step. I had to know.

The road was much longer than I had remembered. The chilled air numbed the tips of my fingers, ears, and nose. The darkness formed into the shadow of a vehicle parked in the middle of the four-way stop. I was too cold and tired to care whose it was, so I sprinted for it.

It took the shape of the minivan. I pulled open the

passenger door. The interior light gave away the young girl asleep across the rear seat. Benjamin's hands tightened around the steering wheel as I climbed in. He kept his eyes on the road and said nothing as we headed toward the bridal shop.

Fire lit the sky in the distance. Smoke choked out the stars. Worn and wounded bodies of infected shoppers gathered around the blaze. *They have to be there.*

Benjamin parked at the edge of the shopping mall's parking lot. I jumped out and sprinted toward the building, pushing my muscles until they burned. Benjamin's fingers slid over my shoulder and grabbed the collar of my shirt, yanking me backwards. My feet flew into the air, my head snapped back, and my spine slammed into his body as he caught my fall. He pushed me off. "You're going to get us all killed."

She can't be dead. I sat heaving my shoulders in defeat. The fire's perfect autumn colors devoured the last white gown.

The hollow shells of shoppers turned their attention to us.

Benjamin pressed his hand against my cheek. Its weight was the only thing I could feel. He eased my head around so my eyes met his and spoke as softly as could be, "Just one more day."

I looked up at him, holding back my tears. He had no right to comfort me. One more day and it could all be over. My body had already given a light nod before I could make the decision. He helped me stand. A shadow moved from the building, running straight for us. The infected never moved that fast at night. It was gaining speed.

4

NEVAEH OPENED HER EYES.

Zach paced back and forth in front of a fireplace. A painting of the Yosemite Valley hung against the room's wood-paneled wall. She knew in an instant where she was: the Library Suite. But why did he bring her back to the Ahwahnee Hotel?

He sat down beside her on the small couch. The warmth of her breath flooded the duct tape sealing her lips. His fingertips picked at the corner of the tape. Handcuffs secured her arms behind her back, pushing her breasts out. He moved his hand to the name badge pinned to her front pocket. She held her breath and a smile crossed his lips. He ripped the pin from her shirt, tearing the grey fabric. "Something tells me you're more than an ordinary park ranger."

You're an asshole.

His hand slid down the curve of her waist and between her thighs. She shifted her weight back from him and his fingers continued down her leg. They stopped at the tip of a knife holstered in her boot. He pushed her pant leg up and grabbed it, slicing the first two buttons of her blouse. The fire's glow danced across her white bra. "I never get tired of seeing women's breasts."

Pig.

He walked over to a table nestled beneath the windows. Moonlight trickled in through the chevron-patterned glass. It danced across the table, finding the dagger and flowing into its design. He picked up the dagger. His thumb rubbed the curves of the glowing moon. His chest rose with a deep inhale. He slid the blade across his empty palm. Blood dripped onto the tip of his shoe. He looked up at Nevaeh, charged her, and tore the tape from her lips.

A moan was the only thing that could dull the pain as she hunched over.

He grabbed her hair and threw her head back against the couch pinning her only inches from his lips. "So you must also know ... who ... I ... am."

Her eyes said everything.

He smiled, looked at the dagger, and pressed it to her throat. His free hand slid up her leg, resting an inch from her inner thigh. Her cheeks burned. He pressed the blade up to her neck and dug his fingers into her leg. Blood soaked into her jeans. "Say it. Who am I?"

She looked away.

He freed her leg, jerked her hair back, and forced her to look at him.

"The Great Spirit," she whispered.

He let go and eased back, sitting beside her in silence.

"If you really are, why don't you just end all of this?" She looked at him.

He said nothing and glanced down at the bleeding palm of his hand.

"You can still change this legend," she said.

Agent Jane stepped into the room.

"I think it's time to pay a visit to the old man." Zach wrapped his hands around Nevaeh's throat and strangled her.

5

THE MINIVAN DRIFTED BACK AND FORTH OVER THE center line, the tires' hum pushing me to sleep, but I wouldn't falter. Benjamin began to nod off. His eyes closed for a second. The tires bumped over something. His body jerked from sleep and he gripped the steering wheel. I held onto the door handle and straightened up in my seat. "Would you like me to drive for a while?" I said.

"I'm sorry." He sat up, keeping his eyes on the endless highway. "It was just a job assignment. I didn't know you, not like I do now. Your parents' death was supposed to look like an accident. Jay and I didn't ask questions. We just did our job. When it was done, we knew exactly where you'd be."

I sank into the seat. I didn't want to hear it.

He cleared his throat and stepped on the gas. "I believe the man you know as Zach is the one who gave the order."

How —

He slammed on the brakes.

Erin rolled off the back seat and thumped to the floor. "Ouch!"

A huge *Yosemite National Park* sign sat to the right of the road.

"Why are we here?" She climbed back onto the seat, rubbing her head.

He handed me a folded piece of paper with the word *Liaw* scribbled on it. Inside was a photograph—of me. *The café*. The woman I thought myself to be. I kneaded a dreadlock between my fingers. I barely recognized myself. He had captured the last moment life had been right. If I could go back to that moment, I'd savor every second, enjoy every breath, and find happiness in every exhale. In that moment, life was wonderful and I had failed to see it. The handwriting looked familiar. My heart pounded and my brain raced to trace its origin. *Zach.* I crumbled it. "You're just as crazy as him."

He stayed quiet.

"I don't understand."

"The order to kill your parents came directly from the Chief of Meadowlark. Zach controls Meadowlark. He always has." He eased my face toward him. "I don't think saving some park ranger is worth your life."

"Really? That's funny since only a few days ago you thought very little of the value of my life. I was just some job assignment. What next? You were supposed to guarantee that I sacrifice myself?"

The van was quiet.

I sat silent, trapped with my thoughts. "You know, I waited up there, beside the waterfall. I waited for you to say something—anything. To give me a reason to live."

He looked at me. He knew he had let me down, but I didn't want to hear it now.

"If you don't want to help me—fine." I jumped out of the vehicle and slammed the door behind me. The world disappeared and all I could do was storm off to the park gates. Pieces of flesh were crusted to the handprints smeared across the toll booths. Movement emerged in the blurred tunnel, forming the background of my path. I stopped and the world came back into focus. Eight campers emerged from the shadows and the damaged buildings. I wasn't going to take shit from anyone anymore. I let adrenaline fill my veins, and tightened my fists. I charged the mob. It was a stupid idea.

The first camper was a thin old lady. She went down with one punch. The second was a middle-aged man. He grabbed my shirt. His fingernails tore into the skin of my arm. *That fucking hurts.* I kneed him and knocked him to his ass. Another one came from my left. Before I could react, he knocked me to the ground. I lost all the air from my lungs. He bit the air a hair from my arm. I shoved my fingers into his eyes. The hard, wet balls popped beneath my fingernails.

Benjamin pounded on the horn.

I ignored the asshole, finger deep in eye sockets.

The van wheels screeched. Benjamin jumped out and snapped my attacker's neck. Two lifeless bodies lay crushed beneath the van's tires. A third had hit the windshield and flown over the van's roof, splattering on the asphalt.

"Whatever you want." He kicked the last camper down and stomped his face. "Whatever you need."

The camper stood up behind him.

I swung my fist toward Benjamin's face. He closed his eyes. I punched the camper to the ground. He opened them and stared at me. "I will help you. Before morning, or there is no hope for her."

I nodded and headed for the van. Erin slid the back door open. A thin female hiker rounded the back of the vehicle and lunged inside. The girl screamed. The woman tore into her flesh. Erin's blood poured onto the floor mats.

The cargo door was thrown open and Jasmine fell out of the back. We had rescued her from the bridal shop, but we were too far away this time. A park ranger stood behind her. His hat sat straight on a crooked head. Crusted blood stained the front of his uniform. Jasmine sprinted around the van and climbed up the hood to the roof and lay down like she would be invisible. Her wedding dress hung over the sides.

The young cries of the girl had died out and snarling filled the van's cabin as the hiker fed. Benjamin ripped the creature out and threw it against the tollbooth. I kicked the ranger to the ground. Jasmine slid off the roof and into the driver's seat. I took shotgun and Benjamin jumped in through the side. His boots slid through the blood-soaked floor. The van sped through the booths. He kicked Erin's tiny body from the vehicle. I picked the photograph off the floor. Jasmine moved us deeper into the valley.

Everything had been right until I saw *him* sitting in my seat at the café — *Nantai.*

6

ZACH AND HIS AGENTS SURROUNDED THE OLD MAN'S cabin. Reports indicated that a large Russian man was staying there. They kicked in the door. Pieces of wood splintered into the air. A solid man was indeed standing beside Nantai. Zach charged him and took him down in one sweep, the floorboards vibrating with his fall. "Take him outside."

Jane lifted a single finger and five men accompanied her to the Russian.

Nantai sat down on the floor in front of the fireplace. He took the pipe from his back and pulled a stick from his pouch. Zach sat down across from him. A breeze slithered through the door, teasing the fire's flames. Nantai offered the calumet. Zach bowed and took the pipe. Smoke swirled from his breath, around the room. The gust of wind pushed the door closed.

The old man took the pipe and puffed slowly against it.

"I will admit I never fully believed it. Until I saw this ...." Zach took the dagger out and set it on the rug.

"Coyote." The pipe fell from Nantai's lips and he looked up. Smoke leaked from his lungs. Silence drifted with the white smoke. He offered the pipe once more to the young man.

Zach declined. "Where is she?"

"On the wind."

"Old man, I have no time for games."

Nantai grinned. "You have changed, then. But, this is your last chance. For without her, you keep the earth in death. You will not get another lifetime."

"What are you not telling me? How do I make her mine?"

"You can not force a flower to grow." He took another puff. "Nor catch a turtle that does not want to be caught."

Blood rushed to Zach's head and his cheeks burned. *I don't have time for this shit.*

"You cannot force love, no matter how much you want it." Nantai reached for Zach's bandaged hand.

Zach allowed the wrinkled fingers to pull the gauze from his skin. Crusted blood tore open and fresh blood drained from the cut.

Nantai opened a different pouch and pressed a leaf against the wound.

Zach's finger's tightened around the dagger. It was as if everyone thought this was a game—funny—just a pathetic mortal life. He shoved the blade into the old man's lower right side.

The pipe fell to the floor.

Zach wiped the blade on his bleeding palm. "Tell her that her path is with me and I will spare you in death."

Blood seeped through the old man's fingers as he fell onto his side, pressing against the wound.

Zach kicked the pipe as he stood and opened the door. Wind pounded against Nantai's headdress. The fireplace's warmth trickled out, bringing Coyote with it.

7

I HAD NOT SEEN THE SOUTH SIDE OF THE PARK SINCE Friday's trip with Jan. *God, I miss her.* The mountain walls framing the valley tore into the sky, high enough that the moon could surely be reached. The beauty found within Yosemite's walls confined the death within them.

Jasmine slowed the van as we approached the exploded Lodge. She parked at the foot of the Lower Falls trail. I led the group up to the empty waterfall. Something was different. Deep footprints tracked away from Nantai's trail and continued away from the fall, toward Yosemite Village. The same path that led to Dominic's corpse.

"Well?" Benjamin stepped beside me. I kept my eyes forward, focused on the path. He took the trail down to the village. Deep footprints led to the edge of a creek. I stopped beside him. My boots sank two inches into the mud. No footprints carried to the other side.

Jasmine groaned, stuffing the wedding dress into her hands and over her head. I stepped into the water. It soaked between the laces of my boots. We walked the creek until we came to a brown building the size of a trailer, on the opposite bank. The footprints continued, straight to the building.

I began to climb up.

Benjamin yanked me back down. "This is the Medical Clinic."

The wind picked up and blew toward the building. A yellow leaf drifted with it. I climbed from the soggy riverbank. My boots suctioned to the mud. A second tug dislodged me faster than expected and my fingers slid through the cold wet dirt encrusted between my fingers. "So?"

"You know, we might be heading into a trap." Benjamin climbed out behind me.

"Or following a fucking zombie." Jasmine shook some mud off her fingers and smeared the brown soil down the side of her dress.

The leaf fell at the building's front corner. I sprinted toward it. The cold air nipped at my damp skin. Benjamin grabbed my shoulder, pulled me back to the side of the building, and pinned me there with his arm.

The leaf disappeared, swept to its inevitable decay in the valley.

I pushed his arm off and peeked around the corner. The coast was clear outside of the building, but anything could be hunting us in the open—anything could be waiting inside. A fresh footprint rested just outside the closed door. The wind pushed my body against the wall. Benjamin stepped around me and took the lead, reaching for the doorknob. As he began to turn it, the door burst open. He fell to the ground.

"Pree-vyet!" Sven smiled at me. His face had been beaten, but he was still as charming as Paul Bunyan. He pulled me into his arms and rushed us inside.

Hospital beds were separated by curtains. In the very back corner rested the old man. His headdress sat on a medical tray beside him. Blood poured from a gash in his side.

"No." I ran to his side, cupping my hand over his. Warm blood ran between my fingers. "Help me!"

No one moved. They all just stood there looking at me.

"Benjamin!"

He stepped up and slid the man into his arms.

Sven stood holding the door open. Benjamin took him out into the night and rested his body beneath a tree.

Pain eased from the wrinkled face as moonlight caressed his cheeks. Nantai weakly pointed at me, beckoning me closer. He pulled the eagle feather from his hair and rested it in my palm. "Tell her, lykj-mhi."

Lykj-mhi.

Nantai rested his head against the bark. Lunar rays trickled through its bare branches. The wind rested and he smiled at me. "Within the moonlight of the empty waterfall, she would find the path." He took a breath and placed his hand against my cheek. "Awanata."

Then he was gone. His hand fell loose to his side, his chest rested, and the light in his eyes disappeared.

Sven hid behind the tree and cleared his throat to hide how we all felt.

I closed my eyes and took a breath. A breeze passed and blew west. I stood and followed its direction.

"Burn him," Benjamin said. "Meet us at the stables."

I stopped at the field's edge. Just beyond was the Hotel.

"They'll see us a mile away." Benjamin stepped up behind me and cuffed my right wrist. I turned to face him and he cuffed the other. "Are you sure you want to do this?"

My shoulders dropped. I stepped onto the road and walked toward the Ahwahnee Hotel. Each beat of my heart burned. We made it to the little stone guardhouse before Meadowlark agents stormed us. Benjamin only had to say my name and two agents were escorting us back to those fucking elevator doors.

"We'll take her from here. Why don't you get something to eat?" The younger of the two men grabbed onto my arm.

I looked to the floor—this was it.

Benjamin's fingers brushed mine as he let go of the handcuffs.

8

I STEPPED INTO THE ELEVATOR. BOTH AGENTS TOOK their places guarding the door. The seconds it took to get to the sixth floor felt like hours. I stepped into the hallway. My knees weakened. It looked as if the corridor went on forever. *What am I doing?* I leaned against the wall. An agent stepped behind me.

A door opened down the hallway.

"Leave us." It was *his* voice.

The agent stepped back into the elevator.

Before I could push off the wall and gain composure, Zach's body was pressed against mine. His hands cupped my face. He kissed me more deeply than ever before, and I let him. He pulled away slow. "I've waited *so long* for you."

I turned my cheek as he tried a second kiss.

He grabbed the handcuffs and led me into the Library Suite.

Nevaeh's body was slumped motionless on the couch.

I jerked my hands away from his and ran to her. My knees slammed to the floor as I bent over, resting my cheek on the couch nose-to-nose with her. Her eyes were closed. I couldn't tell if she was breathing. *No.* Tears filled my eyes. "No."

"She'll be fine. Well, she'll have a hell of a headache,

but she'll be fine." Zach walked over, placed the dagger on the coffee table, and sat on the floor behind me. His arms wrapped around my waist and his chest pressed against my back. His warm cheek lay against mine. He unlocked the handcuffs. "It's been so long."

I closed my eyes. *I could smell algae growing on the lake, hear the sound of baby turtles splashing from the rocks.* I spun in his arms. *I could feel the wet, hard turtle shell in my hands.* I felt his lips before they touched mine. *Warm sunshine braised my arm as he kissed me.* It wasn't real, not anymore. I pulled away. *What am I doing?*

"I can wait." He pulled me back, squeezing me in his arms. His eyes grew wide and anger spewed from his mouth. "When every last one of them is dead, you'll beg for me to take you."

"What happened to you?" I said. He had been so gentle when we were eight.

He looked over at the dagger and loosened his grip. "I'm sorry. I should've never messed up your stars. Silver Fox ...."

Hazel's gift, the necklace.

"I made the moon for you." His hand rested on my cheek. "Awanata, immortality is torture without you."

The tips of my fingers touched the turquoise fox.

"Elizabeth." He leaned into me, his lips an inch from mine. "Come home with me. Stop all this. Give yourself to me."

I took a deep breath and the necklace shifted against my skin. I looked over at Nevaeh's motionless body and back at him. His warm eyes felt so familiar in a world that had become so cold. I whispered, "No."

He pushed me to the floor, pinning himself on top of me. "Once your earth crumbles and its creatures lie rotting in pain, you'll beg for me. I will deny you every single time that godforsaken moon rises,"—a tear ran down his cheek—"every single time its soft glow brings back the eternity that I've waited for your love—every time you scream at it begging for your heart to stop hurting—I will deny you."

"You're scaring me."

His face melted into a calm and normal state. He brushed his finger along my cheek. "Will you stop these games? Elizabeth, it hurts to live without you."

I turned away from his touch.

He kissed my neck and continued to the collar of my shirt. Soft kisses continued down the fabric. His finger brushed the curve of my breast. The warmth of his breath seeped through the cotton covering my nipple.

The necklace shifted and the fox—spinning like a yoyo on a string—fell to the floor. I reached for the coffee table. My fingertips slid across the wood and hit the edge of the dagger.

Nevaeh opened her eyes. She looked at me, to the table and back, without moving. I closed my eyes with a subtle nod. Zach's lips had stopped on my breast. A tear dripped from the corner of my eye.

She sat up, grabbed the dagger, and plunged it down into his back. She tore it out and thrust it back down on him. I threw him off into the coffee table and it snapped. She held her head, fighting a dizzy spell. I took the dagger from her, stowed it in my pants behind my back, and braced her with my shoulder. Adrenaline eased her weight from my frame—it was the only thing pushing me toward the elevator. Nevaeh tapped the *DOWN* button. My heart pounded. *Tap.* The hallway lights flickered. *Tap.* Zach stepped into the hallway with a gun pointed at us. *Tap, tap.*

I held my hand out in front of my chest and walked toward him. With the other hand, I clasped the turquoise fox. I closed my eyes and continued for him. There was no way to know if I'd live through the next step. My hand pressed against his chest. I opened my eyes and he was there—right across from me. I moved my hand to the side of his face. He lowered the gun.

The elevator doors chimed opened.

I pressed my lips against his and reached for the dagger. I shoved the blade into his stomach, kissing him harder, and pushed him. As he fell backwards, the blade slid from his body. His arm fell out to the side and I stomped his fingers, freeing the gun from his grip.

"Awanata!" Nevaeh said.

9

BENJAMIN STEPPED INTO THE DINING HALL. A CROWD of Meadowlark agents filled the tables and food line just as before. It must have been another shift break. He stepped to the end of the line and grabbed a plate. The weight of a single set of eyes crawled up the back of his neck. The room fell completely silent. He turned around.

Agent Jane stood with her sword drawn, eyes fixated on him. The agents beside him pulled back. In training they had always dueled, but the chandeliers hanging from the turquoise ceiling cast an inevitability of death. Someone sitting nearby tossed their sword to him. He recognized the young agent, George. Benjamin thanked him with a nod and charged Jane. She stayed firm until the last second, then spun, shaving his shoulder. He fell.

The sword swung back to her with such grace he almost forgot to shield its swing. The clink of their swords could he heard throughout the still room. He thrust all his weight against the weapon and shoved her to the floor. He could have swung—killed her there—but he stood back. Her foot hooked his ankle and dropped him beside her.

Roll, roll! He rolled, found his footing, jumped onto a chair, and kicked off, swinging the sword so hard that his body twisted with its movement. She swung for his chest. He landed on a table. Plates and food went flying.

She swung again, like a warrior dancer, but missed. The blade chopped through George's forearm. He screamed as blood spurted out. Benjamin's eyes dared not leave her, but he noticed Menendez sitting a table away, front and center—her perfect disciple. Jane thundered toward Benjamin. Menendez slid out his leg. She tripped. Her face smacked the floor. Blood poured from her nose as she looked at Benjamin. He didn't want to win like this. Within a single breath the room inhaled.

Something moved in the corner of his left eye. Elizabeth and Nevaeh sprinted past the windows outside, back toward the field. *That wasn't the plan.*

Jane stood up, swaying on her feet. He uppercut her back down, and swung the sword as fast and as hard as he could. Her arm fell to the floor. The blade stuck in her ribcage. She fell to her knees. Blood pooled from her body.

The room held its reverence.

Benjamin yanked the sword back. *Now. Now!* He turned and ran out of the dining hall as fast he could, slowing at the door just enough to fling it open.

An agent ran out of the elevator yelling, "Medic!"

She did it. Benjamin ran out the back door. His heart pounded. They had gone west, but the stables were east. He stopped. *What was she doing?* There was no wind blowing to guide him. *Stick to the plan.*

10

I KNEW NEVAEH HAD TO SAY GOODBYE, OR IT WOULD haunt her like it haunts me. You never really do get to say goodbye—it's never enough.

The fire beside the Medical Clinic dwindled. Sven had laid logs on top of Nantai, giving his body reserve as it turned to ashes. It wouldn't be long before the dead would come for the burning flesh.

Nevaeh fell to her knees at its edge. Red embers took the last of her grandfather. Tears rolled down her cheeks, dripping into the ground where her people once lived. The fire engulfed the last purity of her culture. Her body slumped into a ball. She cried with no regard for its consequence.

I rested my hand upon her shoulder and knelt, wrapping my arms around her. I never asked for this, but it *was* all my fault. "He wanted me to tell you, lykj-mhi."

"I love you, too." She stared into the flames.

I pulled her toward me and slid the eagle feather into her hand. "He wanted you to have this."

She looked at me with tear-soaked eyes. The rain clouds were rolling in and soon the fire would die. Sven and Jasmine were waiting at the stables for us. The trees marked shadows on the ground with the covering clouds.

"We have to go." I searched the tree line for agents or the infected.

She looked down at the dagger clenched in my fingers and held out her hand.

I gave it to her.

"Pyhij." She read the word on the hilt. "It means to not know or recognize."

The wind swirled.

"Have you found yourself yet?" she said.

My eyes ran from hers straight to the flames dancing behind her. I hadn't found anything but death. "We better go."

"In the empty waterfall, she will remember. And when the earth breathes, she will return." Nevaeh handed the dagger back to me. By now Meadowlark agents would have realized their beloved Chief was dead.

11

NEVAEH GRABBED MY HAND AND HEADED DOWN A trail behind the Medical Clinic. She let go at the trail's head—the Lower Fall. Its riverbed was still empty. I sat at the edge of the forest and looked out at the open sky. Nevaeh took a seat beside me, hugged her knees in, and leaned against the tree.

We sat there in silence. I spun the dagger's point on the tip of my finger. She twisted the turquoise beads into her hair, the eagle feather hanging as it had on her grandfather.

The wind picked up and tore into my pores. The moon reached high in the sky as midnight approached. The clouds pushed out of the valley and moonlight crashed over the land. Lunar rays stretched through the tree line, filling the bone dagger. It glowed. *They could all be wrong. Why can't they be wrong? I'm all alone, so alone.* A tear escaped and I reached to wipe it.

Nevaeh grabbed my hand and held it tight.

I looked at her, but something caught my eye in the tree line. A Great Grey Owl sat staring at us. Its beady yellow eyes floated above the tree branch. *Within the moonlight of the empty waterfall, she would find the path.* I stood up. Rainwater dripped down my arm, over the stitches of my wrist, and lingered at my fingertip.

Nevaeh stood. The owl blinked.

I reached for the necklace, closed my eyes, and held my breath. I could hear Hazel. *Let go, and live for me.* My thumb dug into the dagger's letters, *Pyhij.* It felt warm. I opened my eyes. Its blue glow brightened, blinding me, and I dropped it. The dagger sank into the mud.

Nevaeh picked it up. Its glow had dimmed back to a soft blue. She stared at it, speechless. The owl screeched. She held out the dagger to me and whispered, "Awanata."

I took it. The curves of the word had shifted, spelling *Awanata.*

"Are you ready?" she said.

The ancient winds were still. The valley was silent. The moon cast a steady glow across the clearing. The owl's big yellow eyes stared at us.

"Elizabeth?" she said.

I traced the glowing blue line over the word again and again with my thumb.

"It's time." She placed her hand over mine.

I swallowed hard and nodded. When I looked up, she was already walking down the path we'd come on, toward the owl.

12

IT WAS QUIET AT THE STABLES.

"Oh, thank God Joe put the horses away." Nevaeh ran past a small building to the brown and green stables and peeked in. The smell of week-old shit spewed from the doors. Half the stalls contained horses. They were too busy eating fresh oats to care that we were there. The office was dark. A chill ran up my spine.

Nevaeh gently closed the door and sprinted to a small building that we had passed. She reached for the doorknob, but it turned.

Jasmine opened the door, jumped out, and hugged Nevaeh. She pulled her inside and then moved on to me. The warmth of her body comforted the emptiness I felt.

Sven was passed out in the corner. His cheeks shimmered with the sticky residue of tears. Strong bonds form when society crumbles.

Benjamin had taken the other far corner. He stared at me, dropping his shoulders with a sigh. His left sleeve was torn off and tied around a fresh wound. "You came back."

"So have you guys found anything to eat?" I looked away, diverting my attention to Jasmine.

The biggest, shittiest grin crossed her face. She scooped something from beneath the shelf. "Twinkies!"

Nevaeh looked at me. Benjamin smiled. I let out a laugh—if only it was a movie.

Sven opened his eyes.

Jasmine threw the junk food at Benjamin. "So can we leave now? I don't want to get stuck in some tiny-ass building again for days."

Sven closed his eyes and nuzzled deeper into the corner.

"We'll wait an hour." Benjamin wouldn't stop staring at me.

Jasmine took a seat and tapped her fingers to the song in her head. Grief had caught back up with Nevaeh and she buried her head down against her knees—twisting the feather in her fingers.

The man who killed my parents stared across the room at me. I was stupid to fall for those cold blue eyes.

13

AN OWL'S HOOT FILLED THE AIR.

I woke to a quiet and dark building. I clenched the dagger. Jasmine had slid into Sven's corner and snuggled in his safety. Her soiled wedding dress covered them. Tears had sent Nevaeh to bed quietly. Benjamin's eyes were finally closed. There was no telling how much darkness we had left in the night. I stood up. *They don't deserve this, to have their lives risked for me.* Except Benjamin: he owed me much more.

I pushed the wedding dress away from my feet and tiptoed toward the door. The floorboard creaked. I grabbed hold of the doorknob. It clicked as I turned it and cracked the door. Moonlight trickled over my boots. Nevaeh grabbed my ankle. I pressed my finger to my lips, hushing her. She stood. I placed my hand flat against her chest and shook my head. I couldn't be the one who made her lose more than she already had.

The warmth of her hand covered mine. She nodded me out and followed.

Every shadow shifted in the lunar light. The tree branches looked like witch's fingers reaching down to scoop us up. Moon rays danced over my skin as we walked to the stables. The large door clunked as it closed behind us. Nevaeh grabbed a bucket of oats beside the office. Its door was cracked. I walked past it and tried to look inside, but it was darker than it had been earlier. Goosebumps ran down my back. My spine hurt.

Nevaeh was at the back of the stable petting a brown horse that feasted from a fresh bucket of oats. She smiled at me. "You're not leaving without me."

Something nudged my back. I jumped. The pounding of my heart spun me around. A light brown horse stared at me. The white streak down his nose looked brushed-on. He nudged my arm. I reached out my hand. His wet nose pushed my hand to pet him. I brushed his coarse mane.

A shovel fell over behind us.

A whisper escaped Nevaeh, "No."

A park ranger in his 30s stood outside the office door. His shoulder hung broken and he leaned to the right. A week ago, girls would have thrown themselves at him. Now his skin hung loose, piss soaked his pants, and drool leaked out of his drooping lips.

Nevaeh let out a deep exhale.

"I'll do it." I tightened my grip around the dagger. If I waited, the horses would panic and death would flood this place in a matter of minutes. My heart pounded. I sprinted before I couldn't move—wouldn't move.

"No! Let me," she said.

I skidded to a stop halfway to the mangled man. His ranger hat fell to the dirt floor and rolled to the tip of my boot. The sound of hooves to my right stomped to the back of their stall. The man moaned and took a step toward me. A name badge hung from one clip—*Joe*.

Nevaeh charged past me and crashed into him. They fell to the ground and the man's skull smacked the dirt. A moan sprayed from his bloody lips.

She rolled to the side, off him, and cried, "I can't."

He rocked to get up, stood staring at me, and looked down at her. A pitchfork sliced through his back and out his torso. The three prongs dripped with blood and his corpse thumped to the ground. Sven stomped on the back of the man's head and ripped the fork out. He stretched out his hand to Nevaeh.

"Are you going somewhere?" Benjamin stepped out from behind him.

"I—"

"We were checking on Cymy. Liz was picking out a horse." Nevaeh walked over to the horse with the white brush stroke down its nose. "I think we should call this one Ben. He's always stuck up your ass. What do you think, Liz?"

"Can I talk to you?" Benjamin stepped into the dark office.

I hesitated—*Hazel had called me Lizzy*—and entered. Moonlight trickled through the windows into the bone dagger. Benjamin stopped. His lips easily rested three inches from mine. His breath moved to my neck and he whispered, "Don't leave me. I'm sorry. I will go a whole lifetime to fix this. Elizabeth, I didn't know."

I took a breath and kissed him. *He hadn't known it was my parents!* My lips quivered on the edge of losing all control. I tightened my eyes and pressed my lips harder against his. My heart pounded against my chest, pushing me closer to him. *Does he think I'm an idiot?* I left my lips against his and stepped closer. My hand slid down his back and grabbed his ass, pushing his pelvis tighter against mine.

He fumbled to unbutton my pants.

I slid my hand down his back pocket and grabbed the handcuffs. My finger pressed against something hard—a stone? I tightened the cuffs around his wrists before he could look down, then dug the object out of his pocket and stepped back from him. It was *my mother's stone*. Carved in its center was a dragonfly. She had promised it to me. I looked at him.

"You knew."

He knew exactly what he had done.

His big blue eyes hardened the heartbreak I felt. I pushed him to the floor and walked out, never looking back.

He was still speaking, but I couldn't hear a word.

I closed the door as his sentences grew into yells, but I only heard silence. The darkness of the sky began to lift. In almost a whisper, I mustered the words, "Let's go."

Nevaeh handed a bucket of oats to me and pulled a saddle from the wall.

"What about him?" Jasmine looked at the closed office door.

I looked at Sven. His hand was already extended out to me. I shook it and hung my head in a nod. *Was I doing the right thing?* He cupped my chin, pulling my eyes up to his, and nodded. I grabbed a saddle and walked back to the painted horse.

"Hey. What about me?" Jasmine ran up and the horse backed away.

"You can ride with us, or you can stay with them." Nevaeh fastened the saddle girth on Cymy and walked over to my horse. Once he was properly fitted, I climbed up, yanking on the reins. He neighed and turned his head back at me. Nevaeh hushed him and stroked his mane. She grabbed my hand and placed it against his neck, brushing him. "He is a creature, not an automobile. Understand?"

She didn't wait for my reply and turned towards Cymy.

"Wait!" Jasmine grabbed a bucket and spilled half the oats as she ran back.

Nevaeh didn't speak a word, helped Jasmine mount a horse, and climbed on her own.

Sven threw the stable doors open and stepped out of the way. Nevaeh stopped beside him. Her horse made no movement as he petted its long dark mane. She rested her hand on his and whispered, "Thank you."

Jasmine made her way beside me. "I'm gonna call mine Ferrari."

I smiled, but only for a moment. The Great Grey Owl rested in a tree across from us.

"Where do we go from here?" Jasmine's hair blew with the last pieces of night. The strands of her hair reached for the south. A yellow leaf followed its gust—like a yellow petal leaving the fingers of a little girl.

"He loves you, he loves you not, he loves you ...." Hazel was ten, picking the petals from a buttercup in a field of wild flowers. Her lips pressed against my cheek as she wrapped her arms around me. "I love you."

I wiped the tear that ran down my cheek. The salt water trickled to my wrist, flowing over the sutures. I looked back up at the bird. "South. I have a promise to keep."

About The Author

Julie Dawn grew up in southern Jersey, spending the summers collecting bee stingers in her feet. After graduating from Richard Stockton College, she dipped her toes in the environmental field for a few years, got married, moved to North Carolina, and finally got to become a mom. Four years of living in state parks was enough to make her relocate to the Oregon Coast. Under bright stars, she started writing again, determined to change the world one story at a time.

WWW.JULIE-DAWN.COM

Made in the USA
Charleston, SC
10 September 2015